The Burning Tree: Book 6 Power (Part 1)

Christopher Artinian

CHRISTOPHER ARTINIAN

ISBN: 9798861206006

CHRISTOPHER ARTINIAN

DEDICATION

For Uncle Den. We'll never see another like him.

ACKNOWLEDGEMENTS

This last couple of months have been harder than most, and this book would never have seen the light of day without my wonderful missus, Tina. We've been together for thirty years, and she is the best thing that has ever happened to me. Thank you for everything, wife.

A big thank you to the gang across in Christopher Artinian's Safe Haven. (The new name for the fan club). You'll never know how much your support means to me.

Thanks to my pal, Christian, for another great cover. Also, many thanks to my editor, Ken – an awesome editor and a lovely guy.

Last but by no means least, a huge thank you to you for purchasing this book.

.

PART 1

PROLOGUE

THEN

The arrival of the Wanderers had been tumultuous to begin with, but everyone settled into a routine quickly. Rommy and Becka had become their spokespeople, and at least one of them was always present at the committee meetings.

Rather than being a drain on resources, the Wanderers seemed out to prove themselves quite the opposite. After the first few days and with the loan of some of the tools that had been scavenged and traded, they took over the building projects on their side of the ridge.

The original plan had been for those not involved with that or foraging to begin work preparing fields for the following spring. Instead, Phil suggested that the extra bodies should be used for the harvest, and he would help them with their fields afterwards.

So it was decided, and this one decision brought the two groups closer together. They worked side by side diligently, helping one another, keeping one another's spirits high despite the onerous task that lay ahead of them.

Ebba was allotted a small army of new recruits too. These assisted in preparing the fruit and veg for storage.

The days dragged on and on, and each one seemed colder than the one before, reminding them all that autumn and winter were just around the corner.

Finally, the harvest was over and the committee had assembled once more. The meetings usually took place in the open, but this one was held in the house Susan, Nicola and Wei's families resided in. Not because of the weather, although it had been raining and it was chilly, but because of the noise outside. People were celebrating, and even the builders on the other side of the ridge had downed tools and come across to join in the festivities.

Songs were being sung. Games were being played. Laughter rang out from around the campfires despite the inclement weather, and even though the two groups had lived and slept separately since their communities had been thrown together, there was a oneness now.

Three wide logs had been positioned around the fire, and each of the committee members enjoyed a few minutes of rest while cradling bowls of soup. They were more elated than the people outside.

Susan sat looking around the circle at the faces who still seemed to be in a state of shellshock, not believing it was over, not believing they had managed to pull off this logistical nightmare.

"Well, I suppose we'd better get started," she said. "The sooner we finish here the sooner we can get out there and join the others. First of all, I think we should have a round of applause for our two people of the moment. Phil and Ebba."

Whistles and loud claps filled the room. "Well done, Philly boy," said Jason, who had partaken in a little of the potato peel vodka that he'd been gifted by Woody the last time he went to Infinity.

"Brilliant job, Ebba. Just amazing," Debbie added, placing a hand on the other woman's back.

The words of congratulations and thanks went on for several minutes before everyone calmed down again. "You pulled it off," Susan said, taking the reins once more. "You both pulled off what seemed like an impossible task."

"It was a team effort," Ebba replied humbly.

"Nonsense," said Phil. "Let's face it. It was mainly me."

They all laughed. "Humble as ever, my husband," Debbie replied, shaking her head.

"I'll leave humility to the peasants. You should all bow down before me."

"I'm not too sure if Phil's got a God complex or God has a Phil complex. But either way, I can't thank you all enough for this," Rommy said. "Phil, Susan, Callie, everyone. The way you've brought us in. The way you've included us, made us feel part of the community. In the couple of weeks we've been here, it's given us all a new lease of life."

There had been another journey to Crowesbury since their arrival, and they had returned with a much smaller group of Wanderers, but they had been absorbed into the bigger melting pot too. The hope was that, eventually, all the displaced people who wanted to fit in, wanted to start again and build a new community would hear about what was happening in Redemption and join them.

"Yeah, well," Drake said, glaring at Callie then Susan. "The original plan was to do it in increments, but all that went to hell after that first night, didn't it?"

The others laughed. "Yeah. I think that's what they call baptism by fire."

"Well," Susan said, taking back control of the meeting, "everything is working out. We've managed to iron out the bumps we've encountered along the way, and nothing I've seen suggests to me that we won't grow stronger with the inclusion of other Wanderers when we find them or they find us."

"Provided they're not cannibals or people traffickers, that is," Phil added with a smirk.

"Well, then they wouldn't be Wanderers, would they?" Callie replied. "Arse." She knew he'd said it to wind her up, and his wink and friendly smile told her as much.

"I realise spirits are higher than usual today, and I'm sure I'm not the only one who wants to get done, so let's keep this moving. I just want to confirm," Susan said, turning to Phil. "You called time on the harvest. You're content that everything is out of the ground?"

Phil leaned back a little. Normally, sharing the revelry outside would be the last thing he wanted to do, but this was different. This marked all his hard work, all his worrying, and all his planning coming to fruition. This was probably the single greatest achievement of his life. In the bunker, there were a thousand contingencies in place in case something didn't work. In business, there were plenty of wealthy backers who could always pick up the tab if something went wrong.

Out here, it was all down to him, and those closest to Phil knew that he carried the full weight of that responsibility on his shoulders. His work was literally life and death now. He looked across at Debbie. She'd been his rock. She'd been the one who gave him strength when he needed it the most. He looked at Callie. Her refusal to accept that any problem was unsolvable had been his inspiration. He smiled then turned to Susan and realised that the day's business was not over just yet. "Everything that needs to be out of the ground is out of the ground. I've got a few test crops growing to see how they last through the colder months."

"Test crops?" Susan asked.

"Yes. There are some vegetables that are particularly hardy. Things like parsnips, sprouts, kale and so on. Wei and

I have planted about half a dozen patches and we're going to keep an eye on them across the colder months. It's possible that they might actually grow through the winter. If that's the case, we'll know to plant more next year."

"But I thought we couldn't grow anything in winter. I thought that's why there was such urgency with gathering the big harvest."

"Well, what I should probably have said is that these are crops that can typically grow in the winter months. We've got no idea what kind of winter this is going to be. If this works, then we've gathered some good knowledge and a few extras for the pantry. If it doesn't then, at the worst, we've gambled a few seeds and some labour."

"Okay," Susan replied, nodding appreciatively.

"Of course, if I was able to build more polytunnels that would shore up our food supply no end."

Susan smiled, and the others laughed. "I'm regretting the day I ever traded for those rods," Harper said. "You've been obsessed ever since."

"In all earnestness, though," Susan continued, "I think, moving forward, materials for more polytunnels, cold frames and greenhouses should be put high up on our list of priorities when it comes to both trading and scavenging."

"Seriously?" Phil asked. He found this surprising as every time he had brought this subject up to anyone who would listen, it had been met with shakes of the head and rolls of the eyes.

"Yes. Definitely."

There was no disagreement from the rest of the committee. Phil looked towards Caine, who showed no signs of shock on his face. *This has already been discussed with him.* "Not that I'm not grateful, but why the change of heart?"

"Well, the cabins have proven to be a game-changer with respect to housing. We have most of the materials far more readily available, and this means that we can expand much quicker," Susan said, looking towards Rommy then

Becka and smiling. "So, with the housing situation well in hand, I think it's important that we double down on our food security."

"So this has all come about as a direct result of our new guests?"

"They're not guests."

"You know what I mean."

"Well, yes, that and the fact that Wei gave me a guided tour of the polytunnel and explained what it was allowing us to do and what potential was there."

"I've been trying to explain that to you ever since we built the bloody thing."

Everybody laughed once more. "Ah, yes, but Wei explained it in a way that I could actually understand."

"Well, excuse me if I'm not fluent in peasant. I've been trying to explain that—"

Susan put her hand up. "Look, I'm sorry. Sometimes, you're just a little bit overwhelming, and it needs someone who can break things down to illustrate the benefits of something."

"Well, I suppose I should just be grateful that you've agreed to it anyway, but—"

Debbie placed a hand on her husband's arm. "Yes, you should. This is what we were talking about the other day. When you've got something you've been wanting, don't keep labouring the point. It will only make people regret their decision."

Raucous laughter erupted from somewhere outside, and Phil let out a long sigh. It was true. This was why he needed Debbie, Callie, Wei and others. He had no off switch. His mind operated not just on a different level but in a different dimension a lot of the time, constantly racing ahead. It was difficult for people to keep up, let alone understand him. He turned back to Susan. "Thank you."

Susan nodded. "You're welcome, Phil. Now," she said, turning to the others. "Does anyone have any further business to discuss?"

"Gustav's team finished work on the first hotel this morning," Becka said.

The hotel was a glib description of the giant wooden building that Jason's team had made a start on. It was twice the size of the barn but, for the time being, just on one level, although they hadn't ruled out the possibility of building a second. It meant that over a hundred people would have a solid roof over their heads instead of living in tents.

"Blimey. He doesn't muck around, does he?" Jason said, nodding appreciatively.

"No. He's breaking ground on another tomorrow while a second team begins work on erecting large lean-tos at the left and right of it. We're expecting these will house another fifty."

"Yeah," Rommy continued. "Now that the harvest's done, it's going to free a lot more bodies up, and we're hoping we'll have everybody on our side of the ridge under cover by the time the really bad weather hits."

"That's impressive," Drake said. "You'll have to get Gustav over here to show Jason how it's done."

"Screw you, soldier boy," Jason said, laughing.

Susan turned to Jason. "How are we doing on this side of the ridge?"

Jason looked towards Zep then turned back to Susan. "Well, now the harvest's done with, we should be okay too. Our biggest hurdle is still the stone for the chimney stacks. If we can give Austin some extra bodies, that'll help us out no end."

Susan wrote something down on her piece of paper and looked at Caine. "I know you wanted to head out on another scavenging trip the day after tomorrow, but how do you feel about your full crew going with Austin instead?"

The full crew. Even Caine found it hard to believe the level of responsibility he had been given, but he was also more than a little confused about the request. The full crew consisted of six hundred men and women, and although there was nothing he wanted more than to search new villages and towns to discover what new treasures they might find, he wasn't blind or deaf to the situation.

"Yeah. Of course. But…."

"But what?" Susan asked, leaning back a little.

Caine looked at her nervously. "But I thought you wanted us to help with the fuel situation."

Susan closed her eyes. "Oh, God, yes, I'm sorry. We spoke about it earlier, and now I'm asking you to be in two places at once, aren't I?" She shook her head. "Sorry," she said again.

"The fuel situation?" Jason asked.

"I want to create fuel stores. I think we need a concerted effort to make sure we've got enough wood cut and kindling collected for the winter months."

"I know you've got a lot on, Susan," Jason began, "and what you're suggesting sounds worthwhile, but how are you going to do that?"

"What do you mean?"

"I mean we're cutting and chopping for all the building projects. We can't afford to give up any of our tools or we'll get behind, which will mean we don't have enough substantial shelter for the winter months. I mean, I know the initial idea was to have a lot of people under tarps and so on, but since we've started building the cabins, that hopefully won't be a worry now. If you say you want us to give up some of our tools, though, then there's no way we'll have all the building projects done in time for the winter. So, what do you intend to use for the firewood?"

"Err…." Panic seized Susan. This had been something she'd discussed with Callie the previous evening. Callie had been the architect of a lot of the ideas Susan had put forward. The teenager never wanted credit for them. She wanted to make her mother's life easier. She wanted her mother to appear to people that she was in full control, that she had her finger on the pulse and she was ahead of any problems that might arise. All Callie wanted was for Redemption to succeed.

It had been Callie who had brought up the matter of fuel. At the moment, people collected their own. There was a vast wealth of blackened boughs and branches and chunks of wood lying around from the aftermath of the cabin building. Pickings were good, but anyone with a gram of foresight understood that in the dead of winter, having a consistent and bountiful supply would be the difference between life and death.

"Don't you remember, Mum? You said you were going to have a word with Jason first," Callie said.

Susan flicked over the sheet in her lap and looked at the one below. "Agh. Yeah. I suppose the cat's out of the bag now, isn't it?"

"Go on, Susan," Greenslade said. "What were you going to propose?"

"Well," she said, flicking back and forth between the sheets. "I err … y'see—"

Even by the light of the fire, Phil could see the expression on Callie's face. Most people believed Susan to be the architect of the majority of the ideas she put forward, but he knew better. In Callie, he spotted a kindred spirit, a mind that raced ahead, not just contemplating the next hour or the next morning but the next month, the next year, the next decade. "Good grief, Susan, I was there when you wrote it down," he said, looking towards the others and taking the attention away from her. "See what we've done to this poor woman? We've filled her head with so many of our ideas and complaints and wants that she can't even recall her own thoughts." The others laughed, and he caught the anxious look etched on her face out of the corner of his eye before continuing. "We simply use the tools in shifts."

"What?" Jason and Zep asked.

Both Callie and Susan were looking at Phil, wide-eyed now, fearful of where the conversation would lead and how the others would react. "When you've finished your day's work, you relinquish your tools and our woodcutters use them."

"Are you kidding me?" Jason asked, first looking at Susan and then Phil. "This hasn't been thought through. We work from dawn 'til dusk. Our tools are in use all that time. You're suggesting people who've already worked a full day pick up axes and saws and start again."

"Once again, the gist is so near and yet so far. One day, I'm going to say something and it will be just as blindingly obvious to everyone else what I mean as it is to me."

"I wouldn't bank on it," Debbie muttered under her breath.

"Jason, it's simple," Phil said, ignoring his wife's remark. "We have three collection points. The farmyard, the forest on this side of the ridge and the forest on the other side of the ridge. The wood-gathering crew will be split into two shifts, one that will begin at dawn and one that will begin a few hours later. For the sake of fairness, this can alternate, maybe three days earlies and three days lates, something like that. Some of the wood and kindling won't need cutting or trimming down. Some will. When your work is done, your saws and axes are handed over to the late shift, and they work into the evening cutting and chopping, thereby making use of your tools when you don't need them."

"Okay. Fair enough, I don't have a problem people using our tools when we're not, but you haven't explained how they're going to do this in the dark."

"Aah, I'm glad you brought this up because this is where the science of what we're doing comes into it." Phil still held everyone's attention, and several leaned forward, a little intrigued by what he was about to say next. "Y'see, about seven hundred thousand years ago, our ancestors discovered how to create fire. Ever since that time, it's been used for a variety of purposes, including the generation of heat and—" he turned to Jason and Zep "—this is where you need to concentrate, fellas, light." Some people began to chuckle. Others shook their heads. "Y'see, if you have light, it permits you to see what you're doing even after the sun has gone down. Now, I know what I'm suggesting sounds cutting edge and possibly a little bit crazy, but I propose we try to emulate what those pioneers did and build our own fires in order to—"

"How someone hasn't beaten the shit out of you before now is completely beyond me," Jason said, and everyone laughed this time, including Phil.

"And me," Zep added.

"And me," Debbie replied, causing even more laughter.

"Sorry," Phil said, smiling. "I couldn't resist. In all seriousness, though, when Susan first mentioned the idea to me, I shared your exact same concerns, but when she went into detail, it made perfect sense."

"It's not ideal," Jason replied.

"Tell me something that is these days."

The other man shrugged. "Yeah, true enough."

"I did get it all right, didn't I?" Phil asked, looking at Susan. "That was what you were going to say when you found your notes."

"Err … yes. Yes, thank you, Phil," she replied with a weak but grateful smile on her face. She turned to Caine. "So, do you think you'd be able to coordinate that?"

"Three sites, six teams, two shifts. No problem," Caine replied, and Susan scribbled something onto one of the sheets.

"Excellent. Thank you. Now, I think that's enough of our night gone, don't you? Unless there are any other issues that require immediate attention or discussion, I suggest we get out there and enjoy what's left of the evening."

"Hear, hear!" Debbie replied, and everyone picked up their bowls and began to file out.

"Thanks for that," Callie said quietly as she and Phil were the last to leave the small house.

"Your mum seemed to be floundering a bit."

"Yeah."

"Or was it you? I get confused."

"Ha ... ha."

"I mean, the pair of you are so alike. It's almost as if you're talking sometimes."

"Alright, smart arse."

"So, was it her mistake or yours?"

"Mine, actually. I felt sure we'd have had enough tools after the last visit to New Fenton. I just didn't take into account the scale of the building programme that was underway. I mean, Jason's got five different teams working and Gustav has two more over the ridge."

"Well, no harm, no foul. We've got a solution now."

"Thanks again."

"Considering the amount of times you've been to bat for me, it's the least I can do."

"You've got that right." They both laughed. Together they walked through the farmyard. The rain had subsided to little more than the occasional drizzle. The happiness in the air was infectious, and neither of them could do anything about the huge smiles that broke on their faces as they journeyed towards the edge of the fields. Here things weren't quite as loud, and they could hear themselves talk a little better. "How are you feeling?" Callie asked.

"What do you mean?"

It was dark, but there was still enough light cast by the multiple fires that were burning for them to see each other. "I mean how are you feeling?" She gestured towards the fields. "You did all this. We have food for the winter because of you. There are over three and a half thousand people here, and now they've got a chance where they didn't have one before. They've got a future when they didn't have one before. You must be feeling pretty good about yourself."

Phil shrugged. "I suppose."

"You suppose? What about all that 'I am your God, bow down before me' stuff?" Phil let out a chuckle.

22

"There's just a part of me that's worried it's not going to be enough."

"What do you mean? You said yourself there'll probably be a good surplus if anything."

"I'm not just talking about the food, Callie. I'm talking about all of it. The food, the fuel, the houses, all of it."

"Do you think I haven't thought like that? Do you think my mum hasn't? Anybody with a brain in their head is worried about what's waiting for us, Phil. But all we can do is what we always do. Buckle down and fight. If things happen, we deal with them. It's what we've done since we got here; it's what we'll continue to do."

"And what if that's not enough either?"

"It has to be. Because there's nothing else."

1

NOW

It had been just short of twelve weeks since Rommy and Becka had arrived at Redemption. Other than that first night, there hadn't been a minute of regret. In Callie, Phil and the others, they had found acceptance, understanding and eventually solidarity. They had remarked many times since how they wished they'd had the courage to reach out to each other in the time before. Maybe things wouldn't have been as dire as they were.

The fire continued to crackle away and they both sat in front of it losing themselves in the flames. Behind them seventy souls slumbered in curtained cubicles. It was a world away from ideal, but compared to what they'd had, it was luxury. Their quiet late-night chats had become a tradition. They'd formed their own committee of two. After all, they were the representatives of the people formerly known as the Wanderers.

They each took a sip of their camomile tea. In the ruins of Crowesbury, Rommy would have been lucky to have water. *I'll never take this for granted.*

An uncomfortable look crept onto Becka's face and she placed her hand under her top. There was a tearing sound, and a second later, she flicked a washing instruction label into the fire. It sizzled before vanishing into the flames.

"Bloody thing," she said.

"You forget what it's like wearing new clothes, don't you?" Rommy replied, smiling.

She and Becka had been the last to take clothing supplies from the Redemption store, despite Becka needing them more than anyone. Today had marked the occasion when they had finally afforded themselves the privilege of a new wardrobe. Caine had taken them and a number of their people out a couple of times. The original plan had been for them to keep what they found and vice versa, but even though they were still referred to as Wanderers by some, others called them the Northerners because of their camp being north of the ridge, while others still labelled them Rommy's gang or Becka's gang. But it was clear to everyone that they were just an extension of the Redemption community. So, anything scavenged, farmed or foraged just went into a communal pot. It was the only logical way forward. Us and them didn't cut it anymore. Us and them created unnecessary barriers that would ultimately result in conflict. Us and them had been the way of the time before. Us and them had failed. It was time for something else.

Rommy rubbed her hand down the arm of her hoodie, appreciating the soft feel of the material beneath her fingers. She let out a small, childlike, gleeful giggle.

"What is it?" Becka asked.

"I can't remember the last time I wore something that didn't have holes in it or wasn't stained. I just didn't think I'd get to have something like this again."

"I know what you mean." Becka had changed more than anyone since their arrival in Redemption. She'd let her hair grow back, and even though food was hardly plentiful, there was more to her than just skin and bone now.

Another short, sharp sound left Rommy's lips, and for a second Becka thought her friend was laughing again, but as she turned, she saw tears streaming down the other woman's face. Becka shuffled a little closer and placed her arm around her.

"I'm sorry," Rommy said, wiping her eyes.

"You never have to apologise to me, Rommy. But what's wrong? One second you're smiling, the next you're crying."

"It's just that…." She couldn't go on for a moment, and as she looked into the warm fire, it burned her eyes. "We spent last winter in the sewers. The sewers, Becka. I took my Bea down into the sewers of Crowesbury."

"We all did whatever we could to survive."

Rommy sniffed loudly and wiped away more tears. "Yeah. We did. But trying to keep smiling when you're stuck in a network of tunnels that have served no purpose but to transport piss and shit and all kinds of foulness is tough. Keeping a smile on your face and telling your daughter it's all going to be okay while a storm above ground unleashes torrents washing away the temporary camp you'd made for yourself makes you lose a little bit of your soul. I told her. I told her it was all going to be fine. But I didn't believe it. I didn't believe it for a second. I lied to my daughter because I didn't want her to feel what I was feeling. I didn't want her to feel the desperation, the hopelessness, the … the … torment."

"Jesus."

"I don't know what was worse. I don't know whether living through it or lying to my little girl, telling her it was all going to be okay, was the worst part of it. To this day, I still don't know."

Becka tightened her grip on her friend a little. "But it was okay, wasn't it? You got through it and you're both here now."

Rommy turned to look at Becka. Her eyes were still full, threatening another flood. "But that's the point. I didn't know that. I told her it would all be okay, but I didn't believe it. I didn't think it for a second. They were just words. I felt like my grandad."

"What? I don't understand."

Rommy sniffed once more, using the heel of her palm to dry her eyes. "When my grandma had been diagnosed with lung cancer, I remember him repeating over and over again, 'She'll be okay. Strong as an ox that woman. She'll beat it.' It gave her comfort. She was suffering at the time, but it gave her comfort. She lasted less than six months."

"I'm sorry."

"No. That's not the point. Afterwards, I asked him why he kept saying to her that she was going to be alright. He just looked at me and said, 'Because it's what she wanted to hear, and it made me feel better.'" They both sat quietly for a moment just listening to the quiet crackle and pop of the fire. "So, you see. When I told Bea it was all going to be okay, I said it to make my life easier, not because I thought for a second it would."

"We all have to lie sometimes to save people from the hurtful truths."

"Maybe. Maybe that's the case, maybe it isn't."

Becka sat back for a moment, pulling her arm from around Rommy. "This time last year, we were contemplating going back to the mine."

Rommy had heard Becka talk about the mine only with disdain. It had been where her people had survived the asteroid and the horrors that followed. "And did you?"

A bitter smile cracked on Becka's face. "We put it to a vote. But in the end, we couldn't. There were many who'd rather have died than go back there. Sometimes memories are more dangerous than the sharpest blade, the biggest gun, the deadliest virus. Sometimes memories are enough to bring about the end of everything you've fought for."

"So, what did you do?"

"Ha!" It was Becka's eyes that filled now.

"What does that mean?"

"There were some who said we should just stay put. We should stay put and let whatever was going to happen happen."

"But that would have been suicide."

"Yeah. I think that was the point." She leaned forward, grabbing another chunk of wood and lobbing it gently onto the fire. "On a scavenging trip we'd found the ruins of an old manor house. It was well off the beaten track of any of the traders' routes to Crowesbury, so we discounted it as a permanent base, but we thought it might be somewhere we could last out the winter."

"Why there? Why not in Crowesbury?"

"This place had a big cellar. My guess is that it would have housed wine at some point. Sadly, there was nothing like that when we went. The manor had pretty much been obliterated. Part of the cellar had collapsed, but enough of it was intact enough to house us, and we used the debris from the rest of the house to make it a bit more shielded. We were able to keep fires burning. There were plenty of broken joists and beams up for grabs."

"What did you do for food?"

"We'd done what we could to put a little bit away for winter. We traded what we could with some of the convoys going to Crowesbury, but when the first snow came, we all headed to the manor. Well, most of us did anyway. Some stayed."

"What happened to them?"

"We found their bodies when we returned in the spring."

"So the manor saved you?"

"Most of us. Most of us." Becka's eyes widened as she tried to prevent herself from crying.

"I'm sorry," Rommy said, reaching out and taking her friend's hand.

"Eleven days."

"What is?"

"I went eleven days without food. Once I went eleven days without a thing to eat. Water wasn't a problem. We had plenty of snow to melt. But we had children in the group. We couldn't expect them to go without food."

"How did you last?"

"I don't know. I don't know what got me through. Maybe it was just believing that things couldn't end so badly, so horribly. Maybe it was the stubborn streak inside me that said no way." Another sad smile cracked on her face. "Whatever it was, we survived … most of us."

There's that phrase again. "Most of you?"

"I tried my hardest to keep everybody going, to convince them that the winter would end, that we'd be back in the forest soon enough. We had a few elderly people whose bodies just couldn't take it. To be honest, I'm amazed they lasted as long as they did. But then…."

"Then what?"

"Like I said, it was a big cellar. Lots of nooks and crannies." She took a drink of her tea before continuing. "I used to do my rounds each morning, mainly to check the walls, y'know? Make sure no new cracks had appeared that suggested the whole thing might come crashing down."

"I'm guessing you didn't switch off much."

"Ha. What gave it away? Anyway, one morning, about a month before we went back to the surface, I found six of our people hanging. Five of them had their eyes closed, but Bri … Bri's were bulging out of his head. If I'd have had anything in my stomach at the time, I'd have hurled. Instead, I wretched until it felt like there was nothing but broken glass inside me. In his eyes I could see everything he'd gone through. I could see the doubts and the torturous last few breaths. I won't forget his face until my dying day." She looked down to see Rommy still holding her hand and she pulled it away. *I don't deserve people feeling sorry for me. It was my responsibility to get them all through.*

"I'm sorry," Rommy said, sensing the conflict inside her friend. She understood it only too well.

"Anyway, we lasted until the thaw and then headed back to the forest. We'd found a few empty jars and tools and other things that we were able to use in trade, and we all started eating at least one meal a day again." They both sat quietly for a moment until she continued. "But in all honesty, if we weren't here now, I have no idea how we'd get through another winter out there."

"You're not the only one. And on that happy note, I think it's time for me to turn in."

Becka finished off her drink. "Yeah, me too. Back to preparing the fields tomorrow."

"Oh don't," Rommy said, half laughing and reaching for her back. "I would literally kill for a nice hot bath."

"Mm. With scented candles."

"And a glass of Chablis."

"I was always more of a red girl. Give me a Cab or a Malbec any day of the week."

"And a tub of ice cream."

"Now you're just being cruel. Amnesty International might be a thing of the past but—" She cut off suddenly as she heard a sound. There'd been a cool breeze building outside all night, but now something else had been added to the mix. "What's that?"

"I'm not sure." They both walked down the curtained corridor of what was jokingly referred to as the Hilton. In the evenings, Gustav had carved ornate wooden plaques featuring the names of famous hotels for each of the hostels they were constructing on the northside of the ridge. The two women stepped carefully and kept their noise to a minimum, trying hard not to wake those who were sleeping. As they neared the entrance, the sound became clearer and without even needing to venture outside, they both knew what it was.

Rommy opened the door and raised her lantern to see that a white blanket had already covered the ground around their home. When they had finished their day's work, it had been crisp, but there hadn't been a cloud in the sky. Now, though, not a single star could be seen. In the few seconds they stood there, the snow seemed to have started falling even heavier, and the odd gust hit the side of the building creating the whooshing sound that they had first heard.

"Oh," Becka said sadly.

"Oh," Rommy echoed.

"I'd been hoping we might have a bit longer."

"Me too." The chill was biting as they remained in the doorway, but it was nothing that the pair hadn't experienced before. "Come on, let's get in."

They stepped back inside and closed the door firmly then walked across to the supply corner. The hotels all had their own cooking equipment and food supply. In addition, Susan had ensured that they had spare clothing, blankets and whatever other extras they might need to make the cold a little more bearable.

Almost as if a telepathic conversation had occurred between the pair, they walked over to one of the neatly folded piles and grabbed a thick curtain, which they rolled and placed at the base of the door. Rommy went back across and picked up a roll of the duct tape with which she covered the sides and tops. "It's not the best insulation in the world, but it's better than nothing."

They both went over to the shuttered square that acted as the Hilton's front window just as another light gust made the wooden barrier rattle. Shivers ran through both of them at the same time as the cold bristled over their skin. "Here," Becka said, picking up a section of orange tarpaulin that they'd used to carry over many of their supplies. They squeezed it into the gaps. It wasn't perfect, but it provided some relief from what was going on outside at least.

They stood back as another breath of wind stroked the front of the hotel. This time, there was no freezing rush of air as there had been previously.

"This is it then. This is the start of it all."

"Yeah."

Rommy looked back down the curtained corridor to the fire that still blazed away in the hearth. "We'll be okay. It won't be like last year. We'll be okay, Becka."

Becka didn't speak for a moment but finally turned to her friend and in the lantern light, Rommy could see that fresh tears had appeared in her friend's eyes. "We have to be. I can't go through that again. I can't lose anyone else."

"I promise you. Together, we'll get through and we'll get our people through. I promise you."

*

Tiff and Stu had both lost their families on that fateful night when the Salvation guards had swept into the forest. Neither of them knew how they were going to continue, and for a long time, dark and often suicidal thoughts rang around their heads during every waking hour.

They had lived in a state of bewildered numbness trapped like slaves back in the bunker. It was only when they escaped that they were able to truly mourn what they had lost. With their newfound freedom came survivors' guilt. But it was Redemption that had saved them. It was a giant screw you to the administration, and helping to build it seemed like the best way to honour the memories of their loved ones.

Neither of them had been looking for companionship or friendship, but despite that, they had found it. There was a connection between the two of them, and although the tragic events still pained them like fresh wounds, they had found comfort in each other, and both had a feeling it would lead to more eventually.

They ate together, they confided in each other, and they pulled as many shifts as they could together as respected members of the militia too. They were both proud to have gained esteem the way they had after being such insignificant cogs in the Salvation machine. But tonight, they'd have traded it for a nice warm bed in a heartbeat.

"You okay?" Tiff asked as the snow whirled around them again.

It had seemingly come out of nowhere. One minute it had been cold, colder than either of them remembered in the time before the asteroid. And then the blizzard had begun. They were already heading up the hill to their duty at the east turret when it started. First, there were just a few swirls of snow that seemed almost magical on the breeze as they drifted through the torchlight.

Then the flurries became more persistent. Now, still with another three hundred metres to go before they reached their lookout post, it was ankle deep. What made it worse was that Stu carried a giant backpack full of wood meaning at best all he could do was trudge.

"I-I've never seen anything like this," he replied as his teeth chattered a little.

"Me neither." Tiff looked back to see him holding on to the jutting rocks to his right. In places, the passage to the ridge was narrow, but in the dark and under snow it was even harder to establish whether one was placing their feet on safe ground or not.

"Hang on a m-minute. I need to adjust the pack."

Tiff paused and turned, shining her torch towards him. He struggled with the straps, pulling hard, shifting the position of the pack on his shoulders. Finally, he straightened up once more. "No way should this be left to us. They should deliver these things during the day. Even if it wasn't snowing, it's dangerous lugging this much around on a night."

"I know. Maybe you can give me some of the load," she said, taking a step towards him. "Would that make it easier?"

Stu reached out and took her hand. To his surprise, it was still quite warm. She had her fists balled and curled the end of her sleeves around like giant mittens. He had meant to just squeeze her hand once as a gesture of thanks and friendship, but now it wasn't just the soothing warmth that kept him holding on, and as she gently rubbed her thumb over the top of his fingers, he knew that she felt it too.

They both smiled. It was a simple gesture, and in some ways, it felt taboo, like it was all too soon. In other ways, it felt perfectly natural. The world had come to an end and they had to live their lives at high speed because no one knew what was next.

"Come on," Tiff said. "Let's get to the turret where we can get you warmed up."

"Yeah. Let's."

She turned and started to walk again. It seemed like in that moment's pause, another few centimetres of snow had fallen, but in reality, they were just heading into a drift.

"Be careful here, it's—WAAGH!"

*

To Stu it looked as if Tiff's legs had been knocked from beneath her. One second she was plodding along, the next she was falling. "TIFF!" His voice was lost in the howling wind almost as soon as he shouted her name.

The snow tore at his face as he battled forward, and his heart began to pound harder than any time since that night in the forest when his life was turned upside down.

*

It wasn't so much thought as instinct that made Tiff reach out. Somehow, her right hand grabbed a mound of scrub grass bursting through the rocky face of the ridge. The snow had yet to consume it fully and she felt the sharp, frozen stalks tear at her fingertips, but she managed to hold on. "Stu!" The pleading cry left her lips and soared above the screaming wind.

Her left hand dug into the snow on the other side, finding the narrowest of ledges to hold on to as her legs swung beneath her.

*

Stu could barely move with the weighty rucksack on his back. He shuffled it off, not thinking, not caring where it would land. There was just one thing on his mind and that was saving the woman who had saved him, who had got him through these last few torturous months.

From where he was standing there was no sign of her, but he followed the sound of Tiff's voice and as he leaned over the ridge, there she was. The drop was about forty metres to already snow-covered, jagged rocks below. He fell to his knees, and for the moment at least the cold and discomfort were forgotten as adrenaline began to surge. He reached down with his right hand and burrowed into the snow with his left, anchoring himself to whatever jutting piece of granite offered help. "Reach for my hand, Tiff."

*

Pop! Pop! Pop!

Despite the sound of the rising storm around her and Stu's voice, Tiff could hear the unmistakable sound of the scrub grass tearing. Then she could feel it as more of the life-giving strands began to pull free from the rocky earth that had borne them.

"I can't. I can't."

Stinging tears formed in her eyes as she looked up. Her torch was still strapped to her wrist and in the periphery of the light, she couldn't see Stu's face, but his reaching fingers dangled above her.

*

"Listen to me. You've got to."

He heard a sound to his left, he wasn't quite sure what it was, but that didn't matter. The only thing that mattered was Tiff. "Reach. You've got to reach. Please."

*

The hot tears rolled down her face warming her cheeks despite the storm. *I love him.* It was only now that she was at death's door that she could make this admission. It felt like a betrayal to the family she had lost, but it was so freeing as the thought formed in her mind at the same time. "I love you." She spoke the words only for them to be stolen by the wind.

36

"What?" Stu called down, trying to extend his arm even further but failing.

"I said I love you," she shouted back as the grass in her fist became looser.

Got to say it back. If these are the last words we say to each other, I've got to say it back. "I love you. That's why you really need to take my hand, Tiff."

"I-I can't. I can't reach." Pop! Pop! Pop! Pop! "I can't reach."

Stu took a deep breath, which ripped at the back of his throat. He edged further forwards, his knees displacing more snow, which disappeared over the ledge. He hunted around with his left hand for another raised bump, or crack, or anything that would give him purchase; then he reached further. "Take it. Take my hand. TAKE MY HAND!"

Pop! Pop! Pop! Tiff pulled herself up with all the speed and strength she could muster. At the same time, she could feel the roots of the scrub grass tear. *This is it. This is my one and only chance.* She lunged, whipping her arm around anticlockwise. Clap! At first, she thought she was dreaming when she felt icy cold fingers wrap around her slightly warmer wrist. Then she looked up to see Stu's face as he extended himself at a perilous angle. "Don't let go," she cried. "Please don't let go."

"I won't. But you're going to have to help me. I don't have the strength to pull you up by myself. You're going to need to try to climb." His words were strained as he took her full weight.

Tiff searched the rock face with her left hand hunting for anything that she could grip. She found a crack and squeezed her fingers in then heaved herself up while Stu pulled. She swept her right leg up and the edge of the heel of her boot came to rest on a jutting piece of granite no wider than a couple of centimetres. It wasn't exactly safe footing, but it was something. She shifted her left hand higher and found another thin ledge. Her fingertips held firm. It was agony.

"Don't let go," she cried again.

"You're almost there. Keep going."

She hoisted the full weight of her body upwards, and this time, Stu didn't stop pulling. A battle cry left his mouth as he heaved with all his strength.

She continued to rise until finally her left hand then foot found safe ground on the ledge before the rest of her body rolled into the drifting snow. The whirling, fast-moving flakes lashed against her face once more now the rock was not there to protect her, but she welcomed them. They were a symbol of life. They signified she had survived. She scrambled to her knees then feet and rushed into Stu's waiting arms. "Thank you. Thank you," she repeated over and over as she kissed his face. He reciprocated until their lips finally met and lingered for several seconds.

When they pulled away once more, the cold, the terror of the last few moments was forgotten. A smile, the likes of which neither of them had shared in a long time, lit their faces beyond what the LED torch could ever do.

"We'd better get going."

"I suppose," Tiff replied, kissing him once more.

It was as if the world had frozen around them. Nothing mattered anymore. They'd found each other, really found each other. Stu turned to grab the rucksack. "Shit!"

"What? What is it?"

"I think it went over the side."

"Oh crap!"

"Look. Let's just get to the turret, and we'll have to ask Esme to sort out a resupply for us. Drake won't be happy, but when is he ever happy?"

"Well. Worst comes to worst, I'm sure we can figure out another way to keep each other warm." She winked, and the smile was back on both their faces.

"I like your thinking."

"Come on," Tiff said and set off once more. The blizzard continued to howl around them and each metre they travelled felt like a mile.

They carried on, traversing the overhang, pausing when the gusts struck, turning towards the rock to protect their faces until Tiff stopped again. "What is it?" asked Stu.

She turned to look at him. "We need to be extra careful here," she replied, pointing her torch up ahead at the drift. No rock was visible, it was just a bank of white for ten metres that disappeared around a slight bend, but in the glow of the torch it looked like it went on for an eternity.

"How can it have massed so quickly?"

It was a question she wondered the answer to as well. It was like nothing she'd ever seen before. The snow continued to dance around them and sometimes it was as if it was a solid frozen sheet striking their bodies. Tiff had lived in Norway for a few years as a young girl and she had witnessed some hellish snowstorms but never anything like this before.

"I don't know," she said, turning back to her direction of travel and slowly plodding through the drift. *One foot in front of the other. That's the only way through this. Slowly, surely, make sure I've got a firm footing before moving again.* "It's a good thing we got the new boots from the stores before we set off," she shouted over her shoulder. *One foot then the next.* "I said it's a good thing we got these new boots from the stores before we set off." When no answer came a second time, she stopped and turned, shining her torch directly at the space where Stu should have been. "Stu?" She angled the beam down to see a gap in the snow hacked from the edge of the pathway where he'd vanished. "STU!" she howled this time as the wind competed with her once more.

She battled the short distance to the spot where he had obviously gone over the edge, hoping, praying that she would see him hanging on to something as she had done just minutes before. But as she angled her torch down, all she could see was the twirling snow disappearing into the blackness. "STU!" she shrieked this time. "STU!"

Tiff lost track of time as she stood staring over that ledge. It could have been a few seconds, it could have been a few minutes, but when she came to her senses again, she was covered in snow almost as if it had been shovelled on top of her. She shook herself free, still waiting hopelessly, pathetically to hear Stu's voice calling back to her.

A few minutes ago, she had been the happiest she'd been since that night in the forest. *Now … now this.*

She unstrapped the torch from her wrist and turned it off, dropping it in the snow at her feet. Then she stepped off the ledge. The unrelenting, freezing wind felt like acid against her bare face as she fell. *It'll all be over soon. It'll all be over soon. It'll all be—*

*

Esme had pulled sentry duty with Steve. He was a member of the militia, and she often wondered how he had the strength to pick up a gun never mind fire one. He was like a skeleton, and it was nothing to do with food rationing. By his own admission, he had been like this since childhood. He didn't have an eating disorder, in fact his appetite was good, but he was just someone who struggled to put on weight.

The turret they occupied looked out over the vast swathe of barren land to the north and up until an hour ago, the visibility had been pretty good. Then it clouded over, and now there was a full-scale blizzard in progress.

"Our relief should have been here," Steve said.

"Yeah," Esme admitted reluctantly. "They should have been here about twenty-five minutes ago."

All the turrets were fitted with flues courtesy of Caine and Woody. Originally, no thought had gone into making the simple defence buildings anything other than battle resistant. However, it became obvious that some kind of heat source would be required if the occupants were going to last through the long, cold, dark winter nights. Because this had been an afterthought, there was no fireplace as such, merely a hole dug in the ground with a semicircular row of stones around it, not that there was anything to burn if the fire somehow managed to spread a little.

Steve placed his hands under his arms, hugging himself tightly. The fire was meagre. Neither of them had expected such a sudden drop in temperature and the shift before had used up far more wood than usual. They both glanced into the corner now to see just one more log. "For their sakes, I hope they bring more wood with them because there's no way that's going to last the night."

The little wood there was had barely been enough for their duty. Esme had felt like Ebeneezer Scrooge when Steve had asked if he could put the last log on the fire and she'd said no. "Yeah. Let's hope." She walked up to the normally open aperture at the front of the turret. This had been another amendment to the initial design. On the advice of Rommy, Becka and others, if Drake and his people wanted to keep these buildings operational in the winter months, they would need protection from the elements. Shutters had been constructed for all of them, and although they were far from perfect, they held out the worst of the weather. She reached up towards the long narrow shutter, wide enough to allow two rifles to take aim at any prospective enemy.

"Don't. It's freezing," Steve protested. "The temperature in this place drops five centigrade every time you open that thing."

She glanced back towards him. *He's right.* "We've got a job to do. That's why we're here."

"There are another two turrets facing north. It's not like we're the only ones."

She paused with her hand on the shutter. Originally, there had been more, but now there was a larger one closest to the road and two satellite ones to report back if someone tried to launch a cross-country assault. They were in the one furthest to the east. It was about half a kilometre from the road and nestled behind a small ledge. "You know they've all got different lines of sight."

"Nobody's going to try to launch an attack in this weather."

"We've got a job to do," she repeated, taking a breath and sliding the shutter open.

The icy breeze of an hour before had turned into a biting wind, and even though they had been able to hear it with the shutter closed, it howled like a distressed wolf with it open. A blast of snow hit Esme in the face as if it had been fired from a cannon. She stumbled back a little before steadying herself and squinting in the hope of seeing something beyond the angry flurry. She forced the sliding shutter closed one more time and bent over, wiping her face with both hands hoping to alleviate the painful sting of the blast.

"See anything good?"

"Very funny," she replied. "It seems to be getting worse by the minute out there."

"I told you it was a mistake to open that shutter. I didn't think it could get any colder in here, but feel it. It's like we're in the Arctic or something."

"It's our duty to—"

"Listen to me, Esme. You know I don't shirk responsibility, and I take this and the militia as seriously as anyone, but we're inside and we're feeling the cold this badly. You couldn't keep that thing open for five seconds without nearly falling over. Do you honestly think anybody could launch an attack in this? Hell, the fact that our relief is so late probably means the roads are already a nightmare to negotiate."

Esme let out a long sigh and walked over to the small fire, extending her hands and allowing herself to warm up for a moment. "You're right, I suppose."

Steve suddenly felt a little guilty. "Look. I admire you for being so diligent. But we need to be sensible too. We need to keep it as warm as possible in here. It's not like it's well insulated to start off with, is it?"

Esme let out a small laugh. "No. I suppose you're right." She looked at her watch. Few people other than the guards still kept time, but it was hard for Esme not to stick to a schedule. "They're very late. Do you think I should go out to look for them?"

"Oh yeah. That's a really good idea. Go out into the freezing cold and get soaked into the bargain looking for a couple of people who might not even have set off yet for all we know. You know our orders better than anyone. We stay here until relief comes."

Esme let out another long sigh as she stared into the meagre flames. "In which case, we'd better make that final log last as long as possible."

2

The occupants of the small dwelling Callie called home had listened to the blizzard rage outside. They had insulated the shuttered opening they called a window and stuffed a threadbare, rolled-up curtain beneath the door in order to block out as much of the chill as they could. They had all said at some point in the evening how grateful they were that Susan had pushed for a special wood chopping and fuel gathering detail to get them through the cold months.

There was a large pile of logs in one corner and plenty more stacked against the food storehouses on the edge of the farmyard. If this first night was anything to go by, every soul in Redemption would be thankful for the forward planning before winter was over.

Callie woke with a start and leaned up a little, noticing her mother's sleeping bag was empty. The fire still hissed and crackled away providing enough light through the curtained cubicle for her to see clearly. Si snored at the far end, oblivious to his mother's absence or anything else for that matter.

"Mum?" she called out quietly, a little confused as to why there was no sign of her mother in the dead of night. There was no response, and she shuffled out of her bag and climbed to her feet. She had originally got into bed wearing all her clothes due to the cold, but the fire and the warmth of the bag had made her gradually undress garment by garment. Other than the gaps beneath the door and around the shutter, the small replica blackhouse was well insulated. Earth packed the walls and heat was slow to escape.

Callie drew back the front curtain to their partitioned cubicle and looked towards the fire to see her mother sitting in front of it cross-legged. She stepped out as a loud snore from Wei made the air vibrate. Callie smiled. It had taken some getting used to living in a small house with people who up until a few months ago had been virtual strangers, but she had acclimatised to their idiosyncrasies now.

"Mum?" she said quietly.

Susan jumped, turning at the same time. She had a look on her face resembling that of a child who'd just been found with their hand in the biscuit tin.

"You scared me," she replied, trying to hide her shock with a laugh.

Callie walked up to her mother then sat down beside her. "What are you doing up? Is everything okay?"

"Yes … yes." Susan gazed back into the fire, still forcing a smile. "I just couldn't sleep, that's all. I didn't want to wake you and Si up."

"Mum. You know that you have the worst poker face on the planet. The days of you being able to tell me that there's nothing to worry about are long gone."

Susan laughed this time and reached out, taking her daughter's hand. "I suppose they are, aren't they?"

"What is it?"

Susan took a deep breath. "It's bad out there. It's been non-stop."

"I know."

"What if…."

"What if what?"

"What if we haven't done enough? What if I haven't done enough?" There it was. Susan bore the full weight of every decision she made for Redemption. She knew the choices she made affected everyone, and there wasn't a waking moment where she wasn't second-guessing herself, wondering if there was something she could do better.

"We've been through this, Mum. Over and over and over, we've been through this. There's only so much responsibility you can take. We've got food. We've got shelter. We've got fuel. There are over three and a half thousand people here, and we've made it work. Yes, it's not perfect, but we've got a functioning and growing settlement. We came here as refugees. No. Scratch that. We came here as fleeing slaves. We had virtually nothing, but we've built it into something … all of us. You've done more than anyone to make that happen."

"We both know that's a lie, don't we? Most of my so-called ideas are yours. They just sound better coming from my mouth than my sixteen-year-old daughter's."

"Err … I'm seventeen now."

Susan laughed to herself again. "I'm sorry, sweetheart. I'm still stuck in Salvation and you're still my little girl."

"I get it. But that's pretty much the point, isn't it? You're not the only one who sees me as a kid. It doesn't matter what I've done or what I've come up with, there are those who'll never be willing to listen to someone so young because it's an affront to their sensibilities." She cleared her throat and did her best Jason impression. "I'm not having some kid telling me what to do. Who does she think she is?"

Susan smiled. "Jason's not as bad as that."

"No, he's not. But others are. So, for the sake of Redemption, it's better that stuff comes from you rather than from me. I've learnt this the hard way." It was Callie who laughed now. "But anyway, going back to what we were talking about. What you've done, what all of us have done here is amazing. But at some point, people have to take responsibility for themselves. You can't go around tucking everyone into bed and making sure they've got enough wood for the fire, making sure that they're insulating their houses as best they can."

"But—"

"But nothing, Mum. Everyone has access to the wood. We've made sure each house or hotel has a good supply, has food and has a means to cook. It's up to everyone here to do the best they can for themselves and one another. It's not up to you to become an insomniac and worry yourself to death about it all."

"It burns so quickly," Susan replied, turning back to the fire.

"Oh, so now you're responsible for the speed at which wood burns? Brilliant. Is there anything else you want to blame yourself for? The snow maybe? How about the night? Maybe if it wasn't so dark on a night, people would be able to see what they're doing all the time and not have to crank up their dynamo lanterns so often. Yeah. Why haven't you done anything about the night?"

"You know, they say sarcasm is the lowest form of wit."

"I'm not trying to be funny—" Callie stopped herself and turned to the curtained cubicles, realising she was raising her voice more than she thought. When she continued, it was in a lower tone. "I'm not trying to be funny. I'm trying to explain to you that you can't hold yourself to account for everything. All you can do is control the things that can be controlled and respond to anything that requires it. You can't pre-empt the unforeseeable, Mum. No one can. And all you're going to do if you think about every possibility, every outcome is make yourself ill."

Susan turned to look at her daughter but didn't speak for several seconds. When she did, it was in an almost apologetic tone. "You're right. I know you're right. It's just…."

"I get it, Mum. I do. You want this place to work for everybody. You want everybody to build a better life here. You want me and Si to be happy here and to have a future. I get all of it. But you need to look after yourself too. You're the cog that keeps this big wheel spinning. Worrying yourself to death does nobody any good."

"I love you so much."

"Well … let's face it. I am pretty lovable." They both laughed. "Are you going to come back to bed now?"

"In a minute."

They sat side by side for a few moments as the snow continued to batter the shutter and the door. "First thing tomorrow, we'll dig our way out of here and visit as many people as we can to make sure they're okay. We'll try to take care of any repairs that need doing; we'll deal with any problems that this storm has caused. Whatever's happened, we'll deal with it. Okay?"

Susan nodded. "Okay."

*

Phil lived in the only house with just two families. One of the doctors who had fled Salvation with Drake shared her curtained cubicle with her daughters while Phil, Debbie and Matt had the other. The third section of the dwelling was dual purpose. It was a drop-in surgery during the day, but at night, it became Phil's domain. It was at the far end of the property, furthest away from the fire.

Much to Jason's chagrin, Phil had demanded that he had some lidded boxes built. It was passed at a committee meeting, but Jason still protested. Then, when Caine found out what they were to be made of, he protested too. It took nearly thirty of his people to gather wood from the pews of the church where they had originally found Rommy and Bea all those months back.

At a first inspection, the boxes looked like sturdy blanket chests. There were three of them. Two of them were pushed end to end and doubled as an examination table during the day, but with a strict proviso. Under no circumstances were they to be opened. It irked Phil that he had to share at all, but he and Debbie actually liked Bindi and her children. She was from Australia originally, and despite being in the UK for over ten years, she'd not lost a hint of her original accent. She was intelligent and funny and gave as good as she got if anyone ever tried to talk down to her or over her.

"I hope you're not damaging my examination table," she said in little more than a whisper as she walked into the white LED glow.

"Bloody hell," Phil cried, throwing his hand up to his chest. "I swear, between you, Debbie, Callie and Dani, I'm going to have a heart attack before long."

"Good job I'm a doctor then, isn't it?"

"Oh yes. That makes me feel so much better."

"Where you're concerned, though, I might just forget my Hippocratic for a few minutes."

They both smiled and Phil looked towards the curtained entrance. "Your girls asleep?"

"Ivy went out like a light. Riley read for a couple of minutes then she went sparko too."

"Poor kids. Can't believe you gave one a dog's name and the other that of a creeping plant."

"You do know that if I inject air into your veins, you'll die a pretty unpleasant death, don't you?"

Phil smiled. "Is there anything I can help you with or have you got up with the sole purpose of giving me a hard time?"

Bindi shrugged. "I wouldn't say the sole purpose. It's just a delightful perk."

Phil shook his head. "There are still times when I wonder if I died in Salvation and this is Purgatory."

"I thought you didn't believe in all that."

"I don't normally, but since I started having to share my house with you, it does beg the question."

"Well, for starters, smart arse, we both moved in here at the same time, so don't make it sound as though you're doing me any favours, and secondly, if anyone's in Purgatory or Hell, it's me, my girls, Debbie and Matt. How they put up with you for so long is beyond me."

"You just haven't got to know me properly yet. When you do, you'll realise I'm an absolute joy to be around."

"Uh-huh. Substitute joy with wanker and I'll agree with you."

Phil shook his head. "You Aussies. No decorum."

"I'll give you bloody decorum." The pair smiled again as a murmur came from elsewhere in the house and Phil's face straightened. He waited to see if another sound followed and breathed a small sigh of relief when it didn't. "Debbie?" Bindi asked.

"Yeah," Phil replied.

"You know I have still got some sleeping tablets in my bag of tricks. I could—"

"That's all we need. Get her hooked on those things then what will she do when we run out? She's started drinking camomile tea before bed. That helps most of the time."

For the first few days of sharing the house, Bindi and her girls had been disturbed by Debbie's nightmares. They had started after her and Phil's abduction and although nowhere near as frequent or vocal as they had been, they still occurred from time to time. "Well, the offer's there if you need them."

"Thanks, Bindi."

"So, anyway. How are they looking?" Phil looked down at the small notebook he'd been writing in and placed it beside him. Bindi sat down on the neighbouring chest and squinted at his illegible scrawl. "You missed your vocation in life. You could have been a doctor with handwriting like that."

Phil laughed. "Yeah. Being a doctor would have been fun if it wasn't for all the people I'd have to deal with."

"Err … the people are kind of pivotal to the profession."

"Exactly."

"So, go on. Have you had a look? You said you were going to tonight, didn't you?"

"Yes and yes."

"And?"

Phil stood and picked up the lantern and notebook before unlatching the lid of the long, wide chest he'd been sitting on seconds before. He knelt down and Bindi joined him as he slowly lifted the heavy wooden cover.

The recycled hinges creaked revealing what to most people would have looked like forest floor detritus beneath a clear plastic sheet but to the two observers was much more. Phil peeled back the piece of sheeting that had been carefully taped around the rim of the chest so they could get a better look. A thick bed of straw was laid out over the base and several logs were positioned on top of them. The earthy smell suggested the straw was damp, and as Phil lifted the lantern a little higher, it was clear that hundreds of little buds of white mould were sprouting out of what looked like small pods over the straw and the logs.

Bindi's hand shot out and clutched Phil's arm. "Shit! It's working."

Phil kept the light hovering for a moment. "Well, it's a little too early to say," he replied, starting to seal the plastic into place once again.

"Wait a minute. I just want to look a little longer." Bindi's face resembled that of a child who'd just been told they could have whatever sweets they wanted from the shop display. "It's working, Phil. It's really working."

Phil remained patient, letting his friend take in the full contents of the chest before he replaced the plastic and resealed the edges. He gently lowered the lid once more and the pair sat down on top of it. "As I say, it's too early to tell."

"It looks like it's working to me."

"I got this far before, remember. Then it all went—"

"Tits up?"

"You have a beautiful way with words. But yes."

"But you figured it out. You told me you figured it out."

Phil shrugged. "I hope I've figured it out. Y'know, nature is as baffling as it is wonderful. Tania and the others found those mushrooms growing on the underside of a log in the middle of a forest that had been pretty much devastated by the inferno that followed the asteroid. I mean, there they were, just minding their own business in a place they had no right to be. Nobody was helping them. Nobody picked that spot out for them. Nobody prepared the substrate or made sure there was enough moisture or not too much. Nobody did anything, they just grew. Yet I've tried to create the perfect growing environment for these things and it has been like some kind of battle of wits."

"Well, that's been your problem right there."

"Very funny. Seriously, though, how picky can what is basically a glorified mould be?"

"So, remind me. You say we got this far last time. What went wrong?"

"The substrate was tainted. There was something fighting the oyster mushroom spores for dominance. Don't get me wrong, we grew a hell of a lot of mould, just not the right kind."

"But this time?"

"This time we boiled the straw for about half an hour, sterilising it. The spelt we used to nurture the spores was kept in an airtight container, and we lined the chest with plastic sheeting. I've controlled the temperature as well as I possibly can, and when I check in next week, I'm hopefully going to find that the spores are growing."

"What would you expect to see if they were?"

"Well, little grey dots to start off with."

"Little grey dots?" Phil leaned back a little and smiled. "What's funny?"

"Nothing."

"Well, you're smiling."

"Sorry. I didn't realise that was an offence. Didn't people smile down in Australia?"

"Let me go get that syringe."

Phil laughed this time. "I was just remembering back to when I was a child. During the summer holidays once, my mum and I grew some oysters as a project together."

"That's sweet."

"Yeah. We used a toilet roll."

"Are you taking the piss? What's the punchline?"

"No seriously. A toilet roll makes a brilliant substrate for growing oyster mushrooms."

"You're not joking me?"

"No," he replied, shaking his head and turning to look at her. "When my mum first told me, I thought she was pulling my leg too, but she wasn't. We placed the toilet roll on a plastic tray then soaked it in boiling water. We let it cool down a bit then poured the excess liquid away before emptying the spores into the middle. Then we secured a plastic bag over it and put it in a warm, dark place for a couple of weeks."

"Seriously?"

"Yeah. After two weeks, we started spraying it every couple of days, but within four weeks, these little dark grey heads started to appear from the mould. They gradually grew and grew and before we knew it, we had our own small crop of blue oyster mushrooms." Phil sat there for a moment with a happy smile on his face. "Y'know, I think they were the first things I ever grew."

"That's sweet. I bet your mum loved it too."

Phil shrugged and shook his head. "I doubt it. She probably just wanted to keep me occupied with something. But I remember what a thrill it was seeing the evolution of those mushrooms."

It was Bindi who smiled now. Many people in Redemption tolerated Phil, realising they needed him, but putting up with him only as a necessary evil. She actually liked him a lot. The trick with Phil was perseverance. "Well, let's hope you can pull it off again with these."

"Yeah. Let's hope. If I can, and we can manufacture a custom facility for growing these things, we could be self-sufficient in mushrooms all year round. The possibilities would really be endless for the amount we could produce." His eyes sparkled with excitement as he spoke.

"Manufacture a facility? You start saying things like that around Jason and he really is going to be gunning for you."

"I mean eventually … kind of."

"This is just you and me talking. And bear in mind, knowing how quickly you alienate people, it's not a bad thing to have someone on your side. How much of a game changer is this if you get it right?"

"It's huge. Massive. If I can make this work, if I can start producing mushrooms on an industrial scale it could change absolutely everything. Back in Salvation, they were never seen as anything more than a side dish. I always wanted to advance our fungiculture efforts far more than Bucks and the others allowed me to. We had lab facilities there. It would have been far easier. I was constantly arguing the point that mycoprotein would be a massively cheaper and more nutritious alternative to the lab-grown meat, but…." He stopped and his eyes drifted.

Bindi had noticed this about Phil. Thoughts occasionally entered his head and got stuck there. She snapped her fingers. "Bindi to Phil. Bindi to Phil. Come in, Phil."

He blinked twice, three times, and suddenly he was back with her. "Could it have been something as simple as hierarchy?"

"If I knew what the bloody hell you were talking about, I might be able to tell you."

"The lab-grown meat was expensive. People on Level Three could only afford it once in a blue moon if they were lucky. People on Level Two didn't really eat it on a regular basis, but on Level One … they seemed to have it all the time. Could their reluctance to allow me to develop mycoprotein as a viable alternative to meat and that crappy soya stuff they made to seem deliberately synthetic have been down to something as petty and ridiculous as status? If it was affordable and available to everyone then what would separate the rich from the poor? Could it really have been something so insidious, so sickening?"

Bindi shrugged. "I don't think I ever met Bucks once in all the time I was in Salvation. I met that Paris a few times though. She had all the charm of a pissed-off tiger snake."

"That was on a good day."

"True enough. Anyway, conspiracy theories aside, you were telling me how cracking the secret of growing these could change everything."

Phil looked pensive for a few more seconds before returning to the original conversation. "I have shown you a spore print, haven't I?"

"What? No."

Phil opened his notebook to the back page. It was a beautiful hand-bound creation finished in cork. Susan had brought it back for him from New Fenton from the bookshop they had visited. Once it would have been an expensive gift, but now it was priceless, to Phil at least. This notebook never left the house, and every night before bed, it was like a ritual of his to put it away in a small metal cash box. This book contained vast amounts of his knowledge and expertise, which he was painstakingly sharing on the pages. This would be something future generations could refer to. He removed a piece of paper that was carefully wrapped in a small PVC sleeve. He handed it across to her protective cover and all. "There we go. That's an oyster mushroom spore print."

"Okay. And what does this do?"

"Well, a single mushroom contains billions of spores, but a print like this will probably contain hundreds of thousands. If we can create the right environment to grow these, the sky is literally the limit. And if these spore prints are maintained in the right environment, they can be kept for months if not years, so we've got a while to get this right."

"I still don't know what you mean by the sky is the limit."

"Mushrooms are a good source of protein, of B vitamins, D vitamins, potassium, iron, and the list goes on. It's crazy that something that grows all over in the most unexpected places is so hard to farm when you're actually trying, but if I manage it, if we manage it, we'll never have to worry about food shortages. Infinity won't. Nobody will for that matter."

"What, we'll just give our produce away?"

Phil smiled again. "My priority is always going to be making sure we're okay, making sure our people are okay. We've got a lot of work to do here still. A mountain of work, in fact. But as time goes on, more will join us. More Wanderers will join us and who knows, maybe we'll grow big enough and grand enough for some of the other survivors to abandon their shelters or wherever they lasted out the asteroid and come and join us too. We're trading a lot at the moment so we can grow. But growing isn't an end in itself. The common welfare is the end."

"And you think the key to all of that is these?" she said, tapping the chest they were sitting on.

"I think it could be."

"What could be?" This time, both Phil and Bindi jumped as they turned towards the gap in the curtains.

"It's a moot point because I'm not going to be alive long enough to see it," Phil said, holding his hand up to his chest again.

Debbie shook her head. "Always such a drama queen, my husband." She walked across to join them and sat down next to Bindi. "What were you talking about?"

"Saving the world by the sound of it," Bindi replied.

"Ahh. Mushrooms then," Debbie said with a smile.

"How did you guess?"

"My husband's monologues on the virtues of mycoprotein are something I suffered for the longest time in Salvation and now it seems I'm going to suffer them out here too."

"So, you think this is a fool's errand?"

"Not at all. I think Phil can do whatever he turns his mind to. There's no such thing as impossible for him, unless you're talking about getting a good night's sleep. That's something he always seems to struggle with. The gears in his head go around and around usually keeping him and the rest of us awake."

"Did you have a nightmare again?" Phil asked.

Debbie leaned forward a little to look at her husband. "I kind of woke myself up before it became fully fledged. I'm getting quite good at that now. I think the camomile tea might be helping too."

"I was saying to Phil that if it ever gets really bad, I can give you something."

"That's kind, but I'd like to beat this myself if I can."

"I get that." The three of them just sat there for a few moments listening to the wind howl outside. "Well, I should probably get back to bed. If my girls wake up, they'll wonder where I am. Goodnight," Bindi said, standing up then heading down the narrow corridor comprised of stone on one side and curtains on the other.

"So, how are they looking?" Debbie asked, gesturing to the chests.

"So far, so good. But—"

"But it's too early to say and you don't want to build anyone's hopes up?"

Phil laughed. "Am I that predictable?"

"Pretty much. Yeah." She reached out and took his hand. "I meant what I said, y'know."

"About what?"

"That you can do whatever you turn your mind to."

He let out a long sigh and looked around their meagre surroundings. "The joke is lab conditions are the perfect environment to be doing what I'm trying to do here. I had a lab. I had everything I needed back in Salvation."

"We're not in Salvation anymore, Phil. And I don't know much about fungiculture, but I'm an expert on you. You'll figure out a way to do this. It might not happen as quickly as you want it to, but you'll figure it out. There isn't a doubt in my mind."

He shuffled a little closer to his wife and placed his arm around her. "I love you so much."

Debbie shrugged. "You're only human."

"I'm serious. I'd be lost without you."

Her mind drifted back to their time on Level Two. She'd been looking for a way out then, but she was so grateful she hadn't found one. Phil was the love of her life. Whatever happened to them was nothing to do with Phil. *It was the administration and that damned place.* "You'll never be without me."

3

The turret's walls were packed with earth, much like the replica blackhouses they'd built at the settlement. They weren't aesthetically pleasing, but they were practical. They held a lot of heat in. It was the peephole and the gaps around the door that were the problems. Even when they were closed, the warm air from the fire bled through the cracks.

"I don't think they're coming," Steve said, wrapping his arms around himself a little tighter.

Esme watched as the flames of the fire gradually died further and further. "No," she said distantly.

"What should we do?"

"We should put the other log on the fire."

"I thought you said—"

"I know what I said, but something's obviously gone wrong. There might have been a mix-up with the roster; something might have happened back at the farm. But whatever it is, when we don't show up, our families are going to raise the alarm."

"Our families will be asleep. They won't figure out anything's wrong until the morning. I don't know if you've noticed, but we're not just talking about a chilly breeze out there. These are like Arctic conditions. I've never known a cold like this. We're not going to last the night with just one log. We need to do something."

Esme looked towards the shuttered peephole once more as another blast rattled it. *Dammit, he's right.* She walked across to the door. "What are you doing?" Steve asked as he watched her fingers wrap around the handle.

"I want to see what it's like on the ridge."

"Why?"

"Because one of us might have to head back to the farm." She opened the door and winced as whirling snow tore at her face. She squinted into the darkness beyond the small arc of light from the entrance then pushed the door firmly closed once more. "Crap."

"What?"

"There's no way we're getting out of here, and my guess is there's no way anybody's making it along the ridge."

"What do you mean?"

"I mean it's a whiteout. I've never seen anything like it."

Steve climbed to his feet. "What are we going to do?"

"I'm thinking." She walked across to her rucksack and pulled out the book she'd been reading. It was a hardback biography of Queen Victoria. She'd never really been interested in reading before they'd gone to New Fenton, but with so little to do with one's leisure time since she no longer had her phone, she delved into whatever books she could get her hands on. This one was a lot more interesting than she had thought it would be, but what was even more interesting to her at that moment was staying alive.

"What the hell are you going to do with that?"

There was a part of Esme's life that she'd hoped was behind her once and for all. Nobody who survived the blast knew about it, and other than in her weakest moments, she could pretend it was all just some nightmare. It wasn't though. After a series of atrocious relationship decisions, she had finally hit rock bottom and found herself living on the streets. Her mother had been dead for several years. She didn't even know who her father was, and there were no siblings. She had never felt so alone. It had been terrifying, but it had also been the thing to turn her life around.

One night, looking up at the stars from a cold, hidden alleyway in the centre of London, she decided that she was going to take control of her life once again. She wasn't quite sure how. At that moment, she hadn't eaten in two days. She'd drunk from the taps in a public toilet and was just about as scared as she'd ever been. But she was determined that she was going to find a way out.

Momo, an old street person whose real name Esme never knew, took her under her wing. She showed her which skips to visit for food and at what time so she could beat the rats to the pizza or spaghetti or fried rice that had outfaced wealthy diners. She showed her the best places to go when it was raining or on a weekend when the drunken yobs hunted street people like it was some kind of sport. But more importantly, she showed her how to stay warm.

Staying warm on the cold London streets was the difference between life and death, and it was a lesson she'd learned well.

When Esme had made it off the streets and found a job, then a boyfriend and finally some semblance of a normal life, she went back to find Momo. She wanted to help, to share the good fortune she'd enjoyed. Maybe find a way to get her off the streets too. But Momo was gone. Esme discovered from another street person that soon after she left, Momo was attacked.

"It happened one Friday night," her informant had told her. "They beat her bad then threw her in the river. Police fished her out, but they weren't interested in finding out who did it. Why would they be?"

Esme had felt sick to her stomach to hear that news. Maybe if she'd been with her, it wouldn't have happened. Maybe, maybe, maybe. From that night on, she took her entire experience of living on the streets, locked it in a box and buried it deep down inside. She had not even told her husband. There was nothing about that time in her life that made her happy. There was nothing that made her proud. All she wanted to do was forget it and move on, but there was something about this moment that took her back to that period.

It was a cold night, a freezing night, and the bus stations, train stations and other regular haunts that might have provided them with a little heat were no-go areas. It was the Friday before Christmas week, and more drunks than usual were on the streets. It was dangerous for people like her and Momo, so they'd disappeared down the banks of the Thames, finding refuge underneath a bridge. A small fire burned away in an oil can, not much bigger than the fire that was flickering in the turret now. Momo had taught her a lesson that night that she would never forget. She had torn out the pages of a telephone directory, scrunched them up and stuffed them into her clothes, her sleeves, down her front, down her back, in her trousers. It was a lesson that had saved her life.

"Here," she said, tearing the binding.

"Here what? We're going to read to each other?"

Half a smile flitted onto Esme's face as she realised that all the thoughts, all the memories she'd relived in the last few seconds had been hers and hers alone. "Screw up the paper," she said, tearing a page out and crumpling it. "Not too tight." She proceeded to feed the scrunched-up paper down the back of her tucked-in shirt. They both wore jackets, but she knew they'd need a lot more to fend off this level of cold.

"Err … why?"

"Because your body heat will collect in the air pockets, trapping it against you and keeping you warm."

"Seriously? Where did you get that from?"

"I read it in a book once."

"What kind of book?"

"I don't remember. Listen, just trust me, it'll work."

Steve looked at the half-volume in front of him and shrugged before tearing out one of the pages and mirroring Esme's actions. "I think we're going to need more than just this to survive through the night."

"Yeah. We're going to seal up the gaps around the door and the shutter and peephole too."

"I thought you said we had to keep a vigil."

"That was before I got a proper look at what was going on. Trust me, if anyone's out there, they're not going to last an hour."

*

"W-we cannot continue in this," Nazya said as she and Chloe leaned into the driving blizzard. The snow was already up to their shins, and there was no sign of it ending.

"We've got to go on. We must g-go on," her friend replied.

"We won't m-make it."

"We won't make it if we st-stay out here either."

"The forest over th-there." Nazya pointed, and Chloe reluctantly nodded. They had been travelling for a few hours, but they were still a long way from their destination. What was left of the road had long since been covered by the falling snow, and it would be easy to veer off course and get lost in the whiteout. "We're no g-good to anyone if we die."

They changed direction and headed towards the expansive woodland. Neither of them was under any illusions as to how dangerous this was. They had no idea if anyone lived in the forest. They could end up on someone's dinner plate or worse, but Nazya was right. If they didn't get out of the storm, it would be the end for them both.

It took them fifteen minutes to slog the few hundred metres, and despite the lack of foliage, the skeletons of the mighty oaks, pines and sycamores protected them from the worst of the freezing storm. "W-we need to f-find shelter," Chloe said.

So far, they had managed to avoid using their torches. Out in the open, despite the storm, the white landscape had provided enough reflected light for them to see, but here things were different.

Nazya flicked on her dynamo flashlight, knowing full well that it would act like a beacon if there were any Ferals lurking. The pair scoured the area. The snow still fell, but it did not whip at their flesh as it had done when they were out on the open road. They searched for the best part of ten minutes before they discovered a small rock formation. They circled it, hoping that somewhere there would be a cave entrance or at least some form of shelter. Then they saw it. It was a long way from ideal, but there was an overhanging ledge on the opposite side. It was low, but beneath it lay the first patch of ground they'd seen in hours that was not white.

"C-come on," Nazya said, crouching down and then crawling underneath. Chloe did the same. They both wore thick gloves, but the freezing earth made them shiver uncontrollably as they felt it through the knees of their waterproof trousers and jeans. They huddled together as they reached the back wall of the small overhang.

"We're going to f-freeze to death, aren't we?"

"No. S-stay here," Nazya ordered.

Chloe didn't understand what her friend was doing, but she did as she was told and remained coiled up against the rock. It was the first time she had sat down since they had fled Crowesbury, and as much as she wanted to go after Nazya, she felt utterly exhausted physically and emotionally. To say the events of the past couple of days were bewildering, terrifying and heartbreaking was a massive understatement.

How can any of this be happening? She withdrew her arms from the sleeves and hugged herself inside her coat. *I can't remember a cold like this.* She rubbed her hands over her upper body vigorously in an attempt to warm up. It was no use. Despite being out of the snow, the biting frigidity still found her. *We're going to freeze to death.*

The wind continued to howl like a banshee, and for a few moments, Chloe just stared towards the entrance where her friend had disappeared, terrified that somehow she'd got lost in the storm and would not return. Then she saw a silhouette against the backdrop of the blizzard and her breathing became a little easier. Nazya crawled back underneath the jutting rock, entering the small arc of light thrown out by Chloe's lantern. She shuffled up to her and dropped a small pile of sticks and branches.

"I th-thought you'd got l-lost or something," Chloe said.

"I snapped th-these from one of the trees out there," Nazya replied.

Freezing snow was still stuck to the upper side of a few of them, and Chloe helped her knock and brush it off before they both broke a few of the bigger sticks into smaller pieces. "Do you think they'll b-burn?"

"They h-have to." After the attempted coup at Infinity, Eric had insisted that Chloe and Nazya had go bags ready in case they ever needed to make a quick escape should a similar situation arise. Nobody could have anticipated the events that led to their current predicament, but both women were happy they had heeded his orders. Nazya slipped off her gloves and reached inside. She pulled out a small flask, a book of matches from the Paramount Hotel and the latest copy of the *Post-Apocalyptic Post*, the newspaper that Chloe's cousins had created. She tore the paper into strips and, despite her shaking hands, twisted a few of them into wicks for kindling while Chloe carefully constructed a small teepee configuration with some of the twigs and then a slightly taller one around it. She raised the lantern and searched the ground for a few stones before building a small semicircular wall to guard the fire from any gusts. They were well protected from the worst of the wind beneath the ledge, but the odd sharp draft still hit them, and the last thing they wanted was for the fire to be extinguished before it even got going.

Nazya weaved a few pieces of the paper into the gaps and unscrewed the top of the flask, pouring some of the clear liquid over the top before taking one of the matches from the book and striking it. The small flame lived and died in the space of a heartbeat, and both women cast each other concerned glances. The doctor edged closer to the small pile of wood and struck another. This time, it caught, and she angled it for a second, covering it from any potential blow with her other hand before moving it down to one of the tightly wound paper wicks. Slowly they watched as the fire caught and travelled up the paper, catching another wick and another, then whoosh. Woody's infamous potato peel vodka was a good accelerant, and the blue flame quickly turned orange as the rest of the paper caught too.

"When it is burning properly, I will go get some more wood."

"No," Chloe replied, reaching out and taking her friend's hand. "Don't go anywhere. This will be enough."

Nazya glanced towards the fire and then looked out as waves of snow continued to fall. "We don't know how long this storm will last. It is better to be safe."

The two women watched as the fire caught further. Some of the twigs hissed and sizzled then finally caught. "It's working. It's working," Chloe said excitedly.

"Yes," Nazya agreed. "I will go get more wood. You make sure it doesn't go out." The doctor began to crawl away again before stopping and turning back to her friend. "We will be okay, Chloe."

Her friend gulped, and her eyes filled with tears. "I'm scared, Naz."

Nazya remained there for a moment then nodded. "I am too. But we will be okay. I promise you."

*

Greenslade's eyes flicked open suddenly. It had taken all the occupants of the house the longest time to get to sleep. The wind gusted again outside, and the noise of a hundred icy darts thudded against the shutter.

Flames still blazed away in the fireplace casting an orange hue throughout the small property despite the curtained partitions. He turned slightly to see Grace still nestled into him, fast asleep. Theo slumbered a few feet away, and he wondered why he had been snapped out of his own dreams. *Was it the wind?*

He had been one of the last ones to be allocated a house. Despite everything he'd done since arriving in Redemption, there were still some who believed he didn't deserve it, and he couldn't blame them. But Grace and Theo had worked as tirelessly as anyone to help build the settlement. Trunk and his family were their neighbours, separated by nothing more than a thick curtain, and after much toing and froing, Austin and Clem became their other neighbours.

They were not the troublemakers that he and everyone else had seen them as when they'd first arrived. Grief did strange things to people, and they had been consumed by it after the loss of their children. It was no wonder they lashed out in the way they did. Greenslade was hardly close to them, but he had come to see them for who they really were. Like him and Trunk, some regarded them as pariahs still, but they were decent people who, until Susan had helped make them feel valued again, were lost.

Another loud whoosh suggested the storm outside was nowhere near abating, and it was followed seconds after by movement. He, Clem and Trunk had spent the evening blocking as many gaps as possible. They had cut up a damaged section of tarpaulin and used the pieces to help insulate the property from Mother Nature's rage. But as the model Spitfire that he and Theo had built swung above him like a pendulum, he knew that there was still a gap somewhere. *I'll sort it out tomorrow.*

He was comfortable. He and Grace had never felt closer, and to have her resting her head on him made him feel more needed than he had in the longest time. It was warm in their sleeping bag, and all he wanted to do was drift off once more with his wife by his side, his son sleeping close by, and the model they'd built together urging him back to slumber where he could relive the happiest moments of his childhood. His eyelids became heavier as he focused on the sound of the crackling fire and not the blizzard.

"Help!"

His eyes shot open again. *Did I imagine that or did I hear it?* It sounded distant. It sounded like a fragment of a dream, something not real.

"Help us!" A different voice this time, getting lost in the howling wind outside. The old Greenslade would have rolled over and covered his head with a pillow, but a lot had happened since the days of the bunker.

He slipped his arm out from beneath Grace, amazed that she remained asleep as her head flopped down onto the pillow. He was already half dressed as, despite the fire and all the measures they'd taken to keep the place warm, it was still icy cold. He slipped on his jeans and boots and headed to the shuttered aperture that constituted their window. They had packed it tightly so it no longer rattled with each gust, but there was no mistaking what was going on outside.

"GINNY!" Again the voice sounded a million miles away, but he knew that name. Ginny was the young girl next door. "Help us. P-please, somebody help!"

"Chief?" Greenslade spun around, his breath taken away as his friend walked up behind him. "Sorry," Trunk said, realising he'd surprised the other man. "I thought I heard something."

"Yeah," Greenslade replied. "Something's going on out there."

"What should we do?" Another gust hit the shutter, and the two men cast each other knowing glances.

"If somebody's out there in this, they're not going to last long."

"Why would someone be out there?"

"I don't know, Trunk, but I heard someone shouting Ginny's name."

Trunk looked back towards the curtained cubicle that was his apartment. His daughter, Stef, was nearly eighteen, but he remembered when she had been Ginny's age as if it was yesterday. He remembered how vulnerable she was and how he would have moved the earth to protect her. "We need to do something."

"Let's get our outdoor gear." Both men retraced their steps gathering their coats, gloves, hats and other winter clothes. Speed was of the essence, and in their zeal to get changed, they managed to wake the rest of the house up. Quickly explaining what was happening, they reassembled by the door a moment later. Austin, Clem, Lydia and Grace joined them.

"I'm coming too," Theo said.

"No," Greenslade replied. "You and Stef stay here."

"But—"

"But nothing. We don't know what's going on out there, but we know we don't want the temperature dropping in here. When we're out of this door, block the drafts and get a pan of water on the boil. I'll knock loudly when we're back. That'll be your signal to get the draft excluders off again." The makeshift draft excluders were wedged in the gaps, and there was no way the door would open again without them being taken away.

"Stef can do that."

"No. If something happens, one of you is going to need to raise the alarm and get help while the other stays here."

Theo's shoulders sagged. "Okay," he replied reluctantly.

No more shouts had been heard from outside, but rather than easing any of their minds, this just ratcheted up the concern. "Okay, everyone. Get ready," Greenslade said, wrapping his scarf around his mouth, pulling up his hood, tying it beneath his chin and raising his lantern. He nodded, and Theo pulled away the excluders and released the latch on the door. It flew inwards, and with it, a knee-high white pile collapsed into the entrance. "Everybody stick together."

Greenslade was the first to step into the night, plodding through the snow, trying to stay vertical despite the wind. Trunk powered forward to join him, and they paused only briefly to make sure the door closed behind them before continuing.

*

Marla had been sound asleep when her world suddenly turned upside down. Screams had roused her from her slumber, and she hadn't understood why at first, but then the wind, which had been screaming most of the night outside, was no longer outside. Neither was the freezing snow. Instead, like an Arctic tornado, the blizzard swirled around her home. The curtains and sheets that formed the walls of the families' cubicles lifted and whipped. The fire, which had been keeping the temperature not comfortable but manageable, had extinguished in a matter of seconds, leaving just two dynamo lanterns to illuminate the unfolding horror in a white LED glow.

Part of the roof had been ripped off, and the rest of it looked like it was well on the way to disappearing into the night. Ian and Sandeep, her two neighbours' husbands, had run to open the front door only to find it completely blocked. The pair had been put in charge of firewood for this end of the settlement. They had run shifts of people sawing and chopping. They had made sure there was enough fuel for everyone. And their property was one of the known collection points for those who needed more. Towers of chopped wood stood in meticulously erected monuments to their good planning and hard work all around the stone dwelling. An added bonus was this gave them an extra layer of insulation too, but there was a good chance that their diligence might well result in their deaths and those of the ones they loved most. One of the wood piles had collapsed in the wind, knocking another down too. The snow had drifted, packing it all tight and making the entrance and shuttered window inaccessible.

"We're going to have to try to dig ourselves out," Ian had said. They were his last words. Another deafening sound from above pre-empted more of the roof disappearing and the collapse of a beam, which cracked his skull wide open. Marla had watched it happen like she was watching a movie. It hadn't seemed quite real, but it was. The thick, heavy piece of wood split Ian's skull. The blood had looked like thick black paint for a moment in the white glow of the LED. For a few seconds, despite all the surrounding chaos and screaming, there was a faint hope inside her that willed her to believe things weren't quite as bad as they seemed. Ian remained standing, and if he was standing, then surely that was something.

But the hope didn't last long, and he collapsed just as the beam had. His wife, Paula, and young son, Leon, had started screaming and crying louder than ever, adding to the confusion and terror as the world fell apart around them. For what seemed like an age, Sandeep remained glued to the spot, looking down at his friend in wide-eyed horror, until finally he jerked into action once more, starting to dig and claw at the snow-packed mountain of wood in the doorway.

Slowly, Marla began to stir too, realising that none of them was going to last long in this if she didn't do something. Shouts and pleas for help rose up around her, but she knew no one would be able to hear in the storm, and if they didn't at least try to save themselves, then it was all over. She started to scratch and tug at the snow and logs but stopped just as quickly as another bone-chilling noise erupted behind her. She turned just in time to see Ginny disappear beneath a mountain of falling debris. She had screamed her name louder than she had ever screamed anything in her life. After the death of her husband, Ginny had been the one reason she had carried on. Without her, there was no point.

Marla had leapt over to where her daughter had vanished and begun to rip away the wood and thatch. The snow and wind still lashed at her, but none of that mattered. She would walk over hot coals for her daughter. She would do anything. She looked up to see Paula and Leon still standing in tear-filled disbelief as they stared down at Ian's body.

Sandeep's family were bewildered too. It had all happened so quickly. They had been through a lot since Salvation, and things had been so much better. They were building a future, but now the world was literally caving in on them.

"Ginny. Ginny. Ginny," Marla cried, dropping to her knees, still finding it hard to comprehend the events of the past few minutes but understanding this was all that mattered now. "Ginny. Ginny. Ginny," she said again, pulling away the wood and dried reeds that, up until a short while back, had been protecting them against the elements.

Another loud thud sounded behind her, and she turned quickly, dreading what she might see. It took her a few seconds to process, but when another figure landed next to the first, she realised help had arrived. They had climbed through a space where the roof once was.

"Ginny," she cried again. "She's under here."

*

Greenslade and Trunk both glanced down at Ian's body. They'd seen enough dead people in their time to know a lost cause. They lurched forward, ignoring the others too, and grabbed and heaved the detritus that was the focus of Marla's attention. Within seconds, they were looking at Ginny's little face. Her eyes flicked open, and although filled with fear, they were responsive to the bright LED that shone towards her. She flinched a little, and Greenslade set the lantern down while he, Trunk and Marla shifted more of the debris.

"Mum?" the young girl said.

"Are you okay, darling?"

"My arm hurts."

Greenslade pulled away more of the demolished roof covering to find that Ginny's arm was bleeding badly. "Oh, my God. Oh, my God, Ginny." The panic in Marla's voice was evident, causing the girl to start crying once more.

"What can I do?" Austin shouted, his head appearing over what were the eaves of the roof moments before. Greenslade turned to see his scarf-covered face squinting in the relentless snowstorm.

"We're going to have to get everyone out of here that way." He turned to Trunk. "Pass Austin some of the curtains and sheets. We'll use them to pull people out." Trunk nodded and immediately got to work before Greenslade turned to Marla. "Get me a towel. The cleanest you've got."

"Okay," Marla replied, rushing away and leaving her daughter alone with the man who had been the scourge of Level Three for so long.

"Am I going to die?" the young girl asked.

Greenslade smiled. "No, Ginny. You're going to be okay, but I'm going to have to dress your wound, and it's going to hurt a bit. Do you think you can be brave for me?"

The young girl nodded as her mother returned with a hand towel. "This was the cleanest I could find."

Greenslade took it, immediately tearing a long strip away. He slipped his glove off and reached into his pocket, pulling out a small hip flask. In New Fenton, he'd discovered a half bottle of Scotch tucked away behind a cash register. If he'd had to work in retail, there was a good chance that he'd have turned into a raging alcoholic too, but even though it was only half full, and it was a generic brand, it was too good to waste. He'd split it fifty-fifty with Trunk, and now the last remaining mouthfuls remained in his flask. "This is going to sting." He unscrewed the top and poured it over the wound.

Ginny let out a cry of pain before remembering her promise to be brave. "Will that stop it bleeding?"

"No. But it will kill any germs. I'm going to have to tie a tourniquet now. This is going to hurt quite a bit too, but it'll stop the bleeding."

Marla took hold of her daughter's hand as another icy blast hit them all. Greenslade took advantage of the diversion and wrapped the strip of towel tightly around the young girl's arm before tying it. The blood flow slowed straightaway, and Ginny sat up while Trunk ushered the others towards Austin, who remained frozen like an awkward Humpty Dumpty leaning over the wall, holding on to a makeshift rope of twisted curtains and blankets.

The remainder of the debris fell away from Ginny as she stood, and Marla wrapped her arms around her, clutching her tightly, knowing that, but for a quirk of chance, she might have lost her daughter as well as her home.

More snow twirled around them. It looked enchanting in the white glow, but there was nothing magical about what it would do if they did not find warmth soon. The adrenaline was already beginning to dissipate, and shivers ran through all of them as Marla and Ginny were the last to throw on the rest of their winter clothes and make their way towards the dangling rope. It was only as each of them reached the top that they could see the scale of the storm. The snow continued to lash and bite, but as Clem, Lydia and Grace started the march back to their home, the white line of illumination showed just how vast winter's white blanket was.

Marla dropped down to the other side and waited with open arms for her daughter as Austin did his best to lower her gently. "Hurry," he called out. "It feels like it's dropped another five degrees in the last minute."

Trunk and Greenslade panned their lights around one final time. About three-quarters of the roof had gone, and it was a miracle that there'd been only one fatality.

"Poor bastard," Trunk said as his eyes came to rest on the still, bloodied figure on the ground.

"It'll have been quick," Greenslade replied. "And in the end, that's probably the best any of us can hope for."

"C-come on, for C-Christ's sake," Austin said, taking a tighter hold on the rope. "I'm not up here for fun, y'know."

Greenslade was the first to climb, and then both men helped Trunk up. When the trio arrived back home, they found Theo had built the fire bigger, and Stef had a pot of piping hot nettle tea waiting. Their homeless neighbours were in shellshock as they gathered around the flames. Sandeep and his family did their best to comfort Paula and Leon, but all of them had experienced more than their fair share of loss, and they knew that no words, no gestures and no kindnesses could ever cure the pain. This was the first real night of winter, and each of them wondered what the rest of it would hold.

4

Three loud bangs sounded against the thick wooden door and Drake almost jumped to his feet. People often commented that he seemed to be in a constant state of readiness, and it was true even when he slept. He, Marina and their families resided in the small cabin that was designated the militia headquarters. If ever there was trouble, people knew where to come, and they knew it would always be manned.

Darin, his wife, was on her feet a couple of beats behind him. Although her job in Salvation was to look after their family, out here she had become so much more. No sooner had they emerged from their sheet-partitioned apartment than Marina joined them. Her husband was one of Jason's workers, and her daughter could sleep through a hurricane, so they remained inside.

The embers of the previous night's fire still glowed in the stone hearth. Darin reached for the lantern they had suspended on a hook in the centre of the room. The dim glow extinguished immediately, and she took it down, cranking the dynamo handle rapidly a few times before hooking it up once more.

Drake continued to the door. The previous night's storm had been like nothing they'd known, and they had all gone to sleep with the howling wind as an accompaniment to their fading thoughts, but now it was silent outside.

Another three knocks hammered against the wood, and Drake lifted the latch to open it. Everything was white. The ground was covered in a thick blanket, and if one didn't know the trees were devoid of leaves, some of them were so thick with snow that a person could be forgiven for believing they were in full bloom beneath their coating.

He instantly recognised Esme's husband, but he didn't know the woman who was with him. "Michael. What is it?" he asked.

"Esme and Steve didn't make it back last night."

It was still early morning, but there was enough light to see the concerned expressions on the two faces. Drake nodded slowly. He knew the lookout rosters as well as anyone, and he knew that Esme was on shift last night. "I didn't expect them to."

"What do you mean?"

"Esme's one of the brightest people I know. The way that storm turned in a heartbeat last night would have made it way too dangerous to head back here. Chances are they stuck it out in the turret with their replacements."

"But ... we don't know that. We can't just—"

Drake put his hand up. "Give it half an hour. If they're not back by then, I'll head up there myself."

"What about—"

"Half an hour," Drake repeated before closing the door on the two anxious visitors.

"You're going to go up there?" Darin asked.

Drake nodded. "I was going to head up this morning anyway."

"Why?"

"I haven't been for a few days. It's important that I keep my finger on the pulse, get ahead of any problems that the weather or anything else might cause."

"I'll come with you," Marina said.

"Great. I'll go back to bed then," Darin quipped.

"Ha," Drake replied, smiling. "Your sense of humour was one of the things that first attracted me to you."

"Who's joking?"

"I'm guessing it's going to be a busy day today, and I'll need you here to make copious notes in my absence."

"And there I was thinking I was your wife and not a secretary."

"You're a member of the militia. Sometimes that means fighting. Sometimes it means listening and reporting back."

"You're my husband, and that means that you don't talk to me in such a condescending manner; otherwise, one morning, you might wake up with your nads lying next to you on your pillow."

"I think she makes a good point," Marina interjected.

A guilty expression swept over Drake's face. He found it difficult to speak without being officious sometimes, and although Marina had worked alongside him for a long time and was used to it, Darin was still adjusting. She'd only known him as a husband. "I'm sorry. I can get someone else to man the desk if you'd prefer."

"No. I'll do it."

"Thank you."

*

The rapping on the door almost sounded as though someone was smashing a mallet against it. Callie and Susan were already up. They hadn't been for long, and they were wearily rekindling the previous night's fire and getting the pan on for hot water.

Callie had placed a green rag over the top of the dynamo lantern so the light wasn't so harsh, as she and her mum did their best to wake up slowly.

"That's always a good sign," Susan said. "Someone banging the hell out of my front door before it's even light. It's bound to be great news."

"You never know," Callie replied. "Ebba might have made you croissants and coffee."

"You're probably right. I'm just being paranoid."

The noise had made others stir in their curtained cubicles, and muted conversations began while Susan and Callie headed towards the entrance.

Susan opened the door, and a burst of freezing air hit them. They both jumped back a little expecting the thigh-high wall of snow to collapse, but it was frozen in place for the time being at least.

"Blake?" Susan said, a little perplexed as to what he was doing there so early. "Is everything okay?" She looked over his shoulder to see it was lighter than she expected, and the white blanket of snow made everything appear brighter still. The sun was not yet fully up, but it was getting there, and for the time being, at least, the sky looked clear. The wind had died down to nothing more than a gentle and occasional breeze, but with it, a harsh, stinging cold prickled her skin.

"We lost someone last night."

"What do you mean lost someone?"

"Someone died."

She looked down at the snow once more and took another step back. "You'd better come in."

Inevitably, Greenslade's forward motion caused a small but not total avalanche, and it took Callie a moment to brush enough of it to one side before they could close the door once more. When she had, the three of them headed to the fire, but now Si, Dani and Nicola were there too, having overheard the two words "someone died" and forgotten all about their morning routine.

"Who died? What happened?" Si asked.

Greenslade retold the events of the night and, in doing so, relived them too. To his surprise, as much as anyone else's, he choked up a little in the cold light of day as he described what happened. When he got to the end of the story, a stony silence engulfed the small house. By which time, Wei, Jiang and Lanying had joined them all.

"This is terrible, terrible news," Lanying said, shaking her head sadly. Paula had often worked alongside her in the fields, and although not close, they were certainly friendly towards each other.

Susan sat in silence on the large trunk in front of the fire that was the closest thing they had to a living room couch. The embers had become flames again with the addition of more wood, and now the gentle crackle laid down a backing track to her thoughts.

"Thank you," she finally said, looking towards Greenslade and nodding gratefully.

"What for? I was too late to save the poor bastard."

"You saved the others though. If you hadn't braved the storm, there's no way they'd have survived. I can't believe you were the only ones to hear their screams, but you were the only ones who acted."

Greenslade shrugged. "That wind was really blowing. It was pure chance I heard anything."

"Maybe. Maybe not. But thank you, anyway."

"So, what now?"

"Jesus. You've just sprung this on me, Blake. Let me think for a minute, will you? How's Paula doing?"

"As well as anyone who's just seen her husband die in front of her."

"Okay. Stupid question. I mean does she need any medical attention? Do you think I should get Bindi to go see her?"

"I don't know. She's pretty zoned out, but wouldn't you be? Ginny could do with a visit though. She hurt her arm. I patched it up as well as I could, but I'm no medic."

"I'll ask Bindi to pay a visit. And then I'd better call on Jason and see if there's any way of piecing the place back together."

"People are going to be scared that the same thing might happen to their place when another storm hits."

Susan nodded. "Yeah. We need to find out what happened too. If there's anyone here who can tell us, it's going to be him."

"Okay. Well, I'll get back and let everybody know you're on it."

"Have you got enough blankets and food over there for the extra mouths?"

"We'll manage."

"Thanks, Blake."

"No worries." He climbed to his feet, and Callie walked him to the entrance as a quiet conversation broke out between the others.

"Always lovely to see you first thing," she said, opening the door once more. "We'll have to do this again tomorrow."

Greenslade smiled and looked back towards the fireplace as Susan began to write a list down on a pad while Wei, Nicola and Si spoke about the community's sad loss.

"Listen," he said, moving a little closer so his words wouldn't be overheard. "Stick with your mum today. I think she's going to need you."

Callie looked out at the vast whiteness beyond her front door. "Well, it's not like I'm going to be going out scavenging or anything, is it?"

"I suppose not," he said, following her eyes. "But I think we're going to be lucky if Ian's the only one we've lost. Susan's going to need people around her who she can rely on."

Callie frowned. "Did you see something on the way across here? Were any other properties damaged?"

"No. Not that I saw. But I was out for little more than a few minutes last night, and I've never felt a cold like that in my life. If anybody got stuck in it somehow, then I don't rate their chances."

"That's a happy thought."

"Look. I'm not saying we'll definitely have lost more people. All I'm saying is make sure you're there just in case."

Callie nodded. "And where will you be?"

"You know where I'll be, and if you tell me you need me, I'll be here."

"Thank you."

He nodded and began his trek back home. Callie watched him for a moment before closing the door and returning to the others. "What did he say to you?" Dani asked.

"He said he doubted Ian would be the only fatality from last night."

"That's a happy thought."

"That's exactly what I said." Callie turned to her mother, who was still making notes. "You okay, Mum?"

"Hmm?" Susan replied, looking up from her pad.

"Are you okay?"

"Yes. Yes, I'm just thinking, that's all."

"About what?"

"I should check in with people. I should make sure everyone's okay, that their properties weren't damaged, that—"

"Mum, we've got over three and a half thousand people in Redemption. The snow's up to our thighs. It's freezing cold. Thinking you can make house calls on every family is just insane."

"It would be for just one person," Nicola piped up. "But a few dozen could do it. I bet we could scramble together a team and make sure every property in Redemption was visited before the end of the day."

"Won't people be doing that anyway?" Si asked. "Won't neighbours be checking on neighbours? Won't everybody be making sure everyone else is alright?"

"Some will," Callie replied. "But the second you start assuming everybody will look out for everybody else, that's when problems start. Mum's right, and Nicola's right. We need to make sure people are okay. And if they're not, we need to try to help. It looks like the storm's over for the time being, but that's not to say that another one won't hit us."

"Right," Nicola said, walking across to the lidded pan near the fireplace. "Let's have some breakfast and then we can get to work."

*

"It's alright. It's alright, Chloe. It's alright."

The words sounded distant and echoey as if they were being spoken down a giant pipe. Finally, Chloe roused and understood that her friend was waking her from no doubt what was another nightmare. Her sleep had been littered with them, which was no surprise considering the events of the last couple of days. "I'm awake. I'm awake," she said, finally focusing her eyes on her friend's hand as it gently rested on her arm. "Was I having a nightmare?"

"I think you were going into one," Nazya replied.

The fire was still crackling away. Chloe's bad dreams had not exactly been at regular intervals, but each time she had woken her friend with her distressed noises Nazya had made sure to put more wood on the flames. The temperature had continued to plummet through the night, and if not for the regular additions to the fire, the pair may have slipped into hypothermia and died. The smoke had disappeared into the cracks of the overhang, and with it, much of the heat. But enough warmth had remained in the small alcove to keep them comfortable.

Chloe looked beyond the glow to the entrance. "Oh, God." There was no way to tell whether it was day or night. The snow had massed all around them, almost creating an ice cave. "I can't hear the howling anymore. That's got to be something, hasn't it?"

"I think the storm ended some time ago."

"Do you think it's still nighttime?"

"There is only one way to find out," Nazya replied, starting to crawl towards the point where they had entered.

"No, don't," Chloe pleaded, reaching out and grabbing her friend by the arm.

Nazya looked a little confused as she stopped and turned to her. "I don't understand."

"What if the wind's stopped but it's still snowing? What if it's a couple of metres deep out there? What if we're trapped in here? What if you try to break through and you can't, and the snow floods in, and you suffocate?"

Nazya placed her gloved hand over her friend's. "You need to calm down. We will get out of here. We will get to Redemption." The doctor let go of Chloe's hand and continued towards the entrance. The light from the fire was reflected by the white sheet in front of her, and a thin film of sweat covered the snow. She reached out tentatively and sunk her hand in. She let out a breath of relief to find it hadn't turned into a solid block of ice in the night. It was firm, but it could be shifted. She withdrew her hand, digging out a mound of snow with it. She plunged it in again, this time pushing it up too. She withdrew it once more, and a small shiver of panic ran through her. She had hoped to see daylight, or at least something beyond the snow, but all she saw was the tubular shape of her own imprint extending through the frigid mass.

"What do you see?" Chloe asked.

"Nothing … yet." Nazya shuffled further, knelt up a little more and punched her right hand out and upwards. She held her breath as she withdrew it, and this time, her heart lifted as the unmistakable gleam of sunlight shone down the narrow tunnel she'd created. She turned towards her friend. "Daylight. I see daylight." She began to scrabble and claw at the snow like a cat against a scratching post, and it was only a matter of a few seconds before enough had been displaced for her to edge through and stand. If they'd had more time and more light, they would have probably been able to find a better hideaway from the storm, one that didn't jut out at a right angle providing a perfect vertical face for drifting. But it had served its purpose and got them through the night alive. Nazya felt a disturbance beside her and looked to see Chloe clawing her way up too.

The two friends stood side by side for a moment taking in the view. "It's beautiful," Chloe said eventually.

"It would be beautiful if it was a screensaver or a poster. We have to walk through this, remember."

Where it had drifted, it was up to their waists, but it was considerably shallower in the rest of the forest. "It can't be much more than shin deep, though, can it?"

Nazya looked up to the boughs of the blackened trees, which were weighted down with a thick white covering. "In the forest, it is shin deep. Out there on the road, who knows what we will face?"

*

"Susan, Callie, come in," Debbie said.

"You might want to stand back a bit," Callie replied. "There's not much chance of us coming in without bringing a mountain of this stuff with us."

Debbie did as she suggested, and, as Callie had predicted, snow tumbled through the doorway as the mother and daughter made their entrance.

"Callie, Susan, how nice of you to reduce the ambient temperature of the place by about twenty degrees. Your visits are always such a delight," Phil said, appearing from the narrow, curtained corridor before joining his wife. Debbie scooped as much snow as she could back outside before jamming the door shut once more. "What brings you here at this ungodly hour?"

"It's hardly an ungodly hour," Callie replied, smiling. "How many times were we up and about in the summer a couple of hours before now?"

"Ah, yes, but this is winter. It's a time for sleep-ins and rest."

"Ha," Debbie scoffed. "Like you ever rest. It's like living with a mad scientist. He's always wandering off to do his little experiments." The other two women laughed. "Anyway," Debbie continued. "What can we do for you?"

"Somebody died last night," Susan replied, and in an instant, the light-hearted atmosphere dissolved.

"Oh, God. Who? What happened?"

"Is Bindi around? There's no point in repeating myself."

"Let me check," Phil replied. "BINDI?"

"I was already on my way, smart arse," she said, appearing from her curtained cubicle. "I overheard you say someone had died. What happened?"

Susan and Callie retold the events that Greenslade had conveyed to them, and before they'd finished, Bindi had excused herself to retrieve her doctor's bag.

"That's terrible," Debbie replied. "What can we do to help?"

"Well, I've got Nicola putting together a team to go around checking on everyone. I'm pretty certain she'd be grateful to have a few more volunteers," Susan replied.

"I'm sure she would," said Phil. "I'll let her know if I come across any."

Debbie swiped at him. "Of course we'll be happy to go around checking on people too. So will Matt. Just give us five minutes to get ourselves together."

"I think there are more important things for me to be doing."

"Like what exactly?"

"I need to check on the polytunnel. I've got some seedlings in there that—"

"They're not going to wither away and die within a couple of hours, Phil. I think this is more pressing."

"Look. We had major snowfall last night. I need to check that it's still standing, that—"

"In fairness," Callie interrupted. "I'm not sure how seeing Phil would lift anyone's spirits if they did need help. Maybe we should just let him play in his tunnel."

"My point exactly. Thank you, Callie. Why would anyone possibly want to see me?"

"You're a member of the committee just like the rest of us. People like knowing someone is in charge and that they're being looked after," Debbie replied.

"And I'm looking after them by making sure there's food for next year and the one after that and the one after that."

"God, you are so infuriating sometimes."

"I think I'm inclined to agree with Callie," Bindi said, re-emerging with her bag. "Him going out there won't do anything for morale. Let him go talk to his plants or whatever he does."

"Honestly, I could punch you sometimes, Phil. Your head's so far up your own arse."

"Y'know, I've got something you could put in his tea. He wouldn't feel a thing; he'd just go in his sleep."

The other women laughed.

"There was a time when I commanded respect everywhere I went. Statesmen and kings listened to what I had to say and treated my words with awe."

"Yeah, well. Treasure those memories, y'drongo. This is Redemption, and we're all equal here."

5

Rommy and Becka had only managed a few hours of sleep. They had woken before dawn and begun their rounds in the forest. They knew better than most what to expect from the winter. They had spent the last few hiding away, but that didn't mean they weren't aware of how cold or how unforgiving they were.

They had already visited four of the hotels. Only minor structural damage had been incurred by one. No one needed medical attention. It was a far cry from what they had lived through in previous years.

"You forget how cold it gets," Rommy said, shoving her hands in her pockets as she walked along.

Becka let out a huff of a laugh as she looked at the thick winter jackets they were both wearing. The coats and other all-weather gear were shared between the residents of their particular hotel. Anyone who needed to go outside in the poor conditions got one, but there weren't enough to go around for everybody.

"I started last winter in a torn shirt and a poncho made out of an old burlap sack. At least we've got some proper kit now."

"Yeah. I suppose you're right."

"I remember—OW!" Something hard hit Becka on the back, and she spun around. Rommy did too, and the pair shared confused expressions for a moment as there was nothing and no one to see. "What the hell's going…? Oh, you little bastards," Becka said with a wide grin as small laughing faces peeked out from behind trees. "You want a snowball fight, do ya? Well, we'll give you a snowball fight."

The temperature was still blisteringly cold, and it wouldn't do anyone any good to be stuck out in the open longer than they needed to be, but these kids had lived through far worse. Having a warm, dry home to return to was something they could not have even conceived the previous winter, so nobody could begrudge them this tiny little rite of passage.

The children laughed and hooted loudly as return fire struck the trees they were sheltering behind. They ducked back as the snowballs exploded against the trunks then emerged once more to launch their retaliatory volley.

Two more heads popped out, and Rommy could see one of them was Bea. A look of pure elation lit the devoted mother's face as her daughter laughed and giggled with the other children. The battle lasted just a few minutes and ended with hugs before the children were told to get back into the warmth. They protested a little but did as they were told, and the two women continued their journey. They weren't walking for long before Becka heard a noise and looked over at her friend to see tears pouring down the other woman's face.

"What is it?" Becka asked, reaching out and placing a hand on the other woman's back.

"I … I didn't think I'd ever get to see her smile like that again. She'd lost something. She'd lost the little spark she had before all this happened."

"We all lost something, but this place is giving us another chance. Don't think about the past. Don't think about last winter or what we faced before coming here. Let's just appreciate what we've got."

Rommy wiped away her tears. "You're right," she replied, sniffing.

"Plus, it's too cold to cry. You'll get frozen streaks on your face, and trust me, that's not an attractive look."

Rommy giggled. "I'm sorry."

"Don't be sorry. I get it. But we've got an opportunity here to turn everything around, create new memories, block out as much of the crap as we can."

"Yeah. That's going to take some doing."

"It is. But we've got the rest of our lives."

*

Drake and Marina were well ahead of the rest of the party, but in fairness, they were not carrying rucksacks full of wood and supplies on their backs, so it was only to be expected. They walked with hiking poles, making sure they had a firm footing before each step they took along the ridge. They'd already checked in on the other lookout stations. The occupants were all okay but grateful to be relieved of their duties. Now they were making their way to the final turret where Esme and Steve were stationed.

"It's beautiful, isn't it?" Marina said, pausing for a moment and turning to look at the expansive white vista that stretched out in front of them.

Drake stopped, too, while they both got their breath back. It was hard work fighting through the snow. In some places, it barely covered their ankles. In others, it had drifted to form steep banks against the rock face. "It won't have been beautiful last night for the poor bastards who were stationed on this ridge."

"True enough."

"Come on. Not much farther to go now." They set off again, Drake taking the lead along the narrower stretches of the snow-covered shelf.

"I think it's probably a good idea for us to—" Marina broke off in mid-sentence, and Drake turned to see that she'd stopped again and she was looking down.

"What is it?"

"Oh God," was all she could say, and Drake walked back to join her. He looked down too, but it took him a while to focus on what she was seeing. Two legs protruded from a large white hill that had formed at the base of the cliff.

"Shit," he hissed.

"Please don't let it be Esme." The words came out of Marina's mouth before she had a chance to think about them, and suddenly guilt seized her. "I can't believe I just said that. I'm sorry. I didn't mean—"

"Esme's your friend. You don't have to apologise. It's a natural reaction."

"But it's a terrible thing to say. Me hoping it's not her is wishing it on someone else."

Drake grabbed Marina's arm. "Despite what the administration tried to do to us, we're human. There are those that we're closer to than others. It's just the way it is."

"I know, but—"

"Come on. There's only one way we're going to find out."

They shuffled back from the edge and continued along, probing the path with their hiking sticks until the final turret came into view. Snow had packed the front of it, making it virtually invisible from the north, but the pair could see the black stone and dark wood of the door on their approach from the west.

Drake came to a sudden stop once more, and Marina almost bumped into him. "What is it?" she asked.

He didn't speak for a moment, but when he did, it came out in little more than a defeated whisper. "There's no smoke."

She looked towards the flu as well, and now she saw it. "Oh, God. If they ran out of wood in this…." She didn't need to finish the sentence, and they both set off again, this time with a little more trepidation in their steps. The handle was frozen stiff as Drake tried it. *Another sign that there's been no heat inside.* It finally budged, and he pushed his shoulder against the door. It moved a little, and he looked down to see a makeshift draft excluder wedged at the bottom making their entrance that bit more difficult. He pushed harder, until there was enough of a gap for them to get through.

It was by no means comfortable in the small stone building, but it was noticeably warmer than outside.

"Y-you finally noticed we hadn't shown up then," Esme quipped as they found her huddled with Steve in the corner next to the fire. The last log had long since burned to ash, but they had remained in position, side by side, their hands and arms tucked into their clothes, their scarves up over their faces, their hats pulled down.

"You're okay?" Marina did her best to contain her excitement but rushed over to her friend. She reached into her rucksack and removed a small flask. "Here. Have some of this," she said, pouring the hot dandelion coffee into the waiting plastic mug. Esme was first. She slipped her gloves off and wrapped her fingers around the cup. The heat stung her skin, but she savoured the warming pain.

"W-we thought we were going to die up here," Steve said. "Our relief never arrived."

Drake let out a long breath. "We saw a body at the foot of the cliff."

"Oh God," Esme said, handing the cup to her companion. "Who were due to take over from us?"

"Tiff and Stu."

"That's so sad," Esme replied.

"Yeah. And this is just the first storm."

"It d-doesn't bode well for the rest of the winter, does it?"

Drake ignored the question. "I'm going to see what the holdup is with the resupply then we'll get you two out of here." He disappeared back out of the door.

"Resupply?" Esme asked. "He's had a few dozen poor bastards marching up here with chopped wood, food and water to make sure the turrets are well stocked if another storm hits. He doesn't understand why they haven't matched us step for step on the climb."

Esme let out a small laugh. "That's Drake alright."

Steve handed the mug back to Esme, and she clasped her fingers around it once more. "Did we lose anyone else?"

Marina shook her head. "I don't know. We set off pretty much as soon as we heard you weren't back. I dare say we'll find out by the time we get down there."

"Yeah. I dare say we will."

*

Despite the thick snow on the ground, Redemption quickly became a hive of activity as people emerged from their homes. A team was clearing the area around the communal ovens. Despite every property having the means to be able to heat and cook, Susan had decided it would be sensible to have a central supply of hot food and drink available throughout the day. She knew they would be lucky to escape with a single fatality and a single damaged property, and so having a pool of available workers in a central area, warm, with full bellies and ready to do what was needed for the sake of the community, was well worth the effort.

Jason hastily assembled a crew to begin repairing the house that had fallen victim to the storm, and Susan, along with the group she'd formed, started to go door to door to check on people.

By mid-morning, the scenery surrounding Redemption was still white, but the farmyard had shovelled pathways and Ebba and her team were able to work in an area completely devoid of snow. Despite the wintery conditions, people were starting to come and go as if it was a normal day.

"It's still standing then," Matt said as he found Si near the stream.

A broad smile decorated Si's face as he turned to see his friend. "Yeah." It was obvious what Matt had been talking about. The wind had ripped through Redemption last night, and both of them had wondered the same thing. Would the water and irrigation pipeline they had built together still be upright by morning?

To their delight, it was. The piers were still in place, as was the network of pipes. "I'd be happier if it wasn't all blocked by snow and ice," Matt said.

Si shrugged. "It's not like it's needed for the fields at the moment, is it? Ebba's got plenty of snow melting in the pots. We knew this would happen. It's no biggie."

"I suppose. Maybe when Caine starts going out again, we can ask him to put insulation for the pipes on the shopping list."

Si laughed. "Do you remember how we had to beg and plead to get the materials to build it? I don't think insulation will be far up his list of priorities."

Matt looked down and let out a sad sigh. "I suppose," he said again. He had always lived in the shadow of his father, and building the irrigation system with Si had been the one major achievement he'd accomplished. Now they had finished, there was a void in his life.

"I was thinking though."

"Thinking what?"

"Well, I mean, the other side of the ridge. They've been preparing fields for next year and they're going to have the same problems we had. Maybe we should offer our services and help them build one."

Matt suddenly looked up with an excited glint in his eyes. "Seriously? I mean, do you think we'll be allowed?"

"Allowed? It would be for the benefit of everyone. I mean, we're all one community, right?"

"Right. So … how do we do this?"

"Well, we've got materials still left over from ours. Granted, not enough, but Rommy and Becka have people who go out with Caine, and I'm pretty certain they'd be more than happy to gather supplies for something like this. At the end of the day, it'll be for their benefit."

"Yeah. When can we start?"

Si laughed. "Slow down. I'll have to get it cleared with the committee, but I'm pretty certain it'll be okay." They both turned as Susan led Callie, Debbie and several others into their small house for a meeting. "And they'll have other things on their minds right now, but I suppose when the snow clears, and the ground softens up, we can head to the other side of the ridge and start making plans."

"Okay."

"Well, I'm going across to see Sasha. Make sure you get some warm grub in you. It's freezing out here."

"I will," Matt said as he watched his friend head off towards the forest. Suddenly, he felt happier than he had done in the longest time. He had a purpose again. Something that was his, something useful to do, something he would be remembered for other than being Phil Trainor's son.

*

Susan stoked the fire and put another log on while Callie poured four piping mugs of camomile tea. "We're going to have to share these for the moment, but we'll get some more water on the boil."

There were about a dozen people assembled in the small house. They had been part of the much bigger group who had gone around Redemption making sure everyone was okay and that there was no further property damage.

"I say it's a miracle," Harper said, taking one of the mugs from Callie. "I know it's a tragedy about Ian, but that storm was something else last night."

Susan stood up and leaned back against the wall. All of them still wore their outdoor gear for the time being, and they knew they'd be heading out again soon enough, but this was the warmest they'd been since first thing in the morning, and all of them relished the feeling. "One person dying is one person too many," Susan replied.

"Yeah. I agree," Harper replied. "But honestly, I thought it would be a hell of a lot worse."

"It was like nothing I've seen before," Tania said. "I peeked outside before we turned in last night. I've never witnessed a blizzard like that."

"And this was just the first storm. Hell, for all we know we might have another one tonight. We might get them every day until the end of winter," Susan said.

"You don't really think so, do you?"

Susan shrugged. "I've got no idea. Everybody I've spoken to who's lived through a winter since the asteroid has said that they're relentless, unforgiving."

"We can't do any more than we're doing, Mum," Callie said. "When the storms come, we just have to hunker down and deal with whatever happens afterwards like we are doing."

Susan looked across towards her daughter in the fire and lantern light and, as was often the case, she swelled with pride. "You're right. Of course you're right, but I just wish—"

The door opened suddenly, letting in a burst of freezing air. Drake and Marina stepped inside before closing it once again behind them. "Thought we'd find you here," he said, stamping the snow off his boots as he walked across to where they were all standing.

Nicola took a sip from the mug in her hands and handed it to Marina, who gratefully accepted. "I was looking for you earlier," Susan said, "but I was told you'd gone up to the ridge."

Marina took a sip from the mug and passed it to Drake, who took a drink and then handed it back. "Yeah. We lost two people last night, and then we nearly lost two more."

The temperature in the room seemed to drop further as the sad news washed over them all. "Oh, God. Who? What happened?"

"Tiff and Stu," Marina replied.

"Then we found Esme and Steve doing their best to stay alive in the turret. Because their relief didn't arrive, neither did the resupply. They got stuck up there, and long story short, I organised the transportation of several days' worth of wood and food to be taken up there and distributed between the turrets. I've also organised the same for the other lookout positions to the east and south, but they're more exposed up there and more in danger." Drake waited. He knew that he was meant to get any such decisions cleared.

"That's good, all things considered. I just wish we'd have thought about it yesterday," Susan replied.

"Yeah, well, hindsight's twenty-twenty. We couldn't anticipate that storm to come at us so hard and fast. And there's something else."

"Oh?"

"I think, given what happened, and knowing that this is just the start, we should station people up there for longer."

"What, you mean double shifts?"

"No, I mean a few days or a week at a time. Two people. One sleeps, one watches. They'll have enough food and wood to keep them going, and rather than worrying about fourteen changeovers for each of the turrets in dangerous conditions, there'll be just one."

"I'm not sure how easy it will be to get volunteers for that."

"We'll select people who've got a track record of working together. Marina's already got a few names in mind."

Susan shrugged. "You're running the show up there. Whatever you think."

"How did things go across here?"

"We lost someone too. The wind ripped part of the roof off one of the houses. Jason and his team are rebuilding it at the moment."

"Have we heard from the other side?"

"No," Susan replied. "Callie and Dani are going to head over there soon."

Drake looked across at the two young women. "Keep an eye on the sky. That storm didn't quite come out of nowhere, but it hit us fast last night. Any sign of another one, and you either get back here fast or stay over there. You don't want to get caught out in something like that."

*

Chloe and Nazya had set off soon after digging themselves out. The going had been hard, and they'd paused a couple of times for a breather, but they both knew they wouldn't be able to rest properly until they had reached Redemption.

"At least we'll be able to see if anyone comes for us," Chloe said as the pair continued to drive through the thick snow.

"Nobody will come for us in this. The Ferals will be doing their best to stay alive. Attacking people will be well down on their list of priorities."

"How much farther do you think it is?"

"I don't know. Not far, I hope. It's hard to tell." Both of them shared the same fear. The road, for all its cracks and holes and missing strips, was invisible under the thick white blanket. They hoped they were on it or at least somewhere near it, but they had escaped from the south of Crowesbury rather than the west, and everything was just best guesses.

"Thank you for looking after me last night."

"What do you mean?" Nazya asked, turning to her friend as they walked along.

"I know I'm not much use when it comes to … well … anything really. If you hadn't got the wood and started the fire, if you weren't with me, I'd be dead."

"You need to stop talking like that. You are capable of much more than you think."

"We both know that's not true."

"You have lived in your father's shadow for so long that you have forgotten so much of what you know.

101

Remember when we went camping in Scarborough when we were fourteen?"

"God, that seems so long ago now."

"It was. It was an age ago. But do you remember, you had been reading survival books all summer? You and I used to go off together on our adventures. You were the one who showed me how to build a fire, how to construct a solar still in case we ran out of water, how to set snares, not that either of us would want to. You learnt all of that and more besides, and you did all that and more besides. You used to be much more independent."

Chloe didn't speak for a few moments as she let Nazya's words sink in. When she did, her voice quivered a little. "You're right. What have I let myself become?"

"You have merely regressed a little. It is not something that cannot be remedied, and if there was ever a time to find your inner strength once more, it is now."

"I don't want to feel like this. I don't want to feel so useless, so dependent on others."

"The only thing stopping you is yourself."

Chloe halted, and Nazya came to a standstill too. "I'm sorry."

"What for?"

"For not pulling my weight."

"It is understandable. Your world has just been turned upside down."

"Yeah, but yours has too."

"But my father—" Nazya stopped herself. They had agreed not to talk about it again until they finally reached Redemption. "All I'm saying is that you have had a lot on your mind. You are my best friend. We are like sisters. I will always look out for you."

"I promise. From today, I'm going to start doing more, start pulling my own weight. I love you, Naz."

"I love you too."

6

In the end, and for reasons known only to Phil, he had joined Callie and Dani on their wintry hike over the ridge and down to the forest on the other side where the Wanderers had settled.

The journey took longer than any of them had anticipated. Even though a small army of workers had shifted a channel of snow up to the ridge, the slope down was thick, drifting in places to chest height.

"It's stunning, isn't it?" Dani said, looking at the expansive icy landscape as it stretched out in front of them.

"It would be a damn sight more stunning if we weren't out here trudging through it," Phil replied.

"I don't remember anybody forcing you to come."

"Well, who else is going to protect you?"

"Protect us from what?" Callie asked.

"Who knows? Ferals, people you've alienated or irritated."

"Err … I think you might be getting us mixed up with you. In general, people like me and Dani."

Phil shrugged. "If that's what you want to believe, you keep telling yourselves that."

"So, why are you really with us?"

"Just thought I'd tag along. It was getting far too peopley in our house."

"Well, you were warned. I told you there was a downside to sharing a house with a doctor."

"'I told you so' is going to be written on your gravestone."

"I'll make sure it's written on yours first."

"I have little doubt."

"So, how are the mushrooms coming along?"

"Ugh!" Dani exclaimed loudly.

"What?" the other two asked in unison.

"Can't you have a normal conversation?"

"This is a normal conversation," Callie protested.

"No, it's not. Normal conversations don't begin with how are your mushrooms? Normal conversations begin with how are Debbie and Matt? That was some storm last night, wasn't it? Do you think it will snow again tonight?"

"They're fine. Yes, it was. Don't know, I'm not a weatherman. There, happy now?"

"Ugh!" Dani said again as they continued their slow descent.

"And to answer your question, the mushrooms are coming along well. If you want to come round tonight, you can see."

"There's actually something to see now?"

"Yeah … well … there's mould."

"And it's white?"

"So far."

"That's really exciting."

"It's certainly very positive so far."

"This is surreal," Dani said. "It's like being in some kind of nerd hell."

"You won't be saying that when you're sinking your teeth into a mushroom burger," Callie replied.

"I'd prefer a real burger."

"Do you honestly think what we were eating in Salvation was real?"

"It tasted real enough."

Callie laughed. "Fair enough. What was the stuff we had down on Level Three, Phil?"

"Well, I'm assuming you didn't have enough money for lab-based meat."

"You'd be assuming right. Even the burgers we had were a luxury. It was like once a month if we were lucky. Were they soya-based or something?"

"Well, I was only in charge of growing the crops. I didn't get involved in the manufacture of the end product, but from what I know, the burgers and most of the meat substitutes were a mix of soya and wheat, soya and pea, or just pea protein. And beetroot was often used for colouring."

"Do you think we'll ever be able to make anything like that again?" Dani asked, suddenly taking a little more of an interest as happy memories came back to her.

"If somebody felt they must, then I'm pretty certain they could. But I'm more interested in making sure people have a healthy and balanced diet than satiating fast-food cravings. The big corporations behind the convenience restaurants were just like the worst drug dealers. They weren't interested in what their product did to you. They just wanted to sell more and more of it. They didn't care that it created an epidemic of obesity and ill health. They didn't care that their burgers and their bargain buckets were catalysts for cancer and heart disease and Alzheimer's and a thousand other illnesses. All they cared about was selling you more. Selling you bigger burgers and bigger portions and gaining bigger markups. They were no different to the tobacco companies, but they owned the politicians, and instead of curtailing their activities, putting health warnings on their products like they did with tobacco, they championed them."

"Yeah, but their stuff tasted so good."

Phil let out a long sigh. "And this is why we were on the verge of extinction before the asteroid."

"I'm just saying … they were. Are you telling me that you never had a Super Q Burger with elephant fries, barbecue coleslaw and a summer fruit and chocolate banoffee shake?"

"Are you speaking English right now? I don't even know what any of that is."

"Oh, man. You haven't lived."

"Ah, yes. I'm sure it ranks up there with Parmigiana di Melanzane served with lightly seasoned focaccia and a nice Barolo."

"What?"

"Never mind." They carried on plodding through the snow before Phil gave in. "Okay. So what the hell was it?"

"What was what?" Dani asked.

"All that stuff you came out with."

"Which bit?"

"All of it."

"You never went to Q Burger?"

"May I remind you that Q Burger was owned by AFS, the people who ran Salvation? Their activities before the asteroid struck were just as morally reprehensible as what they did in there."

"Well, why did you take your family into the bunker if you felt that way?" Callie asked.

"Okay. You've got me."

"No, I'm serious. Why?"

Phil thought for a moment. "Because there are no clean hands. Or at least there weren't."

"What do you mean?"

"I mean that for everything good I did before, there was a point where I had to get into bed with the devil."

"That doesn't make it any clearer."

"I mean permits, permissions, funding. It was impossible to do anything without having to shake hands with corrupt politicians or ruthless prospectors who weren't backing you because you were trying to make things better for everyone but were there because you had a good business plan and they saw a pot of gold at the end of it. Drew was different, and when we worked on the bunkers, it all seemed to be for the right reasons, but then when their building needed to be accelerated, a whole load of other people got involved to fund the projects and exert their influence. Organisations like AFS started to gain more power, and in the end, they took over. I took my family into the bunker because there wasn't anything I wouldn't have done to keep them safe, and, again, that meant cosying up to people who sickened me inside. But I hoped that I might be able to help other people too. I hoped that by being there, I could help build a future when we came out, despite how insidious Bucks and the rest of them were … are."

"You did. If it wasn't for you, the farms wouldn't have been possible."

Phil shrugged. "There were others who might have been able to design something similar."

"Yeah, but it was you who did it. It was you who kept everyone fed in Salvation. It's you who's keeping us alive now. And you're right. In the past, it was impossible to try to do the right thing without it being tainted somehow, but that's the greatest thing about Redemption. We're building something pure, from scratch, the right way." She looked across at her friend and could see he was still deep in thought. Callie knew him well enough to read the myriad of doubts and questions going through his head.

"I suppose," he said, snapping out of his daze and turning to Dani. "Anyway, to answer your question, no, I never went to Q Burger, so you're going to have to enlighten me as to what I missed."

"Well, the Super Q Burger was just like a normal Q Burger but bigger and with extra cheese. The elephant fries were thin and crispy but about so big," she said, approximating a dessert spoon size with her gloved thumb and forefinger. "And they were shaped like—"

"Elephants?"

"Yeah. The barbecue coleslaw was made with mayo and a tangy, sweet sauce, and the summer fruit and chocolate banoffee shake was the sweetest, most amazing thing I've ever tasted."

"You do realise that you probably reduced your life expectancy by a month for each mouthful of that meal."

"I don't care. It was so worth it."

"And that's my point entirely."

"What's your point?" Callie asked.

"AFS and the corporations like them were nothing more than street dealers. They created these things to be addictive, and that's all. Bucks was a majority shareholder in APS too."

"APS?"

"Amalgamated Pharmaceutical Solutions."

"What's that got to do with anything?" Dani asked.

"Well, apart from being the market leader in medication to combat diabetes, they produced the Fatbegone pill, which was the number one drug to fight obesity. Very expensive, and you'd need to take it for the rest of your life, but when they brought that out, their share price went through the roof. In addition, they manufactured Bogrow, the market-leading growth hormone in factory farming, as well as the most commonly used antibiotic Bioagriwell. These companies are responsible for creating multiple health crises, and they made sure they profited at every stage. The devil was never a fallen angel with horns growing out of his skull; he wore a suit and sat behind a boardroom desk. The harm AFS and companies like them did to our ecosystems, our human and animal populations, our very atmosphere is unquantifiable. If it wasn't for the asteroid, it would only have been a matter of time before we killed ourselves."

The three of them carried on walking for a while, and then, finally, Dani spoke again. "I'm guessing you and Debbie never got invited to many parties."

Phil laughed. "No. No, we didn't."

"I can't say I'm surprised." They finally reached the bottom of the hill, and Dani looked back up. "It's not going to be much fun retracing our steps."

"Don't worry," Callie said. "With Phil making the conversation, the time will just fly by."

"You never know," Dani replied, "it might be my lucky day. I might get hypothermia and die before then."

"That's the spirit," Phil said, placing his hands on the two young women's backs. "Now, let's go and find Rommy and Becka."

*

"What are you guys doing here?" Rommy asked as Callie, Dani, and Phil appeared in the clearing where her hotel was situated.

"We've come to see you," Callie replied. "Can we help?" she asked, looking at the pile of wood the other woman held in her arms.

"If you want to grab a bundle each, it will save me a couple of journeys."

The three of them had made good time through the forest compared to the rest of the journey. The snow was shallower, there was virtually no breeze, and whether it was their imaginations or not, somehow it felt a little milder. They stocked up from the log pile and followed Rommy into the house. Inside was a sharp contrast to the calm Christmas card view outside. Lanterns and torches lit the dozens of curtained cubicles that constituted the homes of the hotel residents. At the far end of the corridor, a large fire crackled away, and that's where they headed as they heard the sounds of children playing and good-humoured conversations between the adults.

"Are you having a party here or something?" Dani asked.

Rommy chuckled and glanced back over her shoulder. "Sounds like it sometimes." They reached the fireplace to find Bea and three other children sitting cross-legged in front of it, playing one of the many board games that Caine and his team had liberated from their third mission to New Fenton. Their eyes sparkled with delight as they revelled in one another's company. Becka was busy stacking the wood that Rommy and others had already brought in.

"I didn't know we were expecting visitors," she said, rubbing her hands clean and flashing them towards the fire for a moment to heat them up after touching the frigid logs. "To what do we owe this pleasure?"

"Mum wanted us to check in with everybody, find out what damage the storm did and see if there was anything we could do. You're first on the list."

"We've beaten you to it," Rommy replied. "Becka and I did a grand tour this morning."

"Oh ... wow! Well, that's going to save us a lot of work," Callie said, retrieving a small pad and pencil from her back pocket. "I dread to ask, but what's the damage then?"

"There wasn't any."

"What do you mean? That storm was relentless. There must have been something."

"Nope. We checked in with everyone. There wasn't any major damage to the hotels or even the thunderboxes, for that matter." The thunderbox toilets for the hotels were the envy of people who lived in the houses on the other side of the ridge. They were situated in lean-tos at the rear of the properties, and they could be accessed through the back door. Anyone in the stone-built houses had to make a much longer journey, and, in the storm, this had become impossible, so instead, people were using covered buckets, which was far from ideal but beat freezing to death.

"Why were you so sure we'd have incurred damage?" Becka asked.

"Because we did."

"Was anybody hurt?"

"We lost three people. One when the roof blew off one of the houses and two lookouts who got blown off the ridge."

"Oh, God. That's terrible," Rommy said.

Bea and the other children all laughed simultaneously, and the adults turned to see they were still in the midst of their game and hadn't heard a word of the conversation.

"You're sure that everybody's okay, that no one needs anything?" Callie asked again as she slipped her notebook back into her pocket.

"We're all fine," Rommy said. "All the hotels have got a good supply of wood and food. Spirits are—" She broke off, not wanting to sound callous given the news that they'd just received.

"What Rommy's trying to say," interjected Becka, "is that we've all been used to much worse than this." She looked into the fireplace and then around the rest of the giant log cabin. "This place wouldn't win any awards for comfort or facilities, but we're warm, we're dry, and we've got food, which is a far cry from what any of us had last year. When we did our rounds this morning, everybody seemed to be sharing our euphoria. I'm sorry, that's not a nice thing to say after what you've just told us, but before we came here, there wasn't a single one of us who wasn't wondering about the winter, about how we were going to survive, about how many people we'd lose this time."

More laughter rang out from somewhere in the large wooden building. "I suppose as bad as things were in Salvation in some ways, it was nothing compared to what you lived through," Phil said.

"From everything you've told us about the place, it sounded like a nightmare. But we lived through a different nightmare, that's all. We've seen storms like the one we experienced last night before. We've felt that kind of cold before. We were prepared for it. But waking up in a place that's warm, having food, and feeling protected because there aren't any psychos out to murder you or kidnap you or … whatever else … it's given us all an appreciation of how lucky we are."

"I suppose it would," Phil replied.

"Well, at least that's one less headache for Mum to think about," Callie said.

"She's got a lot of responsibility on her shoulders," Rommy replied. "If there's anything we can do to make her life easier, let me know."

"You've made our lives easier by checking on everyone. Thank you for that."

"We'll be doing this every day," Becka replied. "It makes more sense if we come to you if we need help rather than you making that journey to check on us."

"I suppose it does. It just happened so quickly that we didn't really have time to make plans."

"That's what happens in winter. It comes out of nowhere. The wind, the snow. It's so unpredictable. Not last year, but the year before, we lost two people in a hailstorm."

"Lost them how?" Phil asked.

"The hailstones were the size of cricket balls. Most of us managed to get to cover with just a few bruises, but they got knocked to the ground and that was it. By the time storm was over, it was too late. Their heads and bodies had been battered beyond recognition."

"Christ!" Phil whispered.

"Yeah. You even get a hint of a hailstorm and you make sure you take cover."

"Suddenly, I'm looking forward to our return journey even less now," Dani said.

"That's what we mean. No point in you making extra journeys. Any time spent outside in winter is risky."

"'scuse me," Dani said, holding her stomach. "I think I might need to use your thunderbox before I head back."

"Are you okay?" Callie asked, placing a hand on her friend's back.

"Just feel a bit queasy. That's all. I'll be back in a minute." She disappeared into the back and through the door to the adjacent toilet block.

Phil let out a huff of a laugh.

"That's not funny," Callie said. "I've not seen her like that before. She went pale."

He put his hand up placatingly. "I wasn't laughing at her. I'm not surprised her stomach's turning. That's a horrible story."

"What is it then?"

"My mind was drifting."

"I've heard that starts to happen more when you reach a certain age."

"Yes, thank you, Callie. No, I was thinking back to something my grandfather told me once."

"Okay. And are you going to enlighten us as to what that was, or is this a new guessing game?"

"He told me about when he'd moved house as a youngster. There'd been an outside toilet at the old property, and there was another one at the new house, but this one was right next to the back door in the yard. He said it was like living in the lap of luxury not having to trail all the way up the garden path to use the lavatory. At the time, I couldn't understand how anyone having to use any kind of outdoor facilities could think themselves lucky." He gestured to the door that Dani had vanished through. "But now I get it."

"Trust me. When you've lived in nothing but ruins, having a bucket is a luxury," Rommy replied. "It's all relative."

"I suppose it is."

"I have to say," Becka began, "I'm surprised you decided to grace us with your presence. Even when we've been across at the farm, it's rare that we see you. Don't you usually have a thousand things on the go at once?"

"Usually."

"So, what's different about today?"

CHRISTOPHER ARTINIAN

"I needed to get a little exercise. It helps me get my thoughts in order."

"Which translates as there are far too many people traipsing in and out of his house for him to get any peace and quiet."

The other two women laughed. "Yes, thank you, Callie; I'm more than capable of answering for myself."

"So, what thoughts are you hoping to get in order?" Rommy asked, still smiling.

"Make sure it's a potted answer you give, Phil. We want to be heading back long before dark," Callie said.

"Funny," Phil replied. "I'm kind of in a mushroom state of mind at the moment."

"What?" Becka and Rommy asked at the same time.

"Oh God, not this again," Dani replied, reappearing from the back.

"You've lost us," Rommy replied.

"Phil's growing white mould that may or may not develop into mushrooms and solve world hunger, world peace and the meaning of life."

The other women laughed.

"Well, this is just wonderful. My life's work being reduced to a punchline. I'm so glad I decided to come now."

"Oh, don't pout," Callie replied. "You know she's only joking."

"Okay, so tell us, seriously. What's this about mushrooms?" Rommy said.

Phil let out a long sigh. "I've potentially got a crop of blue oyster mushrooms growing."

"Potentially?"

"If I still had access to a lab, it would be the easiest thing in the world, but it's a lot harder out here. If I can get this right, though, if I can master how to grow them and subsequently how to farm them on a mass scale, it will be huge."

The four women could see the stress evident on his face. They'd been joking about it moments before, but it was obvious that every potential failure drove a figurative dagger through his heart. Everybody looked to him and his knowledge to keep them alive. He was a strange, awkward, socially inept eccentric with a bizarre sense of humour. Plenty gave him a wide berth, but the four women he was talking to genuinely cared for him despite often using him as the butt of their jokes. Rommy reached out, placing a hand on his upper arm. "Well, I'm pretty certain if there's one person alive who can do it, it's you, Phil."

There was a sincerity in her voice and in her eyes that took him by surprise. "Thank you. That's kind of you to say."

"And on that note, we'd better be heading back to the farm," Callie said.

"I suppose we should," Phil replied.

"Remember," Rommy said, "we'll keep tabs on everything over here while the weather's like this. If we need help, we'll shout."

"Thanks," Callie replied. "I really appreciate it. I know Mum will too."

"Give Susan our best," added Becka.

"I will."

*

The rest of the day passed quickly, and by the time darkness fell, nearly everyone was tucked up inside their respective homes with a fire burning in the hearth. With every breeze that made the shutters rattle, shivers of dread ran through the inhabitants of Redemption. Winter was only just starting, and their first night had been a bad one.

"I really hope we don't get hit by another storm tonight," Nicola said as the nine inhabitants of the house all sat around the fire with piping-hot bowls of stew.

"If we do, we do," Susan replied. "We got through last night; we'll get through tonight."

"Yeah. Not all of us got through last night, did we?"

"No. No, we didn't." There was a pause before Susan continued. "We lost people in Salvation. We've lost people since leaving Salvation. The one thing that's always going to get us through is if we look out for one another, and that's what I intend to do. I don't know how many people will leave us before the end of this winter, but we need to stay strong. We need to keep going. We'll learn, and next year we'll be even better prepared."

Callie placed an arm around her mum and squeezed her. There was a lot of responsibility on her shoulders, but she was dealing with it admirably.

Everybody stayed in front of the fire all evening, occasionally throwing on another log. The temperature outside had dropped noticeably since the afternoon, but they kept themselves warm with conversation and stories from their past. By the time they finally called it a night, it was warm throughout the whole house. The makeshift insulation around the door and window had remained undisturbed. There had been no unexpected visitors, and subsequently no significant heat had escaped.

They all bid their goodnights and retired to their respective family cubicles. Si went out like a light, and it wasn't long before the sound of heavy breathing elsewhere told Susan and Callie that the others had fallen into slumber too.

"Can't you sleep?" Callie whispered.

"How did you know I was awake?" Susan asked.

"I could hear you blinking."

Susan chuckled loudly. "Don't make me laugh. I'll end up waking everyone up."

"Are you thinking about last night?"

"Yeah."

Callie shuffled closer until the pair were lying side by side. "There was nothing else you could have done, Mum. It was a freak accident. There was no way to predict any of that happening. That storm was like nothing we've ever lived through. You made sure everyone had wood, food and clothes. You've worked tirelessly. Nobody could have done more."

Susan exhaled deeply. "I suppose we'll never know, will we?"

"Yeah, we will because I'm telling you now. Bad stuff's going to happen. You can't control the weather. You can't control anything other than your response to any situations that arise."

"I forget. Who's the daughter and who's the mother in this relationship?"

"I forget too."

Susan wrapped her arm around Callie and kissed her hard on the side of her head. "Love you so much," she said.

"Love you too."

"Brilliant," Si said. "Everybody loves everybody; now, can we please get some pissing sleep?"

The mother and daughter laughed, squeezing each other once more. "Sorry," Susan said. "Night, night."

"Night, Mum," Callie replied.

"Night, Mum," Si added. "And for what it's worth, Callie was right. Nobody could have done more."

*

Everyone in the house was in a deep sleep when the first knocks came on the door. Nobody stirred for a few moments. Instead, they lay still, hoping they were still in the realms of a dream and they wouldn't have to leave the comfort and warmth of their beds.

Tap, tap, tap. The noise sounded a little louder this time, and Susan was the first to rise with a groan. Callie flicked on a lantern and followed her to the entrance. The wood still glowed brightly in the fireplace, but they knew that some of the warmth it provided would be lost the moment they opened the door.

Susan bent down and removed the rolled-up towel they used as a draft excluder before opening up. Any hope of this being a small problem that could be quickly rectified and allow them the opportunity to return to bed vanished in an instant when they laid eyes on Marina and Drake standing there with Chloe and Nazya. Despite the cold,

Susan and Callie just stood in the open doorway for a moment, baffled and fearful as to what the appearance of their friends from Infinity meant.

It was only when Si and the others joined them that their brains jump-started once more.

"Um," Susan began, shaking her head, "what's going on?" She backed away from the entrance allowing Drake, Marina and their two shivering friends in.

When the door was firmly closed once more, it was Callie who spoke this time. "What's happening? What is this?"

"Marina and I will go and round the rest of the committee up. I suggest you get these girls something warm to drink and eat." Drake didn't wait for a response before turning and leaving. Marina followed him but cast one final sad look towards the newly arrived women.

"Nazya, Chloe, why are you here?"

A shuddering breath left the back of Chloe's throat, but finally she spoke. "We've lost Infinity."

PART 2

THEN

DAY 1

There had been lots of day ones. Ever since the Great Escape, Bucks had been scrambling to hold on to power. Paris, as always, had remained his loyal attack dog by his side, but everyone wondered how long the status quo would remain. Mini rebellions on Level Two had become an almost weekly occurrence, and how many of the Salvation guards remained truly loyal was impossible to quantify.

There was something a little different about this day one though. On leaving Salvation, it had always been the plan to set up a new settlement to the north. All the resources were there ready, but what they lacked was the workforce. Not a single Level Three inhabitant remained, and the forced servitude of thousands of Level Two citizens had turned the giant bunker into a powder keg.

They had managed to augment their workforce a little by rounding up strays who their roving patrols had happened across while in search of the escapees. They had questioned them and gleaned little if no worthwhile information before putting them to work. Unlike the Level Two labourers, these new recruits were grateful for the opportunity to have shelter and food. Outside, it had been a constant battle to find either, but here both were available in not exactly plentiful supply but in greater abundance than they had experienced since the asteroid.

Today, though, something was different. Today, the large troop of new arrivals who had entered Salvation possessed more than muscle and a willingness to work for food. They had knowledge. Knowledge that was far more valuable than the tiny scraps the administration had gleaned from the others since the Salvation guards had first started going outside. So much knowledge, in fact, that Paris had alerted Bucks soon after she had begun her questioning of the leader of this one-hundred-and-fifty-strong army.

"Can we believe what he says?" Bucks asked as he and Paris stared through the one-way mirror at the scrawny looking figure who scooped another chunk of soup-soaked bread into his mouth. The man looked and acted like he hadn't eaten in a month. His face was gaunt and pale, but with each mouthful of food a little more life returned to his eyes.

"Carlisle interrogated him and half a dozen of the others who came in with him before he got me down here. They didn't offer any resistance; in fact, it was almost as if they were looking to get picked up by our patrol. Everything we asked was backed up more or less word for word by the others, so if what they're telling us is lies then they're well-rehearsed lies. At the very least, we've got nearly a hundred and fifty new workers, which is no small thing."

It was true. The groups they'd rounded up thus far had been small, and even though they didn't really have a choice in the matter, none of them resisted when they were forcibly recruited to become workers in Salvation. Compared to the existence they were leaving behind on the outside, life in the bunker, even in servitude, was nothing short of luxurious.

"I want to speak to him," Bucks said.

"There's no need for that, sir," replied Paris. "I can easil—"

"I want to speak to him. If what you've told me is true, this could be the difference. This could be the information we've been looking for."

"But—"

"Give us the room," Bucks said, glancing towards the Salvation guards behind them. They immediately disappeared leaving Bucks and Paris alone. "You know what this could mean."

"Yes, sir, but we don't know anything about this man. He could be a cannibal. He could be—"

"He wouldn't be the first one we've brought into the fold." It was true. They had recruited many outsiders, and stories had soon started to circulate as to what they had done on the outside. Cannibalism was not uncommon, but, thankfully, nobody had partaken in human flesh in Salvation since their arrival. "I want to find out exactly what he knows. This could be the turning point for us. This could bring those thinking about rebellion back on side. This could be what we've been looking for. We need a win, Paris. We need to gain the upper hand again."

Paris nodded reluctantly. "Well, let's at least chain him to the chair."

"We're not chaining him to the chair. I'll have two guards at the door."

"It's a risk."

"It's a bigger risk if we don't do this. This could put us back on top, Paris. If the rumours about the Ark are true, how long do you think it will be before they decide to march down from the Cairngorms and pay us a visit?"

"We can't know that. We can't know that they'll be hostile towards us."

"I know Indigo Sharpe. There isn't a conciliatory bone in his body. All he craves is power. He will never be interested in building an alliance."

"But the plan—"

"The plan became irrelevant the day we entered the bunkers. It was always going to be a mad dash when we raised our heads above the parapet. It was always going to be who could grow the strongest the quickest." Bucks' eyes were drawn back to the figure mopping the last drips of soup from the bowl. "But this could give us a flicker of hope again."

Paris could see the desperation in the first minister's eyes. Salvation had slumped from disaster to disaster. Things weren't as bad as they had been when the mass exodus happened, but they were bad. The occupants were trapped in the bunker with not enough people to begin work on the new settlement while maintaining the day-to-day running of Salvation at the same time. All the meticulous plans that had been drawn up had gone to hell, and Paris knew as well as anyone that unless a game-changing event occurred, Salvation was in danger of imploding. "Well, I'll go in there with you."

Bucks smiled. "I'm going in there by myself. You stay here. Make sure every word is recorded. Watch his reactions. Listen. Make notes. But I want to look in his eyes. I want his full attention. I want to know that what I'm hearing is the truth, or at least what he perceives to be the truth."

Two minutes later, Bucks was sitting opposite his interviewee. The bowl and plate had been cleared away and on the other side of the interrogation room door stood two guards ready to storm in should an alarm be raised.

"Where are the rest of my people?" the figure asked.

Bucks leaned back in his chair and clasped his hands over his paunch. Although many had gone hungry in the last few months, he had not. "Right now, they're probably being fed and allotted housing. You'll be joining them soon enough."

"Just like that, you feed us and put roofs over our

heads?"

"Not just like that. You'll work for your food and shelter. But you'll be paid too. You'll become citizens of the bunker. The more you put in the more you'll get out." The two men stared at each other long and hard. It wasn't difficult to see the mistrust behind their eyes.

"Why am I here?"

"You don't want to be here? I was told you practically handed yourselves over to my patrol."

"I mean why am I here in this room and not with my people?"

"You'll be with them soon enough, but you mentioned some things to my colleagues that I want a little clarification on."

"I'm still hungry."

Bucks nodded slowly. "What's your name?"

"Danko," his guest replied.

Bucks turned to the mirror behind them. "Bring Mr Danko a steak sandwich," he said before turning back around to gauge his guest's reaction. "It'll be a few minutes, but trust me, it will be worth it."

"You're mocking me," Danko replied.

Bucks shook his head. "You'll see in a moment that I'm most certainly not." Several minutes passed and the two men sat in silence. Finally, the door opened and in walked a man with a plate and a glass of beer. He placed them down in front of Danko and left just as quickly. "Go ahead. Tuck in."

Danko edged towards the table and examined the food on the plate. He peeled a corner of the thick bread back and saw the steak still sizzling beneath it. He leaned forward, breathing in deeply, and a single tear appeared in the corner of his eye. Since entering the London Underground to avoid the initial aftermath of the asteroid, life had steadily got worse. He had been a town planner, a respected man with status and wealth. He had become something completely different however. He had done things that he would not even have thought possible in the time before. He had robbed and kidnapped and murdered and … more besides. It had been nothing short of a miracle that he had somehow managed to keep his small army together, but they were withering. They had used up the last of their ammunition. Thirty of their number had been massacred after a raid on Crowesbury had gone bad. Another twenty had deserted them, and Danko knew that unless something big happened, the impending winter would take more.

They had been in a forest the first time they had spotted one of Salvation's roving patrols. They had watched as they had rounded up small groups of Ferals and returned with them to the bunker. It would have been easier to kill them than to imprison them, so the only conclusion Danko could draw was there was a need for bodies, for workers. He had discussed this with his lieutenants, and as big a risk as it was to throw themselves at the mercy of one of the patrols, the alternative was to continue the downward spiral with no hope of redemption. Now, though, he was staring at something he had never believed he would see again. He was smelling something that conjured a thousand memories from happier times. Saliva welled in his mouth and he grabbed the doorstep sandwich in both hands before taking a giant bite. He could barely chew it at first, but eventually he manoeuvred it around just enough for his teeth to start breaking it down.

The hot juices dribbled down the back of his throat and the stodgy bread stuck to the roof of his mouth. He knew it was lab-based meat, but it didn't matter. It was the most amazing thing he'd tasted in years and more tears began to roll down his face as he ate. He had lost so much. He had been on the verge of giving up, and now he was eating a steak sandwich. His people were safe and there was some small glimmer of hope that they might have a future.

He chewed and chewed, finally washing the food down with several gulps of beer. It was chilled and fizzy and made the back of his throat tingle. An involuntary smile lit his face despite the tears that continued to fall. He wiped his mouth clean with the back of his hand and took another bite. Bucks just watched him until the last mouthful had been swallowed and the last of the beer had been glugged. Danko sat there for a moment, a little out of breath, before he wiped his face clean with his sleeve. He silently chastised himself for showing weakness in front of the other man. He had always been the strong one for his people, and now he had broken down like an infant.

"Better?" Bucks asked.

"I didn't think I'd ever taste steak again."

"You've had it rough out there, but you're with us now. Things are going to get better. You won't have to wonder where your next meal is coming from. You won't have to worry about freezing in winter. You won't have to worry about being attacked in the middle of the night."

"And all you want from us is our labour in return?"

"Not all."

"What then?"

"Information … and loyalty."

"Loyalty can't be bought."

Bucks smiled. "On the contrary. I think loyalty is one of the most easily tradeable commodities."

"What information?"

"When you spoke to my people earlier, you mentioned a market. You mentioned a giant settlement to the southwest of here and you mentioned a bunker in the Cairngorms."

"What of them?" Danko asked.

"I need you to tell me everything you know."

"Why?"

"Because all our futures hang in the balance."

DAY 2

Danko had spent most of the previous day in the

interrogation room with Bucks. He had not held back. He'd told him everything he knew about Infinity, about the settlement to the southwest and about the bunker in the Cairngorms.

He'd explained that although they had never trafficked women and children north, they knew others who had. They knew how much they had been rewarded, and they knew how the Cairngorms settlement was expanding.

He'd told Bucks everything he could about Crowesbury and Infinity. He'd told him about the comings and goings of hundreds of traders, what was traded, how it was traded. Of course, he'd never seen it firsthand. He and his people had never been allowed into Infinity. He had interrogated captives, however, and they had furnished him with information in the hope that they would be rewarded with their freedom. Instead, they had wound up on spits.

He'd also told Bucks about the giant settlement to the south that had planted fields and fields of crops. There had once been a time when he had hoped his people could take it over, but it grew too big too fast. Each time they had observed it since, it had got bigger, become better defended.

Danko couldn't remember a time when he had talked more. When the day was over, he was taken down in a lift to what the guards called Level Three and he was escorted to his new home to find many of his compatriots waiting there for him. Spirits were high. Beer had been brought down to them in plastic barrels. More food than they had seen in years was laid out on tables lining the street where their blocks of flats were.

Danko's eyes flickered open and despite his head throbbing, a thin smile decorated his face. *I'm lying in a bed, an actual bed.* He wasn't quite sure what had roused him, but it didn't matter. The most important thing was that the previous day had not been part of some cruel dream. *This is real. It's real.*

There was a bang against a door further down the hallway. "Outside in ten minutes for induction," a voice shouted.

Bang! Bang! Bang! "Assemble on the pavement outside in ten minutes for your induction," a female voice shouted this time.

Bang! Bang! Bang! *That was my door.* This time, no barked orders followed the knock. Danko stumbled down the short corridor and to the entrance. A female guard handed him a pile of clean clothes. "Get a shower and meet us outside in ten."

"For induction?" Danko asked.

"No. The first minister wants to see you."

"The first minister?"

"Mr Bucks."

"But what about—"

"Look. I don't know anything other than what I've been told, and I've been told to escort you upstairs."

Fifteen minutes later, Danko was back in the interrogation room. A mug of steaming coffee sat on the table in front of him next to a bacon sandwich. It took him back to the days when he worked as a town planner. Things had been very different then. His small team had taken it in turns to provide this very same breakfast from the greasy spoon around the corner from his offices. This all seemed a little surreal given everything that had happened in between, but he attacked the sandwich with the same gusto as he'd eaten the food from the day before.

This time, Bucks joined him as did Paris whom he had spoken to briefly the previous day too. They sat on opposite sides of the desk tucking into their food and drinks like old friends, not discussing anything other than the quality of the sandwich and whether Danko liked his new accommodation. When the plates had been cleared away, they all leaned back from the table and continued their polite chatter for a while as they sipped their drinks.

The tone of the conversation finally changed and it was Bucks who took the lead. "I think I got about an hour's sleep if that, last night."

"Oh?" Danko replied.

"Yes. Y'see, you gave me an awful lot to think about yesterday, and while the information you provided was insightful, it raised as many questions as it answered."

"Oh? I … I told you everything I know."

Bucks put his hand up placatingly. "Oh, I don't doubt that. Don't get me wrong, what you told me was invaluable, but the devil's in the details, y'see."

"I don't understand."

"I've assembled a team and I'd like you to work with them."

"A team? I thought I'd be working with my people."

"Oh, you will be … eventually, if that's what you want."

"Why wouldn't it be what I want?"

"It goes back to what we were talking about yesterday. Loyalty. I always reward loyalty, Danko. And I think you could have a very bright future with us here. If you want to work alongside your people in the recycling plant or the farms or the reactor then you can. But for the moment, I'd like you to work alongside my people and help us."

"Help you do what?"

"There's no simple answer to that. Our plans are multi-fold, but they're all with a view to advancement for us all."

"Well, what is it you want me to do?"

Bucks looked over his shoulder and signalled beyond the mirror. A moment later, a female guard appeared at the door and a small team of civilians hovered behind her. "Everything will be explained to you."

Danko placed his mug down on the table and stood. "Okay. But I'm telling you, I've told you everything I know." He headed to the door and followed the woman back out leaving Bucks and Paris alone in the room.

"What now?" asked Paris.

"I've pretty much been working through the night,

and I realise it's only early, but I need to get some sleep. I want a meeting with you and Hogarth tomorrow morning, let's say eight o'clock. Everything starts full steam tomorrow morning, Paris." A thin smile appeared on his face. "I want detailed reports of everything they get out of Danko today. I want numbers. I want maps. I want everything."

"But sir. We've only just—"

"Time is running out, Paris. Summer will have been and gone and it will be winter before we know it, and we'll have missed our chance to act."

"Chance to act? I don't understand, sir. What are you saying?"

Bucks smiled. "All will become clear tomorrow, Paris." Without another word, he got up and exited, leaving her sitting there wondering what the hell was going on.

DAY 3

Bucks couldn't remember a time when he'd felt more energised. After so long receiving nothing but bad news and grim forecasts, finally there was the prospect of a future, a bright one too. The ideas were still forming in his head, but they were slowly falling into place like a giant jigsaw. Piece by piece they were slotting together.

He climbed out of bed and a shiver ran through him as his feet came to rest on the cold slate flooring. He and many others on Level One occupied what could only be described as mansions. This particular one was an almost perfect replica of the one he'd owned in Mayfair. While many had lived in cramped squalor on Level Three, he and his compatriots had enjoyed opulence beyond the imaginations of most.

He slipped on his dressing gown and slippers and walked across to the door. The artificial sunlight was already arcing through the vast landing windows. Beyond them lay a huge mowed lawn, landscaped garden and small woodland. Hundreds of apartments could have been fitted into the space, but then how would Level One have been any different to Level Three?

He headed down the stairs and heard pots and plates clanking in the kitchen. It was just past six o'clock when he entered the dining room and sat down at the end of the table. It would be several more hours before his wife and children roused, and up until the arrival of Danko and the others he would have remained in bed too, but suddenly there wasn't enough time in the day. He had made a point of getting a good night's rest because he wasn't sure when he would get to sleep again.

His screen was waiting for him by his breakfast setting, and he swiped across to see several messages forwarded from Paris. She vetted all his mail and only passed on the things that required his personal attention. Today, there was only one thing that interested him, and he swiped past the regular updates to get to the interview files. A smile lit his face as three-dimensional diagrams and designs flashed up on screen.

Someone cleared their throat and he looked up to see his butler standing above him with a tray.

"Good morning, good morning, good morning, Archer. And how are you today?"

Archer had worked for Bucks long before entering the bunker. He and his entire family were in his service, and he knew him better than most. So, when such an uncharacteristically friendly greeting was offered, he was more than a little taken aback. "Err … I'm very well, thank you, sir. And how are you this morning?"

"I couldn't be better, Archer. Couldn't be better."

"I'm delighted to hear that sir," he replied, placing down a cup and pouring coffee into it from a pot. "Will it be the usual for breakfast, this morning?"

Bucks thought for a moment. "To hell with it, no. It's going to be a long day today. Give me a full cooked with all the trimmings."

Archer nodded. "Excellent choice, sir," he replied,

disappearing back out of the large dining room.

Breakfast was a far more protracted affair than usual. Bucks enjoyed every mouthful, every sip of coffee. He made conversation with all the waiting staff. He hadn't done any of these things in the longest time. Since the Great Escape, his love of life had left him. Despite all the privilege, despite having more than anyone else in Salvation, despite being one of the most powerful people left on the planet, he hadn't been able to find his joie de vivre. A couple of days before, he would have looked at the textured protein masquerading as scrambled eggs on his plate with contempt. The pink strips of Fakin Bacin, as it was marketed on Level One, would have tasted like acid in his mouth, despite it costing more than most families on Level Three or Level Two for that matter could afford. But today, he relished every bite.

Something was happening, something big, something that was going to turn the fortunes of this floundering beast called Salvation. He finished breakfast and, rather than showering, took a long, deep bath. He was in the mood for pampering himself today. Unlike those on Level Two and Level Three, Level One inhabitants had no restrictions on the amount of water they could use, and he wallowed in its depths like a hippo in a mud hole. All the time, the cogs in his head continued to whir.

At eight o'clock, he walked into his office to find Paris and Hogarth waiting patiently and a little nervously. There was something about the energy Bucks was exuding that put them both on edge.

"So, how did it go yesterday?" he asked, looking at Hogarth.

"Well, sir … okay … I think."

"You think?"

The tension in the room mounted. Bucks was famous for exploding if he didn't receive the answer he wanted in meetings, and the hairs on Hogarth's neck bristled. "Err…."

A smile flashed on Bucks' face. "Paris sent me some

of your work. I think it went way better than okay. Let's get it up on the main screen, shall we?"

"Err … yes, sir. What would you like first?"

"Needless to say, anything that's discussed in this room doesn't leave it."

"Of course, sir."

"I want to see Trainor's settlement."

The words were followed by a long silence. Everyone on Levels One and Two had heard rumours of the settlement. A thousand stories had been born from those rumours, but no one had any facts, any solid proof of what it was like or where it was; now, though, maps and diagrams began to flash up on the giant screen as Hogarth walked across to it.

"Well, sir, I interviewed Danko at length and he requested that we spoke to several others in his group. They sketched the boundaries, the geography and the defences. We've pieced everything together for you to see here."

Bucks placed his hands behind his back and walked the length of the large screen examining each computerised drawing. "And all these fields have crops sown?"

"Yes, sir."

"Well, they've been very industrious with our seeds, haven't they? When was the last time they visited the place?"

"It was soon after a massive influx of newcomers, which we can only assume was Drake, Greenslade and the escapees."

"And they haven't been back since?"

"They felt there was little point, sir. Their initial intention had been to take the settlement by force for themselves, but when, all of a sudden, the settlement's numbers swelled by several thousand, they realised that there was no way they could do this, so they simply moved on and forgot about the place."

Bucks nodded slowly while still looking at the maps and diagrams. "And how did they happen across it? How did they find the settlement?"

"They followed a trading party back from Crowesbury."

"The market? This Infinity place?"

"That's correct, sir. Yes."

"Okay. What do we know about it?"

The screen went blank before a host of different maps and diagrams flashed up. "We know that it's become a hub for survivors."

"Where are these survivors from?"

"Well, the ones who use Infinity seem to have survived the asteroid in fallout bunkers mainly. Some fared better than others. There are those who barely lasted while others positively thrived. Everything works on a barter system and—"

"A barter system? What do they actually trade?"

"Well, as I said, some fared better than others. Danko's never actually been inside, but they have encountered a number of the trading parties heading to and from the market. It seems anything and everything can be traded. Building materials, tools, farming equipment, seeds, plants, textiles, pretty much everything you can imagine."

"And how are the trades made? On what basis is the value of an item determined?"

"That's something I can't tell you, sir. As I said, Danko and his people never got into Infinity, so all their knowledge is second hand."

"Who runs it?"

"I don't have a name, but from everything I've gathered it's a family that had something to do with the construction of the stadium."

"And presumably they somehow take a cut of everything that's traded?"

"Once again, I don't have this information, sir."

Bucks walked back to his chair at the end of the boardroom table and slumped into it, placing his feet up on the solid wood. "And people come from all around?"

"Yes. It's become a lot more than just a market. It's

become a beacon."

"A beacon?"

"Like a symbol. It's a community and people trade more than just goods. Information, knowledge, news, it's the new internet."

Bucks let out a huff of a laugh. "The old internet, you mean." He reached for his mug and took a sip of coffee before placing it back down and staring at the screen once more. "This is it."

"Sir?"

"This is it," he repeated, turning to Paris. "This is everything."

"I'm sorry, sir, I'm not sure what you mean," Paris replied.

"This is the answer to all of it."

Paris and Hogarth cast each other nervous glances as if they had somehow missed an entire conversation. "What do you mean all of it?"

"If you own this market, you own everything."

"I don't think it actually works like that, sir. It's much more of a community-based affair. It's run for the mutual benefit of—"

"I don't care how it's run or why it's run. I'm telling you that if we take control of the market then we take control of everything."

"If we take the market by force, I think—"

"I'm not on about taking it by force … well … not completely. I'm on about taking it by stealth."

Paris and Hogarth glanced towards each other once more before Paris spoke again. "I'm sorry, sir, I'm not sure I understand you."

"Information, Paris. We need more information."

"Okay. We'll get Danko in again, but I'm pretty certain he's told us everything he knows."

"I'm not talking about Danko. I'm talking about getting firsthand information."

"You want me to send a raiding party in there and

extract information?"

Bucks laughed rather than smiled this time. "Stealth, Paris. Do you even know what that word means?"

"Look, I'm sorry, Mister Bucks. I'm not getting this at all. If you give me orders, I'll gladly carry them out, but I don't understand what you want me to do."

"We're going to create a group of survivors who will become regular traders at Infinity. They lasted out the aftermath of the asteroid in a fallout shelter to the northwest of here. Maybe a hundred or so, so they don't have to worry about Ferals or any other raiders on their journeys to Crowesbury. They're going to be quite well stocked, but they're wanting to start growing crops as their MREs and other supplies are diminishing month by month. They'll want seeds and tools primarily. By working from within, we'll get to see exactly how this place works, what people trade and how they trade. We'll get to see what the most popular commodities are and why. Then, when we have all the information we need, we'll instigate a coup. The place will carry on running, but there'll be a change of management."

"Okay. But to what end?"

"If there's one thing I've learned from all these years in business it's that if you control the markets, you control everything."

"Well, yes, I suppose, but we won't really be controlling the market, will we? You can't control a barter system when there are so many independent trades taking place."

A smile cracked on Bucks' face once more. "You're going to have to trust me on this, Paris. I know exactly what I'm doing."

Day 14

Nothing was being left to chance. There was no way Bucks could oversee every aspect of the operation, but he took more of an active role than he had in anything since entering the bunker. The fictitious band of survivors would be headed by Hogarth and Danko. Hogarth had been a member of his personal guard on Level One; subsequently she had never mixed with the guards on lower levels and it was highly unlikely that even if one of Drake's people saw her they would recognise her. Similarly, most of the people Danko and his clan ran into didn't live to tell the tale, so, there was little chance of him being identified either. But just in case, he had been given a haircut and a shave which had given him a whole new look.

A combination of other Level One guards and citizens along with more of Danko's people made up the rest of the fictitious survivors' group. A solid and believable back story was created and indoctrinated. Everyone knew their place; everyone knew what they must do. The technical department adapted phones, giving them periscopic lenses that could be disguised as a button or pendant within clothing. Everything would be recorded, and each member of the party would be given two spare batteries to last the full length of their stay.

For their first visit, they would ransack the houses on Level Three that had remained unoccupied since the Great Escape. This would give them items to trade but, more importantly, believable items to trade. If they walked into Infinity with fifty kilos of grain or flour or two dozen Q-Eighteens to barter, it would raise suspicions and questions. Going with a hotch-potch of generic blankets, crockery, cutlery, clothing and hundreds of other items abandoned by their owners was more authentic, more believable. Their aim was not to dominate trading at Infinity, merely to gain information.

Bucks was waiting at his desk when Danko and Hogarth entered the office. He had spent much of the morning with them, and this would be the last time he would see them before they embarked on their journey to Crowesbury.

The pair took seats opposite the first minister of Salvation. When they had seen him earlier in the day, he had been energised and excited by the prospect of this venture, but now his face was long and drawn. "How are you both feeling about tomorrow?" he asked, his mind clearly elsewhere.

"Good," Hogarth replied. "Everybody knows what they're doing."

"And you?" he asked, turning to Danko. "How are your people?"

Since entering the bunker, it was as if Danko's people had been given a new lease of life. Yes, they were housed on Level Three and things were far from perfect, but they weren't fighting for their lives anymore. They had a roof over their heads and water coming out of taps and clothes, a little privacy and many of the things they had taken for granted in the time before but were just pipedreams while they were living on the outside. The candidates who had been selected to go to Crowesbury were doing even better. Their training took place on Level Two and they got to enjoy the benefits and perks of being a Level Two inhabitant for a while, although this was not as luxurious as it once had been.

"My people are grateful for this opportunity," Danko replied.

Bucks stared at the other man for a moment. He was virtually unrecognisable from the skinny, weather-beaten, brow-beaten figure who had arrived two weeks before. He had been dead behind the eyes when he had first seen him. He had willingly admitted to all the atrocities he had committed as if it was some kind of confession. "Your people are content?"

Content? The word seemed foreign. Contentment was something from before the asteroid, and even then it was a rarity given everything else that was going on in the world, but as Danko thought about it now, he nodded slowly. "Yes. I think they are."

"You think?"

"It's not a question I thought I'd ever have to answer. Two weeks ago, we had no hope. I…." Tears appeared in his eyes, but he wiped them away just as quickly. "I had no hope. But now there is hope. You've given us that."

Bucks studied the man a little while longer. "I see a bright future for you here, Danko. We recruited a number of those living wild before your people joined us, and yes, they've been happy to work for food and shelter, but they haven't adapted as quickly and as enthusiastically as you and your people. The information you've provided so far has been invaluable, and I have little doubt that you'll be an asset moving forward. You said that in your life before you were a town planner."

"Yes."

"We have a lot of planning to do, Danko. This is just going to be the start."

Danko straightened up in his chair and held his breath. He was finding it difficult to control his emotions today as memories of the last few years came flooding back to accost him. Everybody had hoped for one of the lottery tickets that would have placed them and their families safely in one of the bunkers. Instead, his family had hidden in the depths of the London Underground. He had lost them, but he had kept going, kept fighting. What he wouldn't have given to have them here with him now. He had felt like giving up so many times, but instead he had fought on for the others who were depending on him. He had become less than human, a monster to some, and indeed a monster to himself in many ways.

This was a new start though. Yes, he was having to take a side and swear loyalty to someone whose intentions and long-term ambitions he wasn't sure about. *But isn't that just what life before was like?* The fact that he was still alive was in no small part due to the people he had survived with. He owed them a life. He owed them the opportunity to live and possibly thrive. He wasn't blind to what was going on in

Salvation.

Alarms had sounded the previous night and a lockdown had been initiated as a group of disgruntled citizens attempted to raid one of the Salmarts on Level Two. Salvation was hardly a utopia. All kinds of rumours circulated all the time, but while Danko and his people were being looked after so well, there was no reason to rock the boat.

"I want to help wherever I can," he replied eventually.

Bucks smiled. "Good. Good, that's what I wanted to hear. Now, can you give me five minutes with Hogarth?"

"Of course," Danko replied, standing and leaving the office.

The smile was gone from Bucks' face the moment the door closed. "We lost a guard last night. Things got ugly. We've managed to keep his people separate most of the time. Paris is taking care of the situation here, but I want you to monitor things while you're away."

"I don't think it will be a problem, sir," Hogarth replied. "Other than Danko's people, the rest of the group are made of Level One workers and guards. When I selected them, I made sure they were loyal."

"Do you understand how important this is?"

"I think so, sir."

"You think?"

"I do, sir. I understand."

"Everything, I mean everything, depends on the success of this mission. This is our future."

"I won't let you down, sir."

"Make sure you don't."

Day 18

Salvation was nothing like the place it had been shortly after the asteroid strike. Back then, everyone was happy and grateful to be alive. The reality of the situation and the understanding of what life would be like in the future soon dawned, however. The first to become disgruntled were those on Level Three. Any cutbacks, any restrictions, any hardships were always imposed on them first.

Life on Level Two was far better and, in general, the population there remained happy and optimistic. And, of course, life was always good on Level One. After the fire at the farm and the mass exodus, however, things became volatile. The only way to keep the farms running, the power running, the whole place running was to conscript people into labour. Shops and services were closed to free up bodies. Tech heads suddenly found themselves working in the farm or the power plant. Schools were put on hiatus, and the young were placed in the food production or recycling industries. Level Two fast became the new Level Three. Food shortages, power outages, water restrictions and a whole host of other minor and major inconveniences made the population understand how little they were valued and how they would be treated by the administration on the outside.

Something had to give; otherwise, the whole thing would come crashing down around them. When Danko turned up with the wealth of information he provided about life on the outside, Bucks saw an opportunity. He saw it all in his head, but to achieve his final goal it would require more hardship than ever in the short term. It would be a gamble, but it was one he was willing to take.

Now, as he walked into the operations room with Paris by his side, his hope was restored once more. The trading party had returned the day before. Detailed depositions had been taken from all of them. Everything they remembered was taken down, and that information would prove useful but nowhere near as useful as the firsthand video and audio footage the pair of them were looking at as a hundred different viewpoints played out on a hundred different screens.

Auto-translations were running as subtitles on each one, identifying the main conversations that were going on. The computers were analysing every sound, however. Keywords like Trainor, Drake, Dante, Revell and dozens of other pre-programmed triggers would raise the alarm for the analysts to pay closer attention.

"Let us listen," Bucks said as he approached Burley, the head of the computer division. She was overseeing the one-hundred-and-ten-strong team who currently had the most important jobs in all of Salvation.

Burley unplugged her headphones. Hundreds of conversations were continuing in the background, but they were virtually inaudible. This was Hogarth's camera, and she was in negotiation with a woman behind one of the stalls for a stainless-steel pan. The handle needed tightening up, but other than that, it was okay.

"Well, what will you take for it?" Hogarth asked, obviously getting a little tired of the barter game the woman was playing. The figure on the other side of the stall was tanned as if she'd spent most of the last few months outside. She seemed to enjoy the process, and when she replied, a smile flashed onto her face revealing one of her front teeth was missing.

"I tell you what," she replied, looking through the bag of clothes that Hogarth had handed over to her. "Give me this and this … and this, and we'll say it's a deal." The woman selected a padded jacket, a sweatshirt and a scarf. The value of the clothes far outweighed the pan, but this mission was not about getting value from the trades; it was about getting information.

"Okay, deal," Hogarth replied, playing the part of an inexperienced newbie perfectly.

"Just got a keyword," one of the other information sifters called out, and Bucks headed across to the terminal the man was working at. Rectangles surrounded the faces onscreen. "Unknown subject" was written in red beneath them. Then suddenly a box came up with "Subject identified" flashing in green beneath it. "Tania Potts, sir. She was a teacher down on Level Three." More rectangles lit up as each of the subjects surrounding her was identified. They were all former Level Three inhabitants who were now manning a pitch at Infinity. Multiple trades were going on at the same time, and it was obvious as the camera moved around that this was one of the busier stalls.

"Our den of thieves seems to be doing well for itself," Bucks said bitterly. As far as he was concerned, everything they had belonged to Salvation. The seeds that were stolen became the crops that they grew. The tools they had left with, even the clothes on their backs, were the property of the administration.

"Sir, this is the man responsible for Infinity," Burley called out, and Paris and Bucks headed back to her terminal. It was Danko who was speaking to him. Underneath the rectangular box, the words "Subject self-identified" were highlighted in green. The name "Eric" followed.

Bucks and Paris stood with their arms folded, listening to the conversation.

"…were going to have to stay in the bunker forever. We thought it was going to become our tomb." It was Danko's voice, and Bucks had heard him say those words the first time they had met. He had been talking about the London Underground before, but now he was obviously using the emotion associated with that experience to portray life in their fictional bunker.

"Yeah, I know that feeling," Eric replied. "I don't think winters will ever be the same as the ones we knew."

"No. But this place. This place is going to make such a difference to us."

"How did you find out about it?"

"A group of us were out foraging when we were attacked. We managed to fend them off, and we took one prisoner. I … questioned him at length."

"Sounds ominous."

"I've done things I'd rather not have done. I think

most of us have since the asteroid."

"That's very true."

"He told us about this place, among other things. Apparently, they'd lived for a while around Crowesbury attacking trading parties before it became too dangerous for them with your militia." The camera suddenly angled up towards the stands and the groups of armed guards dotted around.

"Yeah. The Ferals were a much bigger problem than they are now. You still have to be careful, but at one point we were hearing of people being attacked every day."

"We'll be sure to keep a lookout for them on our return journey."

"You do that. We're getting new groups finding us all the time. This place is flourishing more than I could ever have hoped. People have come to depend on it. It's become a big part of their lives."

"I can see why. Our food supplies are slowly diminishing. We had no idea how long we'd be stuck in the bunker, but we hoped that when we came back to the surface, we'd be able to start working some of the nearby fields. We've got some seeds and tools, but this place has more than we could ever have anticipated."

Eric laughed. "Yeah, we've got some serious traders here now." They began to walk down the crowded aisle until they came to a stop at a much bigger pitch than all the others. "This is Woody's place," he said, gesturing to the vast array of goods laid out in front of them. "They were the first ones to start scavenging the towns and cities in an organised fashion. They've found all sorts. Building materials, camping equipment, clothing, bedding, tools, pretty much anything you can imagine they've put up for trade."

"This Woody seems like a useful man to know."

"To be honest, if it wasn't for him I don't think Infinity would have grown in the way it has." They started walking again. "Oh, wait a minute, there's someone I really want you to meet. Phil. PHIL!"

The camera angled around and a rectangle centred around a face. Underneath, it read, "Subject identified. Philip Trainor."

"Holy shit," Paris whispered. "There he is."

"Phil, I'd like you to meet Jonathan Danko," Eric said.

"Okay. Why, exactly?"

Eric laughed. "You have to forgive my husband," Debbie said, walking up behind him. "What he lacks in etiquette, manners and social skills he lacks in virtually every other grace as well."

"Thank you for such a ringing endorsement as ever, my love," Phil replied.

"Jonathan's a newcomer to Infinity. They want to prepare the fields around their bunker for growing," Eric continued.

"I see," Phil replied. "Well, it's a little late in the season to be thinking about a substantive harvest, but I could give you a list of a few quick-growing crops that would help bolster your reserves."

"We have enough MREs to keep us going for a while, but we'd be grateful for any advice you could give us."

"Well, Phil's down to give a talk tonight, so you might want to take notes," Eric replied.

"A talk?" Danko asked.

"Yes. In the evenings, we have lectures, talks and even entertainment on the stage," Eric said, gesturing to the far end of the field.

"Oh yeah. You won't want to miss that," Debbie said. "It will be riveting."

The other three laughed, even Phil. "Yeah. Listen to my talk tonight. I'll cover the basics about crop selection and management, and if there's anything you want clarification on, you can catch me before we head back tomorrow."

"I'll do that. Thank you," Danko replied.

"Now, you must excuse me. I need to talk to Woody about a couple of cold frames he reckons he can get hold of."

The camera followed Phil and Debbie as they disappeared into the crowd. "Interesting man," Danko said.

"You have no idea."

"We're going know these people better than they know themselves by the time we're finished," Bucks said with a smile on his face. "How's all this information being collated?" he asked Burley.

"It's complicated," she replied.

"I don't want the technical stuff. I want to know how it will be referenced, how it can be searched."

"Once it's all been processed, it will be as simple as typing a word in a search box."

"What do you mean?"

Burley turned back to her monitor. "Let me show you. So far, forty minutes of footage have been processed. Say, for the sake of example, you want to listen to, watch or read any conversations regarding Eric," she said, typing the name in. The details of multiple entries appeared onscreen in chronological order. "This will give you a transcript of each of the conversations where Eric's name was mentioned, or…." She tapped one of the function buttons, and multiple video screens appeared. She clicked on one and footage of two stallholders talking appeared onscreen.

"Anyway, I says to Eric that we're carting way too much back and forth each journey, and he says to us that we can have one of the underground storage rooms," the man at the centre of the image said. "Unidentified subject" flashed beneath the rectangle surrounding his face as it did with the woman he was talking to.

"How much is he charging us?"

"He just asks that we assign someone to the chores list each day we're here."

"That's fair. That's very fair."

"Yeah. He's a good bloke. If we're not carting

untraded goods back and forth, that'll give us a real chance to grow. This time next year, we might be as big as Woody or Phil's lot."

Burley tapped her screen once more and the video disappeared. "Or say you want to identify any conversations about trading seeds," she said, typing "Seeds" into the search box. Again, a list of entries came up and she hit a function button, which turned them into tiny video windows.

"There are a lot more of them," Paris said.

"Just from what I've seen so far, seed trading is one of the most common types of barter at the market," Burley replied. She selected one of the small windows and another video began playing on screen.

"These are carrot seeds," said the unidentified subject who was talking to a prospective punter. "Now, you need to be careful about the type of soil you plant these in."

"What do you mean?" the other man asked.

"You need sandy soil for them to grow properly. You put them in peaty or clay soil and you'll end up with tiny stumps that wouldn't feed a baby. Trust me. I had an allotment for years and I learnt this the hard way."

"Doesn't look like I'll be growing any of these then. Our growing patch is pretty dense."

"Well, maybe you can build a raised bed and mix in some sand."

"There's no sand anywhere near us. We're about as far away from the coast as you can get."

"There's a trader here who can supply you sacks of the stuff. And once you've got your raised bed, you can—there's one of them now. Callie. CALLIE!" the man shouted, and a few seconds later a young woman appeared on the screen. Underneath the rectangle surrounding her face, "Callie Bridges, Level Three," flashed up, followed by her address details from when she was an inhabitant of Salvation.

"Hi, Trev," she said.

"I was just talking to this gent about sand. What are your supplies like?"

"Good. We always make sure we bring a fresh batch with us each time we come."

"What's it trading for at the moment?"

"We're not about to start charging people for sand. We've got an agreement with Eric," she said, turning to the prospective carrot seed purchaser. "You allocate one member of your group to the chores list for the next three days you're here or you trade five kilos of produce for the Infinity kitchen."

"The Infinity kitchen?"

"The communal meals they provide for those who need them, for those settlements who are struggling a little. It helps them out."

"And what do you get out of it exactly?" the man asked sceptically.

"We get to know that we've helped Eric keep things running here. We get to know that we've helped you with your crops. We get to know that we've made things for the people who use this place a little better."

"Yeah. But what do you get out of it?"

Callie laughed. "That's enough for us. Infinity is a lifeline for our settlement. It's a lifeline for a lot of people. It's not run for profit; it's run for the benefit of the wider community. By helping it, we're helping ourselves and everyone else."

The man looked taken aback. "So, you're telling me that we can trade labour here for sand?"

"Yeah. We'll need to coordinate it with Eric because the chore list is changing all the time, but, ultimately, yeah."

"And what chores are on this list exactly?"

Callie smiled. "It could be anything from emptying the thunderboxes to patrolling with the militia to helping prepare the communal meals. There are lots of duties on there."

The trader took over the conversation again. "Yeah.

So, if you want to start growing carrots, you go see Callie and she'll look after you."

The man nodded gratefully to the young woman. "I dare say I'll be paying you a visit soon."

"I look forward to it," Callie replied, disappearing into the crowd once more.

"Now. Where were we?" the punter said, turning back to the stallholder.

"Quite the little socialist utopia they're building there," Bucks said bitterly.

Burley hit a button and the video paused. "Yes, sir."

"When will this be available for me to access on the ministerial server?"

"Instantly, sir. You have full access."

"Good. Excellent. And when are Hogarth and Danko heading back there?" he asked, turning to Paris.

"Two days' time. We've got them working with our graphic designers. We're building 3D mapping of Crowesbury and its approach as well as Infinity. Two of our people managed to get into the tunnel system as well, sir."

"This is most promising." He looked at Burley then Paris. "Outstanding work, the pair of you. Any further updates and I'll be in my office."

Day 52

Bucks had rarely left his office since the source material from the cameras had become available. Many nights, he had chosen to catch a few hours' sleep semi-upright in his Eames lounge chair before getting back to work. Few people had seen him in that time, although Paris had kept him abreast of everything that was going on.

There had been further attempted break-ins of the Salmarts on Level Two, but the would-be rebels lacked the organisation and determination of the Level Three rebels. Their revolution had been bubbling from early on, whereas the Level Two population had only recently begun to comprehend what was happening within Salvation and what life would be like on the outside.

Paris had been given free rein to deal with the uprisings however she saw fit, while Bucks concentrated on the more pressing matters. None of the shortages or hardships had been felt on Level One, but if there wasn't a seismic shift in Salvation's trajectory, that would change.

There was a knock at the door and Bucks raised his blurry eyes from the screen. "Enter," he answered.

Paris walked in. Her perfectly pressed business suit, bright eyes and flawlessly applied makeup disguised the fact that she had enjoyed less than three hours' sleep. She was as committed to what they were doing as Bucks was, and although she didn't quite understand his intentions, she was sure he was going to come up with the answer that would guarantee a change in fortunes for Salvation and provide them with a hopeful future.

"Morning, sir."

Bucks looked at his watch and wiped his eyes. "I'll take your word for that."

She walked up to his desk and placed down a mug of coffee. "Our patrols brought in two groups last night."

"Two?" Bucks asked, surprised. Their recruitment drive for those living in the wilds on the outside had slowed significantly, and their continued visits to Infinity had illuminated them as to why. Trainor's settlement, which was now christened Redemption, had been taking in people known as Wanderers, the poor unfortunates of no fixed abode who had by some miracle survived the initial aftereffects of the asteroid only to be left starving and wanting in the bleakness that followed.

"Yes. Thirty-nine people in total."

"That's good. Very good." Bucks still regretted the massacre that had taken place in the forest. He had been convinced by the acting head of the Salvation guards that an unequivocal show of force was what was needed for the escapees to become compliant. When Bucks gave the go-ahead, he had no idea just how devastating that show of force would be. If he'd paid more attention, maybe all their current woes could have been avoided. Maybe that's why all these plans were so important. The successful execution of them would right a wrong. Not the wrong of killing thousands of innocent people, he genuinely couldn't have cared less about that, but the wrong of causing so much upheaval and disquiet throughout Salvation as a direct result of him not taking time to weigh the options.

"I thought you'd be pleased," she replied with an unconvincing smile on her face as she looked at all the papers and pads laid out in front of her boss. Very few people used paper these days, but Bucks was someone who felt that reaching out and touching a page gave him more clarity. "How are things going?"

It was a vague enough question not to insult Bucks, but at the same time, the answer would be sufficient for her to ascertain whether the pressure had finally got to him and the spark of brilliance that she had witnessed so many times had finally given way to a flame of insanity. "I'm getting there," he said, glancing over the sheets on his desk.

"I'm glad you're here actually. I need a full inventory of our weaponry and ammunition."

"That's all on the database, sir."

"No. I mean I want a stocktake. A physical count."

It was a fair enough request. Ever since the Great Escape, it had become clear just how security was lacking. Drake and his people had absconded with a significant amount of their arsenal, way too much for it all to have been snatched on that one night, and since then, there had been discrepancies with the official figures and random stock control checks. "Okay, sir." Paris nodded, pulling out her phone and instant-messaging one of her many assistants.

"And I need to speak to our chief chemist."

"Burke?"

"Yes."

"Err ... is there anything I can help you with, sir?"

"There'll be plenty you can help me with soon, but for now I need to speak to Burke."

"Yes, sir."

"And Lipton."

"In Recycling? Don't you mean Molko, sir?"

"No, I mean Lipton."

"But Lipton's just a manager. Molko's the director."

"Yes, Paris. And we also know that Molko doesn't have the first clue as to what goes on in recycling, but Lipton can pretty much account for every gram of material that goes through the sorting line."

Paris nodded, not wanting to irritate her boss but also a little miffed that Molko, one of her biggest allies and closest friends, was dismissed so glibly. "I'll sort that out for you, sir." Her fingers blurred as she sent another message.

"And I want to speak to Tattersall and Banner too."

Paris looked surprised once more. Justin Tattersall and Amelia Banner were pale imitations of Phil Trainor. Banner was just a bean counter and Tattersall knew little more than an amateur horticulturist. It was doubtful that either of them could add anything to the information submitted in the daily reports from the farms. But Bucks was obviously on a mission and not willing to share what that mission was for the time being. So she quickly typed another message to Tattersall, cee-ceeing Banner too.

"Will there be anything else, sir?"

"Yes. I want to meet Blenkinsopp from Fabrication too."

Once again, Blenkinsopp was a manager rather than a director, but this time Paris did not question her boss's request. Fabrication was a department that had grown and diminished in size depending on the needs of Salvation and all with Blenkinsopp at the helm. The small factory had retooled many times to piece together whatever they needed. From Bucks' request, it was obvious that this was going to happen again. Paris typed another message into her phone and, this time, despite the early hour, got an almost immediate response. "He says he's available now."

"No. I need to see him after Lipton."

"Very well, sir."

Bucks leant back in his chair and smiled. "I know all of this must seem a little random, but trust me, Paris. I know what I'm doing."

"I do trust you, sir."

He stared at her long and hard. "I suppose you do, don't you? You've always been a more than capable lieutenant, Paris. I doubt if I've told you that enough, but it's true."

"Thank you, sir."

He looked back down at his desk and thought for a moment. "I'd like you in on these meetings."

"You would?"

"Yes. I think it's important that you understand what's happening. You have this uncanny ability to ascertain my needs before even I know them, so yes. I'd like you in with me."

"Okay, sir. But maybe I could be of more assistance if I understood what they were about."

Bucks smiled. "Sit down, Paris." He looked at all the papers scattered over his desk once more. "I can only imagine what this must look like. We have multiple issues that threaten our very existence. The sheen of this place has worn off for the people on Level Two. I'm sure it's just a matter of time before they organise themselves and become a bigger problem than they already are. The only way we can win that battle is to placate them, to give them back the lives they had. The problem is there's no quick way to do that, and I dare say there are many who will never trust us again."

"I don't see how we can possibly do that."

"Things will get worse before they get better, but I honestly believe what I'm planning won't just solve the Level Two situation but every obstacle that's facing us. The Cairngorms bunker, Trainor's settlement, everything. We need to expand, and we need to flourish. We do those things by becoming the only game in town."

"But you've just said it yourself. We're not the only game in town."

"No, we're not. Not at the moment. But we will be. I think I'd like some breakfast before the meetings start. I haven't eaten since yesterday lunchtime. Will you join me?" he asked, rising from his desk.

"Yes. Yes, of course."

It was a little surreal. Paris could count on one hand how many times she'd been asked to share a meal with Bucks. They talked about nothing substantive, instead discussing the improvements that had been made to the park on Level One. A basketball court had been built and a second pool had been put in. The majority of the privileged on Level One had no idea what life was like on Level Two or Level Three. They didn't care either. The only thing they cared about was themselves. A plethora of committees existed whose purpose was to do little else but discuss and debate how things could be made that little bit more luxurious. The basketball court and pool had been hot topics of conversation for some time, but they finally won in preference to batting nets and a water feature.

Their breakfast was a relaxed affair, and Paris couldn't remember a time when she had witnessed Bucks more personable. He seemed genuinely grateful for her company. Normally aloof and officious, he laughed and smiled and joked. She'd never seen him so human, so vulnerable.

He took another sip of coffee from his mug and leaned back. "Hogarth and Danko are heading back to Infinity today?"

"Yes, sir."

He gazed thoughtfully at his mug for a moment. "This whole operation has been managed well. The technical department, the training, the logistics of it all. It's been outstanding, Paris, and when it's all over, I'm going to make sure people know just how much you did."

"Thank you, but I just did what you asked me, sir. This was your brainchild."

Bucks shrugged. "If it succeeds, I'll gladly take the kudos. If it doesn't, I'll just play up your role in it a little more."

Bucks rarely made jokes, and there was probably a certain amount of truth in the statement, but as the corners of his mouth curled up into a smile, she couldn't help but laugh. "However I can be of service, sir."

Bucks laughed politely before placing his mug down and looking at his watch. "I suppose we'd better head back, hadn't we?"

"Yes, sir," Paris replied, quickly checking the messages on her phone before following Bucks out of the dining room.

Lipton was already waiting in the reception area as Bucks and Paris made their way back to the office. He was in his work clothes, despite being called to a meeting with the first minister of Salvation. This was one of the reasons Bucks wanted to speak to the managers rather than the directors. The managers were all about the work. There was no point in raising a list of queries with one of the directors only for them to get the information from their managers and relay it. He wanted to hear the answers straight from the horses' mouths.

"Come in, Lipton," Bucks said, opening the door to his office and heading through.

Lipton climbed to his feet and followed. Bucks took his chair behind the desk and the recycling manager sat opposite. Paris placed herself in a chair by the wall with her tablet at the ready to make notes if she needed to.

"Nobody told me what this was about," Lipton said. "I haven't finished next month's forecasts yet if that's what it's to do with."

"No, it's not about that." Bucks studied him for a moment. "You lost a good portion of your workforce when—" it still pained him to talk about the mass exodus from Level Three "—the rebellion took place, didn't you?"

"Well, yes, Mr Bucks. But that's the thing about recycling. Fewer people, less to recycle. The vast majority of the work is done by the optical sorting machines anyway. My staff simply process what comes out of those machines, which a lot of the time means transporting big cubes of plastic, metal or whatever it might be to the storage area until it's needed. But like I say. Fewer people, less recycling, and subsequently less manufacturing too. The whole process has slowed down, so yes, we lost a lot of staff, but we've managed to maintain the operation with the recruits from Level Two."

Bucks stared at Lipton for several seconds before continuing. "The main purpose of this meeting is to find out how the operation would cope with an upswell of material to process."

Lipton shrugged and shook his head a little. "If you're asking about the outsiders who've been recruited, sir, the waste created by them hasn't really had a noticeable effect on our operation." He looked over to Paris. "Obviously, I'm not privy to the numbers, but I've heard we've had in excess of four hundred joining us. They must be living meagrely because our weekly totals have barely gone up by more than a few kilograms."

"No, I wasn't talking about them, Lipton. I'm talking about a sudden and massive expansion."

Half a smile threatened on Lipton's face for a moment until he realised the other man wasn't joking. "That would depend, sir."

"On what exactly?"

"On how big an expansion."

"I'm talking about tonnes of different metals and plastics coming through here. I'm talking about salvaging teams specifically heading out with the purpose of bringing these materials to you for processing."

Lipton looked long and hard at the other man. He had never really cared for Bucks or any of the administration for that matter. His father had been a factory worker who had eventually become a foreman. Lipton himself had started working in recycling straight from school. He quickly became a supervisor, then a section manager, and finally a general manager. Rather than being selected via a lottery, he had been on a shortlist of candidates for the position in Salvation. He and his family lived a comfortable life on Level Two, but he was always more at home with the Level Three workers who had staffed the plant.

They had often told him about life down below. They had told him what it was like living in a police state. They had told him of the shortages. They had told him of the occasional erratic power and water supplies. They had told him about the guards' brutality. They lived on Level Three and lived like third-class citizens. Lipton shouldered a fair amount of guilt for enjoying the life he did.

There was no reason for any of it. It would have been the easiest thing in the world to equitably divide the resources available in Salvation so all three levels could maintain a comfortable existence until their return to the surface. The only thing stopping that was Bucks and the people like him. They wanted the barriers. They wanted inequality. Inequality gave them power.

"Well," Lipton began, "as I said, sir, the optical sorters do most of the hard work. Then we have the magnetic processors and the various other classification machines. My staff are mainly involved with driving the forklifts, scanning the processed product and making sure the machines are fed. Obviously, if there's a significant increase in materials to process, that will have a direct effect on the workload of the staff, but at the moment, I'd say we could probably accept a fifteen to twenty percent increase without changing the current work pattern or requiring more personnel."

Bucks nodded. "I'm anticipating a far, far bigger increase than fifteen to twenty percent, but it's good to know that you're not perturbed by any increase."

Lipton shrugged his shoulders again. "The plant's able to deal with a lot more than it's currently processing. It was originally designed to cope with the recycling needs of Salvation and the subsequent settlement while that was being established, so capacity isn't an issue at all, and we could run the place around the clock if needed, but we would need more bodies."

Bucks turned to Paris. "When Danko and Hogarth come back from Infinity, select forty candidates to join Lipton's team." He turned back to the recycling manager. "That will help to begin with, yes?"

"Err … yes," Lipton said, surprised. "I can get them trained up while we're still running just the one shift, then—"

"That will be just to begin with. I anticipate our population is going to grow substantially in the next few months, Lipton, and I want us to be ready. Liaise with Paris, and if you feel there are any equipment or supply issues before the expansion begins, make her aware of them. Things are going to start happening fast."

"Err … yes … okay, sir."

"Good. Thank you, Lipton. That will be all."

"Thank you, sir," he replied gratefully, nearly jumping out of the chair and exiting the office.

"Sir, I don't understand," Paris began. "I thought we were going to keep the trade delegation at full strength. We're still gleaning a lot of information from the cameras and—"

Bucks put his hand up. "We just need to keep showing up there. We need to continue gaining the trust of Eric and the others. That's all. I've got all the information I can possibly use now. I've learnt more about Trainor's settlement than I thought possible. We're getting close to the end game, Paris."

"Um, okay."

Bucks smiled. "Now, make sure you stay in contact with Lipton. If he needs something, I want him to have it.

The people we're seeing this morning will all be pivotal to this plan working."

"Yes, sir."

The comms portal on his desk chimed, and he hit answer. When he and Paris entered the office, his receptionist hadn't started work yet, but now she was there on screen looking straight at him. "Mister Bucks. Miss Banner and Mister Tattersall are here to see you, sir. I didn't see anything on your appointment schedule, but—"

"Send them in," Bucks ordered, tapping the screen once more and making the image of his receptionist disappear.

A moment later, Banner and Tattersall stepped into the office. Both of them looked more than a little worried. When Trainor had escaped, things went from bad to worse for a while. It was obvious that there were vast holes in their knowledge and capability, which had been covered up by Trainor's omniscience and omnipresence. He was the heart and brain of the farms in Salvation.

"Morning, sir," they both said.

"Sit down," Bucks replied, gesturing to the chairs on the other side of the table. Both of these people were weak links. He knew it and they knew it. His only hope was that they would be so terrified of disappointing him once more that they would do everything in their power to fulfil his requests. "You're probably going to want to make notes."

Both of them retrieved their phones from their pockets. "If this is about—"

"You're about to find out what it's about," Bucks said curtly, silencing Banner and making her shrink back into her chair.

"Yes, sir."

"I want a full stock count of our seed surplus by the end of the day. I want a crop forecast for both farms, including a chronological harvesting schedule. I want a survey of unused shelving and an estimate of how long it would take to turn that into growing space."

The colour drained from both of their faces. Each of them wanted to tell him that such an undertaking would require more than a day, but both could see the unforgiving look on his face. If they didn't do this, that would be it for them. So, rather than questioning or pleading for more time, they tapped the requests into their phones. "Um," Tattersall said, immediately regretting his utterance.

"Yes?"

"With regards to the estimate for turning the unused shelving into growing space. That's not something that's completely within our control."

"Why?"

"The grow lamps and irrigation pipes would need to be installed by our public works departments, sir."

Bucks looked across to Paris. "We'll deal with public works. They'll be at your full disposal."

"Um … very well, sir. But…."

"But what?"

"After the fire at Farm One, we put all efforts into Farm Two. Farm One is probably operating at maybe twenty percent capacity and a lot of that is because of the damage."

"So, what are you saying?"

"I'm saying it would require a vast amount of work and resources to get it running at an increased capacity."

"I know for a fact we have the resources, Tattersall. I know because when you both came to me after the fire, you presented a list of exactly what you needed and Paris put Fabrication to work in order to produce it. So, what you're telling me, in fact, is the pipes, the lamps, the shelving and whatever else was on your list has been sitting gathering dust since we used the valuable resources required to manufacture them."

"But sir, you said it was a priority to increase production at Farm Two to a level that would sustain Salvation until a time when—"

Bucks shot up from his chair and leant forward,

peering over his desk at the other man. "Are you saying this is my fault?"

"Err … no, sir. Not at all. I'm just explaining that the—"

"I don't want your explanations. I don't want your excuses. I don't want anything other than for you to do what I've requested." He looked at his watch. "I expect those reports by the end of the day, so you'd both better get to work."

"Yes, sir. Thank you, sir," Banner said, standing up. Tattersall gulped and did the same. They both started walking out of the office but stopped and turned as Bucks spoke again.

"There are some big changes coming up. This is your last chance to prove your worth. I won't allow either of you to fail me again."

A little more colour drained from their faces before they resumed their journey to the exit. Bucks maintained his glare until they were gone, and then a self-satisfied smirk appeared on his face. He glanced across to Paris to see she mirrored his expression. "I'll keep tabs on them," she said.

Bucks let out a long sigh and slumped back into his chair. "The frustrating thing is that we've got nobody to replace them with. They're literally the best of a bad bunch. As much as I hate to admit it, Trainor was a once-in-a-generation mind. A massive hole appeared when we lost him."

"I'll stay on top of them nevertheless, sir."

"Thank you, Paris."

Bucks hit the comms portal and his receptionist's face appeared onscreen a second later. "Yes, sir?"

"Who else is out there?"

"I've got Mister Burke and Mister Blenkinsopp, sir."

"Good. Send Burke in first." He hit the screen once more and it immediately went blank.

There was a knock on the door and in walked Kyle Burke, the chief chemist. "Mister Bucks," he said with a warm smile. Bucks rose from his chair and extended a hand towards him. The two shook firmly before taking seats. Burke lived on Level One. On the outside, he had worked for APS—Amalgamated Pharmaceutical Solutions, a subsidiary of AFS. The two men had known each other a long time and shared a mutual respect.

"Thank you for coming at such short notice," Bucks said.

"You call and I'm there," Burke replied with a smile.

"I'll cut to the chase, Kyle. A lot will be happening in the next few weeks and months. There are going to be some seismic changes both inside the bunker and outside. Key to those changes will be making sure our guards have the right tools for the job."

It was obvious what he meant by that. Everybody knew that when Drake had absconded, he'd taken a sizeable chunk of Salvation's arsenal of weapons and ammunition with him. But now it was time to replenish those stocks. "I see."

"How are we fixed?"

"We have significant stockpiles of nitric and sulfuric acid, so there'll be no problem manufacturing all the nitrocellulose we need. What we don't—"

"Nitrocellulose?" Paris asked, and both men turned towards her. She suddenly felt a little self-conscious until a warm smile appeared on Burke's face.

"Yes. We use it to create guncotton, which is a replacement for gunpowder." Without missing a beat, he turned back to Bucks. "What we don't have to hand is enough potassium nitrate, which we use to manufacture the smoke grenades, and ammonium nitrate, which we'd use to manufacture more substantial explosive devices should we need them."

"Okay," Bucks said. "And what can we do about that?"

"The supplies for the settlement, Mr Bucks. There are probably tonnes of the stuff there. They're our primary fertilisers."

Bucks sat back in his chair and clasped his fingers over his stomach. If it wasn't for the exodus, they would be piecing together the first building blocks of the new settlement now. They'd sent out an expedition to make sure the bunker that housed all the supplies was still in one piece, and it was, but that was the full extent of their interaction with it. "I can deploy a group to ferry some back. How much will you need?"

"Well, that depends on how much ammunition you want to manufacture. Obviously, I don't get involved with the farms, but I would think that when we start growing outside again, we're going to need a good amount of fertiliser."

Bucks took a deep breath and nodded slowly before looking across to Paris. "For what it's worth, liaise with Banner and Tattersall. Get an indication of how much they anticipate needing for the first growing season outside."

"Yes, sir," Paris replied.

"I'd like to get my team to work straight away on the nitrocellulose, so will that be all, sir?" Burke asked.

"For now. Thank you again for coming by at such short notice," Bucks said and rose to his feet, shaking the other man's hand once more. As the door closed behind the chief scientist, Bucks returned to his seat and looked at Paris. "The only weak links so far are Tattersall and Banner. You will stay on top of them, won't you?"

Paris smiled and climbed to her feet, walking over to the desk. She placed her tablet down and enlarged a window that was running in the bottom left-hand corner of the screen. "…is like some kind of nightmare. How the hell are we going to get all this done by the end of the day?" The screen was black, but the voice was clearly that of Tattersall. A subtitled readout of what he was saying appeared in white at the bottom.

"I don't know, but we don't really have a choice, do we?" The other voice belonged to Banner.

"Oh well. It was nice knowing you, Amelia. Maybe they'll go lightly on us. Maybe they'll just send us to the surface."

"Don't joke."

"Who's joking?"

Paris shrunk the screen once more and picked the tablet up from the desk. "I'll keep an eye on them all day, sir. I won't let you down," she said, walking back over to her chair by the wall.

Bucks smiled. "You never do." He hit the comms console on his desk and this time didn't even bother looking at the screen. "Send in Blenkinsopp."

A moment later, a scruffy-looking man wearing a khaki boiler suit walked into the office. "I'm sorry about my attire, Mister Bucks, but I was already at work when I got the call that you wanted to see me."

"It was the crack of dawn when I asked Paris to contact you."

"Yes, sir. We've recently had a handful of new recruits starting in Fabrication, and I like to review their work on the screens before the start of each day. This way, if they're picking up any bad habits, I can nip them in the bud early on."

"If we had a bunker full of people like you, my life would be a lot easier."

"That's kind of you to say, Mister Bucks, sir."

Blenkinsopp was a rare breed. He relished his work and counted his lucky stars every day that he and his family had survived the asteroid safely in the bunker. He lived on Level Two, and despite things being tumultuous compared to what they had been after first entering the bunker, he was a man of simple means. He worked, he kept his head down, and he went home. He paid no mind to the growing voices of rebellion on Level Two. He had no interest in protests or revolution as some called for. He was loyal to the administration that saved his family. He was grateful to Bucks, and although in many respects he was a simple man, where his work was concerned he was a savant. Nobody knew more about his department, what it needed to keep functioning properly, and what it was capable of.

"I've called you here today, Blenkinsopp, because we're about to embark on a new chapter. It's going to require work and sacrifice, but I can guarantee you it will mean things will improve for everyone."

"Well, however I can help, Mister Bucks, you know I will."

"I know, Blenkinsopp. I know."

Other than food and munitions, there had been a significant surplus of most other things after the exodus. Subsequently, there was little need to have a sizeable staff in the Fabrication department. A vast number of items were manufactured using 3D printers anyway, which literally involved selecting a design on a screen and pressing the print button. Items that were needed in greater quantities required the utilisation of the wealth of machinery and tools at the Fab department's disposal.

"I've just had Burke in here. You probably saw him in reception. We're going to require replenishment of our munitions stock."

"Yes, sir," he replied almost instantly. He had heard the rumours of how much Drake and the others had taken and was surprised that this request hadn't been submitted earlier.

"But we're going to require a fairly diverse range of other items too."

Paris suddenly leaned forward a little in her chair in the hope that this might give her some insight into what was going on in Bucks' head. "If you don't mind me asking, sir, like what?" replied Blenkinsopp.

"I don't know how much you've heard about this market down in Crowesbury."

"Just bits, sir. I don't really have time for gossip and rumours."

Bucks grinned broadly. "That's one of the things I

like about you, Blenkinsopp. It's all about the work. Well, we're going to take over the operation of the market."

Blenkinsopp's eyebrows arched upwards. "Oh."

"Y'see, it's all a muddle down there at the moment. There's this network of survivors, and they're just struggling to get from one day to the next, one week to the next, one month to the next. There's no organisation, no strategy, no hope. They're living on scraps of everything. Scavenged bits and pieces from the burnt wreckage of cities. The world is at a pivotal point, and someone with vision needs to take charge. By commandeering the market, we can help these people. Some will thrive, some will realise that we can offer them a better future in the bunker and, ultimately, when we found the new settlement."

"Okay, sir. And how can my department help with this?"

Bucks reached into his drawer and pulled out a small notebook, which he placed down on the desk. "We've been gathering information for some time now and I've made a list of the most traded and most desired commodities at the market." He opened the first page. "Spades, forks, hoes, without a shadow of a doubt these are some of the most widely bartered items. Barrows are one of the most sought-after. Food and seeds, obviously, but they're not something you'll have to think about. In short, I've got the keys to the kingdom in this book. If we can mass produce what are, for want of another term, best sellers, we will quickly develop a monopoly."

"I'm not sure I understand. If we're offering these things to them, and it's a barter system, what will we get in return exactly?"

"That's a good question, Blenkinsopp, and one that represents the crux of what you're doing here. I mentioned it's essential that we need to flourish. Well, to do that, we have to grow our population and our sphere of influence. We need to build our defences because, mark my words, there are people out there who want to take away what we've got. Bearing all this in mind, I need to know from you what raw materials we will need. This is what we will be bartering for. Bullets, for example. Burke will be taking care of the chemical aspects of production, but what metals will we want for production?"

"Well, sir. In the past, we've used copper, steel, and tin, to name but three. There are—"

"Excellent. Excellent. I'm going to give you a copy of this list, and I want a list from you in return. The barrows. Refresh my memory, but didn't you manufacture plastic barrows for the farms shortly after we opened?"

"Yes, sir. They were polypropylene with a metal frame, and they—"

"Excellent. Dust off the plans; we need to start producing them again."

"Yes, sir," Blenkinsopp replied.

"Now, we're trading just bits and bats at the moment, Blenkinsopp. We won't be able to source any significant quantities of raw materials until next spring." A confused expression appeared on the other man's face. "Don't worry, it's complicated. But anyway, in the interim, I intend to send some salvaging teams into the mine beneath our bunker. There's a short rail track down there. I'm not sure what they used to make those out of but—"

"Rolled steel, sir."

Bucks nodded appreciatively. "Good. Excellent."

"And if they had electricity down there, I dare say there'll be plenty of copper wiring too."

A broad smile lit Bucks' face. "Yes. Yes, of course. Maybe you wouldn't mind heading down with our team the first time. You can point out what's worth salvaging and what isn't."

"Yes. Yes, I'd be happy to do that, sir." Blenkinsopp had never felt so valued, so important. It was as if he'd been given a new lease of life.

"By doing all this," Bucks said, gesturing to the notebook, "we're not just helping ourselves; we're helping all the poor unfortunates out there who, by nothing short of a miracle, managed to survive through the asteroid but are now struggling."

"Yes, sir."

"Thank you, Blenkinsopp. I'll have Paris send a copy of this list to you a little later on today."

"Yes, sir," the other man replied, standing. "Thank you, sir," he said, inadvertently bowing a little before turning to leave.

When he'd gone, Paris walked over to the desk and sat down in the seat the Fabrication manager had occupied seconds before. "Things are starting to make a lot more sense to me now."

"Starting to?"

"I particularly liked the bit about helping all the poor unfortunates."

Bucks couldn't help but let out a small chuckle. Paris knew better than anyone that the man in front of her couldn't care less about the poor unfortunates. He cared about holding on to power and wealth. He cared about seeking revenge on those who had betrayed him, and he would weave whatever kind of narrative best suited him to do it. "What can I tell you? I'm a man of the people."

"I still don't understand how seizing the market will give us a monopoly. There are too many other traders. I'm sure Drake, Trainor and the others have muddied our names enough for a lot of people to avoid dealing with us like the plague. How do you know this will work?"

"Because I know people, Paris. They're stupid and selfish, and no matter how angry they are about something today, dangle a bright glittery object in front of them and they'll have forgotten about it tomorrow."

"And how does that translate to what you're wanting to do at Infinity?"

"Can you imagine what people who have lived through the last few years with barely nothing would make of a burger bar or another type of fast-food diner? Can you picture how they'd react to a freshly poured beer or glass of whisky? Soap, shampoo, new clothes, the things we take for granted. If we gave them the opportunity to enjoy these things again, they would forget about anything else. They would certainly forget about any misplaced loyalty towards Trainor and the others."

"So, we're just going to give these things away in the hope that we can buy them?"

"Absolutely not."

"I'm afraid I still don't understand how it's all going to work."

Bucks sat back in his chair once more. "We're going to introduce a currency."

"Err ... I ... um ... what? How?"

"It won't be as complicated as you think, and, granted, it will be difficult to see the benefit for us in the early stages because it will be skewed towards the traders. We want them to think that dealing with us is the only way to go. We want them to believe that we present their path to happiness and a future where they can enjoy the things that they coveted so much in the past. Of course, this is going to make things a little more chaotic here than they already are. But in the medium and long term, it will pay dividends."

"I still don't understand how it will work."

"It's really quite simple. From everything we've gathered from the recordings, Infinity closes down for the winter months. We're going to launch a coup directly before the shutdown. Our builders will live in the tunnels and rooms underground during that time. They'll have plenty of supplies, fuel and clothes for warmth, and when the weather allows, they will erect some retail units."

"Retail units?"

"Yes. There'll be a couple of bars, fast-food places, but more importantly than all of that, shops," he said, tapping his notebook, "where we'll supply all the biggest demand items."

"And how are they going to pay for all this?"

"As I said, in the early stages, we're not going to see much of a benefit. We'll purchase a lot of what they've got, even if it's superfluous to our needs, and in return, they'll be able to use the money we pay them to buy seeds or tools or food or whatever they want from our stores.

"We'll have a weighing station for raw materials and erect a giant noticeboard with a list of our most wanted items and the current rate we're willing to pay. Again, in the early stages, this will be generously skewed towards the seller. They'll believe all their Christmases have come at once. Gradually, as people buy our products, enjoy our food, and realise that they can get everything they want from us and more, they won't be interested in trading with others anymore, and Infinity will no longer be a free-trading market as such but our one-stop-shop superstore. I doubt if it will take too long. Then, gradually, we begin to lower the buy prices of what we're prepared to pay and raise the prices of our products.

"All the people currently using Infinity will ultimately end up working for us. From early on, we'll offer those who are struggling the chance to join our workforce here in Salvation. The prospect of food, warmth, accommodation and a small wage for some of these people will be more than enough to entice them here after a long winter out there. And the rest will become our de facto employees. The scavengers will be scavenging for us. The farmers will be growing for us, and so on. I'm guessing that before the following winter, our population will have swelled. Y'see Paris, once we introduce a currency and control its value, we control everyone who uses that currency."

"That's … that's ingenious, sir."

Bucks let out a huff of a laugh. "I can hardly take the credit. It's happened ever since the first coins were made. Anyway, that's the first part of the plan. We grow our wealth, our resources and our population."

"Can I ask a question?"

"Of course."

"The bar, the shops, everything you're talking about building at Infinity, it will require power and materials. Where are those coming from?"

"There's already a wealth of materials that we can use and adapt from Infinity. What we can't find there, we can manufacture. As far as power is concerned, there's a methane generator onsite. But I'm going to equip the crew with about two dozen mobile power packs and a good supply of solar panels." After the sabotage of the power plant by Drake, Bucks had pushed forward with a program to provide mobile power sources for the three levels for emergencies should anything like that happen again. These could be charged by multiple means, but solar was the most sensible option for a team that was heading outside.

"How much sun are they going to get in the winter months?"

Bucks shrugged. "It's a fair question. But the packs will be fully charged to begin with, and consequently, if they hook up the panels in the optimum positions, they'll be on a constant residual charge."

"And what about if we have a problem at the plant in the meantime?"

"In that unlikely event, we'll have more than enough packs to keep Level One in operation, but we'll put in an order to Blenkinsopp for the manufacture of some more as a priority."

"He's going to have a lot of priorities by the sound of it."

Bucks chuckled. "Maybe a raise would be in order."

"And what comes next? What's after that?"

"When our armoury is fully stocked, and our guards have trained enough new recruits from the massive influx of people who I'm sure will opt for an easy life in here rather than an increasingly hard life out there, we make a move on Trainor's settlement."

"So we are going to go after them?"

"Of course we're going after them. They stole from us. We'll make public examples of Drake and the other guards. The rest of the population will become prisoners, permanently housed in Salvation. We'll chip them like dogs. We'll know exactly where they are at all times. Any hint of further disobedience will be met with quick and brutal decisiveness that will stop them or anyone else from so much as thinking about rebelling. And for the record, all their property stored at Infinity will be seized; it's ours anyway, and we'll have deployments of guards en route from their settlement to Crowesbury. We'll need to liaise with Danko's people for that. They studied them long enough, they'll know their routes, and if we so much as get a hint that they're heading to Infinity, we'll cut them down."

In the space of a minute, Bucks had changed from a visionary to a heartless dictator. It was the man Paris was most familiar with who was talking now. "And what about Trainor?"

"As much as it pains me to say it, Trainor is too valuable for us to lose a second time. He's proved it with what he's done. He will be vital to the success of our new settlement in the north."

"I doubt if he'll come peacefully."

"From everything I've seen and heard, his family is the most important thing to him. We'll simply utilise them."

Utilise. It was a word with a broad meaning when it came out of Bucks' mouth. "And what about the settlement in the Cairngorms?"

"The fact that they've chosen not to reach out suggests that they won't until they're in a position of unwavering strength. Then I'm fairly certain it will be with a twig rather than a branch from an olive tree. They will want us to be supplicant to them." He pulled out the pile of papers that had been sprawled all over his desk before the arrival of the first visitor. "This is why we need to act now. This plan will mean we take control. We define the path to the future. And the future is everything, Paris."

Day 75

Danko and Hogarth stood with Eric as pitches were tidied away and the bustling crowd readied itself to spend a final night at Infinity before the winter shutdown. Many groups had already stopped coming, nervous about getting caught in an early winter storm.

"It's freezing," Hogarth said, rubbing her arms to warm up.

"Yeah," Eric replied. "We've stayed open a little longer than we did last year. I don't think it will be too long before the first storm hits us."

"That's a cheery thought."

"It is what it is. You can't stop the seasons."

"So, this is it then. You'll be heading out tomorrow too?" Hogarth asked.

"No," Eric replied. "We'll be prepping the place tomorrow, doing our best to weatherproof it before we head back to our bunker."

"Sounds like a big job."

"To be honest, we've been on with it all week, but we're just taking care of the finishing touches tomorrow. Then we'll be hunkering down for the next three months or so."

"How will everybody know when you're open again?"

"It usually happens slowly. When the daily temperatures head back to above freezing for a week straight, people tend to raise their heads above ground again."

"Last year, we were here for two weeks before we saw anyone," Chloe said, joining them. It was only just after four o'clock, but it was already getting dark. "I thought I was going to die of boredom. But then a couple of groups came, and word spread like wildfire."

"Yeah," Eric agreed. "And we've pretty much been running at full pelt since then."

"I bet you'll be glad for the rest," replied Hogarth.

"To be honest, I will. Don't get me wrong. I love this place. It gives me an incredible sense of pride, and I can't help but feel we're building a future here for everyone. There's no hierarchy, nobody taking advantage of the system. You get as much out of it as you put into it. Woody's people and Susan's people work non-stop, growing, scavenging, and learning about better ways to do things, and they reap the benefits as they should. But they don't exploit. The system's set up so that can't happen. It's a fair market, and it's run fairly. The people who come here are good people doing what they can to look after their families, their friends and one another. It's almost like a cooperative. I mean, look at it down there," he said, gesturing to the former playing field.

It was true. Traders who had finished packing their stalls away aided others while different groups helped with the communal meals and others readied the stage for the evening's entertainment. "You've certainly managed to build something important here," Hogarth said.

"There's still lots of work to do. There always will be. But we're growing all the time. New groups of survivors are finding us, trading here. I like to think that we're building a path to the future. And I suppose the future really is everything."

Day 76

"We need to get out of here," Eric said, bursting into the canteen.

Nazya and Chloe both let out stifled screams. They'd been cataloguing the medical supplies all morning, before the shutdown, and now were enjoying a hot cup of tea in the relative warmth before they started their inspection of the storage rooms. "Wh-what are you talking about, Dad?" Chloe asked, taking a step towards him but stopping suddenly as the sound of automatic gunfire began to echo from somewhere outside.

"What's that?" Nazya asked, slamming her mug down on the work surface, causing the hot liquid to spill over her hands.

"I don't know what the hell's going on. Crowesbury's surrounded."

"Surrounded? Surrounded by who, Dad?"

"I don't know. All four of our lookout teams have spotted them. Whoever they are, there are lots of them, and they're armed, and they're moving fast." The last of the traders from the previous day had departed two hours before, so there was no one able to help. "We need to get out of here, now, otherwise—"

A deafening boom interrupted his words and he leaned back out of the doorway to see daylight bleeding in through the entrance to the underground corridor, adding to the weak electric light provided by the generator.

"THERE. HE'S THERE!" a familiar voice yelled before the sound of drumming feet filled the air.

Eric leapt into the room, locking the door behind him. "I don't know what's going on, but that sounded like Jonathan." Despite only being called by their surnames in Salvation, Jonathan Danko and Gina Hogarth were only known by their Christian names in Crowesbury to give them a greater air of friendliness and approachability.

"Jonathan?" Chloe asked.

Eric turned around. His head was in a spin, but all he was concerned about now was his daughter's welfare. His eyes focused on the ventilation grate above the sink. *Too narrow.* Then he looked at the pile of boxes housing the MREs. "Get behind them," he said. "Get behind them," he said again, starting to pull the boxes away from the wall in order to create a space for the two women to hide.

"What are you talking about?" Chloe asked as tears filled her eyes. "No, Dad. We all need to get out of here."

He turned to look at her as he dragged more of the boxes out of the way. "They've seen me, Chloe. They know

I'm here. They don't know you're here. Now hide, and when you can, get out of here. Get to Redemption and get help."

The sound of running feet was getting closer by the second, and as scared as Nazya was, she understood that Eric was right. She helped pull more boxes away from the wall before grabbing her friend, coaxing her into the nook that had been created. Chloe shook herself free and threw her arms around her father. "I love you, Dad."

"I love you, sweetheart. Look after each other," he said before almost pushing her into the small hidey hole and piling the boxes around both of them. A thunderous banging sounded against the door, but Eric continued, albeit as quietly as possible now. *Christ! I hope this works.* He placed the final box in position and stepped back to see if there was any clue as to what lay behind them.

"ERIC!" a voice boomed as more banging sounded against the door, and further gunfire could be heard outside.

That's Gina. What the hell's going on? "What do you want?" he asked, struggling to disguise the fear in his voice. This was different to the time Childs had taken him. He had seen that coming. There was an inevitability about it. Childs had never been his friend, but he didn't feel that way about Gina and Jonathan. He believed they were decent people possessing his values and the values of many others who used Infinity.

"Open the door, Eric, or we're going to break it down."

He cast a glance back to his daughter's hiding place. *Can't tell. It comes a bit further out from the wall than it did, but unless you were really paying attention to where they were positioned originally, there's no way you'd know.* "I don't understand, Gina. What is this?"

"This is your final warning, Eric, and then we're coming in."

"Okay … okay," he said, walking to the door and opening it. Bodies surged into the room. One grabbed him and turned him around, pushing him up against the wall, while another began to search him for weapons. When they were happy he had none, his hands were zip-tied and he was pushed down into a waiting chair.

The woman who stood in front of him now bore little resemblance to the one he knew. She had changed out of her civilian attire into a Salvation guard uniform. Her hair was tied back. She held a Q-Thirty in her hands, and a Q-Eighteen sidearm was tucked away in its holster. There was no smile on her face as he had become accustomed to seeing. Instead, her eyes drilled holes through him. "Where are Chloe and Nazya?" she demanded.

He paused before answering. "The last time I saw them, they were heading to the lock-ups to make sure they were all secure before the shutdown."

Hogarth turned slightly. "Danko. Show Carlisle and his team where the lock-ups are." Without hesitation, Danko headed back out of the room with Carlisle and half a dozen guards following.

"What the hell is this? What's going on?" Eric asked again.

"Let's call it a hostile takeover. Infinity is now the property of Salvation."

"What are you talking about? You don't have a right to—"

She stepped forward, swivelled her rifle and smashed him hard in the stomach with its butt.

"Oof," he cried, doubling over in the chair.

"For what it's worth, I like you and your girl, Eric."

"You've got a strange way of showing it."

"I'm conditioning you into not asking questions and just accepting things from now on. Trust me, the people you meet when we take you back to Salvation aren't going to care a damn about your welfare. If you learn to shut up and do as you're told now, you might just live through this thing."

"What is this thing?"

"You've built something impressive here. But you've

taken it as far as it can go. It needs someone with vision to take it to the next level, to build it to what's needed."

"It's growing all the time. Hell, you and I stood talking about this last night. You nodded in agreement with me, for God's sake. Are you telling me that all this time you've just been gathering information for your bosses so you can make a move on us?"

Hogarth smiled. "You catch on fast. We know more than you could possibly imagine about you, about Trainor and Drake and—" She stopped herself, realising that she'd told him more than she should, but she continued when she understood it didn't matter anymore. His life on the outside was over. He and his daughter and their friends would be taken back to Salvation. They would be questioned as to the whereabouts of their bunker, and they would tell their interrogators everything because they were very good at their jobs. It was easy to get people like Eric to talk. Simply threatening someone he cared about would get him singing like a canary. "And about the rest of the patrons," she finally said.

"You're going to tear it all down? You're going to destroy everything we've done here?"

"You're not listening to me. We're going to make it thrive. We're going to make it into a hub that will—"

"It's already a hub. People depend on Infinity. Ever since it began, it's gone from strength to strength. It benefits everyone who uses it. We help people. We—"

"Oh, get off your high horse, will you? You're a little man, Eric. Yes, this is something, but it's a fraction of what it could be. There's an opportunity here, and Salvation will make sure that the full potential of this place is realised for the good of everybody, not just your merry little cooperative."

"Forgive me if I don't share your optimism. This is a death knell. What you're doing is going to signal the end for a lot of people."

"Like I said before, Eric. I suggest you keep your

views, your questions, everything, in fact, to yourself. And if you're not worried about your own welfare at least think about your daughter and the ones you love." She turned to the other guards she was with. "Get him on his feet. He's got a lot to do before we take him back to Salvation."

Two guards dragged him from the chair, marched him out of the room and back down the corridor. The others followed. Hogarth took one final look around the canteen before turning the light off, closing the door and proceeding after them. Eric wasn't the only one who had a lot to do. She'd been put in charge of the takeover, and she wanted to make sure everything ran as smoothly as possible.

*

Chloe and Nazya remained huddled together in their little castle of boxes. It was pitch black, and now the others had gone they could hear their own breathing above the distant sounds of sporadic gunfire. A single sob left Chloe's lips, and Nazya reached out to place a comforting hand on her arm.

"We will figure something out," Nazya whispered.

"Figure something out?" the other woman replied, her words trembling in her throat. "There's nothing to figure out. It's over; everything's over. We may as well walk out there with our hands up and just give in."

"No, Chloe. Your father hasn't given up. It is important that we don't either. We must get to Redemption, as he said."

Another sad cry left the heartbroken daughter before she continued. "You heard what I heard. We're surrounded. God knows how many of them are out there, but I'm pretty certain they're not going to give up searching for us."

"And that is why we must evade them."

"Evade them?"

"Yes. And the sooner we move the better."

"Move? Move where?"

"I am still thinking. But when they don't find us by the storage rooms, as your father said, this is the first place they will return to." Nazya finally flicked her torch on. In the periphery of the white light, she could see the silver streaks on her friend's face glistening. "We will get out of this. We will get to Redemption."

"And what about Dad and the others?"

"We must focus," Nazya said, starting to push the boxes and try to force a way out without the whole mountain collapsing on her. Chloe reluctantly followed, despite her feeling that it was all a lost cause.

The pair of them shuffled through the narrow box tunnel and finally made it out to the other side. "I can't believe this is happening," Chloe said.

Nazya grabbed her friend's wrist. "You need to stay strong, and we must act quickly." They walked over to a column of lockers and Nazya removed a key to open one.

"I didn't think we'd ever see these again," Chloe said as her friend removed two rucksacks.

"I hoped we wouldn't," Nazya replied. After Childs' attempted coup, Eric had insisted the pair of them have go bags ready for a quick escape if it happened again. They had done it to humour him more than anything, never believing for a second that they'd need them. Now, though, they were grateful. Neither backpack was full, and Nazya unzipped them, placing half a dozen MREs in each from one of the boxes before folding the flaps and pushing it back. They both had a few dried snacks in there, too, but nothing substantial, and something told Nazya that they would be grateful for the food before all this was over.

"What now?" Chloe asked, still finding it hard to believe what was going on.

Her friend looked towards the wall. Their coats and waterproofs were hanging from the pegs. "It will be cold on a night. We should make sure we are as comfortable as we can be." She guided Chloe over, and the pair slid on their coats, folding the waterproof polyester trousers and cagoules and jamming them into their rucksacks.

"Do we really need these? It hasn't rained in days."

"We will not be coming back here, Chloe. We should take what we can carry." Nazya thought for a moment. "Now come, we must make our way to the boiler room."

"The boiler room? Why do we want to go to the boiler room?"

"Because the vent duct will lead us outside without going through the stadium."

"That's not going to help us. There might be hundreds of Salvation guards out there for all we know. They're going to find us, Nazya. They won't stop until they do."

*

"Come on, keep moving," Hogarth said, nudging Eric in the back as they continued across the field. Just the day before, it was filled with traders at this time. Barter by barter, people were making their lives a little better.

A sudden wave of sadness struck Eric just at the thought of it. *It's all over now.*

"Hold up," Danko shouted as he, Carlisle and the squad of guards they'd gone to search the storage rooms with ran across to meet them. "They're not there."

"Are you sure?" Hogarth asked.

"We went through the place with a fine-tooth comb," Carlisle said. "There's nobody down there."

Hogarth grabbed hold of Eric's shoulder and spun him around. "No more games. Where the hell are they?"

It was only then that Eric spotted the bodies of two militia on the stands. Many of the others had been rounded up, awaiting what fate he could only guess, but the image reminded him again that everything they'd worked to build here had come crashing down and, with it, the future too. "How do you expect me to know? They probably heard the gunfire and fled."

"Fled where exactly? We've got this entire place in lockdown. A mouse couldn't have got out of here without us spotting it."

Eric shrugged. "I don't know what to tell you."

Hogarth slowly turned and looked towards the entrance they'd left a moment before. "Damn you, Eric," she said under her breath before ordering the others, "Get back to the bloody canteen." She grabbed her prisoner's arm roughly. "Move now."

*

This section of the building wasn't lit, and Nazya only hoped that there weren't any Salvation guards lurking anywhere because the small torch beam would instantly pinpoint them. The two women walked side by side, their shoulders brushing against each other for comfort. They moved quickly but not so quickly that their boots would echo down the labyrinthine corridors.

BOOM!

Both women froze. For a second, they couldn't understand what had made the thundering noise, but as shouts and the sound of running feet reverberated towards them, they understood that the guards had returned.

"Oh shit," Chloe hissed.

Nazya flicked off her torch and took her friend's hand. They both looked back to the dim glow of the main corridor behind them, but they were otherwise surrounded by darkness. They continued into the black beyond with nothing to guide them but their memories. In all the time they'd been here, they had probably only visited the boiler room and this part of the building once. There was nothing here, and a funny smell remained that some swore were burst sewer pipes but were probably just blocked drains.

"I think we turn left soon," Nazya whispered, and both women shuffled over to the wall, feeling it out in the blackness, hoping they would find the turn before the guards found them.

"I don't remember. I don't remember anything about this place."

*

The guards and their prisoner stopped outside the canteen door, and it was Hogarth who burst in with her Q-

Thirty raised. She turned the light on and walked a little further inside. "Chloe? Nazya? You're not doing yourself, your father or anyone any favours by hiding from us."

She paused, listening for a cry, a breath, a sound of any kind. "What do you want us to do?" Carlisle asked, heading into the room after her.

"Take two teams. Search the rest of the building. This place is like a maze, so make sure you don't miss anywhere. She turned back to look at the others. "You two, in here with me and bring him with you," she said to the pair of guards who had hold of Eric's shoulders to make sure he didn't try to bolt. They pushed him down into a chair while Hogarth walked up to the sink unit.

She paused, glancing back out into the corridor as the two teams departed. Then she turned her attention back to the sink. She flung open one of the doors and quickly stepped back with her rifle raised.

"It's funny. I had you pegged as someone who was pretty bright up until today," Eric said. "Do you really expect to find my daughter and her best friend under the sink?" He let out a little laugh.

Hogarth shot an angry glance towards him before heading over to the lockers in the far corner of the room. They were thin, but if someone took the shelves out, a person could probably fit inside. She paused in front of one of them with her fingers on the handle as shouted orders drifted down the corridor. She turned the latch and jumped back with her weapon raised once more.

When the door opened, Eric glanced across, trying his hardest not to raise any suspicion. *The go bags. You got the go bags. Thank God. Please be out of here by now. Please be on the streets heading towards Redemption.*

"I THINK I SAW SOMETHING. THIS WAY!" The sound of running feet became more uniform.

Hogarth backed away from the lockers. Now that the hunters seemed to be on the trail her efforts felt redundant. She turned and was about to lead the other three back out of the room when something caught her eye. There was a gap between two of the bottom boxes of MREs. It wasn't enough to get a body through, but now she looked at the ones stacked on top they were a little skewed, too, and not quite flush to the wall. She glanced across at Eric, and despite his best efforts, he looked down at the table.

Please don't still be there. Please don't still be there.

"You keep your eye on him. You come here," she said to the two guards before pulling a torch from her belt. She flicked it on and angled the beam into the most distinct gap. Her eyes followed the white light then she looked across towards Eric once more. "So … you don't know where your beloved daughter is," she said, smiling. Hogarth turned off the torch, placed it back in the pouch in her belt, then grabbed hold of one column of boxes and began to shuffle it across the floor. "You're only making this harder on yourself, Chloe."

Eric's heart began to pound faster than ever as the boxes moved. He could feel the presence of one of the guards still behind him, and as he strained against the zip tie, he knew there was no way he could snap it. *Got to do something. Dammit, Chloe. Why didn't you get out when you had the chance?* "Listen," Eric said, clearing his throat.

"No," Hogarth replied. "You had your opportunity, and now you're going to face the consequences. You and your daughter." She tugged hard at the box and jumped back before getting caught in the mini avalanche. Hogarth and the guard with her brought their rifles up in unison, expecting to see two frightened, surrendering figures emerging from the remains of the box cave.

Eric held his breath, leaning up a little from the chair despite the hand on his shoulder. *Don't try anything, Chloe. Just come out and don't give them a reason.*

"Son of a bitch," Hogarth hissed, aiming her rifle back around towards Eric. "Okay. This is your last chance. Where are they?"

*

Nazya loved Chloe like a sister, but she knew that she was one step away from falling apart and she would have to lead them if they were to stand any chance of escaping.

The sounds of their pursuers had sent a shiver of impending doom through them both, but they had finally made it to the boiler room. They opened and closed the door as quietly as they possibly could, and as soon as they heard the latch engage, Nazya flicked on her torch again.

"Come. We will not have long."

"This is madness. We should just give up."

"If we give up, then everything your father has built here will be for nothing."

"What is it you don't get, Naz? It has been for nothing. It's all over."

"Nothing is over. Now come." She led the way further into the boiler room until they reached the largest of the vent grates. They climbed on top of the vast wrought iron structure beneath it that had once provided the heating for the entire Infinity stadium and paused as confused shouts travelled down the corridors outside towards them.

*

"You said you saw them," Carlisle barked angrily.

"I … I thought I did," another man protested.

"Well, I'm no expert, but that looks more like a floor scrubber than two women to me."

"I thought I saw movement."

"You're a useless arsehole, Morton. This thing probably hasn't moved in five years. Now we're going to have to backtrack and check out all the rooms we missed on the way here."

"I'm sorry, okay. I could have sworn I saw something."

*

Both women breathed a sigh of relief. They had stumbled into the floor cleaning machine in the dark, and seconds later, a dim fan of white light had paused on them for a split second, but they had managed to escape it.

"We won't have long before they end up in here," Nazya said, pulling the small snowflake multi-tool that Woody had gifted to all his favourite people out of her pocket. She reached up and started on the screws.

"I don't see the point of any of this," Chloe protested. "The second they come in here and see the grate missing, they're going to know we're in the ducts."

"Then we have to make sure they don't see the grate missing," Nazya replied.

"Oh yeah. Good luck with that."

Nazya continued until all four screws had been removed and the grate was off. "Come, I will give you a boost up."

Chloe let out a heavy sigh. She was so conflicted. Part of her wanted to put her hands in the air, surrender and face whatever fate her father faced. The other part wanted to obey his wishes. Finally, she reached up, grasping the lip of the large rectangle duct and allowing her friend to grab her hips and hoist her up. "Okay. I'm in," she whispered, surprised at how much room there was. She shimmied along a metre or so until she reached a junction, which allowed her to swivel around and edge back to the opening.

"I will pass you our rucksacks," Nazya replied, giving her friend one then the other.

More calls sounded from outside, and this time they were closer than ever. Nazya finally passed up the grate giving her friend the narrow end and allowing her to pull it into the duct. "What are we going to do with this?"

She didn't answer. "Get back," Nazya said, wrapping her fingers around the lip of the opening and heaving herself up. Chloe reached out, clutching the back of her friend's thick winter jacket and pulling. When she was up, they both shuffled back to the junction where Nazya was able to turn. She reached into her rucksack and grabbed the reel of fishing line she had occasionally used to stitch people up with.

"Have you cut yourself?" Chloe asked, a little

panicked.

"No," Nazya replied but offered no further explanation as she cut four lengths of the line.

"What are we doing? You were the one who said we had to hurry."

Nazya glanced at her friend in the torchlight then proceeded to loop the four lengths of line around the thin bars of the grate in the corners.

"...to check in here." The voice bled through the thin opening in the doorway, and Nazya realised their time was up. As quietly as she could, she shimmied back through the duct with the grill in front of her. She held onto the lines tight with her right hand as the fingers on her left gripped the bars of the grate, extending it out and manoeuvring it around until it married up to the opening. Then she edged back as far as she could, using her weight on the four lines to keep the cover in place.

I really hope this works.

Torch beams danced around the cavernous interior of the boiler room. "If you ask me, this is a waste of our time. We should be searching the other side of the stadium where the storage rooms are," said one voice.

"Well, nobody is asking you, are they?" another man replied.

"I'm just saying."

The search continued. Nazya could sense Chloe frozen like a statue behind her while she continued to pull on the four lines, hoping, praying that they didn't slip or snap. She held her breath as she heard footsteps come to a stop beneath the ducting. "Well, well, well. What have we got here?"

Oh crap. Oh crap. Oh crap.

"What?" one of the other voices called out, and multiple footsteps could be heard, all coming to a stop beneath the duct.

"Looks like Miss July had a lot going for her," the man said, and laughter erupted.

The sound of flicking pages ensued for a few seconds before another man said, "Jesus. Will you look at the pair on her?"

Nazya was revulsed to the pit of her stomach. She was holding on to the grate for dear life, and all that stood between her and the leering group below was some fishing line that could have been a decade old for all she knew.

"I thought they stopped making this kind of thing years ago," one of the men said.

The pages finally finished turning, and another replied, "They did. Look. It's from 2005. Braithwaite's Plumbing Supplies, Crampton."

"What the hell is it doing here?"

"Crampton was what Crowesbury used to be. I'm guessing whoever worked in this boiler room held on to this as a little keepsake."

"It beats a mug or a stick of rock." Raucous laughter echoed around the giant room once more.

"Well, come on. We'd better check the rest of this place out before Hogarth comes looking for us."

"She's a bitch is that one."

"I dare you to say that to her face."

"You're alright. I'm too partial to my bollocks." The men laughed again, and the torch beams began to move once more.

Nazya stared towards the grate. Despite the cold, she could feel a bead of sweat forming on her brow. She continued to clutch the lines tightly but not too tightly. A rattle, a snap, just the slightest sound and that would draw the attention of the men and their torches. In the dark, there was nothing to see. The cover to the duct was in position. A close inspection would show the screws were missing and plastic threads were tensing around the bars, holding the thing in place.

"Yeah, come on," another man said. Let's finish checking this place out and move on. Otherwise, she'll be on our backs." The beams of light began to move again, but

Nazya still didn't relax. TWANG!

Her eyes stretched wide as a piece of line broke. *Oh, God. Oh, God. Oh, God.*

"Did you hear that?" one of the men asked.

"Nah," a second replied.

"I didn't hear anything," answered a third.

"I'm sure I heard something," the first man said again and suddenly footsteps started back to the duct.

Chloe sucked in a deep breath and placed her hand on her friend's calf, gently squeezing it as if to thank her, as if to say it wasn't your fault; you did your best.

"We've already been over here. There's nothing," the second man replied.

"He's just wanting another look at Miss July," the third joked, and laughter fluttered around the room. It was spread out, which suggested that it was just the three men who had come back to explore the area.

"It sounded like something snapping," the first man said.

Nazya continued to stare towards the grate. Her heart was pounding in her chest like a timpani drum. There was another sudden noise, and she tensed up even more. She had no idea what it was but couldn't rule out it was something to do with the grate. She continued to stare, fearful that a torch beam would illuminate the inside of the duct at any second.

"It was Miss July, after all," the second man quipped. "That was probably what you heard, the pin shifting."

"You can't have pushed it back in the wall, right, you numpty," said the third man. "Here, give it to me." There was a sound of pages flicking then a grunt as he forced the pin back into the wall to hang the calendar once more.

"Nah. That's not what I heard," the first man said.

"So, what else could it have been?"

There was a long pause before he answered. "I don't know."

"Exactly. You don't know. In the meantime, we're

wasting time when we should be searching the rest of the place, and we're going to get an almighty bollocking from Hogarth. Come on. There's nothing here; we need to move on."

Silence lingered for a few moments before the footsteps finally began to fade once more. Eventually, the sound of the boiler room door opening and closing signalled that it was safe for the two women to breathe again. Neither of them could move for a full minute. They just remained there in the dark, not quite believing that they had evaded capture. When the silence continued, Chloe gently squeezed her friend's leg one more time. "Are you okay, Naz?" she asked in little more than a whisper.

There was a long pause before any reply came. "Yes. Yes," she repeated as she began to breathe normally once more.

"So, what now?"

There was another pause. "We must secure this grill."

"How?"

"Give me a minute," Nazya replied, flicking her dynamo torch on again. The inside of the ducting was smooth, punctuated only by the nuts that secured one section to another. While keeping a firm grip on the lines, she put down the torch and reached into her pocket for the snowflake multi-tool then held it up to the light. "I love you, Woody," she said.

"What?" Chloe asked.

"Never mind," Nazya replied as she fixed the corresponding profile on her tool around the centre bolt head and began to turn. It was stiff but finally came free. She rotated it once, twice, three times before wrapping and weaving the three lines around the threads and ratcheting the bolt back into place as tightly as possible. An unnerving premonition flashed into her mind of the three lines unravelling as she let go and the grill crashing to the wrought iron structure below, alerting every Salvation guard in the building as to their whereabouts. She held her breath as she finally relinquished her grasp of the lines and stared at the bolt.

No movement. Thank God. She exhaled deeply and turned her head to whisper back to her friend. "We must go now."

"Okay. Go where exactly?"

"We need to get our bearings, but this channel will lead us outside. We must do what your father said. We must head to Redemption and get help."

"Crowesbury's under siege by the sound of it, Naz. Even if we get out of the stadium, how the hell are we going to get out of town?"

"We have something they do not. Knowledge. Remember how we evaded even our own people that time when we headed after Callie?"

Half a laugh left Chloe's mouth despite the direness of the situation. Her father had given her hell for that, but Nazya was right. Their knowledge of the town had allowed them to stay hidden when others would have struggled. "Yeah."

The two friends shuffled to the junction and were able to look at each other face-to-face for the first time in a while. Nazya took her friend's hand and squeezed it tight. "We are the last hope for your father, for our friends and for this place. We must be strong. We must try everything we can to get to Redemption. It is not just our future that depends on it. It is everyone's future."

PART 3

7

NOW

The fire continued to crackle away. Nobody had interrupted Nazya or Chloe once as they recounted their story. They had just sat, often in open-mouthed disbelief, as the enormity of what they were being told dawned on them.

"Anyway," Nazya continued. "We navigated our way through the trunking and finally found the exterior vent, but there were guards everywhere, and breaking out of it would have been noisy and taken time. So, we headed back down to a section that allowed us to stretch out at least. We were in there for nearly two days. We had MREs in our rucksacks, but the smell from them would have alerted someone to our whereabouts. So, all that time we were living on nothing but your seaweed jerky and water and listening to snatches of conversations," she said, casting a smile towards Susan. "Then, when we saw an opportunity, we made our move."

"Of course, we didn't know we were going to get caught out there in the mother of all storms," Chloe added, and Callie took her friend's hand.

Susan looked around the wide semicircle of faces to see they mirrored her shock and unease. "I suppose we have to figure out what we do now," she finally said, breaking the lingering silence.

"Well, surely we need to head to Infinity straight away," Nicola said. "We'll rescue Eric and the others and—"

"We don't even know if Eric's still there," Drake said, interrupting her. "And I'm sorry," he said, glancing towards Chloe and Nazya, "but by the sound of it, this plan has been months in the making." He turned towards PJ, who, like everyone else other than Drake, wasn't quite sure why he was there. He looked uncomfortable and unsure of himself, sitting on a wide tree trunk between Phil, Jason and other big hitters in the Redemption community. "PJ, the administration has had a trading party visiting Infinity for weeks if not months. If someone came to you while you were still in Salvation and asked how the tech department could help, what would you do?"

PJ suddenly felt all eyes on him and immediately coloured up. "Put me on the spot, why don't you?" he said, smiling nervously.

"Sorry, PJ. I normally wouldn't do this, but there's no one who knows more about the tech available to Salvation than you. If Bucks or Paris had come to you saying they wanted to gather information, what would you have done?"

"Err … well … I'd equip every member of the trading party with an adapted phone."

"An adapted phone?" Susan asked.

"Yeah. I mean, every phone has a camera and the ability to record. It wouldn't be too difficult to make the camera periscopic."

"Periscopic?"

"Yeah." He reached into his pocket and pulled his own phone out, pointing at the camera lens. "It wouldn't be a big deal to have this lens hidden in clothing with an optic cable leading to the phone. The mics on these things are incredibly powerful. I mean, you could have them in a rucksack and you'd still be able to record any conversations in a ten-metre radius. They were designed that way. It's how we kept tabs on what was going on in Salvation."

"So what could they glean from that data, and what could they do with it?"

PJ let out a short sharp laugh. "You don't understand, do you?"

"Evidently not."

"With the computers, the AI and the processing power available in Salvation, they could learn pretty much everything."

"PJ," Marina said. "Explain it to us as if we were simpletons."

PJ let out a long sigh and resisted the urge to make a derisory comment. "Well, for a start, they'll have identified every single former Salvation inhabitant who visited Infinity while their trading party was there with the facial recognition software. All conversations will have been recorded, processed and indexed."

"I don't understand. What do you mean processed and indexed?"

"They'll have utilised speech-to-text software, so for the sake of example, if the last few minutes of our conversation had been recorded and processed, they could perform a search on recognition or phone or PJ. They'd be able to call up any conversation by subject. So, every time Phil was mentioned or Redemption was mentioned, they'd be able to access the conversations adding more and more information to their database."

A chilling silence hung in the air for a moment before Drake spoke again. "Okay. So, what else could they know?"

PJ shrugged. "It's an impossible question to answer. The filter and the AI available at Salvation were like nothing I'd seen on the outside. You could have twenty conversations going on at the same time and you'd be able to isolate each one of them. I mean, can you remember every conversation you had at Infinity? Can you remember every person you spoke to? For all we know, they could have specifically targeted Redemption citizens. They could know everything about us." He looked across to Nazya and Chloe. "It certainly sounds like they gathered enough information about Infinity to make a decisive move. It sounds like they knew the perfect moment to strike. It sounds like they knew exactly what they'd be up against."

"Jesus," Jason gasped.

"God," Tania said. "We've had conversations about our journeys, what we've seen; they probably know exactly where we are."

"I can pretty much guarantee it," PJ replied. "The fact that we trade seaweed is a bit of a giveaway too. Even if they don't know where we are exactly, it won't take them too long to find us. I'm pretty sure someone would have blurted how long it takes to make the journey at some stage. The Salvation trading party will have seen which direction we leave Crowesbury."

"Well, aren't you just a bundle of lightness and joy?" Debbie said.

"I was never one for fairy tales. I think the safest thing to assume is they know pretty much everything."

"It doesn't matter what they know," Callie said. "We've got to do something. Eric has been our greatest ally. Infinity is vital for us. We can't just let it fall into enemy hands."

Drake cleared his throat. "And what would you have us do, exactly, Callie?"

"Well...." She didn't know how to continue. *What the hell can we do?* She squeezed Chloe's hand a little tighter.

"What I'm about to say won't be popular," began Greenslade, "but being popular has never been a big thing for me."

"Go on," Susan said.

"We can't do anything."

"Well, that's crap," Nicola replied. "Eric—"

"Eric is as good a friend and ally as we could hope for. Not just that, he's a good man as well." He looked at Chloe. "I'm very sorry about your father." He turned back to the others. "If we try to go in guns blazing, it will be a bloodbath."

"We don't know that."

"Yes, we do," Drake said. "We've got a fairly substantial and pretty well-trained militia. But we won't be able to get within a couple of miles of Crowesbury without the Salvation guards knowing we are on the way. They'd be ready, and that means we'd already be at a disadvantage. The militia's purpose is to defend Redemption. They're not an attacking force."

"Yeah," Greenslade agreed. "And the other thing to bear in mind is that we've just lived through the first winter storm. We don't know when the next one will hit. It would be crazy heading out there with the threat of that hanging over us."

"So, what are you saying?" Susan asked. "We just do nothing?"

"Why did you come here and not back to your family in the bunker?" Phil asked, ignoring the other conversation that was going on.

Chloe's head drooped as fresh tears started to fall from her eyes. It was Nazya who answered. "It is what Eric asked. He asked us to come to you for help."

"That's why we've got to help," Nicola said. "If the tables were turned, there's not a chance in hell that Eric would leave us high and dry."

"If we head out with the militia to Crowesbury it will be the end of Redemption," Drake said.

"We can't know that."

"We really can because I know these people. I know what they're capable of, but that's not the half of it. Greenslade was right. We head out there and get caught in a storm; we'll definitely lose people before we even get to fire one bullet."

"Nazya and Chloe made it," Callie replied.

"Yeah. They found a little nook and managed to stay warm. You think eight hundred or a thousand people are all going to be able to find little nooks and enough firewood to stop them freezing to death?"

"But—"

"Listen to me. On top of everything else, they'll be half expecting us to make a move."

"How can you possibly know that?"

"Because I would be."

Chloe began to sob a little louder. "Dad," she whispered between her cries.

"This is madness," Callie said. "We can't let them get away with this."

"For the time being, I think we should concentrate on enhancing the fortifications around this place," Drake replied.

"You think they're going to attack us?" Susan asked.

"I honestly don't know. I didn't see this coming."

"What I want to know is why," Harper said. "Why seize Infinity like that? It's not like it's going to be of any value to the administration."

"Obviously, it is going to be of value to them. They'll have more than enough information telling them that it's a vital lifeline for us."

"Are you saying the only reason they took Infinity is to cripple us?"

"Not the only one, but I'm sure it was a bonus."

"Infinity has become a hub for settlements not just over the region but over the country. Some people travel for days to get to it," Phil began. "If you take control of Infinity, you take control of everything."

"But how?" Marina asked, still not quite understanding.

"Bucks will understand better than anyone that Infinity is crucial for thousands of people. If you take control of that lifeline, you take control of the people."

"But surely, if he shuts it down, somebody will just set another market up. It might take a while, but…."

Phil shook his head. "To be honest, I don't know what he'll do, but I'm inclined to agree with Drake. I think this is just the beginning of an expansion, and we'll be somewhere at the top of that list."

"But coming here would be madness," Nicola said. "They must have some idea of the weaponry and ammunition we have, not to mention the size of our population. They won't have enough guards."

"I wouldn't put conscription past Bucks. What you need to remember is we sabotaged the power plant. We took a big chunk of the Salvation arsenal as well as large amounts of seeds and supplies with us. As far as he's concerned, that's a debt that needs paying back, and Bucks always collects on his debts."

"There's something else we need to think about," Greenslade announced, and all eyes turned to him once more. "Rommy, Becka and the others." He nodded to the two women sitting nearest to the fire. They had remained silent up to this point, as bewildered as everyone else by Nazya's and Chloe's story.

"What do you mean?" Susan asked.

"I mean we're pretty well defended on this side of the ridge. An army could sweep into the forest on the other side and there'd be nothing we could do to stop them."

"Oh, God. I didn't even think about that."

"It might be an idea to start."

Muted and concerned conversations erupted around the fire. "Quiet. Everybody. Please," Callie begged. She rose to her feet, finally letting go of Chloe's hand. "There's obviously a lot we're going to have to think about, but we're losing sight of the most urgent problem. Eric's been—"

"Nobody's losing sight of anything," Drake said, looking towards Susan, then Greenslade and finally Phil. *They get it. They've figured it out.* "There's nothing we can do, Callie."

"But he sent Chloe and Nazya here for help."

"No, he didn't," Phil replied softly.

"What do you mean?"

"I'm not sure why I didn't figure it out before. Eric's a very intelligent man. When he heard the scale of the attack on Infinity, he might not have known who was responsible initially, but he knew there'd be nothing we could do."

"I still don't understand. What are you saying?"

"He sent them here because he knew we'd protect them."

"That doesn't make sense. Why wouldn't he send them back to their bunker, their family?"

"No disrespect to your families in the bunkers," he began, turning to look at Chloe once more, "but they don't have the defence capabilities we have. Eric sent you here because he knew that you'd be safer with us than anywhere else. And he'd have no reason to suspect this, but the chances are your bunkers have been hit too."

A whimper left Chloe's lips. "We can't know that," she said with her eyes watering.

"No, we can't," Drake replied. "But it's what I'd do."

Anger flared in Callie's eyes. "Yeah. None of us have forgotten who you are, Drake."

A sad smile swept onto Drake's face. "Yeah. Regardless of that, what Phil said is right. Eric wouldn't have sent Chloe and Nazya here for help. He'd have sent them here for safety."

For a few moments, the only sound in the room was the crackle of the fire. It was Chloe who finally broke the uncomfortable pause. "Do you think my dad's dead?"

There was another pause before Drake replied. "No. No, I don't. It wouldn't make sense. Bucks would want me and my people dead because that would make a statement about sedition. Your father is a resource. I'm not saying he'll live a life of luxury, but they'll probably put him to work and do their best to extort information out of him."

"Dad would never tell them anything."

"You'd be amazed how people buckle when someone's torturing one of your loved ones."

"Drake!" Susan snapped.

Chloe started to cry once more, and Callie sat down, placing her arm around her while Nazya took her hand.

"So, we give up on Eric after everything he's done for us?" Nicola asked.

"No," Greenslade replied. "We protect his daughter and Nazya as if they were our own. It's not much, but it's all we can do."

"You're damn right it's not much."

"There's nothing good about this situation. There are going to be no magical answers."

"Greenslade's right," Drake replied.

"No disrespect," Jason began, looking towards Chloe, "but let's forget about Eric for the time being. You're saying there's nothing we can do. We depend on Infinity. Not being able to trade there will have a devastating effect on Redemption."

"We'll have to increase our scavenging activities come spring."

"You mean to send more groups out?"

"If we want to keep expanding."

"So, what you're saying is that we'll be under the greater chance of attack from Salvation forces, but you want to send more people out from here, probably in smaller groups, so we can cover more ground, and this will not only leave them vulnerable but us too."

Drake's head dropped. "Yes." His voice was barely audible as he spoke.

"And how do you think that's going to work out for us exactly?"

He didn't respond, and despite the fire, not for the first time that night, a biting cold embraced everyone in the room. Shortly afterwards, Susan called an end to the meeting, and the attendees returned to their homes other than Rommy and Becka. They, along with Nazya and Chloe, shared a corner of the already cramped house and got some much-needed rest.

*

Callie woke with a jolt. In her dream, she'd been falling. It didn't take Freud to understand what that was about. The orange glow of the fire through the curtains told her that she hadn't been sleeping long. She looked at Si to see he was fast asleep then turned to see an empty space where her mother should have been. Callie leant up a little to see her mum's winter coat and boots were missing too. She grabbed her own clothes and tiptoed out of the curtained cubicle, pausing to put them on before stepping out of the door.

The cold hit her like a wall of flying needles, and she stopped for a moment to acclimatise to it before finally going in search of her mother. It didn't take long. Susan was standing at the edge of the nearest field. The snow was up to her knees, but she didn't seem to notice. The reflected moon threw out enough light for her to see well into the distance. The view looked magical, like a Christmas card.

"That's one thing about the snow," Susan said. "Nobody can sneak up on you in it."

"I suppose not," Callie replied, finally forging her way through the last few metres to join her. "I woke, and you weren't there."

"I couldn't really sleep."

They stood in silence for a moment until Callie spoke again. "What are we going to do, Mum?"

Susan did not break her gaze of the white fields as she answered. "We're going to do what we've always done. We're going to survive."

"Listening to Drake's assessment of the situation, that doesn't sound like the sure thing it was before yesterday."

"What can I tell you? I don't have the answers. Everybody's going to be looking to me, and panic will be sweeping through this place again tomorrow morning when

204

people wake up and find out what's gone on. But I'm not going to have answers for them either because there aren't any. We don't know what the administration has planned for Infinity. We don't know what they have planned for us. We don't know anything, and it's that not knowing that scares the hell out of me."

Callie edged a little closer to her mother and looped a hand through her arm. "If it makes you feel any better, I'm scared too."

"I don't know where we go from here, sweetheart. We can prepare and plan and fortify, but I think there's a war coming, and by the time it's over, there won't be anything left worth fighting for."

8

It was a long few months but, gradually, the frigid conditions began to ease. At least twenty major storms had struck, several far worse than the first and lasting much longer, but the plans and procedures that had been put into place by the committee that ran Redemption had ensured that there were no more fatalities as a result of the weather. Two people had lost fingers and toes due to frostbite, but Bindi and Nazya had provided them with sufficient care for the amputations not to become life-threatening.

There had been over thirty deaths, however. All had been suicides. The news of what had happened across at Infinity had shrouded Redemption in what felt like a death shawl. Most people did their best to get on with the day-to-day task of just surviving, but for some, it had been too much.

The last few mornings had seen Callie and Si start running again. Callie was struggling. She'd suffered bouts of depression before, and this time, she wasn't alone. It was hardly an epidemic, but many were finding it hard, and she had remembered how running had helped her in Salvation. It was hardly a cure-all, but it had made her feel a tiny bit better since she'd begun.

"Well, this is nice," Phil said. "It's a long time since you and I have talked, let alone had a little stroll in the fields."

"Isn't it just?" Callie replied.

It was still quite early in the morning, but a noise made them glance over to the forest. In the periods when there had been no snow on the ground and the earth wasn't as hard as a rock, preparations had been made to erect new hotels in the forest across from the farm. Rommy, Becka and the other Wanderers would move to this side of the ridge as soon as possible, and any plans to farm the fields to the north had been abandoned. Despite the early hour, Jason and his team were already hard at work.

"How are you feeling?"

"I wish people would stop asking me that."

"I'm sorry. I didn't realise being concerned about you was an offence. Are you going to report me to the Redemption Gestapo?"

"That's not funny."

A thin smile formed on Phil's face. Drake's activities and demands had been questioned a number of times in the last few weeks. He'd become more paranoid and mistrustful than usual. "Oh, I don't know. You've got to see the funny side."

Tears began to roll down Callie's cheeks. "There is no funny side, Phil. Can't you see what's happening here?" she said, stopping and turning towards him.

Shock painted her friend's face. They had just been talking, and he'd cracked a facetious joke like he had done a thousand times before, but he'd never seen her break like this. He took a step nearer and wrapped his arms around her. "I'm sorry." She didn't reply. She just continued sobbing. "We'll get through this, Callie."

The young woman pulled back, wiping her eyes. "No, we won't. Can't you feel it? We're coming apart at the seams, Phil. Sure," she said, pointing over to the forest, "everybody's still going about their business as if Chloe and Nazya never arrived, as if they never told us anything, but they all know. Everybody knows this is it. We're just waiting."

There had been far fewer committee meetings, and Phil had barely seen Callie over the winter months. Even though he knew she was down, he didn't realise the full extent of what she was going through, what was eating her away inside. "No, we're not."

"Please credit me with enough intelligence to know you're just saying that to stop me crying."

"If I did, it would obviously be misplaced."

Callie laughed through her tears and wiped her face. "Thanks."

"I've never patronised you, Callie, and I never will."

"So, you honestly believe there's a way out of this?"

"Yes, I do."

"How?"

"How can I believe it or how is there a way out of this?"

"Well … both."

"I can believe it because when I was dumped down on Level Three with my family, unconscious, I thought we were finished."

"Oh yeah. This worked out so much better for you."

"The point is we weren't. Some truly exceptional people worked towards a common goal, and we achieved it, defying all the odds. There was this girl who managed to talk a vicious bandit down and get everyone else behind her. She changed the tide of everything. She proved to me that no matter how bad things are, there's hope and a way forward."

"Yeah, well, she's long gone."

"No, she isn't. It's just that she needs a little help now, that's all. And the way she was there for me at every turn, I'm going to be there for her. And so is Debbie, and so is Matt, and so is everyone who cares for her and loves her, and trust me, that's a lot of people."

"Love isn't going to be enough to get us through this."

"No. But Drake and Marina and Dwyer and Revell and the rest of them might be."

"What are you talking about?"

"Your head's probably been elsewhere. They've been having a lot more meetings than usual."

"And that's what makes you think there's hope because Mister Paranoia and his gang have had more meetings than usual?"

"Whatever anyone thinks of Drake, he has only ever had the best for this place at heart. That's why he was so set against anybody talking about some impulsive mission to go off and find Eric. He knew the only thing that would happen would be that some of our people would get captured, and some would die, making us weaker."

"So, what miraculous answer to our problems do you think he's come up with?"

"I don't know. But I'm sure he'll tell us when he's ready."

"That really doesn't help, Phil."

"Greenslade's been in on the meetings too."

"Blake? How come Mum hasn't been told about any of this?"

Phil shrugged. "Don't ask me. It's not like they invited me to join them."

"In fairness, you can probably see why."

"None taken."

Callie smiled. It wasn't a big smile, but it was something. "Take the strain. TAKE THE STRAIN!" Jason's shouted order travelled towards them on the gentle breeze.

"And, y'know, Jason, Zep and their teams have been working full pelt when the weather's allowed. We're going to have Rommy and her people on this side of the ridge before we know it."

"What's that got to do with anything?"

"A lot. Everybody's still working to make this place something better, Callie. It might not feel like that, and I know the mood is generally dark, but we're all still getting on with it, planning for the future. And we'd only bother doing that if we thought there was one."

They started walking again. "So, what have you been doing to contribute to our future?" she asked, only half joking.

"Quite a lot, actually."

"Oh?"

"I managed to successfully grow two crops of mushrooms."

It seemed like an age since Callie and he had spoken about the mushrooms. She'd heard little bits about what he'd been up to, but couldn't muster the enthusiasm to seek him out and talk about it. She hadn't really wanted to talk to anyone. "You did? And did they taste good?"

Phil shrugged. "I have no idea; we didn't eat them."

"You didn't?"

"No. Debbie wasn't that happy about it. She said that due to the amount of time I'd been spending with them, it was almost as if I was having an affair, and at the very least, she and Bindi should be allowed to put them in a risotto or something."

"But you didn't let her?"

"Certainly not. I took each mushroom and used it to make a spore print."

Callie chuckled. It was a genuine laugh, and it felt good. "I don't think anyone would have begrudged you a few mushrooms."

Phil shook his head. "What's more important is that we now have tens of millions of spores, and now that winter's over, I can experiment with growing them on a larger scale. It's very, very exciting."

"I bet that's not what Debbie said."

"No. No, she didn't. I tried to explain to her what it would mean, but she just kept saying, 'We could have had a few, at least.'"

Callie laughed again. "Poor Debbie."

"Poor Debbie? Poor me."

"So, that's it? That's the full extent of what you've been up to?"

"No. I managed to grow a few crops in the polytunnel too."

"You did? I thought it would be too cold."

"Well, it was, originally, but Jason helped me construct a kind of heater. It's very basic. It's made from the base of an old Calor gas container, but it throws out enough heat to raise the temperature in the tunnel. I managed to grow radishes, spinach and some carrots."

"Actually, that is quite impressive."

"What's quite impressive?" Dani asked, appearing from behind them.

"Were you earwigging?" Phil asked.

"I was coming to find Cal. What's impressive?"

"Phil's managed to grow some crops in the polytunnel over the winter," Callie replied.

"Why's that impressive? Isn't that what you're meant to be able to do?"

"Not in temperatures like we had. Not with something that's been cobbled together from old bits of plastic sheeting."

"I'm probably going to regret asking this, but why's that so impressive?"

"Because—"

"Because," Phil said, taking over, "it means if we build a lot more tunnels, we'll be able to grow crops all year round. The main harvest won't be the be-all and end-all. We'll be able to supplement it."

Dani thought for a moment. "Actually, that is pretty impressive."

"Praise from another twelve-year-old. My day is complete."

"I suppose everybody must look young when you get to your age."

"At least I've got to this age, a fate I feel it is unlikely you will be able to replicate with that smart mouth of yours. Anyway, was there some purpose for you coming over here to give me a hard time or were you just bored?"

Dani turned to her friend. "Your mum's looking for you."

"Did she say what she wanted?" Callie asked.

Dani shrugged. "I didn't ask."

"Oh. I suppose I'd better go see then." She started moving away. "Are you coming?"

"In a minute."

"Okay. See you at home."

Dani and Phil watched as Callie headed back to the farm. "How was she?"

The question needed no further explanation. It was the longest conversation he'd had with Callie in some time. "A little better, I think. She's still very, very down. I think maybe the morning runs are starting to help a bit, but I don't know. You spend a lot more time with her than I do."

Dani let out a deep sigh. "I don't know. It's a tough one. Susan says she's never seen her like this before, but Susan spent most of her time in Salvation shi—drunk. She probably can't remember when Callie got really bad."

"So, you have seen her like this before?"

"Yeah. Sort of. She's had a couple of spells where she kind of lost herself, but each time, she came out of it. I'm just hoping she does this time. I don't know what it is with her, but she seems to take the weight of everything like it's all her fault."

Phil smiled sympathetically. "Callie is a very, very intelligent young woman. She's brave and self-sacrificing. We've seen it time and time again. The fact that Infinity has been hijacked, the fact that we couldn't do anything to save

Eric and Chloe's family, there'll be a part of her that blames herself."

"But that's crazy."

"It is, and it isn't."

"What do you mean?"

"She's probably more responsible than anyone for us escaping Salvation. I don't think the onus of that responsibility ever left her. Callie's a special girl, but I think sometimes the weight of her actions catches up with her."

"So, what do we do?"

"We support her. We make sure we're here for her. We keep an eye on her."

"You don't think she'll try anything stupid, do you?" Dani asked, thinking back to the suicides that had occurred through the winter months.

"I doubt it. Despite what she's going through, she has an extraordinary inner strength."

There was a pause before Dani spoke again. "You really love her, don't you?"

Phil thought for a moment. "Yes. I love both of you."

"But you don't think I'm special."

"That's not true. I've always thought you were special."

"You never say it though."

"Again, that's not true. I've told a number of people. Granted, it's always been in your absence, and it's been in a different context to how I use the word in regards to Callie, but nevertheless, don't let it be said that I never use that word when discussing you. In fact, it's probably the most common adjective I use when talking about you. That and gobby."

Dani play-punched Phil on his upper arm. "I'll get Zep to beat you up."

"How is Zep? I've not spoken to him in a while."

"He's okay. Winter really wasn't conducive to us going on long romantic walks and spending time together.

It's kind of hard to be close when you're stuck in a tiny house with eight other people."

"Who'd have thought the apocalypse and near annihilation of humankind could put such a crimp in someone's romantic life? Will the tragedies never end?"

"I don't know how Debbie and Matt put up with you. If I was your wife or your daughter, I think I'd have put a pillow over your face while you were sleeping."

"If you were my wife or my daughter, I'd have let you."

Dani laughed again. "And I really don't understand why Callie enjoys talking to you."

"You're her best friend, Dani. You always will be. But, sometimes, I dare say she needs conversation of a slightly more elevated nature."

Dani laughed again, and this time Phil did too. "Well. I think I've been insulted enough for one morning."

"Oh, really? That's a shame. If you change your mind, you know where to find me."

"To quote Cal, you are such an arse sometimes."

"Just sometimes?"

"Most of the time." She lingered for a few more seconds. "Thanks, Phil."

"For what?"

"For talking to me about Cal. It's not like I can talk to anyone about her in the house. You know what it's like."

"Jesus, don't I just. The second Bindi opens the doors to the great unwashed, I have to get the hell out of the place. Otherwise, I find out who's got rashes around their unmentionables and warts on their whatnots."

Dani laughed. "Sound tends to travel, doesn't it?"

"When you're living in houses the size of ours, it doesn't need to travel; it's just there."

"True."

"But anyway, you're more than welcome. Don't hesitate to come find me if you're worried about Callie or anything for that matter."

Dani smiled. "I didn't know you cared."

"If anybody asks, I'll deny it."

"Fair enough."

*

Woody sat down in one of the many plastic chairs in the stands of Infinity. Ricky, the nineteen-year-old son of Lisa, one of the founders of their bunker, sat with him.

"This is really something, isn't it?" Ricky said excitedly.

Infinity was usually buzzing when it was open, but today it was like a beehive with a constant, droning excited chatter.

"It is that, Ricky. It is that."

Usually, by eleven o'clock in the morning, Woody would have made a start on his first flask of potato peel vodka. He'd be merry, but at this moment, he felt anything but.

They had been greeted on the outskirts of town by a patrol of Salvation guards who had directed them to the register office just outside the ground. Woody had seen the insignia plenty of times, so there was no mistake about who they were. Here, he and Lisa had gone inside as the representatives from their trading party. It had been explained to them briefly how Infinity had undergone a change of management, and subsequently, the procedures were different, but ultimately, it was for the better and it would herald the beginning of a return to the old ways, the ways everyone knew and loved before the asteroid.

When pressed as to where Eric, Chloe and the others were, the friendly administrator simply shrugged her shoulders as if to say, "Way above my pay grade."

But there was something about the woman and the other officials surrounding her that told Woody they knew exactly where Eric was. When he asked about the goods he had stored in the stockroom that had been allocated to him, the official asked which room it was and then looked at a tablet and said, "Infinity has undergone an entire refit, and many of the rooms have been repurposed. As such, and with no means of being able to contact you, we initiated a compulsory purchase order of the items therein." She turned to one of the other administrators. "Bring me the package for storeroom three."

Woody and Lisa had remained in a state of bewilderment, not quite understanding what this was. He had asked, "What's going on here?"

The administrator smiled and said, "It will all become clear when you're inside." It was then that she'd handed him a thick envelope.

He'd opened it up to find a wad of money inside. The currency was all plastic. It was watermarked and printed in the same way money was before the asteroid. Rather than the Bank of England being emblazoned on top, it read the Bank of Salvation, and where the monarch's head had once been now hung three interconnecting rings, the Salvation symbol. "What am I supposed to do with this?" Woody had asked.

"It will all become clear when you're inside," the administrator had repeated.

Well, Woody had been inside for a night and a few hours, and it was all too clear. The day's trading had already ended by the time they got in, but complimentary food had been laid on and a classic film had been projected onto a white screen where the stage usually stood. People were in awe ... even Woody. It had been a long, long time since he had seen a movie.

The vast majority of the visitors had a great time, but as the night went on and their bent-over-backwards new hosts kept them fed and entertained, a sickening feeling began to rise in Woody. Callie, Phil and the others had told them about the administration and everything that went on in Salvation. The people who ran it were not good people; in fact, they were the very opposite of good people. Whatever they were doing here was not for altruistic purposes, and he felt sure that however they had come to take control of Infinity, it had not been through peaceful means.

"Do you think Dani and Callie will arrive tonight? I was hoping they'd be here by now. They must know it's open again. The weather's been getting better and better."

"No idea, Ricky." Normally, Woody was a chatty person. Normally, he would open up to his young friend, but there was something about this place and the patrolling guards that told him he should be on his guard, that he should watch what he said.

"I think I'm going to go grab another burger," Ricky announced excitedly. "I've already had one, but they're so good. Do you want me to get you one?"

"No thanks." No sooner had he said the words than the younger man disappeared.

In the short few months since they were last here, the stadium had been transformed. The trading area was significantly smaller, which didn't seem to bother most people. Rather than spend the day bartering and haggling, many traders just went to the weigh station and traded their goods in for the slick, shiny banknotes, hundreds of which currently filled Woody's pocket. He and his clan had set up their pitch first thing in the morning, as usual, but they'd barely had a handful of punters.

The administration had turned Infinity into a post-apocalyptic shopping mall. Bright stalls sold everything from new barrows to gardening equipment and other tools to clothes to food to everything in between. All the prices were clearly marked. There was no guessing or overbidding. Everything was simple and straightforward.

New shop units were going to be unveiled today, and that was a topic of hot conversation among the Infinity regulars. A few wondered about Eric and the others, but they didn't wonder long. This was like Disneyland or Vegas. This was a one-stop shop for everything they needed.

There was even a booth where people could apply for citizenship in Salvation. It guaranteed a home, food, power, entertainment and a living wage. Woody had noticed that there had been a constant stream of visitors since it opened first thing.

"Don't mind if I join you, do you?" Gina asked.

Woody was snapped from his thoughts as if being shaken from a deep sleep. "No. Go ahead," he replied, gesturing to the chair beside him. He wasn't a fan of Gina or many people in her trading party. They had started coming a couple of months before the winter shutdown, and there was just something about them that made Woody feel uneasy. He was a pretty good judge of character, so he trusted his instincts.

"This took me by surprise when I arrived here last night," she said.

"Yeah. You're not the only one."

"What do you make of it?"

For someone who had never exchanged much more than a few hellos and the odd chat about the weather, this seemed like a more involved question than normal. *Get over yourself, Woody; you're being paranoid.*

"It seems just like old times," Woody replied with a smirk.

"Ha. You've got that right. I didn't think I'd ever get to taste a sausage sandwich again, but one visit to the breakfast bar later and there it was in my hands. Don't get me wrong, I know the sausages are soya or pea protein or whatever, but they tasted like real meat, and the ketchup was just like the stuff I used to get at Q Burger. And it was only three Salvation dollars. It was a bargain at twice the price."

Woody's mouth started watering just thinking about it. He had eaten flatbread and jam for breakfast. They still had a good supply of preserves back at the bunker, and as grateful as they were for them, after all this time, having the same thing over and over got a little dull. "I didn't see you set up your pitch this morning," Woody said.

"No," Gina replied. "I didn't see the point. They're offering fair prices at the weigh station, so we just traded everything in for cash. All the store prices are more than reasonable, and it takes the guesswork out of things. We don't have to worry about making bad trades anymore."

"Hmm."

"Hmm what?"

"I'm just wondering, that's all."

"Wondering what?"

"What's a fair price?"

Gina looked at him, and for one split second, Woody could swear he saw her eyes narrow a little. *Was that a glare of hatred? Was it suspicion? Was there just too much sunlight in her eyes?*

She shrugged. "You make a good point, I suppose," she replied, casting her eyes back to the busy stands on the opposite side of the stadium. "For me, a fair price is getting enough money to buy what we want. This trip, we'll be going away with new tools, barrows, clothes, and plenty of tinned and dried food. And that's to say nothing of the peace of mind."

This woman sounds like a damned cheerleader for the place. Is she going to get her pom poms out and start dancing? "Peace of mind?"

"Yeah. If we have a bad harvest, at least we won't have to worry about starving. At least there's plenty of food available. At least it doesn't mean the end now."

Woody glanced back down to the field and his stall. There were a lot more people standing behind it than in front of it, and nothing was changing hands. "And how long do you think it's going to be before there's no more trading down there?"

Gina straightened up in her chair. "I suppose there'll be trading as long as it's needed. But to be honest, I think Salvation is being more than generous with its offers."

Woody sat for a moment longer. It was as if his mind was an old computer slowly processing everything. Finally, he reached into his pocket for a larger silver hip flask. He unscrewed the top and offered it to Gina. "Fancy a tipple?"

"It's a little early, isn't it?"

"Suit yourself," he replied, taking a healthy gulp. "I think you might be right." He wiped his mouth.

"About what?"

"About all of it. I think we're entering a new age."

Gina smiled and nodded. "Yeah. I really think we are," she said, plucking the flask out of Woody's hand and taking a drink herself for no other reason than to imitate camaraderie.

"Good talk, Gina," he said, climbing to his feet. "I think we might take our gear to the weigh station after all and see what these bright shiny shops have to offer."

9

Susan, Callie and several others were all waiting patiently by the ovens for Drake and Marina. Becka had come up with an idea for how to find out what was going on at Infinity. Drake had taken it to his people, and now they were going to find out if it would get the go-ahead.

Over two weeks had passed since what had been deemed the end of winter, but there were a few who still weren't convinced it was over.

"And it definitely happened like this last year?" Callie asked. "Freezing temperatures, freezing temperatures, freezing temperatures, and then bam, it's noticeably warmer, and winter's over."

Rommy laughed. "Yeah. I'm sure you've noticed that the weather isn't like what it used to be."

"I know, but it feels like…."

"Like somebody's going to pull the rug from beneath our feet and all of a sudden we're going to be waist-deep in another blizzard?"

The others all laughed. "Exactly," Callie replied. Since her chat with Phil, she had begun to feel a little better. Her morning runs with Si had helped no end, and this idea of Becka's had lit a tiny flame of hope inside her that maybe Infinity wasn't a lost cause. Maybe they could find a way to win it back. They'd need information though. Information was power, and this idea would give them a foundation at least.

Drake and Marina finally arrived, and PJ was with them. His appearance was more than a little surprising to the others, but when Drake didn't explain himself and when he suggested they adjourn to Susan's house, everybody followed.

There was no fire burning. It was not exactly hot, but compared to the temperatures of a couple of weeks earlier, it seemed positively balmy. The shutters were open, and the sheets and curtains that provided the walls for the cubicles had all been taken down for the day, so there was plenty of light for people to see one another as they took their positions on one of the logs.

"We're just waiting for a moment," Drake said.

"What for?" asked Susan.

"Greenslade and Trunk."

"What have they got to do with this?"

"You'll see when they get here.'"

"I don't understand what's going on. I thought we were here to get the yay or nay on Becka's idea."

"We are," Drake replied. He had been a different man since Chloe's arrival. The news that Salvation was in the ascendency had first made him feel sick to his stomach then driven him to a dark place. Like Callie, he had struggled, and it had been Marina and his wife who had protected him and supported him. Like everyone else in Redemption, he had felt powerless, and the hopelessness of the situation had ground him down. The standoffishness that he had worn like a protective cloak still shielded him, but, like Callie, Becka's idea had spurred him on a little.

Greenslade and Trunk arrived through the door, and after a few nods and hellos, they took seats at opposite ends of the loose semicircle.

"For Greenslade, Trunk and anyone else who hasn't heard your idea, Becka, could you give us a potted version?" Drake asked.

"Well … yeah. It's simple really. We do what those Salvation bastards did. We pose as newcomers from another settlement that's previously never visited Infinity. We gather as much information as we possibly can. The more we know about them and their operation the better equipped we'll be to move forward."

There was a pause for a moment before Greenslade spoke. "The problem with that is that there'll probably be more than a few people there who recognise us. The second that happens, it's game over."

"We don't send anyone who's been to Infinity before."

"That's a bit of a tough ask. Most of us have been at one time or another."

"That's not the case for our people," Rommy said. "There are probably a hundred and fifty, two hundred maybe who've never set foot in the place."

"And they'd be willing to do this?"

"I know my people," Rommy replied. "I'm pretty certain they want to help however they can. Becka's and Ashraf's will be the same. It shouldn't be too hard getting a trading party together."

"PJ?" Drake asked, and all eyes turned to the computer wizard, who suddenly looked as uncomfortable as ever, chewing the end of his thumb nervously before realising he was the focus of attention.

He sniffed loudly and winced before answering. Like Drake, like Callie, like so many others, the knowledge of what had happened at Infinity weighed heavy on him. Heavier than most, in fact, because he knew that he was responsible for a lot of the technology that had been used.

For a long time, he was a loyal administration dog who did his tricks and sat in eager anticipation of a well-earned treat. Back then, he never thought of the human cost. He was only interested in finding out the bounds of his own genius. It was all a game to him. Then, one day, he accessed footage from one of the interrogation rooms and he realised nothing was theoretical, nothing was a game. He suddenly understood what the administration was and how everything he had done had in some way been responsible for the suffering and oppression of others.

He sniffed again and then turned towards Becka and then to Drake. "It's a risk."

"Why?" Becka demanded. "Why is it a risk if none of the people have been there before?"

PJ twitched a little before taking a deep breath. "How many of your people have been to Infinity? I don't just mean your people; I mean all the Wanderers."

"I don't know," Becka replied. "Maybe a hundred. Maybe more."

"And if you spoke to every one of them, do you think they could recall all the conversations they'd had while ever they were there?"

"Well … no, of course not, but what's that got to do with anything?"

"It's got everything to do with everything. Let's take you, for example. Maybe the last time you went, you talked about how Hansel, your neighbour, or Gretel, your friend, made a great soup last night or found more strawberries when they were out foraging or whatever."

"I really don't see where you're going with this."

"And that's the problem. Through a very innocent and easily forgettable conversation, suddenly Hansel and Gretel are on the database. Your conversation will have been processed and referenced. Everybody, every place, everything you talked about during any of your visits to Infinity might be there ready to call up. The same goes for anyone who's visited the place."

"But if we're only sending people who haven't gone before, then what's the risk?"

"How do we know their names will never have been spoken by the others? How do we know that none of their physical attributes have never been described? They may never have been to the place before, but that's not to say they're not on Salvation's database, and I can guarantee that any newcomers would be put under the microscope."

"You can't know that."

"I really can."

"How?"

"Because PJ and his ilk used to spy on us," Callie said. "And they were really, really good at it."

"Yeah," PJ agreed sadly.

"So, you're saying this is a no-go?" Drake replied.

"It sounds like it, doesn't it?" Becka answered and suddenly deflated as if all the air had left her body. The atmosphere in the room became heavy as others shared in her disappointment.

"Not necessarily," PJ said, and all eyes were on him once more.

"What are you talking about, PJ?" Marina asked.

"Well, we use some of the tricks that Salvation will have used."

"Like what?"

"Every man and woman who went to Infinity would have been coached. They'll have been coached not to let anything slip. They'll have been coached not to act suspiciously; they'll have been coached in what to look for and what to do."

"Okay," Rommy said, leaning forward again. "But that doesn't help us with respect to what you've just said. We might have accidentally talked about them on our previous trips. They might be on the database, and if the administration is going to be putting all newcomers under a microscope, as you suggest, that's not going to solve that problem."

"So, nobody uses their real names," PJ replied. "Nobody talks about any of the people here."

"But what if something slips? What if somebody accidentally talks about the journey or the geography of the place?"

"You do understand the concept behind coaching, don't you?" PJ didn't mean it to sound as condescending as it did, but suddenly a smile was back on Drake's face.

"So, let me get this straight," Greenslade said. "We take a hundred or so people who've never been to Infinity. We give them new names and a fictitious backstory since the asteroid struck. Then—"

"No. You give them a completely different backstory, full stop," PJ replied.

"Why?"

"Haven't you been listening to anything I said?"

There was a time when Greenslade would have risen from his seat, grabbed hold of PJ by the scruff of his neck and beaten him into unconsciousness for talking to him in such a dismissive manner, but that time had gone. Greenslade thought for a moment, and then it dawned on him. "Hansel and Gretel."

"Exactly."

"Okay. You're going to have to explain this to me," Becka replied.

"Because Hansel might have been a skydiver and Gretel might have been a taxidermist or a Channel swimmer or a Commonwealth Games heptathlete. Something might have been mentioned in passing by any of the people who've been to Infinity about the pasts of any of the people who stayed at home. All it would need is that one unusual detail that was just a small fragment of a conversation to raise suspicions."

"Shit. This is real next-level stuff, isn't it?"

"So, how do we do this, PJ?" Marina asked.

"Don't ask me. I'm not an acting coach. I'd suggest you select the people who'll be going then get a team to work with them to develop their backstories. Don't make them too difficult. Make sure their new names fit them, etc."

"What do you mean fit them?"

"Well, you're not going to get someone from a poverty-stricken ex-mining village with a double-barrelled surname like Fortescue-Smythe, are you?"

Laughter rippled around the room. Despite the mountain of work that lay ahead, they suddenly had purpose again.

"Thank you, PJ," Drake said, still smiling.

"Oh, and we'll need a different route too."

"Why?" Marina asked.

"Because it wouldn't surprise me if they've got roving patrols out searching for a trading party coming from this neck of the woods."

"You make a good point."

"I trust we can come to you if we have any queries," Rommy asked.

"You can, but I'm going to be busy."

"Doing what?"

"Well, I did say that those mobile phones would come in handy someday. We might not have Salvation's processing power, but we'll be able to glean some information from them."

"It won't take the Salvation guards long to figure out who we are if we go around taking photos of the inside of Infinity," Susan said.

PJ resisted the temptation to be sarcastic and instead let out a long sigh. "I'm going to adapt as many as I can in the time I have and with the materials I have. Which sadly won't be many, but some are better than none. The cameras will be hidden in clothing, attached to the phones via optic cables."

Drake looked towards Becka, Rommy and Susan. "I can trust you to select the candidates and manage the coaching?"

"Of course," Susan replied.

"Good."

"What are you going to be doing?"

"I'll be figuring out how to engage a far greater and better-equipped force if it all goes tits up."

∗

It was the first time Bucks and Paris had left Salvation since the asteroid strike. There were over three hundred in their convoy. Many of Danko's people who had not become a part of the trading party had been trained by the guards. They were a kind of unofficial militia. On the outside, necessity had made them efficient fighters, so they were easy to mould.

Even though there was an artificial sky on Level One, the real sky seemed a thousand times more magnificent. They had set off in the middle of the night, unconcerned about Ferals or any kind of potential raiders. Word had spread how Salvation offered ... well ... salvation for those that were displaced. It didn't matter what you had done in your past; if you were prepared to work for the administration, if you pledged loyalty, you would be rewarded with food, a roof, warmth and a wage.

The population in the bunker was growing all the time, which solved more problems than it created. Gradually, the children and teenagers on Level Two started to have lessons once more. Some of the sedentary workers returned to their desks, leaving behind the more manual jobs they had been conscripted to in Recycling, the farms and Fabrication. They were not quite there yet, but it was obvious that things were beginning to return to normal. There had been severe food shortages shortly after the grand reopening of Infinity as many supplies were sent down there to wow the traders and convince them that a new day had dawned.

These were alleviated quickly by the pre-planned planting of fast-growing crops. The range in the Salmarts was grim for a while unless you really liked kale, courgettes, spinach, chard and beets. But it was only short-term as the raw materials were quickly processed using small reserves of textured protein to create burgers and sausages and a dozen other convenience foods that contained cancer-causing chemicals but tasted so, so good.

Of course, things on Level Three were very different. For those who had lived from meal to meal on the outside, it seemed like a luxury. For those who valued their freedom, it felt like a prison. Many had barely scraped through winter, wondering if they could get slightly ahead in the warmer months so as not to suffer the same hardship the following year. When they saw the booth at Infinity guaranteeing food, shelter and warmth, they felt it was too good an opportunity to pass up despite what they had heard, sometimes second-hand, sometimes firsthand, about the place. But now they all understood.

The inner conflicts of some of the new citizens on Level Three were Bucks' last considerations, however. All his plans were coming to fruition with staggering success.

When he and Paris entered Infinity for the first time, a wave of excitement rushed through them both. They had watched hundreds of videos. They knew where each of the shops were, what they sold, and who tended them. But the true atmosphere of the place could never be conveyed through a video screen. They stepped out onto the field with their entourage and stood like children in the middle of the most spectacular circus ever to have existed.

"It's more beautiful than I imagined," Bucks said.

It was garish, bright, and noisy, and the smell of highly processed fast food made his stomach turn, but it was everything he could have hoped for and more. They had opened a tavern at one end of the ground and a restaurant at the other, and as he had predicted all those months ago, not a single pitch remained on the field. Nobody was interested in bartering anymore. Nobody wanted to go through the rigmarole of setting up a stall and spending the day on their feet haggling like some peasant on the streets of Marrakesh.

The giant whiteboard positioned next to the opposite entrance was now the only thing that mattered. That provided the list of materials that were particularly sought by Salvation. Copper, steel, tin, zinc, or anything that contained them had a value. In fact, most things had a value, but they were on a sliding scale and one that was nowhere near as generous as it had been when the new, improved Infinity re-opened.

They had already gleaned enough materials from the willing traders in Salvation to manufacture enough Q-Eighteens and Q-Thirties to account for all the ones taken by Drake. But Bucks wanted more. He wanted more guns, more bullets, more people for his army. He wanted his administration to become the only force that mattered, the only governing body in the UK, and he knew at some stage that would mean dealing with the Ark, the bunker in the Cairngorms, but that was some way off yet.

His plan had only just begun, and today was about enjoying his creation in all its vulgar, insidious splendour. Bucks proceeded with Paris and their personal guards further onto the field while others in the party dispersed, keen to experience some of the delights that the traders were enjoying. Everything was bought using credits in Salvation, so each member of the party had been given an allowance of Salvation dollars to partake in the stadium's facilities.

A figure stumbled into their path, and two bodyguards immediately withdrew their Q-Eighteens, aiming them at the man.

"Woah," he said, raising his hands immediately. One of them contained a hip flask, and Bucks had seen enough footage to know who this was.

He placed his hand on one of the guard's arms. "It's alright. Lower your weapons. I don't think this gent intends us any harm."

"My ap-apologies," Woody said, bowing in front of the slimmed-down group. "I might have had one or two too many at that fine establishment over there." He pointed across to the tavern.

"And why not?" Bucks replied with a grin on his face.

"I haven't seen you here before," Woody continued, staggering a little as he focused on the other man.

"No. First-time visitor."

"Ah, well. Don't you worry. They look after you here, and if you need any help, you just come and ask Woody. I'll steer you right."

"Thank you. That's very kind," Bucks replied before continuing across the field.

Woody just stood there, watching them go. The truth was he had barely touched a drop of alcohol since the reopening of Infinity. Unlike the vast majority, he understood what this was. Unlike the vast majority, he knew that the end was coming for their way of life.

Bucks, Paris and the others continued revelling in all the sights and sounds. The area around the tavern was particularly noisy, and the boisterous and good-humoured nature of the vast majority of Infinity's patrons highlighted the fact that they didn't understand what was happening.

Bucks came to a stop at the giant whiteboard. A pair of stepladders stood by it, ready for any updates. He and Paris stood back, and they both smiled. The initial buy prices when Infinity had reopened had been deliberately generous. They had wanted to make the patrons believe they were far better off selling directly to Salvation than trading. Now the buy prices had fallen considerably.

Bucks pulled a piece of paper from his pocket. It was one of the sheets he'd had on his desk the day Paris had stared at him like a madman. On it was a list of materials with figures by the side.

- Copper – $22 per kilogram
- Brass – $15 per kilogram
- Potassium nitrate fertiliser – $15 per kilogram
- Ammonium nitrate fertiliser – $15 per kilogram
- Steel – $12 per kilogram

- Iron – $8 per kilogram
- Plastic – $1.50 per kilogram
- Mixed textiles – $1.50 per kilogram

There were thirty or forty more categories on his sheet and subsequently on the board, and if what someone had wasn't featured, a member of the weighing staff would give them a price. In the early days, nothing was turned away, and this contributed to the Infinity users buying into the whole concept.

His eyes flicked from the paper to the sheet and back again, over and over.

- Potassium nitrate fertiliser – $15 per kilogram
- Ammonium nitrate fertiliser – $15 per kilogram
- Copper – $12 per kilogram
- Brass – $8 per kilogram
- Steel – $6 per kilogram
- Iron – $3 per kilogram
- Plastic – $0.50 per kilogram
- Mixed textiles – $0.50 per kilogram

Some of the prices had been reduced by half and some by as much as two-thirds. It had all happened in increments, and if anyone asked, they were told that the prices were governed by current manufacturing requirements and they could bounce back in response to end-product buying trends at any time. Of course, they never would. They would just get lower and lower, and by that time, it would be too late for the patrons of Infinity to do anything about it. They would be glued to Salvation's teat, desperate for whatever nourishment it could provide.

In addition, when the newly opened Infinity had first begun trading, other generous allowances were made, such as insulation being included in the overall weight for copper wiring and the plastic handles of stainless-steel cutlery contributing to the final buy price. Within a couple of weeks, this was no longer the case, but many patrons were still cash rich from their original sales, and so what if they were getting a little less for their wares now? it didn't matter. There would be good weeks and bad weeks. That's how businesses worked.

Bucks folded the piece of paper and placed it back in his pocket before looking around the stadium once more.

"Tell me," he began, "how many people have decided to become fully fledged citizens of Salvation since we reopened?"

"Just over five hundred, sir," Paris replied. "That's just from here, of course. The figure's closer to eleven hundred if we include all the displaced that our patrols have found."

Bucks nodded slowly as his eyes were drawn to the Salvation citizenship booth and the line of applicants. "You see, Paris. If you immediately rip away everything someone has, they'll consider you a monster. If you do it by stealth, and they're too dim to understand what's happening, they'll believe you're their saviour."

"Yes, sir," Paris agreed.

Bucks turned once more, and this time, his eyes focused on the seed store. The crowd in front of it was four deep. "It looks like everyone fancies themselves as horticulturalists these days."

"Yes, sir."

"Tell me, are we still using a sixty-forty ratio?"

"Yes, sir. It's on your orders, sir; we can ramp it up at any time."

"No. This is good for the moment. If no saplings appear, they're going to believe they've been sold duds. If a few appear, then the others will just seem to be late bloomers."

To someone not in the know, this conversation would seem cryptic at best, but to Bucks and Paris, it made perfect sense. Bucks' plans for Infinity were multi-fold. On the one hand, it was a valuable source of raw materials in the short term. It was also their best chance of luring Trainor, Drake and the others out into the open without them having to go look. But the long-term plan was to make all the patrons of Infinity Salvation citizens. Many would go to work in the plants and farms of Salvation. The talented ones like Woody and his ilk who took the extra risks and dug deep into the heart of towns and cities to find the most valuable materials would become scavengers, not for themselves but for the administration. They would be rewarded commensurately, and those gains could be spent within Salvation. After all, by that time, there'd be nothing to buy on the outside. All trade would have ceased, and Infinity would be nothing but one giant recruitment centre.

Bucks would be able to build not just an army of workers but a proper army ready to vanquish any foes, whoever they were. Part of that grand plan demanded that the free citizens who came and went from Infinity became utterly dependent on the administration for their survival. And what better way to do that than by making sure their harvests were failures? To this end, the chem lab treated multiple consignments of seeds to make them sterile. These were mixed at a sixty-forty ratio with fruitful seeds so as not to arouse too many suspicions at once.

"Sir," Carlisle said, walking up to greet the party. "I didn't know you were coming."

"The first minister doesn't have to make you aware of his movements," Paris replied.

"Of course. I'm sorry. I just meant that I would have made sure you had a proper greeting if I knew."

"I wanted to see what the place was like firsthand. Surprise visits are always the best way to do that."

"Err ... yes. I suppose they are, sir. I'm afraid we haven't had time to—"

Bucks put his hand up to stop him in mid-sentence. "You've done an excellent job here, Carlisle."

"It's a team effort, sir."

"Yes. Of course it is." He suddenly caught sight of Hogarth, still posing as an Infinity patron, still hiding in plain sight.

"You must be exhausted from your journey, sir. Could I offer you some refreshments?"

Bucks looked at him and smiled for a moment before turning three hundred and sixty degrees. When he looked back towards Carlisle, the smile had become a wide grin. "Yes. Yes, I'd like that very much."

10

Eric winced a little as he reached out and plucked a few more strawberries before dropping them in the punnet. From everything he'd learned, these would be going to Level One. A few punnets might make it to Level Two, but things were still in a state of upheaval there.

"Heads up. The Gestapo are on their rounds," the harvester next to him whispered.

Eric glanced down from the elevated platform he was on to see a Salvation guard with his Q-Thirty firmly in hand heading along the aisle towards them. This was nothing unusual. He had gone from being a free man, doing his best to help build a better society, to a prisoner. It beat the alternative though. Not just he but his family and the occupants of the other bunkers they owned had been brought to Salvation too. But for a small rucksack of clothes and personal possessions, all other materials in the bunkers were seized by the administration. Trying to fight back would have been futile.

They were vastly outnumbered and outgunned, and the Salvation guards were notoriously vicious. The first few days were the worst. He was drilled for information. They all were. They were drugged, and often bodily harm was threatened to a friend or loved one to get to the truth.

Eventually, however, they were sent down to Level Three and allocated jobs. Life down there was like something out of a horror novel. He had been with his father and a few others in the market square the night before and a fight had broken out. He'd tried to intervene and got slashed by a blade across his shoulder for his trouble. Kendall Marks, the doctor who shared duties at Infinity with Nazya, was now his next-door neighbour, and he did his best to patch him up with a torn strip of bed linen, but it still hurt every time he reached out and probably would for some time to come.

"Thanks for the warning," Eric replied under his breath, turning back to the shelf of strawberries as if he hadn't even cast eyes on the armed guard.

When the black-clad enforcer was gone, the other man spoke again. "I used to see you quite a bit at Infinity. I was with Melanie's crew. I'm Baz. You're Eric, aren't you?"

He turned to look at Baz. He made a point of not trusting anyone other than his family and friends. They could be a plant. They could have motives he'd not even thought of. "That's right."

"We get paid again tomorrow, don't we?"

"I lose track of the days in here, but very possibly."

"Not that there's anything to spend it on. The last time I went to the Salmart, the only fresh veg they had there was chard. I mean … chard, for Christ's sake. I hadn't even heard of it until I came here."

Eric chuckled as he thought back to the first time Phil had brought him a sack full. "Yeah. I can't say it's one of my favourites, but it fills a hole, I suppose."

"You hear about the trouble in the market square again last night?"

Eric glanced up and down the giant aisle once more. There were dozens of workers on identical elevated platforms but currently no more guards. "Yeah. Every day there seems to be more trouble."

"Well, what do you expect? They bring Ferals in here to live with the rest of us. Jesus, I mean, we lost people to those bastards. Some of them are cannibals, for Christ's sake. How can anybody think you can just integrate them into the population and everything will be hunky dory?"

"There are plenty who are trying to fit in," Eric replied.

"Yeah. And there are plenty who are still feral if you ask me."

"Everybody should be given the same chance. If they misbehave, they should be dealt with accordingly."

"Yeah, well. In my humble opinion, it's just asking for trouble bringing that type in here to mix with the rest of us. The administration must have a collective screw loose to think it will work."

Eric shrugged. "It seems to be working at the moment. They've got a cheap labour force, haven't they? A bit of trouble on Level Three isn't really a great hardship for them."

"I suppose. 'Ere. How's your daughter getting on? Colleen, isn't it?"

Eric stiffened up a little, but not so much that the other man could notice. *He's been friendly. He's been critical of the administration. Was that all to get me on the side so I'd open up? Is he a plant?* "Chloe. It's Chloe."

"Chloe. That's right. How's she doing?"

"Well, I hope. I haven't seen her since the day I was captured."

"How come?"

"Well, they took me and they didn't take her. I've got no idea what happened; I'm just hoping she's safe somewhere."

"Maybe she made it back to your bunker."

Eric studied the other man for a moment before returning to the strawberries. "They abducted the rest of my family and friends from the bunker, so I doubt that."

"So, where do you think she went?"

Yeah. He's a plant. Bastard. "I have no idea. I just hope she's safe."

The other man paused for a moment and half a smile appeared on his face as if he understood that Eric had figured out what he was doing. "Yeah. Let's hope," he replied before getting back to his harvesting duties.

This is what it's going to be like from now on. This is my life. I really hope you made it to Redemption, Chloe. I really do.

*

Callie had made a lot of progress in the last week. The exercise was helping. The longer, warmer days and exposure to the sun were increasing her serotonin levels and making her feel better. All those close to her had continued to be supportive and nurturing, and there were plenty of signs that she was getting back to her old self.

Ebba and her team had been manning the ovens all day. A vast seaweed harvest had been brought in first thing in the morning, and ever since, they had been drying out sugar kelp as if their lives depended on it. They still had a decent supply in storage, but there was nothing like warm, crisp sugar kelp straight from the oven. A long line of people who had finished their afternoon's work waited patiently to get their hands on some for themselves and their families as a tasty pre-dinner snack. What was left over would be allowed to cool and wrapped in the industrial cellophane that they had used for the winter stores.

"So, how are things going with your pupils?" Phil asked as he joined Callie, Dani, Tania and Harper in the line.

"I don't want to talk about it," Tania said.

"Yeah. That goes double for me," Harper added.

"Triple for me," said Dani.

"Oh, come on. It can't be that bad," Phil replied, turning to Callie.

"Ha." She shook her head. "You have no idea."

"But you've been at it for over a week."

"Thanks for telling me, Phil. Having been there for every excruciating minute, I wouldn't have known otherwise."

"What's been going on that's so bad?"

"We were doing roleplaying today."

"Okay. That's sensible."

"Isn't it just?"

"So what's got the four of you so flustered?"

"I'll tell you what's got us so flustered," Tania replied, not giving Callie a chance. "Within three minutes … three bloody minutes, somebody mentioned you."

A smile cracked on Phil's face. "I'm guessing you pointed that out to them?"

"Too bloody right I pointed that out to them. She went on to call the woman next to her by her real name, then later in the conversation actually named Redemption as her home." Phil laughed. "It's not bloody funny."

"Sorry."

"That was all in the first ten minutes of us starting today."

"Surely it couldn't have got any worse."

"Don't you believe it," Callie replied. "The guy I was roleplaying with actually had a cut on his arm. I said to him that it looked really nasty and he should get it seen, to which he replied, 'Nazya put some antiseptic cream on it and said it was nothing to worry about.'" Phil laughed again. "It's not bloody funny," she snapped, echoing Tania's earlier sentiment.

"Well … it is kind of."

"No, it's not, Phil. If they do this at Infinity, it will be disastrous. It'll all be over before it's even begun."

"Salvation managed to infiltrate Infinity without too many problems. I'm sure we'll be able to as well."

"You're forgetting that it didn't matter if the people from Salvation made a small faux pas. There wasn't a massive database of information that someone could cross-reference it with at the push of a button. If our people screw up, that's it. Game over. The entire party will be rounded up. Do you really want a hundred Redemption inhabitants being tortured for information? Can you imagine what they'd give Bucks and his cronies whether they meant to or not?"

"Well … when you put it like that, I don't suppose it's very funny."

"What's not funny?" Matt asked as he and Debbie joined them.

"Your father was just commenting on how amusing it was that our prospective Infinity infiltrators are crashing and burning in quite a spectacular fashion," Tanya said.

"Phil!" Debbie snapped. "Do you have any idea how important this is?"

Phil's shoulders drooped. "I'm not saying the situation is funny per se, but certain aspects of it are quite funny."

"Like what exactly?" Debbie asked, folding her arms.

Phil sighed deeply, realising there was no good way forward with the conversation. "I take it back. It's not funny. It's not funny at all."

Debbie nodded. "That's better."

"It makes my life so much easier when you decide for me what I find funny and what I don't."

"I'm your wife. That's my job." The others all laughed before Debbie turned to Tania. "Is it really as bad as all that?"

Tania exhaled deeply. "Yesterday was a much better day."

"How so?"

"All day, there might have been just three or four slips. We were going at it from first thing in the morning to last thing at night, and that was it. Today, we had that many in the first few minutes."

"Perhaps they were just having an off day."

"But that's it. Don't you get it? They can't have off days. They can't have off minutes. They can't have off seconds. If PJ is to be believed, and I've got no reason to doubt him, one slip and it's all over."

"You're right, of course."

"This is one occasion when I wish I wasn't."

"So, what are you going to do?"

"What can we do? We'll start all over again tomorrow and hope they have a better day than today. And hope the day after that is better still." Tania shook her head sadly. "I don't know why I volunteered to do this. I'm much better with kids than I am with adults."

"Who is looking after all the urchins while you're playing head coach?" Phil asked.

"Greta, Penny and Michelle."

"Michelle?"

"Yeah. She's great with the children."

"As long as she's not giving them swimming lessons."

Debbie punched Phil on the arm. "That's not funny."

"Oh, come on. It was a bit funny."

"No, it wasn't."

Phil sighed. "Fair enough."

"Oh shit, what now?" Callie asked, and they all turned to the brow of the hill to see one of the lookouts running down towards the settlement. By the time he had reached the farm and found Drake and Susan, a much larger crowd had gathered around.

"There's somebody coming," the lookout said.

"How many?" demanded Drake.

"One."

"One?"

"We spotted them with the binoculars."

"Okay. I'll be up in a minute. Return to your post."

The lookout did an immediate about-face and set off once more, a lot slower this time, not looking forward to the steep climb in front of him.

"What do you think?" Susan asked. A slightly bigger crowd had gathered around them now, and normally, this would be a discussion they'd have in private rather than public, but time was of the essence.

"I think we don't know anything until they get here," Drake replied.

"What's going on?" Greenslade asked as he, Trunk and their families joined the rest of the growing crowd.

"There's a single person heading towards us," Callie replied.

"A messenger?" He asked the question that was going through everyone's head. *Is this the administration coming to give their ultimatum?*

"We don't know anything at the moment. I'm heading up there now," Drake said.

"We'll come with you," Greenslade replied.

In the end, over a dozen Redemption citizens made the climb to the top of the ridge. By that time, the figure had come into focus, and when Drake took the binoculars, he immediately identified the lone traveller as Woody.

"Woody?" Callie asked.

"Yeah. It's definitely him." He handed the glasses over to her, and she focused on the visitor.

"Yep. That's definitely Woody."

"But what's he doing here?" Greenslade asked.

"I dare say we're about to find out."

Their friend was greeted with open arms. He told them how he'd been on the road for two days, dodging the odd band of Ferals, sometimes having to retrace his tracks when he came to an impassible section of road. He was given food and water; then he was taken down to the stream to freshen up before finally being guided into Susan's house.

Normally by this time, the curtained cubicles would have been in place, but for the moment, it was all just one wide open space. An extra trunk had been dragged in, and on it sat Woody, looking worn out but seemingly possessing a purpose that none of them thought him capable of.

"Okay," Susan began. "Woody's given us a little heads-up as to why he's here, but I think it's important that you all hear it from him."

Their friend from Infinity went on to give them an account of everything he had witnessed since it had reopened. He was clearly jaded, but at the same time, he was determined. When he was done, he sat back a little. By this time, the shutter and door had been closed, and several lanterns illuminated the inside of the house. It was clear to everyone present that telling this tale had been traumatic for him. A film of tears coated his eyes, and as he took a much-needed drink of tea, one of them trickled down his cheek.

The silence after his words dragged on for the best part of a minute as people processed what they had heard. Chloe and Nazya had been invited to join the extended council, and they were equally horrified.

"And what do your people think about what's going on there, Woody?" Phil asked.

He took another sip of tea before answering. "At first, they thought this might be a good thing, especially the younger ones. I mean, we were in a position like nobody else. We'd been paid off for all the stuff we still had in the storeroom, and generously too. We tried to trade that first day, but nobody was really interested, so we went to the weigh station and cashed in. Again, we were paid well. We bought fast food from their outlets, and we bought dried and tinned food from their market. We even bought some of their tools. They were all new, straight off the production line. It was like they had a top twenty of the most traded items at Infinity, and they were all there, shining brightly, just waiting to be picked off the shelves."

"What about Dad?" Chloe asked. "What about us? Weren't people bothered that we'd mysteriously vanished?"

"I was, flower. And so were a few others. And the administration must definitely have been bothered. They went around putting padlocks on every internal door, locking the place down. But whenever we asked any questions, it was a case of 'Sorry mate, I just work here; I've got no idea about any of that.' It was impossible to get any answers."

Chloe's head dropped, and Nazya placed an arm around her friend. "So they're actually using cash? I mean physical notes?" Phil asked, still a little bewildered by everything he'd heard.

"Ha. Yeah. Here you go," Woody replied, reaching into his pocket and handing out a few of the Salvation dollars for people to take a look at.

"And there's no more trading?" Callie asked.

"Oh, there's plenty of trading. Just not between settlements anymore. Everything's just cashed in at the weigh station."

"And people don't see what's happening?"

"For the first couple of weeks, they really inflated the buy prices. Anyone who went to Infinity during that time would have been mad not to accept what they were offering. The food they were selling in their market was cheap. Everything they were selling was cheap. They sold the idea that this was the dawn of a new age and things were going to start getting better for everyone. You were drowning in cash if you visited Infinity in those first weeks. Most people believed there was no reason to think that things wouldn't just get better and better."

"And that's when they pulled the rug out," Nicola said.

"That's right. Anybody with a brain and anybody who'd listened to you talk about what Salvation was like would understand. But the rest of them just walked into it blindly."

"Walked into what?" Debbie asked.

"The prices in the shops and the tavern and the burger bar and the rest of it started going up while the trade-in prices started going down. It was subtle at first, but then it became more and more obvious. They came up with excuse after excuse. It was due to tooling problems at their fabrication plant, and it was only temporary until they worked through the backlog. Then they said it was due to reduced demand, then something else, then something else. But the prices on the whiteboard just kept dropping."

"The whiteboard?" Greenslade asked.

"Yeah. They've got this giant whiteboard that gives the dollar per kilogram value for materials."

"What kind of materials?"

"What you'd expect for what they were manufacturing and growing. Metals, plastics, fertiliser, that kind of thing."

"And how much—"

"Fertiliser?" Phil asked, interrupting Greenslade.

"Yeah. Um … potassium or ammonium or something or other."

"Potassium nitrate and ammonium nitrate?"

"That's the stuff. It's the only thing on the board that's kept its value too. Not that anyone has any of it."

"That doesn't make sense."

"Why, Phil?" Callie asked.

"Because that's not something we'd use in hydroponics."

"Maybe they're thinking ahead to when they start the settlement in the north."

Phil looked at Callie thoughtfully for a moment, but when he replied, his voice was distant. "Perhaps. But they already have tonnes of the stuff at the storage bunker for the new settlement."

Drake locked eyes with Phil, and a certainty passed between them before the former Salvation guard continued the questioning. "What metals are on the whiteboard, Woody?"

Woody shrugged. "All sorts. Copper, brass, steel, iron. But that being said, I've never seen them turn any metals down. They must have tonnes of the stuff, and it's weird because the vast majority of what they produce doesn't really use metal that much. I mean, sure, the frames of the barrows and the spade heads, fork heads and so on. But most stuff is plastic or composite."

Drake and Phil shared another knowing glance. "Okay, you two," Susan said. "I've known you both long enough to figure out when something's not right. What's going on?"

"They're arming themselves," Phil said.

"What do you mean?"

"They're making munitions."

"How can you be sure?"

"It's the only thing that makes sense with the fertiliser."

"But ... don't you need other stuff?" Callie asked. "I mean sulphur and things like that. And it's not like there's a ready supply available, is it? Are you sure they couldn't just be planning ahead?"

"They don't need sulphur," Drake replied. "They don't use gunpowder; they use gun cotton."

"What's gun cotton?"

"Nitrocellulose. The chem lab manufactures it. Potassium nitrate is the main ingredient in the smoke grenades we sometimes used in Salvation, and ammonium nitrate can be used to make other explosives."

"So, they're coming for us?" Susan asked.

"When they're ready, I'd say there's nothing surer."

It was suddenly as if all the air had been sucked out of the room, and nobody spoke for some time. When they did, it was Callie. "Is there anything else you can tell us, Woody?"

"Like what?"

"Like anything. Anything that you think is important."

"Well, they seem to be recruiting more people every week."

"Recruiting? What do you mean?"

"I mean there's a Salvation citizenship booth. You can become a Salvation citizen and never have to worry about knowing where your next meal comes from or what next winter will be like. You can live in the bunker. You'll be given a paying job and an apartment."

"Huh! We all know how that turns out," Nicola said bitterly.

Woody nodded. "The thing is winter was hard for a lot of people. They barely got through it."

"When you're at your lowest rung, it's easy to believe in fairy tales," Callie said. "Anything else. Is there anything else?"

"Well, I think they've got people undercover there."

"Undercover?"

"Yeah. There's this woman, Gina, and—"

"Gina," Chloe said. "She's still there? She was the one who took my dad."

Woody let out a huff of a laugh. "Well, that makes a lot of sense. Yes, she and her people are still there. They mix with the rest of us, but there's always been something I didn't like about her."

"No wonder they were able to take the place so easily. They must have gathered a tonne of information," Callie replied.

"We're finished, aren't we?" Woody said sadly.

"Nobody knows you came here," Susan replied. "You can go back to your people, and there's no need for any—"

"No, I mean humankind. If it's not Bucks, it'll be somebody like him. There'll always be some greedy, power-crazed bastard who isn't interested in anything but total control."

"That's the way it's always been, Woody," Phil replied.

The other man let out a long, sad sigh. "I suppose."

"So what now?"

"What do you mean?"

"I mean what for you now? Are you going to go back to Infinity?"

251

"No. Not me. I can't speak for others in the group."

"Well, we still owe you a debt to get your fields growing," Phil said.

"To be honest, I'm not sure we'll be staying where we are."

"What do you mean?"

"Some of the younger ones are talking about going to live in Salvation."

"But that's madness. Can't you talk sense into them?"

"My days of being able to talk sense into anyone are long gone. They just think I'm a paranoid, washed-up old drunk."

"Then let us talk to them."

"It wouldn't do any good."

"So, if you don't think you'll stay there, then where will you go?" Nicola asked.

"I'm not quite sure. I might—"

"You should come here," Callie blurted. "You and anyone else in your bunker who wants to should."

Nobody objected to her announcement. They couldn't. An open-door policy for any Wanderers had been introduced, and Woody wasn't only a friend but a proficient scavenger.

"I couldn't. I mean, you've got—"

"We've already got thousands of people here, and we're growing all the time. Everybody pitches in. Everybody pays their way, and I know for a fact that you'd do that and then some."

He thought for a moment. "My people could come too?"

"Of course they could," Susan replied. "We're in the process of relocating Rommy, Becka and people living on the other side of the ridge onto this one, but summer's approaching fast, and I'm sure we could make you comfortable enough until we got accommodation built for you too."

Woody nodded slowly. "I'll try to convince them."

"Do. Convince as many as you can because Bucks won't stop, Woody. If you're not his ally, then you're his enemy, and he won't hesitate to steamroll over you."

"Do you really think he's coming after you?"

"I wouldn't mention that when you're trying to convince your friends to come here," Phil said, and laughter flittered around the room. "But the thing is anybody who isn't willing to bow to Bucks will be crushed by him. The best chance for you and those you can convince is to come here."

"How so?"

Drake stood, walked to the door, placed his fingers on the handle then turned back to the others. "Because we're not going down without a fight."

CHRISTOPHER ARTINIAN

11

After the meeting, Dani had suggested that she and Callie go for a walk before bedtime. It was dark out, but the half-moon and the multitude of stars twinkling away in the clear sky provided them with enough light to see. When Woody had said all that he'd had to, he was shown to Phil and Debbie's place, where a space had been made for him near the fire. It wasn't like the bed he was used to sleeping on in the bunker, but he was so tired from his journey that it didn't matter.

The second half of the meeting continued in his absence. Drake had left to get Dwyer and Revell, giving them a brief overview of Woody's account of what had happened before the trio joined the others. The extended committee had talked for several more hours, coming up with plan after plan. With this wealth of new information they'd received, it seemed pointless taking the risk of sending their people to Infinity. So despite all the hard work of Tania, Harper and the others, the idea was scrapped.

None of the participants objected. In fact, relief consumed them.

Finally, though, they called it a night with a promise to have another meeting the following day after some sleep and more time to process what they'd heard.

"Are you okay?" Dani asked nervously. She'd watched her friend all evening, but Callie's face had been unreadable.

They carried on walking for a few moments before she got a reply. "Yes."

Dani laughed nervously. "That's it? Yes."

"Yes," Callie said again, laughing a little herself. "Yes. This sounds weird considering what we heard today, but I feel better than I have done in a long time."

"I don't understand. Why? How?"

"Because for so long we've wondered what's going on. We lived through that horrific winter with this threat looming over us, but we weren't quite sure what the threat was. It was just like some big black cloud on the horizon. But now we know."

"Oh yeah. I feel much better. Uncertainty was so much worse than knowing for a fact that the administration was gathering a massive army and a huge arsenal together to completely obliterate us."

Callie laughed. "I told you it sounded weird."

"In fairness, you did."

The pair continued walking for a moment before Callie spoke again. "Don't you see, Dani? Now we know for sure we can do something about it."

"Do something about it? I didn't imagine things, did I? You were there with me when Woody was telling us everything?"

Callie laughed again. "Yeah. I was there."

"So, what are we going to do exactly?"

"I guess we're going to find out tomorrow morning."

"It worries me that I can still hear a smile in your voice."

"I'm actually starting to feel like my old self again."

Dani stopped and pulled her friend around to face her. The white light of the moon made Callie's teeth glimmer as she smiled. "Seriously, Cal. You're weirding me out a bit. I'm more scared than ever after listening to what Woody told us. Bucks is getting on a war footing. Hell, he might already be there. An army might come marching towards us any day for all we know. Given how you've been the last few months, I think I've got a right to worry about you when you're telling me that you feel better than you have in a long time."

Callie stepped forward and hugged Dani tightly. "You don't need to worry about me, Dan. I'm not losing it. I'm getting it back. I'm just about as angry as I've ever been right now, and yes, that's not healthy, but it beats being depressed."

"What do you mean?"

"I can do something with anger. I can direct it. I can turn it into a tool. What I was feeling before was like this heavy black shroud crushing me. I could feel it first thing in the morning when I woke. It held me down under the covers. All I wanted to do was pull the sheets back over my head and stay there, block out the world, not talk to anyone, not deal with anyone. I couldn't see through it or beyond it. It felt like there was no purpose to anything anymore. It felt like I wasn't really there."

"You were there. We were all with you."

"It's hard to explain. It wasn't like an out-of-body experience or anything, but it was like I was on autopilot, not living, not registering, just a passenger in my own skin trying to get through the day as quickly as I could before I could bury myself beneath the sheets once more."

"I was so worried about you."

"I know. I knew you were worried. I knew everyone was. And there was a part of me that really appreciated it. I saw how you all ran around after me, how you supported me. But in some ways, that just made me feel worse. It sounds horrible and ungrateful now as it's coming out of my mouth, but I just wanted to be left alone."

"Good luck with that in a tiny house with seven other people."

Callie laughed. "Yeah. I thought I was prepared for the winter. And that day after the first storm, I felt really positive, even though we'd lost people. It was a tragedy, and I knew there'd probably be more to come, but we'd all been through so much since leaving Salvation that it felt like there was nothing we couldn't deal with. I was so proud of my mum, the way she got everybody organised that morning. I was proud of us, the way we went over the ridge, prepared to do whatever needed doing despite the dangers of another storm kicking in at any time. But then … when Chloe and Nazya appeared and told us what they told us, everything started to fall apart. I didn't feel so sure about anything anymore."

"I get that."

"I know. Probably everybody did. But it just made a light turn off inside me. When I finally started listening to other people and realising that there was nothing we could do to save Eric and Infinity, that's when it took over. I went to bed that night, and the next day, I felt it. The following day, I felt it a little bit more. The feeling kept growing until it was this huge physical effort just to get up in the morning. I mean literally. It sounds dramatic, and it probably sounds crazy to someone who hasn't experienced it. That shroud I'm talking about is a figurative thing, but in another way, it's as real as the soil beneath our feet or the clothes on our backs. It weighs you down; it keeps you down. It constantly whispers in your ear, 'There's no point in going on. It's all over. Give up. Give up. Give up.'"

Callie's words lingered in the air for a moment as Dani thought about all the others who'd taken their lives. "And why didn't you?"

Callie exhaled deeply. "'Cause I couldn't get two bloody minutes to myself," she finally said, laughing.

"That's not funny," Dani snapped.

"I'm sorry," Callie replied, placing a hand on her friend's arm. "You're right. It isn't."

"I don't know what I'd do if anything happened to you, Cal. You're like my sister. I love you so much."

"And I'm pretty certain that's the reason I didn't do anything."

"Because of me?"

"Yeah. Because of you, Mum, Si, your mum, Phil. Because of everybody who was there for me. Even though it might not have seemed like it to either you or me, I'm pretty certain that's what kept me going. And I'm not somebody who believes things happen for a reason, Dani, but I'm out the other side now, and suddenly a reason's presented itself, and I'm fired up. My brain's sparking again, connecting the dots."

"What do you mean?"

"I mean I see where this is going, and I know what we have to do. We can take back Infinity. We can win this war, and we can help people build the lives they deserve."

Dani giggled. "I don't know which one's scarier, depressed Callie or crazy Callie."

They both laughed. "Trust me. You haven't seen anything yet."

*

"Tim wanted to try for another kid before the lottery was announced," Nicola said as she and Susan did their last rounds of the farmyard before turning in for the night.

"Oh?" Susan replied.

"What a bloody nightmare that would have been."

"Oh, I don't know. There's a definite upside to having two."

"No, I mean having a young child with everything that went on. And, y'know, with him the way he was. He wasn't a good father, and I don't know if I'd have been able to do what I did with a four-year-old as well as Dani to think about."

"I suppose that would have been a bit of a nightmare."

"Things worked out for the best."

"You're still young, Nicola. There's nothing to stop you from having another child at some point."

Nicola laughed. "Apart from the whole war with Salvation thing."

"Yeah. Apart from that," Susan said, smiling.

"What do you think's going to happen?"

"They'll come. We'll fight, and one side will be left standing at the end."

"Uh-huh. And who do you think that might be exactly? Because I can tell you, there are a lot of people around here who are thinking that this time next month, they're going to be back on a production line in the bunker."

"Well, it's up to us to prove them wrong, isn't it?"

"And how do we do that exactly?"

"We talk to them."

"That's it? That's your big plan?"

"No. But when we've got our big plan in place. Then comes the talking."

"And what will our big plan be?"

"I'll leave that to more suited minds than mine."

"What does that mean?"

"All I'll say is don't underestimate Drake."

"Do you really think he can come up with a way to help us win?"

"Drake has made more compromises than anyone here. He's had to completely change his attitude and way of thinking. But he's told me about some of the things he's done in the past. He's put up a wall between them and who he is now, but make no mistake, to protect his family he'll bulldoze that wall in a heartbeat."

"For all our sakes, I hope you're right."

*

"No offence," said Greenslade, "but going for a moonlit walk with you doesn't do much for my reputation."

"Well … we're not walking," Drake said, handing the other man his hip flask back. "That's good stuff."

"It does the job. I finished mine, but Trunk gave me a refill from his."

"Where did he get it from?"

"New Fenton."

"That place just keeps on giving, doesn't it?"

The pair remained a foot or so apart, perched on the same rock, their legs dangling over the side as they listened to the stream rush by and watched it glimmer in the moon's rays.

"So, I'm guessing you didn't ask for this chat just so you can drink my whisky." Greenslade took another swig and handed it back to the other man.

"No."

"So, are you going to tell me what this is about?"

"If we're going to go up against Bucks and the administration, I'll need your help."

"What makes you think I'm not going to grab my go bag and hightail it out of here?"

Drake took another drink and passed it back. "That's a good question. I think you would have done … once. But now I think you've become a believer like me."

"A believer?"

"That there's a better way. That there's an alternative to the old ways. That everybody working together for the good of everybody else is the only sustainable way forward."

"Doesn't seem like much of a way forward at the moment."

"True enough."

"So, what it is you want me to do exactly?"

"How many of your old crew do you think you could conjure up?"

"What do you mean?"

"I heard all about what went on when the lights went out. I know you had a pretty big gang of thugs who helped you take control of the Salmarts."

"You're mistaking desperation for loyalty. The only person I can really count on is Trunk. The others went along with me because they couldn't see an alternative. Some tagged along because they thought it was a way to get into my good graces. I didn't have an army, Drake. I had a flock."

"I see."

"I don't. You do have an army. Why do you need me?"

There was a long pause before Drake spoke again. "Marina, Dwyer, Revell and the others have trained the militia well. People know what they're doing, but as I've said before, their training's being geared towards defence rather than attack."

"When you're pointing a gun, you're always attacking. It doesn't matter what you've been trained for; if you can hit a target, that's pretty much all that counts."

"I suppose. And tomorrow, we're going to start training in offensive manoeuvres."

"Okay. But that's not why you asked me here."

"No. I need someone who'll do what needs doing besides me. I need someone—"

"Uncompromising. Vicious. Soulless. Someone who will do whatever it takes, no matter how disturbing normal people will find it."

There was another long pause before Drake answered. "Yes."

Greenslade placed the flask up to his lips again and took a hefty gulp. "I don't suppose we can ever escape our pasts, can we?"

"You have. You've become respected here, despite your past. But I'm asking you to revisit it for the good of Redemption. I'm asking you to do what needs doing. Will you help me, Blake?"

It was the first time Drake had ever called him by his Christian name. "On one condition."

"I'm listening."

"We see this through to the end."

"What do you mean?"

"I mean I'm not going to live with this threat of invasion hanging over us for the next year or two years or five years. I mean, no matter what, we finish this one way or the other."

"That's my intention."

"Okay then," Greenslade replied, extending his hand. Drake shook it firmly. "Okay then."

*

"You're up late," whispered Bindi as she joined Phil in the doorway.

"I didn't wake you, did I?"

"No. I've been lying there listening to Riley and Ivy sleeping and seriously thinking about waking them up just out of spite. Little bastards. Why should they be able to sleep like logs when the rest of us can't get a wink?"

Phil chuckled. "You're a great parent."

"Thanks. I've always taken great pride in my self-discipline." They stood side by side in the doorway for a moment, occasionally seeing movement.

"All the little cogs whirring," Phil said distantly.

"Hmm?"

"The war machine. It's starting up."

"We all knew this day would come."

Phil sighed. "I suppose."

"It was bound to happen."

"Yeah, but…."

"But what?"

"I didn't think they'd be as organised as this."

"What do you mean?"

"I mean Bucks and the other fat cats never impressed me with their forward planning and initiative. They just trundled along, letting everything happen around them while their minions did their bidding. All this seems way too proactive."

Bindi shrugged. "I don't know. I mean, the whole of this plan centred around money, didn't it? That's all people like Bucks have ever understood. They've never created anything other than wealth. In times of recession, people like that made more money than ever by profiting from the misery of others by short-selling and manipulating the markets. I think he's just finally figured out a way to do it post apocalypse."

Phil let out another long sigh. "That's a cheery thought."

"It is what it is. People like that have always existed, and they probably always will. It's up to the rest of us to make sure he and they don't succeed."

"And do you really think we can?"

There was a pause before Bindi answered again. "Honestly? Yes, we can."

"I never had you pegged as an optimist."

"I'm not. You can't have the two devil children I've been cursed with and still be an optimist."

Phil laughed again. "They're not that bad. They're just full of life."

"Yeah. And sometimes they have no idea how close they come to losing it."

Phil laughed again. "Remind me never to get on your bad side."

"But going back to your question. We've built something special here. Yes, we're still learning, and it's a huge experiment, but everybody is playing their own vital role. Everybody has a place. It's fair. What went on in the bunker was abhorrent. I mean, I certainly never understood for the longest time. When I did, I knew I had to get myself and my girls out of there."

"Okay. I grant you we've built something special, but that and winning this war don't equate to the same thing."

"That's true. But our souls have gone into this. They live in the fields, they live in the houses, they live in the irrigation system, the defences … they live in everything. I can guarantee not a single person here will be willing to give that up, and they'll fight to the death to defend it. Do you honestly think the Salvation army will feel the same? Sure, you might get a couple of diehards who've bought into Bucks' great plan, whatever that might be. But most will be just trying to get by."

Phil shrugged. "I hope you're right."

A lone figure suddenly appeared in the farmyard and headed in the direction of the woods. "And even if I'm wrong, we've got him."

They both watched as Drake disappeared into the darkness. "Drake's just one man."

"Yeah. But sometimes one man is all it takes."

12

Ricky and Lisa were both worried about Woody. Everybody was. It had been over a week since he had disappeared. He'd vanished before, but never for more than a day at a time. Usually, it was due to getting stinking drunk, wandering off into the woods, and only returning when he'd sobered up enough to remember where he lived.

This was different though. They both knew it, and they both felt it. He had shown increasing disillusionment with Infinity. He had never publicly complained or demonised the administration while he was there, but back in their bunker, he had gone on incessantly about it being the beginning of the end. He had told of how they would all become slaves if they fell into the trap that Bucks was setting.

At first, it just sounded like drunken ramblings, but as the trading prices of materials continued to fall and the purchase prices of the wares in the shops kept going up, many began to realise there was an air of truth to what he was saying, but what could they do? Eric was gone. The old Infinity was gone. New management was in place, and they didn't look like they were going anywhere.

The mother and son now sat at one of the tables outside the tavern. It was a warm day and, as usual, Infinity was buzzing, particularly the Salvation citizenship booth. At the other end of the beer garden were five traders from one of the other bunkers. Neither could remember their names, but they'd been there when they had arrived and were well on their way to being drunk.

Visits to the tavern had become a luxury for most, compared to the early days of the new Infinity. Few could afford that luxury. Woody's crew still had plenty of currency, however. The money they had received for the stock in the storage room, and the fact that they had traded more than anyone else in those early days, meant that they had managed to put quite a bit away.

It was of little consolation, though, as things gradually continued to unfold around them.

"Nah. Screw it. I'm going to settle this once and for all," one of the men said, standing up and staggering a little.

"Don't be daft, man. You can't go around saying things like that," urged another.

"We're not the only ones. It's a scam. It's all been a scam."

Ricky and Lisa looked at each other then took another drink of their beers as they continued to listen.

"Yeah. It may very well be, but I don't know if you've noticed, there isn't a customer service booth in this place."

"Yeah, well. They'd better bloody open one," the man replied, staggering away.

"Duffo. DUFFO!" his friend called, and the rest of the men climbed to their feet, too, trying their hardest to stifle the Dutch courage that the alcohol had given their pal.

Ricky and Lisa looked at each other once more, swigged back their drinks quickly and followed.

"Duffo. Duffo, come on, mate, please. Think about this," one of his friends said, taking hold of the other man's arm, but he just shook it free as the small procession continued.

They finally came to a halt at the seed store. This was one of the most consistently busy places at Infinity. Virtually all of those who had not yet succumbed to the offer of Salvation citizenship had bought bags and even sacks of seeds from here.

"'Ere," Duffo said, pushing to the front. "The seeds you're selling are shite. They don't grow."

All those around who were angry at first that this man had pushed his way to the front suddenly wanted him to go on.

"I—" one of the serving assistants began before being pushed out of the way by a trading manager. The trading managers monitored several stores, making sure things ran smoothly. The arrowhead of figures led by Duffo that had arrived at the seed store was plain to see from some distance away, so the TM was ready should a problem arise.

"What's the problem?" he asked.

"We bought seeds from here and they're duds."

"What do you mean they're duds?"

"What do you think I mean?" Duffo replied, his words slurring a little. "They're not growing."

"You do realise, sir, that different crops require different soils, different environments to grow in. We're not responsible for the ground you planted them in not being fertile enough or too sandy or too acidic. You need to—"

"Yeah, you can quit with your clever talk too. We bought some of the same crops at the end of last year. We planted them side by side with yours, and they're sprouting now, whereas less than half of yours are. What have you got to say about that?"

"Without knowing what conditions you stored them in, without being able to inspect your fields, I wouldn't be able to comment."

"Oh no? And what about all the other people who've been complaining about the same thing?"

"I can assure you there's nothing wrong with the seeds we're selling."

"Are you calling me a liar?" Duffo asked.

"I'm saying that everybody's desperate to grow crops for their independence, but very few have the experience and the knowledge to do so properly."

"Now you listen here, you little shit. I had an allotment for fifteen years. I know how to—"

"I won't allow you to use that kind of language with me or any of the staff here. This is your one and only warning."

Ricky and Lisa suddenly noticed several Salvation guards hovering on the perimeter of the growing crowd. "And I'm telling you this is a con. You're conning us. Our takings are going down. The prices are going up, and you're ripping us off." Duffo turned to the others gathered around. "We're getting conned. These bastards are—"

The TM gave a barely perceptible flick of his head, and before Duffo could get another word out, he was on the floor convulsing as the current from a taser flowed through him.

"What the hell are you doing?" one of his friends demanded. "He has a right to—" He collapsed too, then the man next to him, then the other two in their small group. The bustling crowd were stunned into silence. On the odd occasion, tavern visitors had got a little boisterous, and the tasers had been used, but never had someone with a legitimate complaint been subdued in such a manner.

"Come on," Lisa said, leaning in to Ricky. "Let's get out of here." The pair backed away as the bewildered crowd became something else. Angry shouts and jeers rose, causing many more Salvation guards to close in. The threat of being tased or worse … much worse meant the small rebellion ended as quickly as it had begun, but afterwards, the atmosphere at Infinity was very different.

Those who hadn't seen it had heard about it, and the movie screening that night had only a handful of people paying attention. Most just congregated quietly in their own clans. Duffo and the others had been dragged away, and no one had seen them since. It was a warm and clear night, yet still, a figurative black cloud hung over Infinity. Today had changed everything.

*

There was a part of Revell that felt this was nothing more than a babysitting job. Caine's scavenging team was around three hundred strong today. They were all armed. Those who didn't carry guns carried spears or bludgeoning instruments. It was hardly business as usual, knowing what was going on at Infinity and Salvation. But the key to Redemption continuing was to carry on growing. Scavenging was an important part of that equation, but Caine and his army served another purpose too.

They were travelling north today, something they had not done since their missions had first begun and something that many weren't comfortable with, but to the north lay villages and towns where they could smash and grab. They had started early. They could spend two or three hours picking the bones of their chosen sites, and they could be back home before nightfall.

"So, this is the place up ahead?" Susan asked, looking over Revell's shoulder at the map they had found on one of the New Fenton visits.

"Yup," he replied, tracing the red circle with his finger.

"Doesn't look like much more than a pile of rubble from this distance."

"No," he agreed. "Let's hope it's worth it, shall we?"

They continued along. A vast forest lay to their left while hills stood to their right. "We've seen a few places that look like this, but when we get there, they've got all sorts of goodies waiting for us," Caine said, earwigging on the conversation.

"I suppose," Revell replied.

"How long do you think before we're there?" Nicola asked.

"About half an hour."

They carried on for another few minutes before Callie and Dani caught up with them. "Err … I'm pretty certain we've just seen something," Callie said.

"Yeah," Revell replied.

"Wait a minute. What did you see?" Susan asked.

"There was a flash."

"A flash?"

"Yeah. They're signalling between the peaks."

"Oh, well, thanks so much for keeping us in the loop."

"I thought you'd noticed. Hard not to, really. Your daughter didn't seem to have much trouble spotting it."

"So I don't have the eyes of my seventeen-year-old daughter. I'm sorry."

"Apology accepted."

"Funny. So, what do we do?"

"We don't do anything."

"I really don't like this."

"Nobody asked you to come."

"I thought it was important with this being our first scavenger mission since winter, and … y'know."

"We're just carrying on?" Caine asked fearfully.

"That's the plan," Revell replied.

"I really don't like this."

"Yeah," Nicola agreed. "You and me both."

*

In the end, and despite a number of volunteers coming forward who he didn't expect, Greenslade had decided he only wanted Trunk alongside him on the mission that Drake had passed down. Drake had been less than happy about it. He wanted a decent-sized assault force, but Greenslade had argued that two people were harder to spot than a dozen, and stealth was everything in the wasteland.

Drake had finally conceded that it was Greenslade's neck on the line, so he couldn't really complain.

They had been on the road since the early hours of the morning, but neither knew how long this particular task would take or if they'd ever return home.

"We're in it now, I suppose, aren't we?" Greenslade said as the pair continued along.

"We're in what?"

"It. This is it. There's no turning back. There's no hope that Bucks and the others will just let us be."

"I suppose this was always coming."

"How do you figure?" There was a time when Trunk's opinion would not have mattered to Greenslade. And yes, he wasn't the brightest bulb in the pack, but there was always a straightforwardness to his thoughts and words, which Greenslade appreciated.

"The day Drake broke us out of there. Whether we saw it as taking what we'd all worked for or not, people like Bucks will always see themselves as the victims."

It was a level of astuteness that Greenslade had no idea Trunk was capable of, and he thought about his words for a moment before replying. "You're right. I suppose I was just living in hope."

"I think we all deserve a little hope, chief."

"That we do, Trunk. That we do." They carried on for a few more moments before Greenslade withdrew a compass. It was brass and obviously an antique.

"Nice bit of kit is that."

"Yeah," he replied, taking a reading. He reached into his pocket and pulled out a hand-drawn map that had been traced from one scavenged from New Fenton. "This way." They adjusted direction slightly and continued.

The pair had spent as little time as possible out in the open, instead heading from woodland to woodland where possible. When that wasn't possible, they stayed on low ground or clung to the face of tall cliffs, doing their best to blend in with their surroundings. So far, so good.

They'd been in the forest for about fifteen minutes when the unmistakable sound of a twig snapping underfoot alerted them to the fact that they were not alone.

Before the asteroid, they could have put it down to a wild animal, a fox or maybe even a deer. But here, now, there were no excuses for this sound other than another human.

The pair shared a momentary glance, their eyes asking the same question, *Is this the end of our mission?*

*

"Are you okay?" Phil asked as he joined his wife in the farmyard. She was watching people at work in the fields. Despite what was hanging over them, everyone still had a job, still had a purpose, and were carrying on as normal, or as normally as they could.

"I think so," Debbie replied. "It's a bit of a whirlwind. I don't know how Susan manages it all. There's always someone coming up to you wanting something or wanting to know something."

"That's people. They're like a stubborn rash. Irritating and hard to get rid of. The best thing to do is just avoid them."

"Yeah. I think that might be a bit tough as I'm Susan's stand-in for the day."

"I'm still not convinced it was a good idea for her to go."

"At the end of the day, she couldn't very well ask others to join Caine on a scavenging mission north and not prove that she'd be willing to go herself."

"Of course she could. That's what being in charge is all about. What's the point of having nearly four thousand peasants at your disposal if you can't order them about?"

"And the mystery deepens as to why she asked me to look after things rather than you."

"Doesn't it though? I'm guessing she realised that I'm way too busy to waste my time with the mundane day-to-day stuff."

"Sure, that must be it. It couldn't be anything to do with the fact that you'd alienate every single person here and probably end up beaten to death and thrown in a ditch somewhere."

"Are you saying I lack the communication and people skills needed to make this place run smoothly?"

"That's exactly what I'm saying."

Phil shrugged. "You make a good point, I suppose."

"Is it just me or have you got far fewer people working the fields this morning than usual?"

"No, it's not just you. It's all part of the militia expansion. Drake wants everybody to be trained and ready in case of an attack."

Debbie let out a long sigh. "Do you really think that could happen? I mean here?"

"I have no idea."

"Liar."

"What do you mean?"

"I mean that I can tell when you're saying something to make me feel better and when you're telling me the truth."

Phil smiled. "Am I that transparent?"

"Only to me."

"Do I think Bucks is enough of a megalomaniac to try to take this place? Yes, probably. Do I think he can do it? There's part of me that wonders and another part that thinks he'd be foolish to try. We've got the geography of this settlement on our side, a significant number of weapons and ammunition, and an awful lot of people who call it home and are prepared to shed blood to keep it."

"That almost sounds optimistic for you."

"What can I tell you? I'm having a weak moment."

＊

It had taken Rommy days to make the bow that she now carried around. She had once interviewed a survivalist for a magazine article before she started to work for the *Tribune*, and he had shown her the basic steps of how to do it, many of which she had forgotten by the time she actually came to need them. After several attempts, she had found a suitable beech sapling that wasn't so charred that all the bark had been burned away. Then she had gone about the task of crafting it, carefully removing the tiny branches and carving the wood until it finally had near to perfect form. Her hunting knife and her dad's Swiss Army knife were the only tools she'd had, which made her achievement all the more impressive.

For a woman who had spent most of her life behind a screen, the sense of self-worth she'd gotten from this one act was almost spiritual. She then whittled notches for the bowstring, securing it at the top with an overhand knot the survivalist had shown her.

Then, as her interviewee had demonstrated, she placed the bow on the ground and pulled at the string to make sure the limbs were flexing evenly. There was a loud cracking sound, and the weapon snapped in two. Bea had laughed, thinking it was all part of some game or trick, and Rommy did her best to hide her sadness and disappointment. She had thought about giving up. She had thought about sticking with the spear, but she persevered. Her second and third attempts failed too, but she still carried the fourth around to this day.

"How's it going?" Jason asked as he appeared from through the trees. He and his people were erecting another hotel in the woodland across from the farm.

Rommy straightened up, arching her back a little and looking at the small line of workers as they used the borrowed tools to build more bows. Another small enclave worked on arrows. Some used small strips of rag or cloth for fletching, some used PVC, while others used strips of dried oarweed. Everyone was hard at work, young and old alike, and all under her watchful gaze.

"If someone had told me a few years ago that I'd be running classes in bow and arrow production, I'd have said they were mad."

Jason laughed. "I get what you mean." He looked at the finished weapons and missiles and nodded appreciatively. "You seem to be doing a good job though. Saying that I've never seen arrows with trailing bits of cloth for flights."

She remembered using the term flights when she had gone to interview the survivalist, and he'd nearly snapped her head off. "Fletching. Fletching," he had said twice so she wouldn't make the same mistake again. "Yeah. I was told it's how the Chinese used to make them. I was sceptical until I saw them in action, but they work well."

Jason nodded. "And I see you've pinched some of my thatching," he said, nodding to a pile of rushes on the ground in front of the fletchers.

"Sorry. Clem said it wouldn't be a problem."

"I'm only pulling your leg. It's not as if it's in short supply. I'm just curious what you're using it for."

"It makes good cord for tying the flights in place before we glue them." On one of the visits to New Fenton, they'd gleaned a dozen tins of bitumen from a steel-shuttered hardware store that had been in the basement of an old stone building, just waiting for them to smash the padlock and reap the rewards of what was inside. Up until now, they had used it for the odd repair and to waterproof, Phil had even used some of it on his polytunnel. But it provided an excellent adhesive for the fletching.

"It's sturdy stuff. That's why we use it for thatch. I suppose it only makes sense that it would make good cord as well."

"Yeah, well, it does." They stood in silence for a moment, watching the workforce go about their tasks. "Was there anything you wanted?"

"Hmm?" Jason said.

"It's just we don't see you around here often."

"Actually, I was coming to see if you needed anything. With Susan and Nicola away, I thought I'd better check in, but I can see you've got everything in hand." At that moment, loud hammering echoed through the forest. "Well, I suppose I'd better get back to my crew."

"Thanks, Jason. I appreciate it."

"Welcome," he replied and started back through the woods again. In all the time Rommy had been here, she couldn't recall a longer conversation with the man. She and Becka had always got the distinct impression he didn't like them, or any of the Wanderers for that matter, but now she realised he was just a little awkward. Like her, though, like everybody, he just wanted what was best for the people of Redemption. She smiled as she watched him go and looked forward to telling Becka of her encounter with him when she returned later in the day.

13

Revell slowed once more as Becka walked up beside him. They had all been casting more than the odd glance towards the hills for the last half mile as the suspicion that someone was watching them turned to a certainty.

"I reckon about here," Becka said.

Revell let out a long breath and looked back towards the forest. If this turned bad, then that would be their refuge. "If you say so," he replied and then watched as Becka tied a large square of white cloth to the end of her spear and walked to the verge in the direction of the hills and whoever was watching them.

She waved it from side to side in an exaggerated sweeping motion so there was no mistake that she was signalling to the lookouts. Susan, Callie, Nicola and Dani walked up to join her. "I really hope you're right about this," Susan said.

"Me too," Becka replied.

"That's reassuring."

"I told you it was a long time ago."

"In fairness, you did."

They all remained in position, occasionally casting glances back to the rest of the scavenging team, who clearly shared their nerves. "I really don't like this," Revell said, walking up to join the five women. "It's taking way too long."

"Wait a minute," Callie replied. "There."

They all followed the line of her finger to see a few figures appear from around the side of one of the hills, then a few dozen, then at least a couple of hundred. "Alright," Revell said, returning to the others. "Nobody make any sudden movements, but be ready."

"What is this?" Caine asked. "What's going on?"

There was a good chance that there would be no encounter, despite what Becka had said, and if that was the case, there was little point in making the majority of the scavenging team aware of what was going on. They'd all had militia training and were all armed and ready, but there would probably have been far fewer volunteers for the mission if they'd known a confrontation was more likely than usual. However, they were in it now, and there wasn't a man or woman who wasn't holding their weapons tighter than a child clutching its comfort blanket.

"We should get into the trees," someone called out to the approval of those around.

"We stand fast," Revell replied, and the others fell silent. Revell was not someone to be toyed with, and they all knew it.

The two hundred-plus figures slowed to a stop barring half a dozen who continued towards Becka and her group. When they finally arrived, Becka's heart sank a little. "I'm looking for Selby," Becka said.

"I'm Selby," a young woman replied. Her face was red as if she'd spent half her life outdoors. She had thick black hair, knotted in places. Her clothes were worn, and a single tear on the thigh of her dirty jeans revealed dark, unwashed skin beneath.

"I'm looking for a man called Selby."

"What do you want with him?" one of the men asked. He was tall with a long beard and wild scraggly hair. His eyes punched holes through Becka and the others as he stared at them.

"We were in a tight spot together once. I helped him out, and he told me if I ever found myself in trouble, then I c—"

"He's dead," the woman said, stopping Becka in her tracks.

"Oh. I'm sorry."

"What tight spot?" the Selby woman asked.

"My people lived in a forest near Crowesbury. A tribe of cannibals were hunting Selby. He'd led them away from his people in order to save them. It was a bloody fight, but in the end we won. He thanked us, stayed with us that one night and then he was on his way."

"So that was you," the woman said, her face warming a little. "He was my husband. He told us about you."

"Again, I'm sorry," Becka said. "He seemed like a good man."

"He was." There was a pause before the other woman continued. "So, now you find yourself in trouble?"

"Not quite."

One of the men let out a derisory laugh and looked at all the figures assembled behind. "You thought you'd come here and ask for permission to raid our town for supplies?"

"I—"

"You try to take anything from here and there will be blood."

"Listen," the Selby woman continued in a more conciliatory vein. "Like everyone, we're struggling to get by. We tried to trade in Crowesbury in the early days before we found this place, and they wouldn't let us. We tried to trade on the outskirts, and we got chased off. Market Galson has been a godsend for us. We've had to fend off—"

"If this place is yours, that's fine," Callie interrupted, stepping forward.

"Callie," Susan said, placing a hand on her daughter's shoulder, realising her openness, honesty, and forthrightness was not what the situation required.

"There are plenty of other places for us to scavenge. We brought a team with us because, to be honest, we didn't know if you'd still be alive. A year's a long time."

"You hoped us dead?" one of the men asked angrily.

"My daughter didn't mean—"

"That's not what I said," Callie replied, interrupting her mother.

"So, if you didn't come to ask my husband for permission to pick over the bones of Market Galson, why did you come?" asked Selby.

"We want to form an alliance with you."

Selby and the others laughed. "Just like that. With one story of how this woman met my husband, you want to form an alliance? We know nothing about you."

"Okay," Callie said, shrugging. "We live in a place called Redemption, which we founded ourselves last year after we escaped one of the lottery bunkers. We grow our own crops; nobody goes hungry. We build our own houses; nobody goes to sleep without a roof over their heads. We forage, and we scavenge, and what we can't find, we try to make. We have defences and a militia. We have a good supply of weapons and ammunition, and in total, there are getting on for four thousand of us. We have a school for children, and their days are split between learning the stuff we learned in school and learning the skills that are going to keep them alive out here. What else do you want to know?"

"You lie," one of the men hissed. "Nobody has those things. What kind of trap is this?"

"My daughter doesn't lie," Susan said. "Sometimes I wish she would. It would make everyone's life a lot easier."

Half a smile cracked on Selby's face. "Okay. Say all this is true," she said. "Say you have all these things. Why are you interested in forming an alliance with us?"

"Because there's a war coming."

Silence hung in the air for a moment before Selby continued. "The war's been and gone. The war was an asteroid that practically destroyed the planet. There are no more wars to be had. There's nothing left to fight for."

"You'd think, wouldn't you?"

"Listen," Callie said, taking over again. "We were lottery winners. We were in one of the bunkers, and yes, I know in many ways that made us the lucky ones, but in the end, we were little more than slaves. And—"

"Oh, our hearts bleed for you," one of the men said. "You have no idea what—"

"What you went through? No, I don't. I've heard Becka's stories. I've heard a hundred stories, and each one has its own horrors. You're right; I can't imagine what it was like. The fact that you're standing here now is a testament to you because billions of people died. However we got here, we're here now." She turned back to Selby. "And we've come here today to tell you that every free man, woman and child is going to have their freedom taken away unless we do something."

"Okay, I'll bite. By who?"

"The administration. The people who ran the bunker. They've already taken over Infinity. They've—"

"Good. Bastards wouldn't let us trade there, so what good was the place?"

"Infinity was a good place that was run by a good man. He tried to help people, but he had others under him who had their own agendas. He wanted to make it somewhere for everyone. The administration has taken it over, and now, suddenly, there's no more trade. They've established a currency, which they're in complete control of. They're using it to indebt people, to subjugate them, to force them to join their ranks, to work for them."

"And this settlement of yours ... Redemption ... how's that different? There are no free rides. Never have been, never will be."

"You're right," Callie said, putting her hands up. "There aren't any free rides. Everybody in Redemption works. We have people working the fields, foraging, building, scavenging. Everybody has a role. Everybody has a vested interest in making the settlement a success. Because everybody knows that this is our last chance."

"Sounds like you've got it good down there. And you're with them now?" Selby asked, turning to Becka.

"Trust me. I was as sceptical as you to start off with. The first night, we got attacked, and we thought it was some double-cross. But it was people traders. They swooped in, and Callie, Susan and the rest came to our defence. They saved us twice in one day. Before my people joined them, there were plenty of times when we went to bed starving or freezing. You never go hungry or cold in Redemption."

There was a pause as Selby and her people exchanged glances. "The people traders. We ran into them. I lost friends. They lost plenty too."

"Yeah, well, it's not just one tribe. There are lots of them. They're supplying another bunker in the Cairngorms," Becka said. "Listen to me. We're stronger together. I didn't realise it until I was a part of it. I thought it was everyone for themselves, and that was the way. But it doesn't have to be. At Redemption, if someone needs help, they get it. We all pull together as a community. We share the victories and the losses alike. Things aren't perfect. Things will never be perfect, but we're free. We're in charge of our own destinies. The alternative is slavery.

"If you joined us, you'd have a say in your own future. You might not think the administration is your problem right now, but trust me, it will be. They'll dress it up as something else, but it will be us and them, the peasants and the overlords, because that's how it's always been, and that's the way they want to keep it."

Selby looked long and hard at Becka then Callie and the others. "You're saying we can join you? We can be part of this Redemption place?"

"Err … well—" Susan began.

"Yes," Callie replied. "We've taken in hundreds of people. We're growing bigger and stronger every day, and if you wanted to join us, then yes, absolutely you could."

"Let me speak to my people," Selby said, and she and her small entourage returned to the mass of bodies they'd left further back.

"What the hell are you doing, Callie?" Susan asked when they were out of earshot.

"This is why we're here."

"Actually, it's not. In an ideal world, they wouldn't have been here, and we could have scavenged what was left of Market Galson."

"We're stronger together, Mum. And at the end of the day, what's the difference between integrating them into Redemption and integrating the people we gather together after a few trips to Crowesbury? When we went down the open-door route, it was for a good reason. We're trying to build back, Mum. The more of us there are the stronger we'll become as a society."

Susan let out a long sigh. They'd taken plenty more souls in on subsequent visits to Crowesbury after Rommy, Becka and the others. But two hundred all at once and out of the blue when they had supposedly been going on a scavenging mission was excessive. "Does anyone want to adopt a seventeen-year-old girl?" Susan asked, looking at the other women. "She's headstrong, argumentative and has a messiah complex."

They laughed, but Becka placed her arm around Callie. "I'll take her any day of the week because I'm pretty certain that a lot of people I know and love wouldn't be here without her."

"Good. It's a done deal then. She's yours. I'll get her bags packed when we get back."

They stood around for a few more minutes before Selby returned with her entourage. "Myself, Dan and Silas would like to come back with you. If this place is as you say it is, we will put it to a vote."

"Can I ask you something?" replied Nicola.

"What?"

"How have you survived here for so long? What do you eat?"

The woman's face suddenly changed. Gone was the strong leader they had seen before; now there was someone in pain, hurting, sad. "We took supplies into the caves before the asteroid. They kept us going for a long time, but not long enough. The winter was still in full flow when we realised that we were going to run out before it was over. It was a twist of fate that helped give us a little extra time. Two children went missing in the cave system. They'd gone down, deep down. They had dropped their lantern, and it had broken. The caves are labyrinthine. It's easy to get lost and stay lost. We found them huddled together in a cavern near an underground river. There were fish in the river."

"Fish?"

"Cavefish," Dan replied. "They don't taste good, but we started mixing them with what was left of our reserves. It got us through the long winter, but not without casualties. We found a few things in Market Galson, and we've been foraging in the forests. Found some mushrooms once, but mainly it's nettles. My grandma used to make nettle tea and nettle soup, so I figured we could too. We've pretty much been living off a thin stew of cavefish, nettles and whatever else we've found that we can throw into the pot since then. When we heard about Infinity, we hoped we'd be able to trade there, but we got chased off. We know a lot of people like us were attacking the traders, and that's why, but we would never do something like that. The only time we've fought is when we've had to defend ourselves."

"I'm sorry," Nicola said. "I'm sorry it's been so hard. But if you join us, things will be much better. We grow everything you can imagine. Potatoes, carrots, parsnips, courgettes, onions, peppers, peas, beans, blackberries, strawberries, and dozens of other crops besides. You'll never have to eat cavefish again."

"Is this true?" Selby asked, looking towards Becka.

"Every word," she replied and watched as a single tear ran down the other woman's face.

"Come on then," said Susan. "I'll go tell Caine that our scavenging mission is over. The sooner we get back to Redemption the sooner you can see for yourself."

*

Greenslade and Trunk had carried on walking after they'd heard the branch snap. If, somehow, their pursuer was in sight of them, then a long pause would give the game away that they knew they were being followed.

It had been several minutes since they'd heard the sound, and it was clear that whoever was behind them had been much more careful since. "They carried on for another couple of hundred metres before Trunk threw a glance over his shoulder.

"D'you think they're gone, chief?"

Greenslade carried on walking, his eyes fixed ahead, looking for any signs of an ambush set up by Ferals. He didn't answer. Instead, he put his right arm out, signalling for his friend to stop, and put his left index finger up to his mouth, telling him to be quiet. They just stood there in the middle of the vast charcoal forest for several seconds, listening. At first, they could hear nothing other than the gentle wisp of the breeze, but as they concentrated, there was the definite sound of footsteps on the detritus of the woodland floor. They remained glued to the spot for a moment before Greenslade whipped the Q-Thirty from his shoulder and started to charge back the way they had come.

Trunk followed the other man's lead and, although not as agile as his friend, stayed no more than a few paces behind. "There. Up ahead," Greenslade cried as he caught sight of a figure diving behind a tree.

He skidded to a stop and raised his rifle as he zeroed in on their pursuer. A second later, Trunk did the same, and for a moment, neither of them could speak or believe their eyes. Theo had his hands raised, only now realising how close he had come to meeting his end. "Hi, Dad," he said, almost apologetically.

"What the hell are you doing?"

"I-I wanted to come with you."

"I could have bloody killed you."

"I'm sorry."

"What are you doing following us?"

The teenager's face looked pained as he spoke. "I wanted to help."

"You could have helped by staying at home and looking after your mother and Lydia and Stef."

"They've got everybody else to look after them. I wanted to come with you."

"What we're doing isn't something I want you involved in. That's why when you asked me if you could come last night, I told you no."

"I heard you. But I'm sick of it."

"Sick of it? Sick of what?"

"Of people avoiding me because I'm your son. Of people not asking me to get involved in things because I'm your son. Of people thinking that I have no worth, that I don't contribute anything. I see how they all look at me, and I thought that if I could do something big, if I could do something important, something that mattered, then they wouldn't look at me like that anymore. Maybe they'd start seeing me for who I am and show me a little respect."

It was only then that Greenslade realised he was still aiming his rifle at Theo and suddenly lowered it. "Nobody thinks those things, Theo."

"They do, Dad. You might not see it, but they do."

"I'm sorry. But this is the last place I want you."

"Why, because you're worried that I'll screw things up?"

Greenslade placed a hand on the teenager's shoulder. "No, Son. It's because I have to do something that I don't want you witnessing."

"I'm not an idiot, Dad. I know why people treat me the way they do. What you did in Salvation you did because you thought it was the best way to do things. Right or wrong, you did it, and now we're out here, and things have changed, but you're still doing what you think is for the best."

Greenslade glanced towards Trunk for a moment before returning his gaze to his son. When he spoke, it was in a softer tone. "Son. In Salvation and during the time before, the only thing I was interested in was me. I never gave a damn about other people. I mean, look what you're going through. You've got people avoiding you because of what I did. That's proof."

"But you tried your hardest for the people who followed you."

He looked at Trunk again. *This isn't the time to come clean. Not totally clean.* "Look, Son, what I did, and for whatever reasons, it was the wrong thing. There was another way. There was always another way, and I didn't see it for the longest time. But I was made to see it, and now—"

"You're trying to make amends."

Greenslade thought for a moment. "Yes. Yes, I suppose I am."

"Well, that's what I'm trying to do, Dad. I might not have done the stuff that you did, but everybody treats me as though I did. Everybody sees me like they see you. If I come with you, if I can help do something that makes a difference, then maybe they'll start seeing me for me."

A forlorn look swept across Greenslade's face. At that moment, he looked more vulnerable than Trunk or anyone had ever seen him. *The sins of the father.* "What we're going to do is incredibly dangerous. More than that…." He didn't quite know how to continue for a moment, but then he finally got his thoughts in order. "More than that, Son, it requires the very worst of me. The reason Drake asked me to do this is because he knows I've got it inside me, and it's the last thing I want to expose you to."

"Look. I get it, Dad. But this is like a war, isn't it? And lots of bad things happen in wars. People have to do lots of bad things. Drake sent you and Trunk out here to help Redemption. Whatever you're doing, it's to help Redemption, and I want to be a part of it too."

Greenslade ran his fingers through his hair and looked up at the blue sky. *Give me strength.*

"It's not like we can send him back, chief," Trunk said.

"Right," Greenslade replied. "You can come on these conditions. You do exactly as Trunk and I say. You don't question anything. If it comes from our mouths, you take it as gospel."

"Okay, Dad."

Greenslade looked at the rucksack on Theo's back. "Have you got a weapon?"

The teenager proudly produced a hunting knife. "It's the one you gave me."

This kid. All the time Greenslade had been in Salvation, and all the time before, he had never really appreciated or understood the depth of love and admiration Theo possessed for him. He had been a distant father, and he believed his wife and son felt suitably estranged, but no. He reached into the back of his jeans and handed him the Q-Eighteen. "You only use this if we get into a tight spot and only if I say so. You understand me?"

Theo's eyes lit up. His father had taken him to the shore twice to show him how to use the weapon. He had also told him that it was a massive responsibility to possess a firearm, and the lessons proved how much trust he placed in him. The fact that he was now handing him a loaded gun made Theo as proud as he'd ever been.

"I won't let you down, Dad."

"You never have, Theo. You never have."

14

It was only just after five o'clock, but Bucks had poured himself a cognac. There was a knock on the door, and he turned to see Paris open it. "You want one?" he asked with the bottle still tilted.

For the last few months, they had been working closer than ever, and although she would never be his equal, their late afternoon meetings had become a little less formal. "That would be nice. Thank you, sir." She closed the door and walked over to the desk, taking a seat in the waiting chair.

Bucks poured her a double then topped his own glass up to the same level before heading across. He placed the drink in front of her, and the thick amber fluid sloshed a little, coating the sides of the glass before finally falling still. She reached out, cupping it in one hand, letting her body heat slowly warm the two-hundred-pounds-a-bottle booze that she didn't really appreciate other than the fact that it was an opportunity to spend time with the most powerful man in Salvation, probably the most powerful man in the country.

"I've come to look forward to our afternoon meetings. Things are always so much nicer when it's all good news," Bucks said with a smile on his face.

"Yes, sir," Paris replied. She leaned forward, placed her tablet on the desk, and relaxed back into her chair.

The pair sat in silence for a moment, relishing the peace and quiet. Bucks occasionally sniffed the cognac, revelling in its aroma. Paris did the same, although it could have been cheap hooch for all she knew.

"So," Bucks said finally, "I suppose we'd better get on with it."

"Yes, sir," Paris replied and picked up her tablet. "Farm Two, the recycling plant and water treatment are all now operating at full capacity with no conscripted Level Two workers. Farm One still has a twenty-two-percent-conscripted contingent, but we've split their shifts, so they're only working part-time in there."

Bucks took a sip of his drink and nodded appreciatively. "How long do we expect it to be before we're able to replace the Level Two contingent completely?"

"Well, sir, obviously, the skilled positions at the farm have always been Level Two, but at the current rate of citizenship enrolment, I anticipate we'll be at full staffing within the next three weeks."

"Good. Excellent. And Fabrication?"

Paris smiled, and Bucks did too. "As you're aware, sir, Blenkinsopp is rather fussy about who he has working for him."

Bucks' smile became a chuckle. "Yes. Yes, he is."

"Saying that, out of the new recruits, we've found eleven who he's happy with."

"That's something, I suppose."

"Yes, sir."

"And how are things at Infinity after the little rebellion?"

"Settling down again, sir. Three of the trading parties haven't visited in the last few days, but we anticipate they'll show up sooner rather than later."

"How so?"

"There's nothing else for them to do, sir. They've become dependent on Infinity. Yes, winter is a long time away, but it will always be there in the back of their minds. With the real possibility of failing crops hanging over them, their only option is to come back."

Bucks swilled his cognac thoughtfully. "What's to stop them heading over to Trainor's settlement?"

"From everything we've gathered since we first set up the operation at Infinity, although many of the different trading parties are on good terms, they don't tend to deal outside of the market. It's questionable whether one party would even know where another was based. I can't rule the possibility out completely, but I've cross-referenced the database with the parties that have been absent, and although on cordial terms with Trainor's people, they didn't seem particularly close."

"Okay. Good."

"And Trainor's pal, the drunk. What about him?"

Paris smiled. "It was a false alarm, sir. He showed up. He'd gone on a bender to end all benders. Apparently, it had happened before, and I dare say it will happen again."

"There's no helping some people."

"No, sir."

"Good worker though."

"Yes, sir. I suggest that when they finally become citizens, we continue letting them do what they do best … with an armed escort, obviously."

"Obviously. And you think they will become citizens? They seem to have held out better than most."

"They were as dependent on Infinity as anyone. More so, in fact. They have no one to trade with but us now, and as time goes on, it will become harder and harder as it will for all of them."

"Any new trading parties?"

"Just one this week, sir. They received their signing bonus and spent most of it on the first day."

Bucks chuckled. "I have to say, Paris, the signing bonus idea of yours was pure genius. Sign a contract that says you'll only trade your wares with us and get a big wodge of cash. It's not like there's anyone else to trade with, and it's not like you can spend the money anywhere other than Infinity. Brilliant," he said, smiling again and taking a sip of his drink.

"I was just taking your idea that extra step."

"You don't do yourself justice, Paris." He raised his glass. "Truly an excellent idea."

"Thank you, sir," she replied, raising her own too.

"And our patrols, have they picked up many new recruits this week?"

"A few, sir, but they've run into quite a few hostiles too. People traders mainly."

Bucks took a deep breath. "Our friends in the Cairngorms are becoming troublesome."

"Yes, sir."

"And how are things in general on Level Two?"

"We reopened four more bars and restaurants this week. As fewer people are able to afford the wares down at Infinity, we can divert more of it back here. It's amazing how quickly satisfaction levels start to return to normal. We still have the main culprits behind the attempted Salmart raids in isolation, but things are getting better. We had a grand reopening event for Bella Mozzarella and Piece o' Pizza. They were a huge success. The day after, we had a voucher event at the Tipsy Turvy for its reopening, and, again, that was well attended. Sales have been buoyant in all the entertainment venues ever since. I think the worst of our troubles are behind us."

"Good. Good. And Level Three?"

Paris's left eye twitched a little. "It's a different scenario with Three, sir. We have a much broader mix. As you know a few weeks ago, I deployed a detachment of guards down there on a permanent basis. That was one of the things I wanted to talk to you about, actually."

"Oh?"

"Well, sir. I think we've learned as much as we're going to learn from Infinity. We still have a trading party heading down there on a regular basis, and it's not so much them as the tech staff and processing power it requires to trawl through all the footage."

"You'd prefer us to be monitoring Level Three?"

"I would. I mean, we're monitoring about twenty or thirty phones of known troublemakers, and obviously that means as long as their phones are on, we can hear anything they're doing. But quite a few of them are wise to this, sir."

Bucks leaned back a little further in his chair and took another sip of his cognac. "Tell me. In the last week, have we gleaned any further pertinent information regarding Trainor? Have we established if he had alliances with any other trading parties? Have we found out anything at all?"

"No, sir."

"Very well. Where are they at the moment?"

"Where are who, sir?"

"Our trading party."

"They'll probably be arriving back in the next few hours."

"Okay. Redeploy them here however you see fit. That will give us more labour and free up the resources we need to take a firm hold of what's going on."

"Yes, sir. I'll get on to that straight away." She glugged back her drink and quickly realised that was a mistake. She winced, causing Bucks to laugh.

"Yes. You don't really want to do that with a good cognac."

"No, sir," she said, climbing to her feet. "Thank you, Mister Bucks."

"No. Thank you, Paris. Excellent work. Truly excellent."

*

Greenslade, Trunk and Theo had continued east until they'd hit what had once been a dual carriageway. Then they had waited in the trees that punctuated the long open wasteland. The information they had gleaned from Woody told them the rota the Salvation trading party was working to would see them heading back today.

Even though they entered Crowesbury from a different direction, they would, at some point, have to rejoin this route. Drake and Greenslade had studied numerous maps and established that this was their best option. Like most trading parties, they had a routine, and if they kept to it as they had done up until now, then they would appear in the next couple of hours.

"I see them. I see them." Theo said excitedly.

They were positioned at the edge of the forest, and as Greenslade and Trunk joined the teenager who had volunteered for the first lookout duty, they saw them too as figures began to emerge over the brow of the hill.

"Okay, then," Greenslade said, "remember what I told you. You do exactly as I say."

"I will, Dad. But I don't see how we're going to do this. There are loads of them."

"About sixty."

"Well, how—"

"One step at a time, Theo. This forest stretches for about five miles. We see if there are any opportunities, and if not, we make an opportunity."

"Make one? How?"

"We give them a reason to come in here looking."

"But … this is really dangerous, isn't it?"

"Yeah, Theo. That's the reason I didn't want you to come. There's a good chance that we might end up running for our lives or…. Look, the important thing is that we just stick to the plan."

The colour seemed to drain from the teenager's face. "Okay, Dad."

"Come here." The teenager walked over to his father, wondering why, and was even more confused when Greenslade crouched down, scooping up a handful of ashy bark that had collected between two roots of a charred oak. He crumbled it in his hands then gently rubbed it over Theo's face and arms, making all his visible skin dark grey in colour, just like the trees.

"Camouflage?"

"That's right, Theo," Greenslade said before he and Trunk did the same thing.

It was fifteen minutes before the procession drew level with the forest, by which time the trio had drawn back into the trees. They followed them, continuing to give them a wide berth, but it was only another five minutes or so before the convoy slowed to a stop.

"Get ready," Greenslade whispered, placing a firm hand on his son's shoulder. They were about forty metres back, but the slight incline, coupled with a thinner distribution of trees as the forest met the road, meant that they could see what was going on while using the more densely populated treeline and thicker forest behind to disguise themselves.

Greenslade stayed low as he gradually moved forward. Trunk mirrored his actions before Theo finally followed. The teenager's stomach was in knots. *This is crazy. They're going to catch us and kill us, or … worse still, they'll take us back to Salvation. I can't go back there.* It had been a culture shock for a lot of the younger people, leaving behind the technology that had become their best friend in the bunker. But now the thought of going back to that bleak dungeon sent shivers through Theo.

From here, there was still a couple of hours' hike before the trading party would reach Salvation, and it was the perfect place to take a pit stop. Good-humoured calls and shouts echoed through the trees as many in the party took the time to grapple with their rucksacks and have a well-earned drink while others disappeared into the trees on either side to relieve themselves. Women and men alike searched for a small refuge of privacy where they could ease the pressure that had built on their bladders since the last break.

"Ohh-uughh-oogghh!" Bourne exclaimed as he began to urinate. Others laughed while more still echoed his sentiment. "Jesus. Did I need this?"

"Tell me about it," someone called out a little further back.

Bourne had been sceptical about the plans for Infinity when he had first heard them, but it was an opportunity to get out of the bunker on a regular basis, and so he had taken it. He had quickly proved his worth ten times over and had now become Hogarth's right-hand man. He continued to relax, breathing deeply as the pressure on his bladder eased further. He finished, and his zip was halfway up when a hand closed around his mouth.

*

Greenslade hadn't asked what was in the syringe Bindi had given him. He guessed it was the same stuff that had knocked him and Trunk out when they had been held in Salvation. He depressed the plunger fully, just like the doctor had shown him, and finally released some of the pressure on his victim's mouth. Conversations were carrying on no more than a few feet away. *Shit. Going to get spotted. Going to get spotted. Going to get spotted.* The thought chimed over and over in his head as he wrapped both arms around the figure as if he was giving him the Heimlich manoeuvre then struggled with him around the tree where Trunk was waiting. It was a wide sycamore, probably hundreds of years old, but it had died the day of the asteroid, and so had its magnificence.

The conversations behind continued, but without a word passing between the two men, Trunk hoisted the unconscious figure over his shoulder and waited for Theo to give the nod. The teenager had been crouched down, watching for movement during the whole thing. He turned to the others and signalled that it was clear. The three of them retreated to the next line of trees. Theo popped his head out once more, checked they were safe, and signalled again. They repeated this until they were back in thicker woodland then set off at as much of a sprint as they could.

*

"Bourney? Bourney, did you hear what I said?" When there was no reply for a second time, Piper peeked around the corner. "He's gone."

"He probably realised he needed a shite and went a bit further in," another man said.

Piper laughed. "Yeah, probably. DON'T FORGET TO WIPE!" he shouted, and a few others laughed.

The group returned to the road, but five minutes later, when Hogarth wanted to resume their journey and there was still no sign of their friend, they were back in the forest.

"And this is definitely where you were?" she asked as Piper and his pals stood around the trees where the wet trickles still marked what was left of the bark.

"Deffo," Piper replied.

"Well, we'd better spread out and look for him."

*

Trunk had managed to run for a short way with the unconscious man on his back, but now his pace had slowed to a brisk walk. Of course, for a man whose strides were as big as Trunk's, that was like a jog for others. The nerve damage that had affected his walking months before was now nothing more than a distant memory, and the good diet, coupled with the physical nature of the jobs he did at Redemption, meant he was in better shape than he had been at any time since entering the bunker.

"Do you need to stop?" Greenslade asked as he looked back the way they had come.

"I'm alright, chief."

"We need to use the cover of the forest as long as we can."

"Whatever you say, chief."

*

Over forty men and women entered the woodland looking for Bourne while the others stood guard. Although there were still a few roaming bands of Ferals, Wanderers, Displaced, or whatever they wanted to be called, the vast majority wouldn't risk targeting a party as well-armed as theirs. However, desperation was a cruel master, and staging a diversion in order to make a smash and grab on the supplies piled on the road wasn't something that Hogarth could dismiss.

"What do you reckon?" Piper said as he drew up next to their leader.

"What do I reckon?" Hogarth snapped angrily. "I reckon you should have been using the buddy system like you were told on your first day of training."

"We were."

"Okay, Piper. Then tell me where Bourne is."

"I … I don't know."

"Exactly. You don't know." She put her hands on her hips and looked down the long line of searchers in both directions. It was clear that hundreds of people had used these woods for shelter or foraging in the past month, so the hope of finding a trail was virtually non-existent. "I really don't like this. We need to head back to the convoy."

"But we haven't found him."

"What, really? I hadn't realised. That changes everything then. Let's stay out here all night."

"So, we're going to leave him behind?"

"Unless you and your pals are volunteering to keep on looking."

"Err…."

"Look. I don't like this any more than you. Bourne was a good man … is a good man. But obviously, something's happened. I'm sorry, but I don't think he walked fifteen minutes into the woods to take a dump because he was worried about being seen. And he liked his job. He liked life in Salvation, so I know he didn't just get up and walk out. Something's happened to him. I don't know if it's part of a plan to split us up and get our supplies or if it's…." She didn't want to go on. She didn't want to think about what could have happened.

"Cannibals?"

"We don't know what it is, but the fact is by the time we get back to the road, and by the time we take into account how long we waited before the search even started, we'll be well behind schedule, and I don't want to be travelling in the dark. That would make us ripe for the picking."

"So, he's gone then? That's it?"

"Yeah. That's it. And before you start crying to yourself, I'm going to have to explain this to my boss, and she is going to be beyond pissed."

"But he's got to be somewhere."

"Yeah. Once again, a very astute observation, Piper. I'll use that reasoning to justify keeping us out here another hour and losing another fifty people to whichever psychos got hold of Bourne before we get back tonight."

"He was my friend."

Hogarth's icy glare melted a little. "He was my friend too. That doesn't change the fact that I can't justify us spreading out further and further in the hope that we might find him. If we had a drone, if we had a sniffer dog, if we had anything that I thought could give us a fighting chance, then I'd keep looking, but the fact is whoever took him could have gone in any direction, and this forest might very well go on for miles. It would be like looking for a needle in a haystack."

Piper nodded sadly. "I suppose."

"WE'RE HEADING BACK TO THE ROAD. PASS IT ON."

The order spread down the line in both directions, and Piper's head dropped even further. *Bourney's gone. I'm never going to see him again.*

*

"You see anything?" Greenslade asked his son as the trio continued.

"No, Dad. Not a thing."

"Keep looking." He turned to Trunk. "How're you doin', big fella?"

Sweat was pouring down Trunk's face as he walked with the unconscious figure on his back. "Fine … chief … don't you … worry about … me," he managed to say between laboured breaths.

Greenslade could see the other man was seriously struggling, but he also knew that he'd die rather than let him down. They carried on for another few minutes, Greenslade jogging ahead with his Q-Thirty ready, scouring the treescape for potential threats. "There," he said, "up ahead. We'll stop at those rocks to catch our breath."

They all came to a halt at the jutting rocks. Trunk placed his cargo on the ground, and the three of them eagerly reached into their rucksacks for water. They knew better than to gulp, instead sipping at the contents of their bottles until they were quenched.

Theo was the first to put his drink away, and he climbed to his feet. "I'm going to keep watch."

"Rest, Son."

"I'm fine, Dad." He wandered a little further back the way they had come.

"Stay in sight, Theo."

"I will, Dad."

The two men relaxed for a moment, catching their breath before Trunk spoke. "He's a good boy."

"Yeah, he is."

"He did a good job back there. Most kids his age would have been too scared to keep watch."

"Yeah, he did that."

"He's a chip off the old block is that one."

"Christ, I hope not."

The pair laughed and turned towards their captive. "Do you think they're still looking?"

"Possible, but I doubt it."

"So, we're safe?"

"From them. We've got a long way to go, and there are all sorts of people out here, Trunk. We're going to need our wits about us. Drake and the others are depending on this. The whole plan's depending on this."

"Do you think Drake will get him to talk?"

"If Drake doesn't, then I will. On that, you have my word."

15

Darkness had fallen several hours before, but Drake was still working. Even though it had been a long time since the tents had been used for accommodation, he now occupied a family one. He sat in it, cross-legged, with papers spread around him and two dynamo lanterns making the whole thing glow in the dark like a giant nightlight. Time was running out fast. Woody had ended up staying for a few days, and Drake had spoken to him on numerous occasions. During their final conversation, Redemption's military commander had formed an idea. Woody and his people would join their community eventually, but there was a more pressing purpose for them in the short term.

Everything was happening all at once. The trip north to Market Galson, the manufacture of primitive weapons to complement the guns. It was a vast amount of work on a giant scale, and although everyone was taking care of their own little part, ultimately, the security of Redemption fell firmly on his shoulders. It was a massive responsibility, and being up against the clock did nothing to help Drake's peace of mind.

"Knock, knock," Marina said, stepping inside.

Drake looked up for a moment, but it was as if a stranger was standing there. Finally, his brain clicked into gear. "Hi," he replied with a weak smile.

"I brought you some soup," she said, handing him a travel mug.

Again, for a moment, he just stared before reaching out and taking it. "Thanks."

"Are you going to call it a night soon?"

Drake let out a huff of a laugh. "Soon."

"What's so funny?"

"You sound like Darin."

Marina sat down opposite her friend. "I'm guessing she's just worried about you like the rest of us."

He took a drink of the soup. "Worried about me?"

"How much sleep have you had in the last two days?"

"There'll be time for sleep when this is over."

"Is there anything I can do to help?"

He looked up from all his notes. "You're already doing enough."

"You should really try to catch a few hours."

Drake rubbed his hand over his face. "Maybe I will when—"

"Knock, knock." They both turned to see Callie standing there.

"Has somebody pranked me?" Drake asked. "Is there an 'All Are Welcome' sign on the outside of the tent that I don't know about?"

"That's almost funny for you," Callie said with a weak smile.

"Thanks. I've been working on my material," he replied, tidying up some of the papers.

"I'm not here to spy on you."

"That's a relief. And not that it isn't always an absolute joy to see you, Callie, but what are you doing here?"

"I couldn't sleep."

"So, you thought you'd come and keep me company? My luck just keeps getting better and better."

"Don't pay attention to him, Callie. He hasn't slept in a while," Marina said.

"Yeah, don't pay attention to me. But while you're not paying attention, would you like to share why you're really here?" Callie sat down opposite Drake. "By all means, make yourself at home."

"Selby and her friends set off before dark."

Drake looked at her blankly. "Who?"

"The people from Market Galson."

"And?"

"Hard to say. They didn't exude excitement."

"Visiting a settlement of strangers on the edge of war probably takes the sheen off for some people."

"I suppose."

"I'm sure your mum would have told me all about it in the morning, but thanks. Was there anything else?"

"Yes, actually. I need to come with you."

"You're going to have to narrow it down a little bit for me. Come with me where?"

"To Crowesbury."

Drake laughed. "Oh yeah. That's a conversation I want with your mother."

"I've already spoken to Mum, and she's not happy about it, but she understands."

"Okay, I'll bite. Why do you want to come to Crowesbury?"

"Because Chloe is freaking out, and I don't think Nazya's attempts at stoicism are helping."

"And you're the all-calming influence that's going to help?"

"Chloe's like a sister to me and Dani, and—"

"Wait, what? You want Dani to go as well?"

"And Nicola and—"

"Why don't we just get some invitations printed up?"

"You need Chloe and Nazya, and they need us."

"We could just take Nazya."

"You're the one who's always talking about redundancies. What if something happens to one of them?" She looked at the pile of papers. "I know you think I'm just a kid, and I know I irritate the hell out of you sometimes, but—"

He put his hand up. "Yes, you irritate the hell out of me and more than sometimes. But no, I don't think you're just a kid, Callie. If it wasn't for you, this place wouldn't exist. If it wasn't for you, we'd never have brought Rommy, Becka and the others here. You're everyone's better angel. Like I said, that's as irritating as hell, but more often than not, you get to the right answer long before the rest of us. You're hope."

"Hope?"

"You make people better versions of themselves. And that's why I really don't want you heading out there. The chances of us all coming out of this alive are slim at best. Nobody's irreplaceable; I know that. But part of this place would die if you didn't come back."

Callie laughed. "Okay. What's the punchline?"

"No punchline. I'm serious. I really don't want you to go."

"But I really need to go."

Drake looked towards Marina and shook his head. "Can you try talking some sense into her?"

"I'm guessing her mother and brother have already tried, so I don't know what you're looking at me for."

"Thanks for your help."

"Don't mention it."

Drake looked at his watch. "Tick-tock, tick-tock, tick-tock," he said to himself.

"What?" the two women replied in unison.

"This," he said, picking up the papers and throwing them down once more. "Everything I've been working on. All the planning. It all has to happen in a certain order, and

308

the various wheels have to be in motion at a certain time, and if anything misfires, that's it. The whole bloody thing comes tumbling down." He took a drink of soup, scooped up all the papers and placed them into a folder then climbed to his feet. "I'm going to get some rest." Without saying another word, he walked out of the tent, leaving the two women alone.

"Err … is he okay?" Callie asked.

"He just needs some sleep."

"He's under a lot of pressure."

"We're all under pressure, Callie."

"Yeah, but I mean we're kind of all relying on him."

"I've known Drake a long time. He won't let us down."

"And if he does?"

"Then I'm here, aren't I?"

"Where did Greenslade and Trunk go?"

"Scouting mission."

"Why don't I believe you?"

"You're a very mistrustful young woman. I've come to learn this about you."

Callie laughed. "Fine. Don't tell me. You heard Theo went after them?"

The half smile that had formed on Marina's face was suddenly gone. "Yeah."

"I hope he's okay."

"I hope they're all okay."

*

"I need water," Bourne said. The zip tie around his wrists was attached to a rope, and he was being dragged along like a dog being taken to the vet. But it beat the alternative.

"You can wait," Greenslade replied.

"Hey, kid. Let me have some water."

Greenslade whipped around, grabbing hold of Bourne by the scruff of his neck. "How many times? You don't speak to him."

"That stuff, whatever it was you gave me, it makes you thirsty."

Greenslade let out a frustrated sigh before reaching into his backpack and retrieving a bottle. There was enough moonlight for him to see what he was doing, and he placed the rim up to Bourne's lips and tilted it. "There. Now shut the hell up."

They carried on a little further before Bourne spoke again. "I know who you are, y'know. All three of you."

"And?" Greenslade replied.

"And nothing. You were featured in our training. Regular stars. Well, you and him. The boy's just a background actor."

"We've still got a way to go, so if you don't want the gag put back on, I really suggest you stop talking."

"Or what will you do? Kill me like you did Maria Rogin and more besides?"

Greenslade turned around angrily. Bourne's teeth shone white in the moonlight. "How—"

"How did I know? Like I said, we learnt all about you and your friends." He turned towards Theo. "Did you know your dad was a murderer?"

Greenslade pulled hard on the rope that was attached to Bourne's zip-tied hands then unleashed a hammer blow. There was a cry and an explosion of blood as the prisoner fell to the ground. Greenslade didn't miss a beat. He dropped to one knee and continued to punch; each time, Bourne cried out, trying his hardest to defend himself but failing. Greenslade could see the cocksureness was gone. *I don't know why he thought he was untouchable.* Strike! Strike! Strike! And still he continued, again and again. Blood poured out of Bourne's mouth as he desperately tried to shuffle away.

"Chief," Trunk said, finally placing a hand on Greenslade's upper arm.

He stopped, looking at his clenched fist in the moonlight as blood dripped from it. He glanced towards

Theo and saw him standing there in open-mouthed horror as the prisoner continued to squirm on the ground.

He finally climbed to his feet, and Trunk pulled the other man up. "I think you've broken one of my teeth," Bourne cried out.

"Trust me. You got away lightly." He handed Trunk the rope. "You take him for a while. I swear if he mouths off again, we'll be carrying his corpse back home."

"Sure, chief," Trunk replied.

Bourne remained silent as they continued west along the moonlit dual carriageway. "I'm sorry you saw that, Son," Greenslade said, not loud enough to be heard by the other two men as they carried on further ahead.

Theo didn't say anything for a moment but then passed his father a rag from his backpack. "You should clean your hand."

"Thanks, Theo," Greenslade replied, pouring water over his knuckles.

They walked a little further before the teenager spoke again. "I already knew."

"Knew what?"

"I knew about Harry and Ollie's mum and dad."

There was an uncomfortable pause before Greenslade replied. "How?"

"I overheard Michelle talking once."

"I see. Listen, Son, you've got to realise—"

"Things were mad in the bunker, Dad. People were scared, and you were trying your hardest to get us to safety."

Jesus. If he only knew the truth. "I'd do things very differently if it happened today."

"I know you would."

"And how does it make you feel, knowing that?" *I sound like a bloody shrink.*

"I don't know. You're my dad. You'll always be my dad. You've done lots of good things since we left the bunker. You've saved people's lives. Redemption wouldn't exist if it wasn't for you, and we're out here now, trying to save it again. What happened happened. You're my dad, and I love you, but I wish you hadn't done it."

There was another long pause as they continued walking. "Yeah. Me too, Son."

*

Eric woke with a jolt. He'd been having another bad dream. They were the only kind he seemed to have anymore. He looked at the clock next to him. He'd be heading to work in another hour, and from past experience, he knew it was doubtful he'd get back to sleep.

He sat up in bed and swivelled his feet out onto the floor. He was about to turn the light on when he stopped. *BOOM!* The deafening sound made the building shake.

He turned on the lamp, threw his clothes on and ran out into the hallway.

"What the hell's going on?" Hugh asked, running out of his room too. Even though Eric's family had been taken from the bunker, they were not allowed to live together. Hugh had been a Wanderer. In his life before, he was an accountant, and other than being very untidy and a bit of a chatterbox, there were far worse people Eric could have ended up sharing with.

Shouts could suddenly be heard from all over the building. "We'd better get—" His words and thoughts were cut off as more loud noises travelled towards them.

BANG, BANG, BANG, BANG! "W-what's that?" Hugh asked nervously.

"It sounds like it came from down the hall."

"SALVATION GUARDS. OPEN UP!"

"They must be going door to door."

"But why?"

"I've got no idea, Hugh, but I'm guessing we're about to find out."

BANG, BANG, BANG, BANG. "SALVATION GUARDS. OPEN THE DOOR."

Their turn had finally come, and Eric unlatched the door and stood back in the narrow hallway as three armed and uniformed men burst in. They pushed Eric back, and his head smashed against the thin hollow wall.

"Who else is here?" one of the guards asked.

"No one. It's just us," Hugh replied.

This did not stop the guards from going room to room, tipping furniture over, and dropping to their knees to check under the beds. Terrified screams and shouts continued outside as more guards raided the other flats.

When the three men were happy there was no one else in the property, they rejoined Eric and Hugh in the narrow hallway. One of them held a phone up. "When was the last time you saw him?" he demanded, revealing a picture of a man who lived on the ground floor.

"Err … I don't really know him well. He—"

"That's not what I asked. When was the last time you saw him?"

"Um. Yesterday, maybe, when I was heading out to work."

"You," the guard said, turning to Hugh. "When was the last time you saw him?"

"A few days ago. Err … he held the door open for me in the stairwell when I was coming back from the Salmart."

"Did he say anything?"

"Let me get the door for you."

"Are you trying to be funny?"

"N-no. That's what he said." The guard took a threatening step towards Hugh and glared at him, making the other man look down at the carpet.

"I can take you in just like that," he said, snapping his fingers, "if I've got any reason to believe you're withholding something."

"I'm not. That's what he said, and I said thank you, and that was it."

The guard's eyes narrowed a little more.

"What's he done?" Eric asked, trying to diffuse the situation.

"Never you mind what he's done. If you see him, you alert the authorities immediately; otherwise, you'll be in as much trouble as he is." Without another word, the three guards marched back out of the flat.

Eric stood there for a moment until he returned to the still-open entrance. He peeked out and looked down the long corridor. It was awash with uniforms. Shouts, cries and screams continued not only from his floor but the rest of the building. He closed the door, sliding the bolt across once more.

"What the hell do you suppose that was about?" Hugh asked.

"Well, they wouldn't be going door to door if he was late for work, would they?"

"You think he's got something to do with the attacks?"

"Keep your voice down," Eric said, heading back down the hallway and ushering the other man into the small open-plan kitchen, diner, and living room.

No explanation was needed as to what attacks Hugh was talking about. In reality, they were not attacks at all but smash and grabs on the Salmarts. It was obvious that the scale of the attempted robberies and the organisation was what concerned the administration. Dozens of people were involved, and so, rather than announcing them as what they were, desperate people trying to feed their families, they called them terrorist attacks by rebels wanting to undermine the administration's efforts to make things better for everyone.

Whenever anything went wrong in Salvation, they were the ones who were blamed. A small handful of Level Three citizens believed the official line, but most knew. Some had come to Salvation willingly, others had been forced, but very few people on Level Three were happy with their lot.

"Where do you think he is?" Hugh asked.

"How would I possibly know?"

"Do you think they'll take his family?"

Another shriek of fear sliced through the early morning, rendering the pair silent for a moment before Eric continued. "I'd say that's a given ... unless they got out before the guards came."

"Every day, they say things are getting better here. They say food supplies are getting back to normal levels. They say there'll be no more rolling brownouts soon. They say the pubs and cafes in the market square will be opening up again soon. But every day, things are just getting worse and worse down here."

"You'd do well not to say anything like that outside of this flat." Eric looked towards his mobile phone on the table. "In fact, you'd probably be better off just not saying anything like that, full stop."

*

Four hours was more rest than Drake had gotten in the longest time. When he'd curled up next to Darin, she had been asleep. He had eased his arm around her, and she had mumbled something. He'd hedged his bets and said, "Love you too." Another mumble of approval sounded before she gripped his arm and fell back into a deep slumber. He had too, and it was glorious, but when his eyes had sprung open once more, he knew he would not get back to sleep.

He climbed out of bed and was on his way back to the tent where he had spent most of the day yesterday when a figure holding a lantern approached out of the darkness.

"Dad reckoned you'd probably be awake," Theo said.

A smile cracked on Drake's face. "A lot of people were worried about you. I'm guessing you caught up to him and Trunk."

"Yeah. They're waiting for you in the hotel that Rommy and Becka used to live in."

It was sad that so much effort had been put into building on the other side of the ridge only for the properties to be abandoned, but there was a small hope in

Drake that, one day, they could be used as homes again. "I'll head over there."

"What are you going to do to him?"

"We need information."

"Yeah, but how are you going to get it?"

"That's not something you need to worry about."

"He's scared."

"What?"

"He wasn't at first, but then my dad beat the hell out of him, and he's scared. You can see it in his eyes."

"Well, that's good. He should tell us what we need to know without any problems."

"And then what happens?"

"We'll see."

"Are you going to kill him?"

"You need to go and find your mother. She's been worried sick about you."

Theo saw the look on Drake's face and knew not to pursue this line of questioning any further. "Okay."

When Drake arrived at the large wooden building that had once housed so many Wanderers, Greenslade, Trunk and the prisoner were waiting. "Good to see you back," Drake said.

"Good to be back."

The prisoner remained silent. "Things go okay?"

"We're here, aren't we?"

"You had a helper."

"Yeah. Turned out he did help too."

"You get anything out of him?" Drake asked.

"He let slip that he was a Salvation guard, but that's about it."

Drake picked up one of the lanterns and held it closer to their prisoner's face. Bourne's hands were still zip-tied, and he was huddled in one corner of the room. Just like Theo had said, there was fear in his eyes.

"Never seen him before. Maybe he was one of the elite guards on Level One."

Greenslade shrugged. "If you say so. He didn't seem that elite to me."

"Yeah, well. If you hadn't drugged me while I was trying to take a piss, we might have had an even match." It was the first time Bourne had spoken in a while, and Drake crouched down in front of him.

"So, was that it? You were one of the elite guards?"

Bourne turned towards his questioner, and for the first time, Drake saw the extent of his facial injuries. "Yeah," he replied.

"That nose looks broken."

"You can thank your rent-a-thug for that," he said, gesturing towards Greenslade.

"I'm sure he was just doing what he saw fit."

A huff of a laugh left the other man's mouth. "I don't get you, Drake. You had a good job. Your family was looked after. You didn't want for anything in Salvation, and you just flushed it all away. What the hell is wrong with you?"

"Maybe I couldn't live with myself anymore."

"Yeah, well, I'm pretty certain that won't be a problem for much longer," Bourne said, grinning.

Drake rose to his feet and placed the lantern down. He removed his jacket and walked over to a corner, dropping it on the floor, then grabbed his hunting knife from the sheath on his belt. "One thing I do miss from Salvation is having a washing machine."

"What?"

"A washing machine. Y'see, here, we have to wash everything by hand. Well, I say we. Darin … that's my wife, Darin. She does all the washing for me and the kids. Y'know, Michael, Thomas and Zuzu. I'm sure you had extensive files on me and my family. Anyway, that's the one thing I miss, having my clothes laundered. Because out here, we might have freedom, we might be building a better life, a more decent life, a more just life than we ever could have done in the bunker, but I do miss having my clothes washed properly. Y'see, bloodstains are a nightmare to get rid of. I do my very best not to get blood on my clothes 'cause I get some real earache from Darin, but sometimes it's just impossible, like now. Chances are I'm going to get a lot of blood on my clothes. There's a part of me that knows it's absolutely necessary, but there's another part of me that regrets it because I'm creating a lot of work for my wife, and in the end, there'll still be stains. No matter how hard she scrubs, there'll still be stains."

Drake crouched down once more and brought the blade up in front of Bourne. "What's the point of bringing me all this way if you're just going to kill m-me?"

"Because I've got a list of questions that need answers."

"I'm not going to tell you shit."

Drake smiled a smile that even sent chills through Greenslade and Trunk. "Oh, you say that now. But you will. You will."

*

"I knew you were trouble that first day I met you," Phil said as he and Callie took what could possibly be their final evening stroll around the fields. "I thought to myself, *This girl's a nightmare. Stay clear.*"

"Says the man who was coated in soot when I met him. As far as bad first impressions go, you had me beat."

"Fair enough. I'll give you that."

"How's Debbie?"

"Worried like the rest of us. Y'know, Callie, there's absolutely no reason for you to go."

"There really is."

Phil let out a sigh. "I don't suppose there's any point in trying to talk you around."

"It's taken all this time, but you're finally getting to know me."

"I…."

"You what?"

He stopped walking and turned towards her. It was a clear night, and even though she couldn't see the look on his face, she could imagine it. "I'm not ready to say goodbye to you."

"Well, that's good because I've got no intention of going anywhere."

"You might not have any intention of it, but you're going into harm's way like never before tomorrow."

They started walking again. "We either take the fight to them or they bring the fight to us. One way or another, this is happening."

"We can't possibly know that. We can't know what's going on in Bucks' head."

"You're not that naïve, Phil."

"It's possible that he might just forget about us."

Callie laughed. "Yeah. Sure."

"I don't mean literally. I mean write us off as a bad debt. He's a businessman before he's anything else. He's already made a huge loss, and coming after us would do nothing but compound that loss. He'd use valuable resources, and that's to say nothing of the death toll on both sides."

It was Callie who stopped this time. "Do you honestly, in your heart of hearts, think that?"

Phil thought for a moment. He wanted to with every fibre of his being, but in truth, he couldn't. "No," he admitted sadly.

"Uh-huh. Which is why I'm heading out tomorrow."

"What about your mum?"

"I've talked this to death with her. We need to make a stand, Phil. This war is coming whether we're ready or not, whether we like it or not. Here or Infinity, it's coming, and it's better that it happens sooner rather than later. It's better that we take it to them before they get too strong."

They started walking again. "Sometimes logic isn't enough."

"What?" Callie replied.

"Logic is normally my comfort. It's not doing a good job right now."

"So, you're admitting that I'm right."

"Would that make you feel better?"

"It would normally. I'm not looking forward to this, Phil. We're going to lose people. I might be one of them. I'm scared."

"If it helps, I'm scared too."

"It does … a little." They carried on for a few paces before Callie spoke again. "I need you to promise me something."

"What?"

"If something does happen to me, you'll look after my mum, won't you?"

"Don't talk like that."

"No, I need you to promise me."

Phil exhaled a long breath. "Callie, you're the daughter I never had. Susan and Si are family to me. I promise you on my life, on Matt's life, that I'll always watch out for them, but nothing is going to happen to you."

"No. Course not." They continued for a few more steps before Callie reached out, looping her arm through Phil's. "I love you, y'know."

He couldn't reply at first, but when he did, his voice shook, and it was clear he was crying. "I love you too."

16

Becka and her clan had not returned to the forest they had left all those months before until now. This time, she had more than a thousand people with her. They had travelled all day, leaving the place that had become their home. Everyone knew just how dangerous this was, but there wasn't a soul who didn't understand that, one way or another, this needed to happen.

She and Ashraf were on one side of the fire, while Dwyer and Revell sat on the other. It was a warm night, but similar fires lit the entire forest. "I searched for the ones we left behind, but there was no sign," Becka said.

"Maybe they decided to become Salvation citizens," Ashraf replied.

There was a time when such a notion would have been laughable, but Becka wondered. "Or maybe they just moved on."

"I don't know how you guys lasted out here for so long," Revell said.

"We found strength in one another."

"Do you regret it?"

"Regret what?"

"Regret leaving them behind."

"I regret them not coming with me."

"You don't regret joining us?"

"Not for a second."

"Even now?"

Becka lifted her head, glancing from fire to fire as they stretched out of sight and deep into the forest. "Even now." She took a sip of tea and gazed into their own flames for a moment before saying anything else. "If I die tomorrow, then I'll die fighting for people I care about, and I'll die with people I care about. I can't think of a better way to go."

*

When Becka and the others had veered into the forest, Drake and his team had carried on the same road they had walked a hundred times before in order to reach Infinity. A couple of miles out, they had taken a detour, however, circumnavigating Crowesbury and approaching from the east rather than the west. Now they were in what had been a park on the outskirts of the town. It had once been a place of beauty, with a giant lake in the middle. The trees around it had burned like all the others, but the lake had survived, and around its shore, life had started to grow back quicker than the norm. Saplings had grown fast and strong. Young sycamores already stood over two metres tall, and despite the gravity of their situation, it gave Drake and the others a small glimmer of hope that there might be a future beyond this night and the next day.

"Okay, so what now?" Esme asked.

"Um…. It's around here somewhere," Nazya said, scouring the giant parking area.

"What is?"

"The manhole cover."

"I thought you'd used this route before."

"At night. When we were fleeing for our lives." She turned to Chloe. "Can you remember where it is?"

"If we were allowed to use our lanterns, it would be a lot easier."

"I told you," Drake said. "No lanterns. No lights of any kind."

"Okay. I'm just saying it might take a while."

"Sure, by all means, take all the time you want," PJ said. "It's so nice out here in the open where a roaming patrol could find us at any moment."

"I doubt if they'd come this far out of town on a night," Nazya replied.

"Oh, well, I feel so much better then."

"Y'know, you're a real—"

"Keep it down. Let's just look for this bloody manhole," Drake snapped.

The thirty-strong group split up. Susan and Callie walked side by side. "I still say this was a bad idea. They need you in Redemption," Callie said.

"They don't need me. They just need somebody. Debbie can do just as good a job."

"I'm not even going to get into that, but we both know that your presence there is more important than what you do. And you brought Si along too. It's like a bloody family outing," Callie said the last sentence under her breath.

"Look, daughter dearest," Susan began, pulling Callie around to face her. There was just a crescent of a moon, but that and the starlight reflected on the still lake provided them with enough light to see each other's outlines. "You said it yourself."

"I said what?"

"Whether here or in Redemption, we've got this fight coming. I want to be with my family when it happens, and Si feels the same."

"Yeah, well, I still say this was a mistake."

"And I'm telling you that I'm your mother and I know what's best."

Callie couldn't help but let out a quiet giggle. "Trust me," Nicola said as she and Dani searched the ground a few feet away, "I've tried that line. It doesn't work."

"You got that right," Dani replied.

They were doing their best to remain positive and upbeat, as if this was just another night like any other, but they all knew what awaited them.

"I've found it," called out Chloe, and they converged on the spot where she was standing.

Drake and Esme dropped to their knees. There were two small holes in the cover, and workmen usually used a tool to lift it, but they both knew they were going to have to fudge it. Drake pulled out a straight-edged screwdriver from his backpack and jammed it into the gap along the top edge. "Get ready to grab it when I've levered it up," he said.

"I'll give you a hand too," replied Si, kneeling down to join them.

A loud metallic scrape heralded the raising of the cover, and Si and Esme hoisted it up and out of the way. "We need to put this back on when we're down. Okay," Drake said, turning to the others, "who's first?"

"I suppose it makes sense for me to go first, doesn't it?" Chloe replied. She sat down with her legs dangling through the hole for a moment before she shuffled across and placed her right foot on one of the metal rungs that would take her into the sewer system. The new town of Crowesbury had been built around the bones of an old market town, and this stretch of tunnel certainly belonged to another time.

She reached across, gripping another rung as she started her descent. She paused a couple of metres down and looked up from the blackness that engulfed her to the much lighter night above; then she clicked on the dynamo torch she had attached to her jacket.

Rung by rung, she climbed down. There was a clatter, and she looked up once more to see Callie's silhouette following her. She finally reached the bottom and waited there for just a few seconds until her friend joined her. They both looked up to see Nazya, Susan, and the others making the climb down too.

Callie flicked on her torch to find they were on a small plateau. To their right was a short flight of concrete steps leading to the actual sewer. Any waste had long since decomposed, but there was still a stale, unpleasant smell in the air. There had been no rain for a few days, which they were grateful for because even though the sewer system no longer carried waste to the treatment plant, overflow drains still ran into it.

"We'd better make our way down," Chloe said.

"Yeah. The sooner we're out of here the better."

"Normally, I'd agree with you, but on this occasion, a sewer might be the lesser of the two evils."

*

Marina had spent most of the day touring the turrets to the north, east and south. She had not been by herself. A squad of fetchers and carriers had been with her. Food, water and ammunition, both bullets and arrows, had been delivered. Tents had been set up next to or near the turrets, and these housed militia reserves, ready to take up arms in an attempt to buy the Redemption citizens more time if an attack took place.

It was unlikely that Bucks would choose to move on Redemption at the same time they had chosen to begin their operation, but it was a possibility, and for that reason, Drake had left the one person in charge he could depend on more than any other.

By the time she reached Debbie and Phil's place, night had long since fallen, and many had turned in.

"I thought I'd better check in before I get a couple of hours," Marina said.

"You look exhausted," Debbie replied, taking her by the arm and leading her into the house.

Phil, Bindi and Matt were sitting by the small fire with a cup of tea. "We've just made a brew," Bindi said. "You look like you could use one." She climbed to her feet and poured from the camping kettle into a waiting mug.

Marina accepted it gratefully and sat down. Debbie joined her but shuffled back a little so everyone could see their guest.

"You look like you've had a day," Phil said.

"Ha," Marina replied. "And then some."

"So, did everything go to plan?" Debbie asked.

Marina took a sip of her tea. "Yeah, pretty much. We've got twenty people for each turret on a rotating shift basis. The tents have been set up behind the turrets where possible. Where that isn't possible, namely on the north-facing ridge, we've got our people camped on the nearest safe plateau.

"There are caches of weapons and ammunition at each one, so if the alarm is raised, they're all there and ready. There are also stashes of food and water enough for a few days, and—"

"But won't we be checking on them every day?" Debbie asked.

"Drake wanted to make sure they had plenty of supplies just in case. The turrets to the east and south aren't really the problem; we can access those from behind safely. The only way to the ones facing north is along the ridge, and that means any resupply teams would be exposed."

"It sounds like Drake's thought of everything," Bindi said.

"He does that," Marina said, smiling and taking a drink. "I've known him a long time, and he nearly drove himself mad with the planning for all this."

"What's the signal?" Matt asked.

"Sorry?"

"What's the signal if we do come under attack?"

"One would guess lots of people screaming, running and dying," Phil replied drily.

"That's not funny," Debbie snapped.

"Sorry."

"If we come under direct attack, there'll be three gunshots followed by three flaming arrows," Marina replied.

"Why the arrows?" Phil asked.

"I don't know if you've noticed, but sound travels in a weird way around here. If we come under attack, we can't afford uncertainty or deliberation. The shots let us know we need to be looking; the arrows tell us where we need to go."

"Let's hope their lighters work."

"They won't need to. They've all got good supplies of wood, and they've been told to keep a small fire on the go at all times."

Phil nodded appreciatively. "He really did think of everything, didn't he?"

"I told you."

*

The journey through the tunnel had been more unnerving than either Chloe or Nazya had remembered. The fear was compounded by the fact that Drake had pointed out just how close they had come to being captured before.

During their escape, on making it to the sewer, they had kept their torches on, not even considering that their lights would be spotted by any guards who happened to be passing one of the overhead grates.

Tonight, however, Drake insisted everyone turned their lights off long before the grates. The dribbles of moonlight from above, although weak, were like beacons in the deathly darkness of the tunnel, so it was easy to see the shafts of light emanating from the grates. He also insisted on complete silence.

On one occasion, they had heard the conversation of two Salvation guards above, and again shivers of fear ran through Nazya and Chloe. It was a danger they had not even contemplated before, and it proved to them once again just how out of their depth they had been.

"It-it's up ahead, I think," Nazya whispered.

"You think?" Drake hissed back.

"No. Definitely. It's up ahead … to the left."

"Okay. Lead the way."

Nazya and Chloe sped up a little until they reached a gap in the tunnel. They had discovered a small handful of these on their journey. They were for maintenance access, and in general they all looked the same, but Nazya had noticed a substantial growth of bright green algae when they had first made their escape from Infinity. It had caught in the LED light, and as dire as their situation had been, she had been struck by its beauty.

At the time, she firmly believed that she would never see such a specimen again. *Funny how things turn out.*

They climbed the steps side by side, their shoulders occasionally touching until they finally reached the ladder leading up to the cover. "Up there," Chloe whispered to Drake. "That leads out to the rear car park. The one for players and press and VIPs."

Drake stepped forward, panning his torch around but making sure not to shine it directly towards the manhole cover. There were two small holes as there had been on the one they'd accessed in the park, and he didn't want to waste all the good work they'd done so far by alerting someone to their presence now. He turned to PJ. "Okay. You're up."

"Just for the record. If anything happens to me, I want you to know that I blame you fully."

A smile cracked on Drake's face. "If anything happens to you, they'll probably hold a parade for me."

"Thanks."

"Be careful, PJ."

The young tech wizard took a deep breath and began his ascent of the steel ladder. Although tarnished in places, it did not look like it was as old as the one they had come down in the park, so that was one less thing for him to worry about, and PJ was one to worry. He was close to the top when he glanced down to see all the dimly lit faces looking up at him. He looped his arm around one of the rungs and reached into his inside pocket to remove a mobile phone. It was something he'd specially adapted. He'd only had the most basic of tools, so it wasn't something he was particularly proud of, but it would do the job. A cable extended from the device, and he selected the camera option. For a moment, the screen went black, and then he angled the end of the cable down towards the others.

Suddenly, there were Drake, Chloe, Nazya and the rest of the gang looking up at him. The phone he had used had not been one of the handouts that the administration had given to all the Level Three citizens. Instead, it had been a high-spec model given to the Level Ones. Of course, PJ had one because PJ had most things. There were a few extra features on the Level One phones, but the most significant for this job was the fact that the cameras operated well in low light.

PJ tapped the menu button and selected night scene, immediately making the image brighter. He angled his head up once more and ascended the last metre. With the phone in the hand that was looped around the final rung and the pliable cable grasped between the thumb and forefinger of his other hand, he reached up slowly and fed the tiny lens through one of the slim apertures in the manhole cover. Again, it took a couple of seconds for the camera to adjust, but then PJ was able to make out familiar shapes, and he hit the record button. Bollards, palisade fencing, the remains of a burnt-out food truck and … *dammit*.

Two guards, a male and a female. They were standing together, almost leaning into each other, suggesting they were more than just colleagues. He couldn't hear the conversation and, obviously, had the mute button on to avoid any giveaway sounds, but the content of what they were talking about was irrelevant. What was important was that they were there in the first place. Their very presence meant that he and the others would not be able to escape the sewer unnoticed.

PJ stayed there a full minute, doing another three-hundred-and-sixty-degree sweep before focusing on the guards once again. Finally, he climbed down and moved back onto the small staircase.

"We're stuck here. There are two guards," he whispered as he pressed play on the video he'd recorded.

Drake and Esme watched. "That's Myers and Shilton," Esme said. "I had my suspicions about them for like … ever. They were way more than friendly."

"It doesn't matter who they are. They're screwing up our plan," Drake hissed. They watched the rest of the video in silence. "Play it again."

"It doesn't get any more exciting," PJ replied.

"Just play it again, will you?" PJ did as he was asked, and the three of them watched the video once more.

"See. Told you."

"It doesn't make sense. There's no strategic value to guarding this spot."

"What do you mean?"

"I mean it's nowhere near an entrance of any kind. There's nothing here."

"Unless they've figured out how Chloe and Nazya escaped. Unless they're guarding the sewer," Si said.

Peeking over Esme's shoulder, he'd not been able to see all of the video, but he'd got the gist from what the others were saying. "Well, aren't you just a bundle of lightness and joy?" Esme replied.

"It's possible," said Drake.

"I doubt it," replied Nazya. "I made a point of putting the cover back on."

"There is a small outside chance. Dammit."

"I'm with Naz," Chloe said. "The likelihood of them figuring it out is like a hundred to one."

"In this situation, I still don't like those odds."

"Okay," began Callie. "Let's say they did figure it out. "Why waste two guards standing watch twenty-four hours a day? Why not just put something really heavy over the manhole cover to stop anyone from accessing it? And also…."

"Also, what?"

"Do you think for a second that they'll be expecting us to attack them? I mean, seriously, do you think the administration would think we'd try making a move?"

"The fact that we haven't been back here since the takeover means that they know we know. That being the case, they'll also know that I'll be expecting them to come after us, and that may lead some to believe that I might decide to make the first move. So, on the one hand you're right, but on the other hand you don't know these people like I do."

"Who's a bundle of lightness and joy now?"

"You get used to him," Esme replied.

"Okay, so what do we do?"

"There's only one thing to do," Drake answered. "We watch."

17

Phil had lain awake for a couple of hours before finally deciding to get up for a while. He'd tried to make as little noise as possible as he'd left the small house. He looked up at the crescent moon and wondered if Callie and the others were looking at it wherever they were.

He started to walk towards the fields. They were always his refuge in times of upheaval. The feel of the soil beneath his feet, the smell of the different sprouting plants was life-affirming to him, and if ever he needed their comforting aromas, it was now.

"Don't mind if I join ya?"

"Jesus wept," Phil hissed, turning to see Bindi walking to catch up with him. "Between you and Debbie, it's a wonder I haven't had a coronary before now."

"Lucky for you I know CPR then, isn't it?"

"Oh yes, absolutely. That would make the near-death experience complete. Waking up to see you pumping my chest."

"Duly noted. Do not resuscitate."

"Funny."

"I have my moments." They continued walking towards the fields. "I'm guessing you couldn't sleep either then?"

"I'm guessing it's your years of medical training that brought you to that conclusion."

"Well, aren't you just a smart arse?"

"I have my moments."

"You worried about the others?"

"I'm worried about all of us."

"Drake's not my favourite person, but I'll give him this; he knows what he's doing when it comes to all this."

"I'll give him that," Phil admitted. "But a million things could go wrong."

"True enough. But if there's anyone who can think on his feet, it's him."

"I'm not just talking about what he's doing over there. I'm talking about all of it." They paused on the edge of the fields, and Phil sucked in a deep lungful of air.

"All of it?" Bindi replied after a short pause.

"Yeah. I mean, we've had enemies. We've faced foes before, but nothing like this. This seems a lot more…."

"Dangerous?"

"Final."

"That's a big word to use."

He resisted the impulse to joke that it was only five letters and instead conceded the fact. "Don't you feel it?"

"I feel everyone's on edge, apprehensive, nervous."

"You know they all pretty much mean the same thing?"

"Note to self. Sneak up on that pompous-arse Phil more often."

"Funny. But it's true. I was talking to Jason and Wei tonight. You can see the same thing on their faces. It's like everybody's just waiting for something bad to happen. It's as if it's inevitable."

"I don't think anything's inevitable. I didn't think you did either."

"I … don't … normally. This is different though."

"How?"

"Because we were completely outplayed."

"What do you mean?"

"I mean that we never saw this coming. Drake always thought that at some stage the administration might come for us, but it would be, maybe not an even fight, but a fight that we stood a fair chance of winning. But what they've done has turned everything on its head."

"I don't get you."

"The planning and execution that went into this was way beyond anything I believed them capable of. Taking control of Infinity, bolstering their resources, all of it. It's brilliant."

"Brilliant? You sound like you're regretting ever leaving Salvation."

"I don't mean it like that. I mean it's ingenious. It's way beyond what I could ever imagine them doing, and it destabilised us into the bargain. It took away a resource that we'd come to rely on to continue growing. It took away our key ally. In one simple move they did all that, and it makes me wonder what else they've got planned for us."

"What else?"

"I mean, think about it. When you, Drake and the others escaped, you left them in a huge mess. There was a big part of me that thought that would be the death knell for Bucks and the administration. You left them with workforce issues, supply issues, and that's not to mention the sabotage of the power plant. It was the perfect recipe for total disaster. But, somehow, they clawed their way back, and now they're stronger than ever."

"Well, we can't know that for sure. That's just speculation."

"It's not speculation. Woody revealed plenty to us. They're continuing to recruit; they're continuing to grow minute by minute, hour by hour, day by day. They're continuing to grow while we're stagnating."

She could hear a quiver in Phil's voice and suddenly realised that this was something he'd wanted to share, not necessarily with her but with someone. She'd learnt a lot about Phil since she'd first met him. He was a genius, of that there was little doubt. He was articulate and honest, but there was a side to him that struggled to communicate sometimes. She got the impression that this was that. This was all the stuff he'd held in that had been playing over again and again in his mind, finally coming to the surface.

"I think stagnating's the wrong word, don't you?"

"Oh, really? Then what would you call it? When was the last time we had a fresh influx of Wanderers? When was the last time we went on a successful scavenging mission? When was the last time we expanded? In fact, yes, you're right. Stagnating is the wrong word. We're deflating. We used to occupy the forest on the other side of the ridge, but now we've withdrawn from there for fear of it getting attacked. The administration is stronger than ever, and we're weaker than ever, Bindi."

Phil's words chimed in her head for a moment. "I was going to go for a walk along the stream. I'm so glad I decided to follow you instead. I feel much better now."

"I'm just telling you the truth."

"Y'know, Phil, I can't even imagine what it's like in that mind of yours. I mean, I'm pretty bright. I've got certificates to prove it. But there's a big difference between the way my brain works and the way yours works. You seem to go down a lot of rabbit holes and get stuck."

"I don't understand."

"You talk about our resources, Phil. Well, our greatest resource is our people. Yeah, the administration might have played a good hand, but we've been beating the bank ever since we got out of the bunker. I mean, struth, look at this," she said, gesturing towards the fields. "We built this from nothing. We cleared the fields of debris, we dug out rocks and boulders, we made the soil right for growing. I mean, hell, how many tonnes of sand did we barrow from the beaches to make the far fields suitable for growing carrots and tomatoes and asparagus and ... screw it, I don't know what else? I'm a doctor, not a farmer, but I have been in a constant state of awe at what our people have done here, and I know that if the administration wants to come after us, then they're going to have the battle of their lives because we've got something special here and I don't know a man or woman who won't be prepared to fight to the death to keep it."

"I wish I possessed that kind of certainty."

"I can give you some pills to help if you like."

Phil laughed. "If only pills could help me."

"True. I'd need a whole pharmacy to help you."

"You have a lousy bedside manner, has anyone ever told you that?"

"Frequently."

The two stood in silence for a moment, looking out across the fields. "Thank you," Phil finally said.

"For what?"

"For talking to me. For being patient. For helping me get my head a little straighter."

"That's what I'm here for."

"A doctor's work is never done, I suppose."

"It bloody is. I stopped being a doctor when the sun went down tonight."

"What do you call this then?"

"I call it being a mate. And this is what mates do."

*

"Okay, it got kind of heavy and a little gross for a while," PJ said as he joined Drake and the others at the foot of the ladder once more.

"What do you mean?" Esme asked.

"You told me to keep my eyes on them, and I felt like a perv. You were right, they're bumping uglies in a serious way."

"Uh-huh. When I said watch them, PJ, I didn't mean quite so literally."

PJ shrugged. "Spilt milk. Anyway, they're gone."

"You're sure?"

"Hundred percent. I waited like a full minute or something after they disappeared from view. I did two three-sixties, and they're gone, goneski."

Drake nodded. "Okay, good. Great." He turned to the others. "So, we head up there. Chloe and Nazya will take us to the vent ducts, and I want total silence until we reach the boiler room. Then we wait until first light when the others attack."

"And you're sure that Woody guy is going to let us out of the boiler room?" PJ asked.

"We've been over this and over this. He knows what he's doing. He'll wait for the sound of gunfire, and then he's going jump into action. Hell, he's going to have bolt cutters with him, for Christ's sake. He'll be prepared for anything."

"It's just that when I've seen him in the past, he's been less than impressive. He's reeked of booze, and it's been a miracle if he can stand up straight for more than a minute at a time."

"Woody won't let us down," Callie said.

"Yeah," Chloe agreed. "When it counts, we've always been able to rely on him one hundred percent."

"Well, let's just hope nothing happened to him on the way here, then, shall we?" PJ replied.

Suddenly, a thousand doubts were awash in all their minds. This wasn't like the old days. They couldn't confirm by text or a quick call. These arrangements had been made some time back, and what if, with all his best intentions, Woody had got the day wrong, or something had indeed happened to him on the journey to Infinity, or somehow his intentions had been discovered?

"Way to boost everyone's morale, dick face," Esme said.

"Just saying what everyone's thinking."

"Okay. Enough of this," Drake ordered. "Let's get the ball rolling. PJ, I want you right behind me."

"Alright."

Drake started to climb. PJ was next, then Esme, Callie and the rest. Greenslade and Trunk brought up the rear.

Drake paused at the top and PJ passed the adapted phone up to him. The former Salvation guard proceeded to feed the lens through one of the narrow holes and then angled it around. "It's clear." He handed the device back to the tech head. "You did well with this, PJ. Nice work."

"Thanks."

Drake reached up and pushed against the cast iron cover. *Jesus, this thing's heavy.* Eventually, it shifted a little, then a little more. He heaved it forward and cringed as it scraped on the surrounding tarmac. The grating noise travelled down the shaft, and the entire party held their breaths, sure that they would hear the sound of shouting guards or, worse still, gunfire. The seconds ticked on to a minute, then beyond. Drake heaved once more, sliding the cover further out of the way until there was enough of a gap for him to get through. He unslung his rucksack and fed that through first, then his rifle, and finally he climbed up and out into the cold night air. The slip of a moon had fallen behind a thin cloud, and it took him a moment for his eyes to adjust. He put his backpack on once more and picked up his Q-Thirty. "Okay. Come on," he whispered down into the darkness.

PJ had always been slight, and he managed to squeeze through the gap without even removing his rucksack. Esme was next, then Callie. As each of them made it to the surface, they drew their weapons, ready. A firefight in the dark was the last thing any of them wanted, but if they were discovered, then they would have few options.

Chloe was next, and then, one by one, the others popped their heads up through the hole before climbing out. The thin cloud gave way to a clear sky once more, and suddenly they could make out their surroundings a little clearer.

"It's over there," Chloe said, pointing to a cordoned-off area with shuttered doors behind it. A small annexe jutted out, and on top of that stood four exhaust vents.

"Okay, we need to—" Drake's whispered words were cut off by another sound.

"...Mother's. It's all I have left of hers, and I know it sounds stupid, but I need to find it," said the female voice.

"Look. We'll come back tomorrow when it's light."

"Oh yeah, sure. And how do we expl—Oh, shit! Oh, Jesus!" Myers immediately threw her hands into the air as she saw the silhouettes of multiple people pointing a variety of Q-Eighteens and Q-Thirties towards her.

Shilton came around the corner a second later, and for the briefest moment, his attention was on his companion, puzzled as to why she'd stopped talking and what had caused her outcry. Then he saw it too. "Oh shit." He thought about reaching for his weapon. Then he thought about shouting out for help. Both options would result in his immediate death, so instead he put his hands in the air.

"Myers, Shilton, long time no see," Drake said as he stepped out of the darkness.

"Oh, double shit," Shilton replied.

"That's no way to greet old friends," Esme said, joining her leader.

"Esme?" Myers replied. They had never been close, but they had been out after work a couple of times. Before the escape, they'd been on good terms, but Esme had never trusted the other woman enough to bring her on board with Drake's plan.

Trunk and Greenslade were the last two to emerge from the hole, and they immediately brought their weapons up, not sure what they'd walked into. "You fire and you're going to have every guard at Infinity on top of you in thirty seconds," Shilton said.

"Yeah," Drake replied. "I suppose this is what they call a conundrum. You shout; you die and we die. You stay silent and everybody lives."

"You've known me long enough to know that I'm not a hero."

Drake's teeth glinted in the moonlight as a smile flashed on his face. "I suppose I have."

"Y'know," Myers began, barely noticing Drake but keeping her eyes firmly on Esme. "There are a lot of people in Salvation who'd have gone with you if we'd known about the escape."

"Shut the hell up," Shilton hissed.

Myers turned around and looked at him. They both still had their hands in the air, but they could have had their fingers on the triggers of their weapons and they'd still have been no closer to shooting. "It's true."

"You've been coming here for months," Drake said. "You've had plenty of time to break away, to make contact with us."

He wasn't sure if it was a sob or a laugh that came out of her mouth. "Oh yeah. With all the surveillance, with all the mistrust. You can't trust the punters; you can't trust the storekeepers; you can't trust the other guards. You don't know who's wearing a camera. It's worse out here than it is in Salvation."

Drake stared at her for a moment. "Take their weapons, tie them and gag them," he ordered, and two militia stepped forward with zip ties.

Drake and Esme headed back over to the others. "What are we going to do with them?" Greenslade asked.

"I don't know," replied Drake.

"What do you mean you don't know? I thought you were the one with the plan."

Drake thought back to the piles of notes he had made. He'd never accounted for this. He'd never contemplated the fact that there were other guards within Salvation who longed for freedom, who would have gone with them on that fateful night, who were now here at Infinity. "This is what the Americans call a curve ball."

"Yeah, well, it's what I call a total clusterf—"

"We're still going ahead with the plan, aren't we?" asked Susan.

Drake glanced across at Esme then looked back towards the two guards as they compliantly allowed the captors to bind their hands and gag them.

"I don't know."

"Well, this is just a suggestion," began PJ, "and I know I'm not a military strategist or whatever, but do you think this is really a discussion we should be having out here in the middle of a freaking parking lot?"

"He's got a point," Susan replied.

"The maintenance shed," Chloe said, pointing over to the annexe from which the vent exhausts protruded.

"Get that covered up," Drake said, pointing to the hole they had all climbed through minutes before. Greenslade and Trunk heaved the heavy iron rectangle back into place then joined the others as they disappeared into the small maintenance building.

*

"It'll be getting light in a couple of hours," Becka said as she joined Dwyer by the fire they had sat around just a few hours before.

Dwyer reached forward and threw a few more pieces of wood on it. "I've never been a good sleeper. Especially out in the open."

"You thinking about what's facing us?"

"I'm thinking about Drake and the others. We've got the easy job. There are a thousand of us. We outnumber them by more than five to one. Drake's team is just thirty strong."

"Yeah, but they're all armed to the teeth."

"Well, so are we," Dwyer replied.

Becka reached for her bow. "Good luck switching one of these things to automatic fire."

Dwyer smiled. "You make a good point. But even with just the Q-Eighteens and Q-Thirties, we outnumber them two, maybe two and a half to one."

"Doesn't make it any less dangerous though. We'll lose people. There's nothing surer."

"That's a pretty safe assumption. We just need to make sure that they lose more."

"Yeah. Piece of cake."

18

The maintenance building was bigger than it appeared on the outside. Ducts ran through it from the stadium leading up to the flat roof. It had been stripped of all useful tools and fittings, but two floor-sweeping machines and even a hydraulic lift table told the story of what this place had once been used for.

"Well, if you're going to call this thing off, you'd better make your bloody mind up 'cause a thousand of our people will be descending on Crowesbury in a few hours and, y'know, it'd be nice if we gave them a heads-up before they all walked into harm's way."

"Yeah, thanks, Nicola. That's really helpful," Drake replied.

He stared across to their two captives who just remained seated on top of one of the sweepers, their gags on, their hands behind their backs. "What's the problem?" Greenslade asked.

"What do you mean what's the problem? You heard what I heard."

"I did. I also know that there are ways to get the real truth if we want it."

"You don't mean what I think you mean?"

"You didn't have a problem with it before."

"What's he talking about?" Callie asked.

"It doesn't matter."

"What are you talking about?" She turned to Greenslade this time. They only had a couple of LED lanterns on, but she could see the guilt in his eyes as he looked down at the floor.

"Like Drake said, it doesn't matter."

"What's he talking about? What did you do?"

"We got one of them," Drake finally admitted. "We questioned him."

"You tortured him?"

"We did what had to be done to get the information we needed."

Callie gestured towards their two prisoners. "And how did that work out for you? Did he tell you about the contingent of the Salvation guards who'd have followed you if they'd known about the escape?"

"He wasn't one of them."

"Who was he then? Are you saying you just randomly picked a stranger and ripped his fingernails out until he told you whatever you wanted to hear?"

"This isn't helping," Drake said, looking at Susan.

"What do you expect me to do about it?" she replied.

"Nothing, I guess."

"Yeah, well. You guess right."

"None of this is helping," Esme said.

"Did you know?" Callie asked.

"I…."

"What she knew and what she didn't know is irrelevant," Drake spat. "I made a judgement call, and I believed—"

"You did this?" Callie announced, looking at Greenslade and then Trunk. "Your surveillance mission wasn't a surveillance mission at all, was it? You kidnapped someone and—"

"What they did they did on my orders."

"The second we start acting like them, we become no better than them."

"This is not the time or the place to have this discussion."

"No. The time and place was before you kidnapped and tortured someone."

Drake turned to Susan once more. "Bleeding hearts are all good and well in principle, but—"

"I'm right here," Callie said, putting her hand up. "You can talk to me, Drake."

"Fine. You want a lesson in reality? You want to do this now … here? Fine."

*

Myers felt sick to her stomach. She was so confused, so conflicted. When Drake and the others had escaped, there was a big part of her that had wanted to go with them. Yes, she would have taken her family, but then she would have broken it to her husband gently that she'd found someone else. That was not a conversation that could be had in Salvation. Break-ups and divorces didn't happen in Salvation. Not officially, anyway. There was too much to tally. It wasn't simply a case of moving in with someone new. There were the children to consider, joint credits, the joint allowances. It gave her a headache just thinking about it.

She had lived in blissful ignorance until Trainor's escape and then the massacre in the forest. Ever since then, she and many others had come to understand the insidious nature of the administration and that they were all slaves in one way or another. She had thought Shilton was on the same page. She had thought he understood her better than anyone. But now, as she sat there alone, she looked to the door that he had just left through. He hadn't urged her to follow him; he had simply and silently slipped away.

The two guards who had been charged with watching them were, instead, standing wide-eyed, listening to the war of words raging between their friends, the people they looked up to, the people they relied upon. They were as stunned as Callie to hear of the covert mission.

The bastard left me. Should I go after him? Should I raise the alarm? What the hell should I do?

Tears continued to stream down her face, and her breathing got heavier and heavier. *I'm going to pass out. I swear, I'm going to pass out.*

"MMMMMM. GHGHGHGH!". The sound was unintelligible, but it was loud enough to gain the attention of one of the guards assigned to watch the pair.

"Oh SHIT!" he cried, turning towards the remaining prisoner and then to the open door.

*

The war of words suddenly came to an abrupt end as all eyes looked first at the remaining prisoner and then moved to the door.

"Shit!" Drake cried, launching into a sprint and nearly knocking Callie, Susan and Dani over as he tore towards the entrance. Shock stopped the others from following for a moment.

By the time Drake re-emerged into the night air, there was no sign of Shilton. His eyes pierced the darkness in every direction, looking for some clue as to where he had gone, but there was none.

"That's it. We need to abort right now," Greenslade said as he and the others joined him.

Drake didn't say anything; he just ran back inside. "What the hell's he doing?" Si asked.

"I don't know," replied Esme.

"If you ask me, he's behaving pretty erratically," Nicola said. "I think we should get out of here while we've still got a chance like Greenslade said."

348

Trunk moved across to the manhole cover and started to lever it up.

*

The lanterns were still on inside. For the first time, Drake noticed the tears running down Myers' face. He untied the gag from her mouth. "What you said, is it true?"

Her breath shuddered. "Yeah. There were plenty who'd have gone with you, and that's to say nothing of the people on Level Two. Things got really bad after you left. We were putting down mini rebellions all the time."

"The guards that are here. Some of them would have joined us?"

"The guards, the people running the outlets. Nothing's what it seems, Drake. It's not black and white."

"Drake. It's too late. They're coming." He looked up to see Esme standing at the door. A second later, the others came piling in, readying their weapons as they did.

Drake eased Myers off the platform of the hydraulic lift and cut her zip-tied hands. "No point you dying with the rest of us," he said, pushing her towards the door while the remainder of his team filtered in.

"No," she said, turning back. "Maybe if I'm in here, they won't open fire. Maybe they'll let you surrender."

"We surrender, we're dead."

She didn't want to tell him what she knew. It was common knowledge that any of the guards involved in the escape would be put to death. The former citizens, however, would be put to work. Salvation needed workers for its great expansion more than anything. "You don't know that. Me staying in here could be the only option."

"It's your choice."

"That's the thing, isn't it? Out here, there is a choice. I choose to stay."

Drake nodded. "Thank you, Myers."

"This is it? This is how it ends?" Si asked incredulously as he took up his position behind the hydraulic lift and took aim towards the entrance.

Greenslade was the last in. There was no lock; he simply closed the door behind him and then joined his friend Trunk as he crouched down behind one of the sweepers with his rifle raised.

"I love you, Mum," Callie said.

"I love you too, baby girl," Susan replied as they all cast sad eyes towards the doorway.

The tension mounted with each second that passed. "A couple of us should have tried to make a run for it at least," Greenslade said. "The others are going to be left high and dry."

"Should haves don't help us now," Esme replied.

"Nothing can help us now," said Drake.

Several people looked towards him. The tone of his voice made him sound like a different person. It was the voice of someone who had lost all hope. It was the sound of someone who knew the end was at hand.

*

Shilton and the others skidded to a stop taking up positions behind bollards, burnt-out vehicles or whatever might give them a little cover. If someone had offered him a million credits to guess how this night was going to end, he could never have imagined this.

"Well?" Rhodes said as he took up his position next to Shilton by the burnt, rusted remains of a Saint John's ambulance.

"Well what?"

"Well, it's obvious we're going to have to make a move 'cause they ain't going anywhere."

Shilton glanced around at the others. "Shit."

"This was your call."

"Yeah. Thanks for the reminder," he replied.

"My pleasure."

Shilton's Q-Thirty was still inside, but he'd borrowed a Q-Eighteen from one of the others, and now he looked down at its black outline as he broke cover and ran to the door. The shuttered windows told him the occupants were just as blind as he was. He paused outside and looked back to see the silhouettes of the others as they remained in position.

He banged hard on the entrance three times. "It's me. It's Shilton."

*

Drake and the others glanced towards one another with confused expressions on their faces. They were expecting a breach, a few stun grenades followed by deafening gunfire and to hell with Myers.

"How many are out there with you?" Drake called.

"Five."

"Yeah, right."

"I'm serious."

The tension continued to mount. Nobody could figure out where this was going, and the uncertainty was unbearable. Finally, Greenslade climbed to his feet and started walking to the door. "What the hell are you doing?" Drake demanded.

"Talking through doors isn't going to get us anywhere, and if there's a hundred of them out there, I'd rather this was over sooner rather than later." He pulled open the door, and the small amount of light that escaped revealed Shilton standing there.

Greenslade remained in the entrance for a moment, blocking his access but surveying the surrounding area. Finally, he stepped aside and let Shilton in. The Salvation guard raised his hands above his head with the Q-Eighteen still in his right. He walked to the hydraulic platform then placed it down before putting his hand up once more. "Are you okay?" he asked, looking at Myers.

She nodded. "I thought you'd left me."

"I didn't really have time to give you a briefing."

Greenslade walked up behind Shilton. "I see a handful of them out there at the most. They're armed, and they're taking cover, but there are a lot more of us than there are of them."

"That's not to say there aren't more coming," Drake replied.

"There aren't," said Shilton.

"Says you."

"That's right. Says me."

"Okay, so, what's this? You're here to negotiate our peaceful surrender?"

"No. I'm here to prove to you that Naomi was telling the truth."

Drake was about to ask who Naomi was, and then it dawned on him that it was Myers. In all the time he'd known her, he'd only ever used her surname. "And how are you going to do that?"

"The others I brought with me. I want to bring them in here."

"Ha. Yeah, good one. To be honest, you had me going there for a minute."

"I'm serious."

"I bet you are."

"What have we got to lose?" Callie asked.

"Hostages."

"Are you going to torture them like you tortured the other one?"

"Callie!" Susan said. "She's right though. What have we got to lose?"

Drake glanced around. He was confident that every man and woman there would have been willing to die for their freedom, but if there was some vague possibility that could be avoided, then surely it was worth it. "Okay, Shilton. But I swear to you, if I see a double-cross, you're the first to go down."

"Duly noted," Shilton replied; then he went to the door and beckoned the others in. One by one, they entered, making their way to the hydraulic platform and placing their weapons down.

"Rhodes!" Drake said. Rhodes was on the maybe list when Drake had been compiling the names of whom to inform of his plans to escape. He was pretty high up, but he wasn't a hundred percent sure he could be trusted, so in the end, he left him behind. He walked up to Drake and stared him straight in the eyes.

"One day, you and I are going to have a discussion as to why the hell you didn't tell me what was going on. But right now, none of us are safe. I've got colleagues here who I don't trust as far as I can throw them. There's a pretty hefty bounty on your head, and if any of them saw us together, they wouldn't think twice about selling me, Shilton and the others out too. But there are more here who think like we do. I've had long discussions with them."

"Anyone who wants to join us can walk out with us right now," Susan said.

"Wait a minute," Drake replied.

"If only things were that simple," Rhodes said, ignoring Drake and turning to Susan. "There are plenty of us who'd leave Salvation in a heartbeat. You think it was bad when you were there?" He turned back to Drake. "It's a hundred times worse now." His eyes moved back to Susan. "But none of us will go anywhere without our families."

"I'm guessing they don't let you bring them down here with you?" Esme said.

"Well, that would solve a lot of problems, wouldn't it? We do this in two-week rotating shifts. We carry out the orders we're given, knowing full well that they've got our families there if we step out of line or if we even hint that we're dissatisfied with our lots. Being sent to the surface isn't a punishment anymore. They used to plant that there as an abstract, terrifying thought, but now people know that it's not an uninhabitable wasteland the penalties are far worse. If they knew I was talking to you like this, they'd arrest me and torture me until they'd got every last bit of information they could and then they'd kill me. I'd die with the knowledge that my family would be sent down to Level Three. And trust me, the Level Three you knew is paradise compared to what it is now."

"So, what is this, Rhodes?" Drake asked. "You want to join us but you can't? I don't see the point of this."

"I just wanted you to know that there are people there who would have come with you if you'd given them the chance, Drake. There are people there who would still gladly come with you. There are people who hate their lives there, who hate the thought of what awaits their families and their children when they finally establish the new settlement. My boy has already been enrolled into the guard academy. That's what they're doing now, they're not giving them a choice. He's thirteen years old and he's been separated from his friends. He's being trained as a Salvation guard—the noblest pursuit they call it. Defenders of Salvation. He's a kid and you want to hear the shit that's coming out of his mouth. It's terrifying."

"But you put him straight, I'm guessing."

"Surveillance and monitoring have entered a whole new level since you went. They used to think their biggest problems were the reactionaries on Level Three. They could be listening to any of us at any time."

"On the subject of which, I'm assuming you all left your phones outside?" Myers said.

"We're not amateurs, Naomi. When Shilton came to find us, we knew what this meant." He moved his flat hand across his throat. "We put all our phones in a locker and headed outside into the corridor. Technically, they shouldn't be able to monitor them all the way down here, but it doesn't hurt to be a little paranoid."

"And nobody spotted you?"

"We're on ground night patrols. The others who aren't sleeping are outside, but the changeover won't be long, and we need to get you the hell out of here," he said, turning back to Susan and Drake.

"Why are you helping us if you're not going to come with us?"

"Because, hopefully, one day, we'll get to join you. When we heard about the escape, it was excruciating and elevating at the same time. As I said, there were a lot of us who would have gone with you given half a chance, but the fact that you did it, the fact that you got out gave us all a little hope."

"The people," Chloe said, coming forward out of the darkness. "The people they took from here, my father. Is he there? Is he in Salvation?"

"Yeah. He's there. They rounded up everyone from your bunker and the other bunkers in your network. They're under strict surveillance, but they're alive and they're there."

Tears flooded Chloe's eyes. "Dad," she whispered.

"Organise another breakout. We managed it. Surely you can too," Drake said.

"Weren't you listening? Nobody knows when they're being watched or when they're being listened to. Your trap door, the one in Block Seventy-One, there are cameras all over now, and they've installed another coded metal door at the end of the tunnel. The thing's blast-proof. If you don't have the code, you're not getting through it."

"PJ?" Drake asked, looking towards the young tech wizard.

"If I could get access to the server, I could get it, but that would mean being in Salvation."

"You don't think we've been through this?" said Rhodes. "We've been through everything. It's no good."

"I can't believe that. There's got to be a way."

"When you did what you did, that kind of took the element of surprise away for everyone. They're monitoring everything."

"If there are all these guards and all these people so pissed off, surely if you start the ball rolling then it will just keep gathering pace," Susan said.

"There's no ball to get rolling. It's not like before. You had a movement on Level Three." He turned to Drake. "And obviously you had enough key allies to make a move on Level Two. Nobody dares even use the word revolt now. And as pissed off as they are down on Level Three, the situation's hopeless. People are just trying to stay alive. They've got a squad of guards stationed down there all the time now, but there are certain parts that even they won't head into."

"What do you mean?"

"I mean that just because we brought some of the Ferals into a more civilised environment doesn't mean that they've become more civilised. There have been three missing persons in the last few weeks. We found bones, and that was it."

"Cannibalism?"

Rhodes shrugged. "I'm guessing they're not just making lampshades out of the skin."

"Why isn't something done about it?"

"You still don't understand, do you? Bucks and the others are using everything at their disposal to control the situation. Who needs curfews when you have murderers roaming the streets who are looking to put you in their stockpots? Of course, in the morning bulletins it's all shock, horror, 'We're doing everything we can,' yada, yada, yada. In reality, the administration couldn't be happier. Fear and uncertainty are powerful weapons in the right hands."

"Jesus."

"Is there anything we can do to help you?" Susan asked.

Rhodes shook his head. "No. If there was any sign of Level Three getting organised, then maybe I could see a way forward, but a few dozen guards and their families initiating a jailbreak will do nothing other than get a lot of innocent people killed."

"But you said there are guards down there now. Surely you've got some you can trust," Callie said.

"There are a couple across the three shifts, maybe."

"Can't they reach out to someone?"

"To whom? Nobody trusts anybody, and with good reason."

"So you keep waiting," Drake said.

"Yeah," replied Rhodes. "We keep waiting and hoping for an opportunity to present itself. But I think it's going to be a long wait, and in the interim…."

"In the interim, what?"

Rhodes looked towards Shilton, Myers and the others, then back at Drake. "Bucks has been building up stocks of weapons and ammunition like there's no tomorrow. It's not like he's doing it for fun."

"You think he's coming after us?"

"My guess is he'll strike just before winter. If he doesn't wipe you out, he'll leave you floundering through the cold. The weather will do a lot of his work."

"It might be harder than he thinks to take us out."

"Hey, no doubt, but it's not like he's the one in the firing line, is it? Like I said. It's coming, I just can't tell you when."

"And you'd take up arms against us?"

Rhodes looked down at the ground. "Not if I can help it. But whenever we're out here, our families are back there. If they so much as got a hint that we were trying to help you, that would be it."

A long, deep, dark silence fell. It was Chloe who finally broke it. "I want to go to Salvation."

Susan laughed nervously. "What do you mean, love?"

"I mean I want to be with my dad and my family."

"Sweetheart, you don't know what you're saying."

"Now I know they're alive, I want to be with them."

"But … you heard what it's like in there. And they probably won't even let you go near him."

"It doesn't matter. You heard what he said. They're coming after us sooner or later. Whether it's in there or out here, there's no hope. But I'd rather be in there."

"I can guarantee your father wouldn't want this for you."

"No, he probably wouldn't. But I'm not a kid, and even if I can't be there with him, I want to be in there with him."

"You're not thinking properly," Nicola began. "What kind of life is it going to be for you?"

"If you do this, I will come too," said Nazya.

"No, Naz," Chloe replied. "This is my choice, not yours."

"It is my choice whether I join you. We are like sisters, Chloe. Where you go, I go."

"Err … neither of you are thinking straight," said Drake. "You can't just waltz in to Salvation, y'know. It's not like—"

"We wouldn't waltz in," Chloe said, turning to Rhodes. "You've found us. We were sneaking back in here to see if I could find out what had happened to my dad. As far as they're concerned, I disappeared all those months ago and haven't found out anything since. Maybe I thought they'd let him stay here as an unwilling participant."

"That might work," Rhodes replied. "But I doubt if they'd let you see your father again."

"This is madness," Susan said. "Chloe, Nazya, you can't seriously be talking about this."

"It's what I want to do," Chloe replied. "And let's face it, Susan, the picture's just as bleak out here. The only difference is that I might at least be able to get some news about my dad in there."

Susan was about to respond when all the air left her. *I don't really have a comeback for that.*

"Look," Rhodes said. "Whoever is doing whatever, we need to wrap this up quickly, otherwise we're all screwed."

"Are you sure about this?" Susan asked, taking Chloe's and Nazya's hands.

"Yes. Thank you for everything you've done for me … for us … for all of us. Dad only ever said good things about you."

"I really hope you get to see him."

"Like I said. Even if I don't, I might be able to find out about him, maybe even get a message to him."

"They'll probably split you up, y'know," Rhodes said, trying to sow a final seed of doubt.

"If it happens, it happens."

"Yes," Nazya replied, taking her friend's other hand but looking far less sure.

Susan was the first to throw her arms around the two women. "Be careful. I'm really going to miss both of you."

"I'm going with them," Callie said. And for the second time, a long, stark silence hung in the air.

"Don't be so bloody ridiculous," Susan said.

"Not a chance in hell," added Si.

"Over my dead body you are," Greenslade suddenly piped up.

"Listen to me," Callie persisted. "We—"

"Not up for discussion, Callie," Susan snapped.

"Listen to me," she said more forcefully this time. "Rhodes confirmed what we've all been thinking. They're going to come after us, and the longer we give them before we make a move the more organised and better armed they're going to be."

"What does this have to do with anything?" Si demanded.

"If there's somebody on Level Three that can get messages in and out; if there's somebody who can form alliances and build a movement from the ground up then—"

"Jesus Christ, I can't believe I'm hearing this," Susan said, leaning back against one of the carpet sweepers for support. "You'll be lucky if they don't lock you away or worse."

"We've got to try something, Mum. We'll end up going to war with our own kind. We'll end up fighting people like Rhodes, like Myers, like Shilton, people who don't want to be there, people who are being forced, or their families will face God knows what horrors."

"That's the way it's always been," Trunk announced, and everyone turned around, surprised to hear anything coming from his lips. "Wars have always been fought by the people who just wanted to get on with their lives, people who wanted to look after their families, try to carve out a little bit of happiness for themselves before they died. The guilty never die in wars. It's always the innocent who die at the guilty's behest." He looked up to see everyone staring at him, and he suddenly felt self-conscious. "That's what I think anyway."

Another few seconds of silence were broken by Si this time. "Callie's right."

"What?" Susan and Greenslade said at the same time.

"She's right. The only way we're going to be able to stop the inevitable is if we start something of our own from the inside."

"But—" Susan began.

"But she's wrong about the fact that it should be her. You came here all the time," he said, turning to his sister. "You and Dani and Nicola and dozens of others. They'll have got so much information on you and them that what Mum said was right. They'll lock you away. You'd be too much of a risk. Any of you would. But me … I've only been here once in a while. I don't get involved in things; I have my own little projects. Despite being related to you two, they won't consider me a threat. People barely notice me. They'd probably put me to work and forget about me."

"You can't know that," Callie said.

"I stand a better chance than you. Even if they don't lock you away, you won't be able to fart without a report going back to Bucks and the others. But I could blend. I could shrink into the background unnoticed, just doing my job. Me and Chloe and Nazya have a chance of making this work."

"How can you possibly think that?" Susan asked. "You don't think suspicions will be raised that you turned up with Chloe and Nazya?"

Si shrugged. "Chloe and I have had a thing ever since she came to Redemption. She was wracked with guilt about leaving her father and she wanted to come back to see if he was still here, to see if there was any hope of helping him escape too. Nazya refused to let us go alone, and that's how the three of us wound up at Infinity."

"It needs a bit of work, but it's plausible enough," Rhodes replied.

"No, Si," Callie said. "You're only doing this because it's me who volunteered." Stinging tears ran down her face. She hadn't thought for a second that her brother would try to take her place.

"It can't be you, Cal. But you're right, it's got to be someone." He turned to Rhodes. "I'll do what needs to be done on Level Three. You figure out a way we can communicate through your proxy or whatever. We're only going to get one chance at this, and if we screw it up, it's all our families who are going to pay."

Rhodes stared at the younger man for several seconds before looking at his watch and turning to the others. "We might have three or four minutes before suspicions are raised. The rest of you need to get the hell out of here. Don't worry about putting the manhole cover back on; that's how we found these three. Now say your goodbyes."

Callie threw her arms around Si. Tears continued to pour down her face as she held him. "I'm sorry. I'm sorry, I should never have said anything. I'm sorry." He held her tightly.

"You should," he replied. "It's going to be okay, Cal. It's all going to be okay."

"Thank you for everything," Chloe said, squeezing Susan. The older woman's body was shaking as she returned the hug. Both women were crying. Even though Chloe had said she had wanted to go to Salvation, she could never have imagined the turn the last few minutes had taken. "I'll … I'll look after him."

"If you ever see each other again," Susan said, still sobbing. Chloe brought her chin to rest on the older woman's shoulder. It was true. No one knew what lay ahead. Finally, their embrace broke, and Susan grabbed hold of Si. "I thought I only had one child who made rash and stupid decisions." She held her son tighter than she ever had. "You're breaking my heart."

Si kissed her on the side of the head and then pulled back. "I've always been the selfish one, Mum. I've always got on with my own thing and let you, Cal, and the others make all the hard decisions, do all the heavy lifting. This is what I need to do. You'll explain to Sasha, won't you?"

"Yes," she replied with a shuddering breath.

"Oh … and leave out the stuff about me and Chloe having a thing."

Susan laughed through her tears and grabbed him again. "I love you. I love you, I love you, I love you, I love you."

He squeezed her back and gulped. "I love you, Mum. Look after Cal."

They all said their final goodbyes and left Chloe, Nazya and Si with Rhodes and the other guards. Callie and Susan cast one final glance back to the lantern-lit circle of faces before exiting, still in floods of tears, both of them hoping Si's plan would work but deep down inside knowing that they'd never lay eyes on him, Chloe or Nazya again.

EPILOGUE

The death toll from the trek to Crowesbury could have been high. In the end, not one person lost their life, and yet the absence of Si, Chloe and Nazya was felt by all. It was what it represented more than anything. This was the beginning of the end. However it was dressed up, whatever spin was put on it, the reality was inescapable. This was the last chance to put a stop to a war that nobody wanted.

"If I'd have known you were going to be so miserable, I'd have gone for a walk with Jason or one of the other peasants," Phil said with a wry smile, doing his best to make Callie laugh.

"I'm sorry. You're right. I should go," she replied, turning to leave.

"Hey, hey, I was only kidding," he said, grasping her arm firmly. It had been two days since their return from Crowesbury, and this was the first time Callie had ventured anywhere but the farmyard and the stream to wash.

"I'm sorry," she said again. "I'm not good company, Phil. I nearly ripped Dani's head off earlier."

"Your mum still not talking to you?"

"She's barely talking to anyone. Debbie must have told you; she's hardly come out of the house."

"She did mention something."

Callie let out a huff of a laugh. "I'm sure lots of people have mentioned something."

"It's perfectly understandable that—"

"She blames me, Phil. She blames me for Si heading to Salvation, and the worst part of it is that she's right."

"Listen to me, Callie, all joking aside. You were absolutely one hundred percent right. We need someone we can trust in Salvation. But Si was one hundred percent right when he said it couldn't be you. Your name was synonymous with the rebellion. Hell, he wasn't even there when it happened, and on his best day, he's not half the loudmouth you are." Finally, a small giggle left Callie's lips. "He was also right in saying they won't have much on him. He's always been in the background, even here. Don't get me wrong; he's a good worker, a great worker, but he's never shouted about it. He won't come across as a threat to them. They'll just put him to work."

"You can't know that."

"Well, no, I can't, not completely. But what's the benefit of doing anything else with him? Sure, they'll probably interrogate him and Chloe and Nazya until they're blue in the face, but they won't get anything out of them that they probably don't already know from the surveillance footage. From what you said, they were going to get their stories straight, and that probably included what they were going to discuss about here. They'll have an inventory of what Drake left Salvation with, so that won't be any great revelation. They'll know what crops we're growing, they'll know we've got a sizeable militia, they'll know plenty.

"Once they're done with them, they'll just put them to work. Nazya might get a job in the pharmacy or something. Chloe and Si are young, fit and bright. They could be useful wherever they go."

"You honestly think so? You don't think they'll make an example of him?"

"If it was you or Drake or, God forbid, me, then absolutely they'd make an example of us, but there's no rational reason with Si."

Callie lifted her head to look at her friend. *He's telling the truth. He believes what he's saying.* "Thanks, Phil."

"For what?"

"For talking to me."

Phil shrugged. "Beats talking to myself … just."

Callie giggled again. "Arse."

Three rifle reports made the air tremble and the half-smiles on their faces vanished in an instant. They turned towards the north ridge and watched as three flaming arrows launched into the air. "Oh shit," Phil said in little more than a whisper.

Drake, Marina, Dwyer and Revell appeared out of nowhere, sprinting across the farmyard.

"This is it. All our plans. They've all turned to shit, Phil. Si's dead, and we won't be far behind." Callie burst into a run heading towards home. Long before she even left the field, she saw her mum, Dani and Nicola emerge from the house with weapons in hand.

She turned the other way to see Becka, Rommy and their people charging out of the forest with bows and spears. *It's really happening. This is it.*

Three more shots boomed, and everyone other than Drake and his small band came skidding to a stop. Confusion reigned as people looked around nervously, not sure if they understood the signal. Callie reached her house just as Jiang, Lanying and Wei filed out, looking far less sure of themselves with the weapons they were carrying. "A false alarm?" Wei said.

Susan looked dazed. She had not been herself since that night at Infinity, but now, as she saw dozens of pairs of eyes looking towards her, she realised she had to take control once more. "I think so. I think that's what Drake said three more shots meant." She and the others began to move towards the hill but with less purpose than before.

Drake was already more than halfway up by the time they reached the base. They remained there as a massive crowd gathered around them. Everybody knew where they had to be if there was a legitimate call to arms, but the second signal had raised doubts. "I suppose we'd better head up too," Callie said.

Susan looked towards her daughter and reached out, squeezing Callie's hand. She had felt nothing but resentment towards her since Infinity, but now she felt guilt. It wasn't Callie, it was the situation, and she had taken it out on her daughter. "I'm sorry, darling. I'm sorry."

Callie just squeezed her mother's hand as tears appeared in both their eyes. "Come on." Nicola and the others all followed.

By the time they reached the summit, the concerned looks that had been etched on Drake's and Marina's faces had gone and been replaced with smiles. For a moment, Callie, Susan and the others didn't understand why. An army of at least five hundred was approaching. It was only when they looked a little harder that they saw a white flag bearer several paces ahead.

Drake turned and handed Susan the binoculars. "What do you reckon? Should we let them in?"

Susan adjusted the focus wheel and zeroed in on the figure with the flag. "It's Selby," she said. Callie burst into a sprint down the hill. "Callie," Susan called after her, but it was too late. The journey down the other side was faster than the one up the ridge, and within a couple of minutes, the seventeen-year-old was throwing her arms around Selby.

"You came," she said, hugging the other woman tightly.

Selby was taken aback. It had been a long time since she'd had physical contact with anyone, but her surprise soon turned to happiness. She had sold the idea of Redemption, but a part of her had feared the people were not all they seemed. This one gesture had laid any underlying doubts to rest, however, and she reciprocated the hug.

"I kind of told a couple of other tribes about you too. I hope you don't mind."

"The more of us there are the better this place works," Callie replied, pulling back from the other woman as tears of happiness ran down her face.

"Why the tears?" Selby asked, not comprehending the depth of emotion behind the hug.

"I was having a bad couple of days. But you've just made everything better."

Selby gulped now. "That's the nicest thing anyone's said to me in the longest time." The older woman reached out and gently wiped the tears from Callie's cheeks. "Seriously, are you okay?"

Callie smiled. "I am now."

The End

A NOTE FROM THE AUTHOR

I really hope you enjoyed this book and would be very grateful if you took a minute to leave a review on Amazon and Goodreads.

If you would like to stay informed about what I'm doing, including current writing projects, and all the latest news and release information; these are the places to go:

Join me on Facebook
https://www.facebook.com/groups/127693634504226

Like the Christopher Artinian author page
https://www.facebook.com/safehaventrilogy/

Buy exclusive and signed books and merchandise, subscribe to the newsletter and follow the blog:
https://www.christopherartinian.com/

Follow me on Twitter
https://twitter.com/Christo71635959

Follow me on Youtube:
https://www.youtube.com/channel/UCfJymx31Vvztt
B_Q-x5otYg

Follow me on Amazon
https://amzn.to/2I1llU6

Follow me on Goodreads
https://bit.ly/2P7iDzX

Other books by Christopher Artinian:

Safe Haven: Rise of the RAMs
Safe Haven: Realm of the Raiders
Safe Haven: Reap of the Righteous
Safe Haven: Ice
Safe Haven: Vengeance
Safe Haven: Is This the End of Everything?
Safe Haven: Neverland (Part 1)
Safe Haven: Doomsday
Safe Haven: Neverland (Part 2)
Safe Haven: Hope Street
Safe Haven: No Hope in Hell
Before Safe Haven: Lucy
Before Safe Haven: Alex
Before Safe Haven: Mike

Before Safe Haven: Jules
The End of Everything: Book 1
The End of Everything: Book 2
The End of Everything: Book 3
The End of Everything: Book 4
The End of Everything: Book 5
The End of Everything: Book 6
The End of Everything: Book 7
The End of Everything: Book 8
The End of Everything: Book 9
The End of Everything: Book 10
The End of Everything: Book 11
The End of Everything: Book 12
Relentless
Relentless 2
Relentless 3
The Burning Tree: Book 1 – Salvation
The Burning Tree: Book 2 – Rebirth
The Burning Tree: Book 3 – Infinity
The Burning Tree: Book 4 – Anarchy
The Burning Tree: Book 5 - Redemption
Night of the Demons

CHRISTOPHER ARTINIAN

Christopher Artinian was born and raised in Leeds, West Yorkshire. Wanting to escape life in a big city and concentrate more on working to live than living to work, he and his family moved to the Outer Hebrides in the north-west of Scotland in 2004, where he now works as a full-time author.

Chris is a huge music fan, a cinephile, an avid reader and a supporter of Yorkshire County Cricket Club. When he's not sitting in front of his laptop living out his next post-apocalyptic/dystopian/horror adventure, he will be passionately immersed in one of his other interests.

Printed in Great Britain
by Amazon